PRAISE FOR LINDSAY MCKENNA'S
WIND RIVER VALLEY SERIES!

"The believable and real romance between Tara and Harper is enhanced by the addition of highly dimensional supporting characters, and a minor mystery subplot increases the tension by a notch. This is a fine addition to a strong series."—*Publishers Weekly* on *Lone Rider*

"Captivating sensuality."—*Publishers Weekly* on *Wind River Wrangler*, a Publishers Marketplace Buzz Books 2016 selection

"Moving and real . . . impossible to put down."—*Publishers Weekly* on *Wind River Rancher* (starred review)

"Cowboy who is also a former Special Forces operator? Check. Woman on the run from her past? Check. This contemporary Western wraps together suspense and romance in a rugged Wyoming package."—Amazon.com's Omnivoracious, "9 Romances I Can't Wait to Read," on *Wind River Wrangler*

"Set against the stunning beauty of Wyoming's Grand Tetons, *Wind River Wrangler* is Lindsay McKenna at her finest! A *tour de force* of heart-stopping drama, gut-wrenching emotion, and the searing joy of two wounded souls learning to love again."—International bestselling author Merline Lovelace

"McKenna does a beautiful job of illustrating difficult topics through the development of well-formed, sympathetic characters."—*Publishers Weekly* on *Wolf Haven* (starred review)

WIND RIVER UNDERCOVER

LINDSAY McKENNA

ZEBRA BOOKS
KENSINGTON PUBLISHING CORP.
www.kensingtonbooks.com

ZEBRA BOOKS are published by

Kensington Publishing Corp.
119 West 40th Street
New York, NY 10018

All Kensington titles, imprints, and distributed lines are available at special quantity discounts for bulk purchases for sales promotion, premiums, fund-raising, educational, or institutional use.

Special book excerpts or customized printings can also be created to fit specific needs. For details, write or phone the office of the Kensington Sales Manager: Attn.: Sales Department. Kensington Publishing Corp., 119 West 40th Street, New York, NY 10018. Phone: 1-800-221-2647.

Zebra and the Z logo Reg. U.S. Pat. & TM Off.

First Printing: April 2020
ISBN-13: 978-1-4201-4754-4
ISBN-10: 1-4201-4754-4

ISBN-13: 978-1-4201-4755-1 (eBook)
ISBN-10: 1-4201-4755-2 (eBook)
10 9 8 7 6 5 4 3 2

Printed in the United States of America

To all the men and women who live undercover,
unsung heroes and heroines.
Thank you for your service to our country.
You are truly patriots of the highest order.
And to your families,
who will miss you for weeks, months, and
sometimes years while you infiltrate crime for all of us.

Chapter One

April 1

Anna Navaro lay on her belly, covered overhead by pungent-smelling juniper boughs. Sharp little Southern California desert stones bit into her thighs and knees, below the Kevlar vest she wore, and were like needles bruising her skin through the tough military camouflage duck fabric. Darkness surrounded her. Her mission for the Drug Enforcement Agency, the DEA, had taken her to an area south of Descanso, California. It was quiet except for some yips from coyotes on the prowl around the rocky hills surrounding her. She pushed a strand of her dark black hair away from her eyes.

Through the infrared scope on her rifle, she followed three gray pickups down a dirt road toward a nearby dirt airstrip located below her position. The Mexican border wasn't far away, and a plane flying across it was expected to drop drugs. Six drug soldiers would be waiting to haul off the goods when they landed on the US side of the border. The tiny radio in her left ear quietly broke the silence and she heard Border Patrol taking five vehicles—three following out of sight behind the enemy and two in front of them on that road, also unseen—to box them in and capture them.

It was a thin, narrow valley, the slopes steep, boulders the size of cars, filled with thousands of spidery-armed ocotillos. There was no way for the druggies to escape this time. The corners of her mouth pulled grimly upward, watching the whole scene play out below her hide. With her rifle resting on a tripod, all she had to do was lie on the ground, remain hidden, communicate what was going on, and continually survey the surrounding area to make sure no other drug soldiers were in the hills waiting to jump her Border Patrol agents. The night air chilled her even though she wore a Kevlar vest and a heavy dark green Guatemalan Marine military jacket. It was not that warm in the dead of night, especially for someone from a hot, humid jungle country who was dropped into the dry Southwest of the US to work in the chilly mountains above San Diego. Still, her country's jacket was better than nothing.

Her mind drifted for a moment, although her gaze hovered near the scope, watching the Border Patrol close in on the unsuspecting pickups that had just loaded a tremendous amount of bales and smaller packages into the beds of the vehicles. The drug plane, a single fixed wing, took off, swiftly gaining altitude and banking toward the border. There was satisfaction in her that whatever was in those trucks wouldn't find its way onto this country's streets. She spoke into the mic and reported the trucks moving onto the dirt road and away from the airstrip, heading east at twenty-five miles an hour. She knew the druggies wanted to get onto a highway ten miles from that point and then scatter east and west.

At twenty-seven years old, with years of experience in Guatemala busting drug runners and taking down major players as a sniper, she found this type of work in the US boring in comparison. The DEA had invited her up to the US based on reports from the Guatemala military that she was their best "force multiplier," someone who could take this type of assignment and carry it out with success. She didn't mind taking out higher-ups or a drug lord himself in her country, either, if she got the chance.

After all, her beloved father, Marine General Marcos Navaro, had been shot and killed by a drug lord sniper when she was fifteen years old. His murder had changed the course of her life as well that of her mother, Maria, a prosecuting attorney. It was on that horrible day that Anna swore to destroy the cancer of drug lords killing her people in Guatemala. Later, she went to Marine sniper school in the United States, learned her trade and craft, and came back to her country and applied that knowledge with deadly precision.

She listened intently, hearing something light-footed scuttling near the tree she was hiding beneath. Her gold-brown eyes were well adjusted to the half-moon light that reminded her of a watercolor, a thin wash across the dark, shadowy desert hill landscape. Sensing movement, she lifted her chin, twisting her head slowly to the left. It was a mother raccoon with six kits in tow, heading off the hill and down to a nearby creek below. They were all in a line, like a gaggle of geese. Probably to hunt for freshwater mussels, crawdads, fish, or other unnamed denizens that lived beneath the surface as well. The babies were probably four or five weeks old, cute, fuzzy, curious with black, shiny eyes, but religiously following their big, ten-pound mother who waddled and wove between the bushes, ocotillos, and junipers toward her objective.

Anna returned her attention to the drama playing out less than half a mile away and didn't see any other human activity. Her heart, however, was elsewhere. Of late, she'd wake up feeling lonely. There was a gnawing sensation in her chest, and it would come and go at times when she wasn't focused on her job. Lonely? Her? She was well respected by the Marines in her own country, and here in the US by the DEA agency. They were glad to have her on assignment with them. She'd been here a year, mostly tramping through the Southern California desert, finding drug-drop off points and then patiently waiting to discover where the drug soldiers would pick them up for distribution. Then, she would coordinate with the DEA, ATF, and Border Patrol with her information. With a sniper scope she could hone in miles away on a target and give them vital, real-time information as well as location and movement directions of the quarry. Then, another group would be netted along with the drugs they were carrying on them.

Pushing her sense of loneliness away, she grudgingly admitted it had started stalking her even while she was on the job in the dark of the night. That bothered her a lot. She had to devote a hundred percent of her focus on her mission, not on some errant emotion that would steal upon her in quieter moments. Lonely for what? Her nostrils flared, drinking in the dry scent of the surrounding vegetation as she kept her gloved hand near the trigger mechanism. She carried a pistol on her right thigh in case she got jumped in her hide.

The Border Patrol vehicle boxed in the three drug pickups from both ends after they emerged from around a long curve. She saw the drug soldiers braking, leaping out of their trucks, running away, not fighting. The Border Patrol officers had more men and women, and very quickly, without a shot being fired, they captured all those who had fled. They cuffed them with plastic ties tightened around their wrists, hands behind their backs, and made them sit down after searching them for weapons. A bright light carried by one Border Patrol truck flashed on from its position on its rooftop. That was to give the agents the light they needed to frisk the soldiers thoroughly, take information from each of them, and then march them into the awaiting trucks and take them back to their station for processing.

Her job was done. She signed off with the Border Patrol and they released her. Rolling slowly to her left side, she pushed a thick juniper limb gently behind her shoulders. In moments, she had shut down her special sniper scope, and then waited, listening intently to the surrounding area. Anna knew these hills were alive with possible enemies and she could become a target herself. Her vehicle, a black, dusty pickup with no markings, was a quarter of a mile away, hidden behind a very old juniper tree.

Pulling the thin leather flap off her watch, she saw it was 0300. Time to close up shop for the night. She would drive back to the DEA headquarters in La Mesa, a suburb east of sprawling San Diego, and write up her report. After that, she could go home and sleep for the rest of the day. Depending upon the time of year, she would set her alarm for dusk, shower, eat dinner, and head to HQ. There, she'd receive her nightly orders, pick up her weapons and gear from the underground basement armory, and find her dusty black truck parked within the cyclone-fenced area. Then she would drive out to her hide to set up surveillance once more. Drug runners usually liked working at night, hiding like the vermin they were from daylight hours.

Slowly easing to her black-booted feet, she pulled her black baseball cap from her pocket and settled it on her head. Her desert-colored camouflage clothes faded into the surrounding night. Never relaxing, Anna surveyed the area for several minutes, listening, inhaling scents, noting the direction of the breeze, her hearing honed like a wolf's ears, trying to pick up, sense, or see anything that was minutely out of place. Because what was out of place she regarded instantly as a potential enemy waiting to take her out. She leaned slowly over to pick out dried plant material that stuck on her thigh and had rubbed into her skin for hours on end, dropping them back into the dry, hard, rocky soil. Easing upward, satisfied that everything was in order around her, she walked soundlessly, like the jaguars that lived in her country, pistol locked and loaded, safety off, and ready to fire at a moment's notice, if need be. She had half a mile to walk to get her ride home.

The DEA HQ was busy, but it always was. They handled so many drug-related missions out of the cinderblock, single-story building painted a Southwest tan color that it had surprised Anna at first. It was like a squat beehive, busy 24/7/365. It was now near dawn, the horizon a dull reddish-brown polluted-looking color, indicating that soon enough, there might be a pretty eastern dawn. Anna looked forward to that quiet time of day. She loved the silence, as if the world were holding her breath before putting on a spectacular sunrise provided there were some clouds to frame the horizon.

On her way to the women's locker room, she stopped first at the armory and placed her weapons, vest, and ammo into the hands of the armorer on duty. Her rifle would be cleaned and ready to go when she picked it up the next evening.

Leaving the basement area, she climbed the stairs to the first-floor locker room. The military clothes she wore were dusty and dirty. In no time, she was stepping into a hot, delicious shower, washing her long black hair that gleamed with reddish highlights among the strands. She always carried a special lemony-scented bar of Herbaria soap her mother sent her every three months, to wash her hair. It left the strands luxuriously fed with natural oils that were contained within it. The other bar was orange citrus and oatmeal, and Anna loved that it not only gently removed the sweat and dust, but also the dead scales off her skin. She later stepped out of the shower, a dual fragrance of lemon and orange surrounding her. Opening her locker, she began to dry off.

"Hey, Anna."

Looking up, naked, her wet foot resting on the bench in front of her locker as she dried it, she saw it was Vicky Brown, part of the office staff, peeking her head inside the door. "Hey yourself. Come on in. What are you doing in here at this time?"

The woman was in her late twenties like herself, dressed in a light gray two-piece suit, a cream silk tee beneath it. Her short blond hair was cut in a pixie style. Vicky grinned mischievously as she stepped aside to allow the women's locker room door to automatically close and lock behind her.

"Have you heard the whispers?" she asked in a low voice, looking around the quiet area.

"No one's here," Anna promised, continuing to towel dry off her other foot. "And no, there's no bugs in here, either. What rumors?" Usually, Vicky was at her desk promptly at 0900, five days a week. She was married to Tom, part of the planning staff at the HQ, and they had two children, a girl and boy who were five and three.

"Got called in early. I hear you participated in a major drug bust this morning. Congrats." She came and sat down primly on the end of the wooden bench anchored to the gray concrete floor.

Anna opened her locker and pulled out a dark navy blue tee, socks of the same color, her Levi's, and a pair of brown leather loafers. After shimmying quickly into her jeans, she straightened and threaded her fingers through her damp hair, pushing it across her shoulders and down her back. Anna settled the blue tee in place.

"It's that bust you called in this morning. I'm hearing from the night crew that it's a whopper."

Giving her friend an evil look, Anna said, "Wow. Think I'll get a raise from it?" That was a common joke. They were federal employees. They got cost-of-living raises if the president okayed it. Raises weren't normal except when an agent evolved upwardly from fieldwork and was assigned to management. She was a field agent, with no wish to evolve anywhere near pushing papers around on a desk eight hours a day. Besides, she was "on loan" to the DEA in a three-year contract agreement with the Guatemalan government. They wanted her back, pronto, but the USA had a lot of behind-the-scenes clout and wanted her to stay put on their soil instead.

Vicky chortled. "No. But they're saying they found over a hundred and fifty pounds of packages of cocaine in those pickup trucks."

Whistling, Anna straightened and walked over to the dressing room area, picking up a hair dryer. "That is a lot."

"There's more," Vicky said. "They've found fifty pounds of fentanyl. That's a huge amount!"

She turned on the hair dryer, lifting her thick, damp strands. "Fifty? Seriously?"

"Yes. A scary, phenomenal amount. Unheard of, until now, sadly. China was the one making it and sending it through the U.S. Postal Service. Now, it looks like the drug lords in Central and South America are making it, too. Do you realize how many people could die if that fentanyl is laced in other drugs they're taking?"

"That's so frightening, Vicky. You could kill a million people with that much."

"Opioid-addicted people often get drugs laced with that deadly substance. You're right."

She leaned down, swishing her hair once more, the dryer whistling loudly, drying the straight strands. "I'm sure someone will figure out just how many people's lives were saved tonight. Part of the stats they keep."

"But it all was hinging on you."

Shrugging, Anna said, "It's my job."

"You're good at it." She gave her a proud look. "You're our Wonder Woman here at the DEA."

Snorting, she continued moving thick strands. "We had five Border Patrol trucks with us to take those druggies down. I was just the spotter. The force multiplier," Anna said, and she flashed Vicky a savage grin laden with black humor, wanting to give credit to the others, as well as the Border Patrol.

"Well, everyone's talking about it. They're excited and stunned." She rubbed her hands across her thighs and stood up. "Director Hardiman sent me down here to tell you to come to his office at 1500 today. I know that's cutting your sleep short, but he wants to meet with you."

Arched brows rising, Anna turned off the noisy machine. "Probably wants to give me an attaboy clap on the shoulder and a double handshake." Anna tried to keep the derision out of her voice. She appreciated the management pat on the head, but she knew how good she was at her job. No need for outside praise.

"Maybe," Vicky said, heading for the door. "Hope it's a raise instead of a handshake, though."

Laughter erupted from her as she tucked in her tee and slid a brown leather belt around her waist. "Sure. Don't hold your breath, Vicky."

She slipped through the opened door, laughing with her. "I won't. But you DESERVE it! Maybe it's a promotion?"

An even louder and noisy snort came from Anna as she slipped on her shoes, grabbed her leather purse, and slung it across her left shoulder. "In your dreams. Have a good day, okay? Stay out of trouble, unlike me."

"Yeah, after seeing the director, you get to have an early dinner and off to the desert in your black gear to hunt more druggies."

"Roger that," she said, shutting the locker door. What she wished for right now was a change from the boring missions she'd been assigned to since arriving here a year earlier. Anna knew the DEA wasn't about to move her into any other position. Being a sniper wasn't for everyone and it took a lot of stealth, an understanding of one's environment, knowledge of how to track, and being one hell of an operator, not to mention a 4.0 shooter. She knew the present Guatemalan general in charge of the Marines had not wanted to release her to the States, but given the US's largesse, a Central or South American country couldn't say no to a humanitarian package deal they were receiving in trade for her services.

Anna didn't blame the general. Her country was very poor, and every US dollar that flowed into it was a good thing. She hated the idea of being the modus operandi of currency, however. Feeling tiredness pull at her, she was happy to be going home and hitting the sack. Who knew what lay ahead of her when she met her boss at 1500 today? She cringed, not wanting an attaboy.

April 2

Gabe Whitcomb forced himself to sit quietly, looking relaxed even though he wasn't. His boss, Randy Hardiman, fifty-five years old and his San Diego DEA supervisor, was at his desk, focused on a stack of papers that begged his attention. The midafternoon sun shed bright southern light into the man's corner office, showing his importance to the HQ.

While Ace, Gabe's eight-year-old Belgian Malinois, played in the DEA dog pen in an air-conditioned area of HQ, Gabe scrolled through his iPhone for text messages from his old haunt, an undercover mission that had lasted two years. He grimaced inwardly while keeping his expression neutral. A lot of his old friends from the past were glad to hear he was done with that assignment, which had taken him into the snake pit of Tijuana and other towns along the border with the US.

There was a text message from his adoptive mother, Maud: When are you coming home? We want to celebrate! Don't you feel like Persephone coming out of Hades and standing on the Earth during springtime?

Gabe smiled inwardly. In his business, no one knew more about body and facial language than a survivor of a long-term undercover, covert mission. He was a master of it. And while it had served him well, saved his life innumerable times, he was free of it—finally. He texted back: I'm a male Persephone? ☺ I'm with my boss right now. I hope to find out what my next assignment will be. He's already promised me some "away" time with all of you. As soon as I find out, I'll call you.

His adoptive parents, Steve and Maud Whitcomb, had raised him from when he was three years old and a foster family didn't want him anymore. He had very few memories of that time, but one thing that had always stuck in his chest like a warm embrace was the love that spilled from Maud and Steve as they adopted him immediately. He became part of a noisy, affectionate family. He was the fourth child to be adopted by them, his whole life changing as he moved from San Diego, California, to Wind River, Wyoming, to grow up on a huge, sprawling cattle lease ranch on the western border of the state. All he knew was love as a child in that incredible family. They didn't care if he was Hispanic.

Maud had spent a lot of time with private detectives, trying to ferret out the mothers of the four children they called their sons and daughters. She and Steve had wanted them to know their family roots, understanding how important it was to have them. Gabe's mother, whoever she was, had placed him in a cardboard box on the steps of a firehouse—that was his beginning in life. A firefighter had opened the back door that led to the trash bin area and nearly stepped on the box, not expecting it to be there. Gabe had no memory of that awful time. He'd seen enough orphans in Mexico, lost to the world, parentless, their safety net gone, their loveless lives, making them horribly vulnerable in the world of the drug trade. It sickened him.

Looking up, he saw it was 1455, or 2:55 P.M. Hardiman said his new partner would show up at 1500. He glanced toward the open door and saw people walking quietly up and down the pale blue tile floor. There wasn't much noise, just people with their heads down, focused and intent.

What would his next assignment be? He'd spent the last year in Tijuana; before that, he'd been in Guatemala. He wanted to know because he'd told Hardiman months earlier in a clandestine meeting that this was his last undercover job. He missed his family. He missed home. And only when he'd gone undercover did that become abundantly clear to him.

He tried to shrug off and ignore that his biological mother abandoned him, for whatever reason. That was an open wound in him whether he wanted it to be or not. Living in the scum of Tijuana slums as a middle-level drug buyer and seller, he saw families torn apart, orphans by the handful, and the dregs of society surrounding him, all struggling just to survive to the next morning.

God, how he wanted to go home, wanted to smell that clean, unpolluted Wyoming air, inhale the sweet scent of grass growing a foot a day in the spring, hear the lowing of cattle that was like a song to him, and the snort of a good horse between his legs. He wanted Ace to enjoy the last half of his life in safety and just be a dog, not an IED specialist. He really missed his family, his siblings, Andy who was thirty, Skylar, now twenty-eight, Luke, who was twenty-nine. Sky was like him, of Hispanic blood, although Maud and Steve and he suspected that each of them had had one unknown parent who was Caucasian. They both had golden skin, not the darker, reddish skin of a Hispanic who was a pureblood. Luke and Andy were Caucasian. They'd all had their genetic map from Ancestory.com. And yes, it showed Gabe was Hispanic on one side and British and Irish on the other. He supposed it was his father who was Irish. Gabe had brown-reddish hair and gray eyes. Neither were hallmarks of his Hispanic heritage. When undercover, that part of him was key. He spoke Spanish like he was born to it, which he was. He had the color of skin that drug lords preferred. They wanted mules and lower-status males of Hispanic blood who tended never to question anyone. They just bent their backs and carried the loads they'd been assigned for hundreds of years in Central and South America, without rebelling. Without getting out of that prison. And it was a prison, Gabe thought, pushing all thoughts of his unknown parentage away. With his lighter skin, he could pass without notice. Border Patrol definitely profiled, no question.

It was 1500. He looked expectantly at the open door and the hall. After placing his iPhone on OFF, he slipped it into the pocket of his plaid shirt. To this day, he wore cowboy shirts with pearl snaps and mostly plaids and leather boots. His straw hat sat on a chair next to him. His belt buckle was the only thing he allowed of his "real" life to follow him into undercover. He'd been on the teen rodeo circuit in Wyoming, riding bareback broncs, winning a state championship at seventeen. That well-worn gold buckle was a part of him, of who he was, of what he loved to do. He liked being around cattle and horses. And he was looking forward to thirty days of leave to do just that. There was no way Hardiman was going to drop him into another assignment without a good rest from the last harrowing one. That wasn't DEA policy.

Gabe caught movement and switched his glance to the doorway. There was a Hispanic woman with long black hair coming toward them. She wore a dark blue short-sleeved tee, a pair of comfortable jeans, sensible leather shoes, and a slender brown leather belt. She was around five foot eight inches tall, shoulders back with pride, and it struck him that she was or had been in the military. Her face was oval with full lips a bit thinned, high cheekbones, and large, alert eyes. As she drew closer he saw that her eyes were a gold-brown. Maybe she was only part Hispanic like him? *Maybe.* He saw the sleek muscling of her upper and lower arms. This woman was athletic as hell, no office type, for sure. She wore a black baseball cap and it gave her a dangerous look. Although she wasn't wearing any weapons on her that he could see, Gabe thought she felt lethal, her gaze always ranging around, like everyone in their business would do. Being in the DEA meant one did not have their eyes and nose glued to a cell phone, never looking up or around. No, she was damned alert and as she drew closer, he appreciated her easy gait, the gentle sway of her hips, the mega confidence surrounding her. He liked her. Liked her chutzpah, which seemed to be a natural part of who she was. She wore no jewelry, either, another indicator of a military background.

His curiosity was piqued. Big-time.

Hardiman looked up as she knocked lightly on the doorjamb. "Ah, Anna, come in! Right on time. Close the door after yourself, please?"

She stepped forward. "Yes, sir," she said, and she closed the door. Anna glanced to her right at the man sitting slouched in a chair near one end of the desk. There was another chair at the other end.

"Agent Anna Navaro, meet Agent Gabe Whitcomb."

She turned toward him, expecting a nod. Instead, he got to his feet, holding her gaze and extending a work-worn hand toward her. "Nice to meet you," she murmured, noting that he had a steely gaze akin to that of an eagle checking out prey. His hand was warm, dry, and calloused. So was hers. He clasped it and she could feel him monitoring the amount of pressure he placed around her hand. At least he wasn't one of these cocky dudes who tried to impress her by crushing the bones of her hand into dust. Anna exerted just enough strength in her returning handshake to let him know she wasn't some limp woman who sat at a desk. There was a flare of surprise in his eyes, his black pupils large, that ring of gray around them, telling her that he missed nothing. *Nothing.*

"Nice to meet you, Ms. Navaro," he said, and he released her hand.

"Same here," she said, trying to ignore his blatant maleness. Her senses told her he was hiding a hell of a lot from her, appearing like a field hand working on picking up produce from the rows of some big white man farm here in the US. His hair was military short, he was clean-shaven, and she liked the faint scent of his skin. Nostrils flaring, she drank it in and then looked back at her boss.

"Have a seat," said Hardiman, and he gestured to the only empty chair in the office.

"Yes, sir."

The Cowboy, as she silently dubbed him, sat attentive in his chair, his gaze on her. Skin prickling, she didn't mind his perusing her. There was curiosity and interest in his eyes. He must be single. Well, she wasn't looking for a hookup, so he could forget that. Even though his face was deeply tanned, as if he'd been working out the in fields, her instincts told her he really wasn't doing agricultural stuff at all. It just appeared that way. She wondered if the cowboy outfit was a ruse and Gabe wanted people to think he was a farmhand. Hiding who he really was? She'd been around black ops and undercover mission men for too long not to bet on what she saw, and in her gut she knew she was correct.

"The reason I've asked you to come here today," Hardiman began, hands clasped on his desk, "is that we have a very special assignment." He lifted his chin and drilled Anna and Gabe with a look. "You two will be going undercover."

Anna opened her mouth to protest, but saw the seriousness of Hardiman's heavily lined face, his green eyes narrowed. Better to wait for all the info he was going to divulge instead of interrupting him. There was no way she was going undercover! Friggin' no way! She was a sniper. Not counterespionage.

Gabe had sat up even straighter, shoulders tensing as he stared in disbelief at his boss. He too opened his mouth to protest, thought better of it, and compressed his lips into a thin line, waiting for the rest of the explanation.

"Gabe, this is a very, very unique and delicate operation. There is a Guatemalan drug lord by the name of Pablo Gonzalez making heavy inroads to the southern portion of Wind River Valley in Wyoming."

"Gonzalez?" Anna hissed, nearly coming out of her chair, hands white-knuckled around the arms of it.

"Yes," Hardiman said heavily, giving her a sympathetic nod. "It was his soldiers who murdered your father when you were fifteen."

Anna felt gut-punched and sat abruptly down in the chair, her grip tightening. "That bastard is here? In Wyoming? Right now?"

"A contingent of his drug operation is setting up shop," Hardiman said. "We don't know if Gonzalez is in Wyoming or not. Most likely, one of his lieutenants has been assigned to the state."

Gabe scowled. "I don't understand why we're undercover."

Anna shot Gabe a look of, *yeah, you got that right. What the hell!* She was getting hotter by the minute. There was no way she wanted undercover work!

"Whoa," Hardiman told them, "both of you, stand down, please?"

Anna forced herself to loosen her grip on the arms of the chair. Lips pressed tightly, she held back a barrage of questions about Gonzalez. There was no one she wanted more than that murdering bastard. Hatred soared through her as the past flashed before her eyes. Her father, in a casket, and her standing in front of it, crying so hard that she couldn't see him. Her mother was beside her, arm tightly around her heaving shoulders, holding her while she sobbed out her heart over his death. Pushing that painful time in her life away, Anna swallowed convulsively, reinforcing the shove of all her emotions down, deep inside herself.

Hardiman gave her an apologetic look. "This is going to be a very emotional mission for both of you for different reasons," he warned heavily. He glanced in Gabe's direction. He was still scowling. "Here's the gist of it," Hardiman offered. "Gonzalez is widening and deepening his operation in Wind River Valley. He's enlisted people who live there, which is a common strategy, to become part of his ring. Namely, the Elson Gang."

A low growl emanated from Gabe. "That's a family steeped in drug selling and running. Most of the brothers have already been to prison at least once, on drug charges. Their old man, Brian, was a wife and child beater, plus an addict, until he was killed by the local sheriff."

Anna gave him an assessing look. "You know them?"

"I grew up in Wind River Valley," Gabe answered tightly. "The Elsons had four sons. One is dead now. I heard from my parents that Cree Elson was killed when he tried to kidnap a local woman. Another, Hiram, was just tossed into prison for ten years. That leaves Kaen and Elisha on the loose and they must be hooking up with Gonzalez, then?"

"Yes. Okay, here's the broad brushstrokes on this mission. First, Gabe, I can't give you any time off for a thirty-day leave that you more than deserve. The good news is that your parents, Steve and Maud Whitcomb, have been working with my people for a good three months. They have agreed to help us on this mission."

"What?" he croaked. "What the hell are you talking about?" and he came out of the chair, standing tensely, glaring hard at Hardiman.

Anna saw the fear in Gabe's darkening gray eyes, looking more and more like an eagle ready to pounce.

Hardiman's voice lowered. "My team has been working with them, with Sheriff Sarah Carter of Lincoln County, and other agencies, to set up this mission. Basically, you are going home as Gabe Whitcomb. You're not fully undercover because you're retaining your real identity, but your story is that you've quit your job, with no mention that you were a DEA agent, and are coming back to live in the valley. There's a broken-down ranch, the Rocking G, right next to where the Elsons live. We've faked the purchase of it and your name is on the title for the ranch. This proves to any resident who might be curious, including the Elsons, that you want to make a home in the valley and settle down."

Brows flew upward as Gabe stared at him. "You're putting me in that situation?"

"Yes. The cover story that your parents are going to tell everyone in the valley is that you wanted to strike out on your own, so you, not them, bought the Rocking G as a starter ranch. You're going to become a land and ranch owner." He gestured toward Anna. "She's been hired to help you as your wrangler. To the Elsons, she's nothing more than your employee. Together, you will eavesdrop, lay certain listening devices in and around their house and barn, and start watching them daily. In the meantime, you will be repairing this ranch that has sat empty for twenty-five years, and bring it back to life. We're hoping the Elsons accept you as their neighbor and won't think anything of someone buying the ranch and bringing it back to life. It's perfect cover for what we need you to do."

"So," Anna said, "this is more surveillance than anything else. Who are we hooked up with?"

"Yes, you're right. We need several things from the two of you and both of you are perfect for this mission. I'll be handing it off to the Salt Lake City, Utah DEA HQ. Because you're a sniper, Anna, you are going to be key in surveilling. Both of you will ride up into the Salt Mountain Range to find out where Gonzalez has his eye on drug dumps by airplanes. That will be important, too. We think they're making drops in high mountain meadows west of the valley. We need to find out where their camp is located, how many soldiers, when and how the drugs are dropped, and see if you can't both establish a pattern of drops. Once all that's done, you can form a mission to move in on that gang after a drop and we arrest all of them."

Anna sat back, the air whooshing out of her lungs as her head spun with the unexpected mission. She saw a lot of different emotions playing out across Whitcomb's face, too. He wasn't exactly happy about it, either, for a lot of obvious reasons.

"You enlisted my parents to help you in this?" Gabe demanded harshly, his hand moving into a fist on the chair as he sat down.

"We did. I flew out there months ago and laid out what was going on and I asked for their help and they gave it."

Nostrils flaring, he glared at Hardiman. "This is damned dangerous work, Director. I do not like the idea that my parents are wrapped up in this mission. For all we know? Gonzalez could send an ambush team and get on my parents' ranch and kill them if they find out they're involved. Did you tell them that side of our business?"

"I did," Hardiman said quietly. "We do not want your parents in harm's way. That was why the purchase of the Rocking G surfaced and was placed in your name only. There's eighty miles between your parents' ranch and this one at the south end of the valley. This is top-secret clearance only on this particular assignment. No one outside of those working on it know about it. There's no way that your mother and father or their ranch can be implicated in this except from the standpoint that you are their son. And, you are striking out on your own, which would seem normal, once you got home. They are sworn to secrecy and your mother assured me, they would not ever tell anyone. Not even your brothers or your sisters know about it. They know nothing about it except that you've bought the Rocking G."

"Hell!" Gabe growled. "You're putting my whole family at risk!"

"There's some risk," the director admitted, spreading his hands out across the desk to try to lower the level of emotion rising, "but we feel it's minimal. You'll be living next to the Elson clan. Your parents are not going to visit your ranch. I've asked them to stay away and disappear, so to speak, and not drive south to visit you."

"And I could have a drug soldier tail me up the highway from the Rocking G to Wind River Ranch, too. They could find out."

"All they'll find out is that you are their son and you've bought the Rocking G as a starter ranch. So long as the Elsons don't catch on to what you're doing there, we feel the odds of the Gonzalez ring putting this together are very, very low."

"God," Anna muttered, shaking her head, "how would I feel if you told me I'd go home and do the same thing? I'd worry nonstop about my mother. Drug lords are inventive, creative, and they are like spiders that find cracks in security all the time."

"Got that right," Gabe bit out angrily, glaring at the director.

Chapter Two

Gabe thought his chest was going to expand and burst open right then and there. All his career he had to rein in his emotions which were easily triggered, stuff them away so they couldn't impact his focus. He held Hardiman's patient look and the man seemed unmoved by his concern for his family. The DEA had sent someone to convince his mother and father that it was easy-peasy to get embroiled in a highly volatile and dangerous mission. *Son of a bitch!* He consciously uncurled his fist on the chair arm, cutting a glance to his new partner, Anna Navaro. She had a distraught expression, her attention on their boss, disbelief in her husky voice tinged with high emotions.

"Look," Hardiman soothed, giving them both a look of understanding, "I want you to go down to planning. Tom Brown has worked up the mission and you sit with him. See what we have created and then you come back and see me. Fair enough?"

Gabe gritted out, "I'll listen," he said, "but my next order of business is to call my parents. By that time, I'll be armed with the basics of this crazy scheme." Right now, he could give a rat's ass if Hardiman decided to fire him on the spot for his insubordination. And the look on

Anna's face was one of terror resting in her eyes. He could tell she wasn't for this plan, either.

"Fine," Hardiman said. "I'll stick around until 1800 to be here to answer any further questions you might have that Tom didn't cover."

Some of the anxiety left Gabe. "Okay," he muttered, standing up, "thanks." He glanced over at Anna, who stood and turned on her heel, saying nothing. She was a woman of action and had little patience, he would guess, with things that didn't count in life. She pushed her long, dark hair across her shoulders, jerked the door wide open, and stepped out, heading down the hall to planning. She was pissed off too, for different and tragic reasons. He was sorry her father had been murdered. Was she a sniper because of that, he wondered?

Gabe caught up easily with her, his six foot height and long legs eating up the distance between them. "I'm sorry you got snagged in this," he offered, giving her an apologetic look. "I knew nothing about this mission."

"Don't worry about it." She punched her chest with her thumb. "I damn well know what happens when a drug lord decides to kill one of your parents, and what happens next to the rest of a family." She gave him a fierce look. "And you won't like it."

Halting, he said, "Stop. Tell me?"

She spun around and came back to where he stood in the hall, looking up and down it, making sure no one was nearby to hear her. Keeping her voice low and raspy, her feelings raw, she said, "My father was a Marine general in Guatemala, where I was born. He headed up a country-wide taskforce to eradicate several drug lords, including Gonzalez, and get stability back into where we lived. My father was VERY good at destroying these filthy animals and where they hid and moved their drugs. A year later, it was Gonzalez who ordered a sniper hit on my papa." Her voice became choked and she looked away, blinking rapidly a few times, forcing back tears that came naturally whenever she replayed this event. Swallowing, she turned and lifted her chin, meeting Gabe's narrow-eyed look, his full focus on her. "They murdered him. It was a sniper. I had just come home on Christmas vacation from Yale, my mother's alma mater, and I was in my first year of law school, when it happened . . ." Her voice became clogged with tears she fought to stop. "My mother had to have six security guards at our estate from that day forward. She could go nowhere without an armed escort. Her life is no longer her own." Making a dismissive gesture to push away the tears threatening to fall, she stepped back, seeing the sudden sympathy come to his tight expression. Anna did not expect that. "My mother is hunted to this day, a price on her head by the drug lords, including Gonzalez. It's horrible. It will happen to your family if you let this mission go forward. You have to stop it if you can."

Gabe stood there, wavering inwardly. The mask of the sniper had fallen from Anna's unreadable features. "I-I'm sorry," he managed, his voice hoarse. "I didn't know. . . ."

"I'm not telling you this for nothing!" she hissed, stepping up to him, drilling him with a dark look. "You said you have two brothers and two sisters, not to mention, your parents. Who's going to protect all of them?" She jammed her finger down the long, quiet hall. "It sure as hell won't be the DEA! No, you know what they'll force your family to do? To go into the Witness Protection Program. Is that what you WANT?"

"Hell no!" he snapped.

She stood there, breathing hard, assessing him. "I don't know you. I've never heard of you."

"I was undercover for two years in Tijuana, Mexico,"

he muttered, running his fingers through his short hair in an aggravated gesture.

"Oh . . ."

"I don't know you, either."

"I'm on loan from the Guatemalan government for a three-year contract with the DEA as a sniper."

"I want to know who threw this mess of a mission together and then picked us for it," he growled. "Let's go talk to Tom and get the facts, first. He's a decent guy and he'll give us the lowdown." He wanted to hold out his hand out to her, cup her elbow, but stopped himself. This was a twenty-first-century woman. He assumed she knew only too well from the past few years that a lot of white men—or men of any color in power in any country—disdained women. All they wanted was to use women for their own pleasure and keep them under their boot, never allowing them to become fully empowered human beings. Maud had taught him and Luke early on to respect women, to always see and treat them as equals, and never consider them as sex objects to be used. Still, he saw the suffering in the way her lips twisted, and his protective side instinctively wanted to comfort Anna. It was a compassionate response on his part, not sexual, but his gesture could easily be read differently by her, and he had no wish to step into that bear trap right now. He knew she was a fully empowered individual and didn't need his antiquated helpful male hand.

"Okay, let's go hear him out," she agreed, her voice rough with remnants of her own tearful, gut-wrenching truths. She hadn't entertained baring such a deep, painful part of her life that she'd always carried within herself. What was it about this guy that made her feel safe when there was nothing safe about her life or this world? Ever since she was fifteen, Anna understood her life was worthless if she was captured by the drug cartels. On some days, she felt eighty, not twenty-seven. Sometimes? She yearned for a safe place. But there were none for people like her. *Ever.*

The mission planning office was near the end of the hall. Gabe opened the door for her. She gave him an odd look.

"Habit," he said, "my mother drilled into me and my brother Luke that we were always to be gentlemen."

A sour grin came to her lips. "Yeah, okay, I'll deal with it. Thanks."

Curbing a grin of his own, he liked her spunk and solid confidence. She was a sniper by trade. Lethal. Dangerous. So why was he so powerfully drawn to Anna Navaro? She could be married, but didn't wear a ring to prove it. In her business as a military sniper, they never wore anything that might give away who or what they were. Having no explanation for this ache centering in his chest once more, he entered and shut the door, seeing Tom just coming out of the planning room. Hailing him, he made a gesture with his head for Anna to follow him.

In a matter of minutes, Tom had taken them to another room and sat them down with a screen up in the semi-darkened space. They sat on either side of him at the end of the rectangular table. Both had yellow legal pads in front of them to take notes, although they would be given a full briefing on a thumb drive they could read and study any time they wanted.

"Sheriff Sarah Carter from Lincoln County, where the Wind River Valley sits, requested federal help in trying to stop the encroachment of serious and heavy drug movements through the southern area of her county by the Gonzalez cartel. We did a satellite flyover and spotted this, the Rocking G Ranch, which was up for sale. Best of all, it sits right next to the Elson home, which is five hundred acres." He pointed to the picture of the Rocking G. "It has been standing unlived in for twenty-five years. The last owner, Mr. Gardner, died at that time, and there was no relative to claim it. The attorney who was in charge of the last will and testament died, and gave it to his younger partner, telling him to try to sell it."

"That place is in rugged shape," Gabe said, scowling. All the paint had long ago been wind- and snow-blasted off the graying wooden sides of the structure. The roof was in sorry shape. In fact, everything about the ranch was in a nasty state of disrepair.

"I'm not a cowboy like you, Gabe, but even I can see it's pretty bad off," Tom admitted.

"What kind of hectares come with it?" Anna wondered.

Tom, who spoke Spanish and French, quickly made the change from hectares to acres in his head. "This was a cattle grass lease and lumber ranch in its heyday, and there's ten thousand acres to it." He moved the pointer, showing the land spreading up into the thickly wooded slopes of the Salt Mountain Range to the east of the main ranch house area. "The family settled in the area in 1875. First relative was a trapper turned logger. He saw logging as a way to make money, and for over a hundred years, the Rocking G was a very rich ranch. The family made money on cattle grass leases during the spring through fall, plus logging that nine thousand acres of trees up on the slopes of the mountain range. They were a pretty ecological family because they replanted young trees in the wake of their logging activities. That guaranteed them more harvesting over the decades."

"I remember my father telling me about the Ghost Ranch, as he called it," Gabe said. "It was the Rocking G."

"Right, it carries that name, too," Tom agreed. "The most important element of this is the fact that it's less than half a mile from the main ranch house on the Elsons' small spread. It sits right next to it, a barbed-wire fence in between them."

Eyes narrowing, Gabe said, "My parents always told us to avoid this area because of the Elson clan."

"With good reason," Tom said, flipping to another photo. "The grandfather is in federal prison in Montana for life. Brian Elson, the husband, was killed by Sheriff Sarah Carson a year ago. Cree Elson, the youngest, was also shot and killed that same year when he kidnapped a local woman and tried to run off with her. Hiram is in prison for ten years. The two brothers who are left, Kaen and Elisha, live at the ranch with their mother, Roberta." He grimaced. "This family has a rap sheet a mile long. Brian used to beat his wife. She's been to the ER in Wind River for a broken nose, cheekbone, and jaw, not to mention both arms being busted up by that guy."

"You ask me," Anna snarled, "it was a good thing Sheriff Carson killed him. He's a piece of vermin."

Tom gave her a sympathetic glance. "Yeah, for sure, Agent Navaro. Nothing good about Brian Elson."

"Do the two brothers beat up on their mother too?" she demanded.

"Not that we can tell. They're a tight-knit, dysfunctional family. We don't know much because no one has gotten close to observing or surveilling the family to understand their interpersonal dynamics. And that's one of the things that we want to know that, hopefully, you two can provide us over time. Further"—he flipped to a photo of several men standing outside the house at dusk—"we want to understand, through video reconnaissance, who these dudes are. We think they are Gonzalez drug soldiers, but aren't sure."

"And any photos can be run through our extensive

facial recognition software and potentially ID them," Anna
said with satisfaction.

"Right on."

"So," Gabe said warily, "we're basically setting up a
surveillance and ID site on this ranch?"

"Yes, the deed to the ranch is in your name, Gabe. Do
you still have Ace? Your dog?"

"Yes. He's always been a part of my cover since I joined
the DEA after leaving the Marine Corps. My hitch in Tijuana undercover, the men called me *El perro soldado*, the
Dog Soldier, because Ace is an ex-IED-trained military
dog. I could easily fold in my four years in the Marine
Corps as a dog handler. Plus, Ace has saved my butt more
times than I can count. He's my friend, my buddy and he's
a helluva guard dog."

"Good to know, because you can utilize Ace as a warning system if anyone is snooping around the property. The
story that your parents are telling everyone is that you're
coming home to stay and wanted to strike out on your
own, starting up your own ranch in the valley."

"And yet? My parents' name is involved because I'm at
that ranch."

"It is, only because you are their son," he agreed. "But
there's eighty miles between the two ranches. And we have
plenty of info on Gonzalez and his activities down in
Guatemala"—he nodded in Anna's direction—"because
we debriefed her a year ago on his strategies and tactics.
We found with him, when he wants to establish a new
territory, he always goes and looks for a local gang, if
possible, as cover and to work with them."

"Then," Gabe said, "the Elsons were perfect for the
way he operates."

"Correct."

"Gonzalez moves slowly compared to other drug

lords," Anna added. "He's very strong in family dynamics, hires carefully and not quickly. He thoroughly vets who's working for him from the lowest man on the totem pole up to and including the men who are closest to him at the top. He does a lot of background checking. He trusts no one. As a consequence, his cartel has a stronger loyalty rate and he knows all his men." She gave Gabe a sad look. "Someone like you trying to break in as an undercover agent? He'll suss you out in a heartbeat and kill you before you ever got a chance to get into his organization even at the lowest level."

"Correct," Tom agreed. "This is why Hardiman and the other agencies are looking to take Gonzalez down in a different way. We can't get inside his organization." He allowed a bit of a satisfied smile to creep onto his lips. "But we can move next to the Elson gang family he's chosen to work through in the valley. There's a half a mile between the Gardner main ranch area and the Elson main ranch house. We have long-range lenses on our video camera's abilities to see clearly who is coming and going from that house. Further, we'll put a twenty-four-hour-a-day video loop on the property, and Anna will be the one who will run that footage daily, to see the day-to-day activity. You, Gabe, will be the owner and you'll be doing a lot of outdoor work around the house and nearby property, like mending fences, to keep an eye on what's going on, as well."

"This is a perfect setup," Anna said, giving Gabe an apologetic look. "We're close, but not too close. We've got state-of-the-art equipment to ID everyone easily at that distance. We can time their movements when they leave the house and for how many hours or days. Gonzalez will establish drug drops and we'll be able to know over time where and when they occur. Plus, your dog, Ace, will be a front-line warning system all of his own."

"Exactly," Tom said, praising her. "And then, the next phase is to go by horseback or ATV up into the largest part of the Gardner property, which is on the slope and mountain range. We've had satellite recon sporadically over that area and seen drug bales that had been dropped in a high mountain meadow right on Gardner property up there at seven thousand feet. What we don't have is a schedule of those drops, who's dropping the bales, and we need to know that."

"Too bad they can't park a satellite over that meadow," Gabe said.

"Too expensive. They can't do it. This is a drug cartel trying to put deep roots into your valley over a long period of time," Tom said. "We're at the front end of Gonzalez's plans. But if we don't get a handle on this now, the whole valley and its citizens are going to become cannon fodder, one way or another, to this cartel. There will be a lot of death."

Gabe sat back, arms crossed, chin on his chest, grim. *The whole valley.* He sighed and unwound, looking at Anna and then Tom. "I grew up in that valley. There's a lot of good people, hardworking, who love that place like me and my family do. None of us deserve to become targets of those killers."

"Well, if we don't hit this opportunity," Tom said, "it won't be only the southern end of the valley that is going to see gunfire, violence, and shootouts. Eventually, this cartel is going to infect the entire valley and its populace. There's a lot of good people who don't deserve to get caught in between gunfire and violence as this cartel takes hold and will eventually rule the entire county. And that's what is going to happen, Gabe. That's why Hardiman flew in to tell your parents what was happening. They immediately wanted to help out of patriotic duty and service to the people in their valley. The director spelled out all the things you're concerned about, that if Gonzalez and his soldiers find out that they have agreed to play a part in taking him down, that they, too, could become targets. And so could your siblings."

Squirming in the chair, Gabe wanted to deny all of it. But Tom was right. His gut felt like a nest of angry, churning snakes right now. Glancing to his right, he looked over at Anna. Her expression was just as torn as his was. She understood from real-time experience, losing her father to the cartel. "Maybe I need to adjust how I'm reacting to this," he muttered unhappily.

"It's different when your own family, where you live, is involved," Tom offered sympathetically. "I know I'd be really upset if a cartel moved into my town. It's never a good thing, and it always has a bad outcome for the innocent people who live in that vicinity."

Rubbing his jaw, Gabe rasped, "Then . . . we have to stop this while it's in the buildup stage."

"Yes," Tom said, nodding. "As it stands, Anna will be your wrangler. She's our force multiplier in this situation and is familiar with surveillance methodologies. Ace should be trained to remain in the barn where all this equipment is at. He should be your guard dog when you leave the ranch to go snoop around up on the mountain range. I know you'll have sensors that will warn you on your cell phones, but up on that range there are no cell towers. That's why I asked if you still had Ace, because he'll be one heck of a guard dog in your absence. You will be, more or less, the 'face' of our undercover operation: the cowboy who has just bought a broken-down ranch and is trying to bring it back to life with daily hard work. Anna will be seen in daylight hours, but it's the night hours that count because cartel movements happen under cover of darkness. She'll be responsible for moving the twenty-four-hour video into the DEA cloud and our people in La Mesa, California, will be viewing every foot of it. They'll be the ones who do the ID work on all of them. Anna will also be there with a camera, too. She'll send those shots to the DEA as well. Doing this will help us build a picture of the cartel, who's involved in it, and keep tabs on their movements. You'll work with her on putting together a weekly report on any and all movements."

"What about that drop area in the mountains?" Anna demanded.

"Well," Tom said, smiling a little, "you're both wranglers and no one on the Elson property will find it odd or unusual that you're riding into the forested areas of your own ranch. But you'll be hunting for hidden trails that the cartel has either set up or are in the process of doing so. You can map them with GPS. That info will also be in the cloud and La Mesa HQ will disseminate that info, building a large file on Gonzalez. It will then be shared by all main HQ DEA stations across the USA."

"Is Gonzalez working with any other cartels?" Gabe wondered.

"Not that we know of, but that's a big question mark. Many cartels will work on the peripheral territory they've established with one another when wise to do so."

"Because Gonzalez is family-centric," Anna objected, "he will not trust outsiders. Especially another cartel boss from another or adjoining territory. He always went to war on them and he never lost. I doubt he'll make any deal with any other drug cartel trying to push into new territory where he's establishing his soldiers."

"We agree with you," Tom said, nodding in her direction.

"He's the outlier of the cartel bosses. Most of them hop into bed with one another when feasible and it serves both their long-range purposes."

"In a way," Gabe said, "we might have lucked out with this particular cartel coming into our valley. If he has few or no connections with other cartels, if we can stamp out the footprint he's trying to put into our valley, we'll be free of him and his soldiers, making our valley safe once more."

"That's the thinking from the top," Tom agreed. He turned off the projector and hit a button that raised the screen back to the top of the ceiling. Turning, he flipped on the overhead lights. "Well?" he said, looking at them. "What do you think?"

"I like that it's well thought out," Anna said. "I know the worry Agent Whitcomb will feel during it because his family is in that valley."

Gabe heard the lowering of her husky voice, emotion clearly in it as she spoke those words. He felt he could work with Anna. She was all business, but at the same time, she had a heart and was able to understand another person's pain. "You've already had that experience," he said to her, his voice low. "And I'm really sorry that happened."

She shrugged. "We'll just make sure it doesn't happen to your family or the people of your valley. I like this plan. I feel it will work. We have better cover than normal on a mission like this. I feel very confident that we can add a lot of intel to the DEA on the Elsons and whoever they are working with to get a toehold in Wind River Valley."

"I'm glad you have a background in dealing with Gonzalez," Tom said to her.

Anna tapped her forehead. "Burned permanently into my brain."

"Thought so," Tom said, and grinned boyishly. He reached over to a red file on the table, handing it to Gabe. "Yours to memorize."

"Who do you suspect is running this phase for Gonzalez in the valley?" Gabe asked, opening it up and seeing photos of six men, all hardened-looking soldiers, their eyes dark, flat, remorseless, and all killers.

"We don't know. Our guess is he's sent one of his trusted lieutenants to get it done, but we don't have a name yet. When we do, you'll be the first to know about it. We're hoping that the surveillance Anna sets up in the barn, which directly faces the Elson home and outbuildings, will be able to suss out that intel for us."

Anna was studying her file, riffling through the papers to find the technical requirements, things she'd be responsible for. Finding the list, she perused it. "This is good, Tom. I've got what I need to set up that surveillance."

"And you can always let us know if you need anything else," he assured her. "The Salt Lake DEA HQ is the closest to your area. If you need any type of help, you can reach out to them. We'll be in the background here," he said.

Gabe looked over his technical sheet as well. "Glad we have the firepower we might need," he said.

"We're hoping that you do not interface with the cartel members. We can't guess what you may find up in the mountains, though. What we're looking for are entrance and exit points from that one drop meadow we luckily caught on satellite. How are they doing it? What vehicles, if any, are used? How often are they dropping a shipment? How many men involved? Photos of an encampment up there, if any. Photos of all drops in the meadow that you discover over a period of time."

"And photos in real time if we can catch them picking up the bundles," Gabe said.

"That will be pure luck," Anna pointed out. "They don't hand out their drop and pickup zones or when they schedule them to anyone. That's one of the most tightly held secrets that Gonzalez has and he's not going to entrust it to many."

"True," Gabe said. "We'll have a video and camera on us anytime we ride up into that area."

"Just be really careful when you do it. Let us know when you leave the ranch, always alert Salt Lake HQ on that one. You'll also let them know that Ace is in that barn, guarding it. Up there? No cell phone coverage. You'll be on your own."

"But you've included a satellite phone," Anna said.

"Have to," Tom agreed. "You'll have to carry it on you anytime you're out in the boonies."

"Roger that," Gabe said. "Ace is one helluva guard dog. His growl is enough to make anyone think twice before going into an area he's guarding."

"How much contact do you want us to initiate with the Elsons, if any?" Anna asked.

"As long as it's neighborly and friendly? Keep your cover and go along with it. There's notes in Sheriff Carson's reports that Roberta is lonely, always wanting friends, but doesn't have any."

"Hmmm," Anna murmured, "she may be a door into that family of hers. I'm a woman. I can be friendly. Maybe gain her trust over time?"

Scowling, Gabe said, "I worry about her two sons, Anna. What if they suspect you?"

Snorting, she gave him an irritated glance. "Women know how to kibitz without raising suspicion, believe me. I think once we get situated, I should go over and make connections. Besides, isn't it a Western courtesy to know and welcome new neighbors? There aren't many people very close and if something happens, you have to rely on the goodwill of the ranch next door. Right?"

"Right," Gabe answered. "It might not be a bad idea. By going over there and introducing yourself, you might create trust rather than suspicion."

"We'll get a feel for the Elsons after we arrive, and then we'll consider it," Anna said.

Gabe liked her common sense. "Sounds solid."

"Any other issues?" Tom asked, looking at his watch. An hour had flown by.

"Not for me," Anna said, standing and gathering up the paperwork.

"Me either," Gabe said, rising. "I'll drop by and tell Director Hardiman to go home, that we've been properly briefed."

Tom opened another file. "Here's pin money. You've got two weeks to get yourselves packed up and moved out of your apartments here in La Mesa. Either of you have a car?"

"I do," Anna said.

"So do I," Gabe volunteered.

"Want to keep both of them?"

Anna looked at Gabe. "I like my black, beat-up pickup."

"Being undercover for two years, the car I was using is in Mexico."

"You can ride with me," Anna said. "We'll go together. I have room for your dog, too. My truck is an extended cab type."

Gabe liked that idea and thanked her. Tom handed out further information and they stuffed them in their individual files. They each had a thumb drive with the info on it, as well. Before they left La Mesa, the files would be turned back in to HQ. They didn't want to take any chance that someone could get their hands on the info by accident or otherwise. "Are you a good driver, Agent Navaro?" He watched her beautifully shaped lips curve upward into a wry grin.

"You'll find out, Agent Whitcomb."

Tom laughed genially. "Oh, you two are going to get along just fine," he said, and he waggled his eyebrows.

"Hello?"

Gabe relaxed on his couch after hearing his mother's low voice. "Maud, it's me, Gabe."

"Steve and I thought we might hear from you."

He heard the wry tone in her voice. "Well, since you pulled the wool over my eyes, I imagine you knew you'd hear from me." He kept his teasing light because in the past two years, there had only been rare times that he could talk to his parents, who missed him sorely. His heart swelled. Damn, it felt good to be free of undercover! Well, sort of, he reminded himself. He eagerly absorbed Maud's husky laughter and he laughed with her.

"Steve is out with the boys tonight, a chess tournament in town, so you got me to talk at. I assume you had your conference with Mr. Hardiman?"

"Sure did. Kinda took me around the bend for a while, Maud. I was more worried about you and the rest of the family being in the line of fire. Some of that dissipated when I met my new partner, Agent Anna Navaro, and then we went to mission planning to pick up our orders."

"Well," Maud said, becoming serious, "we talked a great deal for several weeks before we agreed to the plan with the DEA, Gabe. I know Steve and I are not military black ops like you've been, nor have we been anywhere near the military, but we knew there were risks involved."

He lay on the couch, back propped up with a lot of pillows. "What made you decide to do this?"

"The fact that if we didn't cooperate, Gonzalez was going to eventually poison this valley, and everyone in it. We felt strategically it was better that we knew and the people of the valley didn't, and maybe, just maybe, we could stop this incursion by this cartel when it was in its nascent stage."

Mouth quirking, he said, "You realize you're still at risk?"

"Yes and no. We aren't going to leave the valley, change our names, and disappear after the mop-up operation to get this cartel out of here is done, either."

His voice tightened. "You two are patriotic in the best of ways, trust me. You're doing something not for yourselves, but for everyone else, too."

"I guess we were born that way?" she teased gently.

"You taught all us kids to be of service to others. So why wouldn't you agree to do something like this. Right?"

"You aren't upset that we volunteered?"

Hearing the worry in her voice, he wished he was home just to wrap his arms around this wonderfully strong, clear-headed, compassionate woman who became his mother. "Of course not. After I got over my reaction, I came to understand why you'd agreed to it."

"This place is worth fighting for, Gabe. But you know that. We taught you high morals, values, and integrity. We live by them. All of us. And when Mr. Hardiman called us to fly in and speak to us in person, we knew that we'd been called by our country to serve it, albeit in a different but just as important way as enlisting into the military."

He withheld his comment that cartels were military in every aspect, frequently hiring men out of the services, mercenaries, who fought and killed for them. "I'm proud of both of you," he rasped, love for them welling up inside him. "And I've missed the hell out of you. At least this way? I'll be home, back in the valley and only eighty miles away from you two and the ranch."

"Yes, we're celebrating that, believe me," Maud said. "We can hardly WAIT to see you! It's been a year since the last time. How are you, Gabe? Are you well?"

"Glad to be out of that undercover with the cartel in Tijuana, believe me. And I'm fine. Just glad to get an assignment like this. At least I can play myself," he said, and he chuckled.

Maud laughed. "I'm relieved, then. When this mission is done, Gabe, are you going to continue to be in the DEA as an undercover agent?"

"I don't know, Maud. I honestly don't. Maybe I'll have a better answer for that after we get this one played out."

"We want you to come home, we really do. Sky and Andy live here. They're happy and you missed Andy and Dev's wedding. Luke is coming home soon, too. He's been offered a job with the wildfire unit at the airport on their hotshot team. At least he's off the smoke jumping team out of Montana. No more jumps. I lived in fear all the time of him dying being stuck on a huge pine tree somewhere near a wildfire."

"You've really got a creative imagination," he teased her gently, knowing that beneath that confident exterior, Maud was really a genuine worrywart regarding her family.

"I guess I do. Maybe because we're older, we want our adult children home, and closer to us. Maybe that happens with age."

"Well, I'll take your dreams into serious contemplation," he promised. "I miss being home, too."

"Really?"

He heard hope in her tone. "Yes, really. I've kind of

wondered that since I get to play cowboy and ranch owner, maybe I'll find out if the call of Wyoming is stronger than that of a DEA undercover agent. At the end of the mission, I'm sure I'll know which way I want to go."

"Just think," she said, "Andy being married to Dev? We might have grandkids soon and I'm so excited about that!"

"It would be nice to hold a baby or two, huh?" Maud had been the best mother growing up. Never had four children been lavished with so much love and affection. It was exactly what they needed, having been abandoned by their biological mothers.

"Ohhhh, I dream of that happening!! I think Andy and Dev still want to wait, but they're close to thirty years old."

"Women are having children later," he agreed. "Career first and then family, which is okay."

"I know," Maud grumped, "but I'm in a hurry to be a grandmother. And so is Steve."

"Both of you," he said, a catch in his voice, "were so loving to all of us. I never realized just how much care and attention you gave us until I got out into the real world. I saw a lot of crappy, broken homes. Places where parents should never have been parents at all. And the kids always suffered. I used to hold a lot of anger against my unknown mother, but after seeing what I've seen, and what you two gave all of us? I think we were the luckiest, most loved and cared for children in the world."

"We love all of you, now more than ever," Maud whispered. "We'd better stop this or you 're going to make me cry, Gabe," and she managed a wobbly laugh.

His hand tightened around his cell phone. "Sorry," he said, meaning it. "Listen, Hardiman gave us two weeks to get out to Wind River. Agent Navaro said she's ready to roll in two days. So am I. How about we drive out there and stay with you two birds? That way, we can see Sky and Andy, plus you."

"Oh! We'd love that!"

He could hear the joy vibrating in her voice. Warmth flowed through him. "Hey, it's all going to work out, Maud. Now stop your worrying."

"You can have your old bedroom back for the stay. Agent Navaro, as I understand, is a woman?"

"Yes."

"She can choose between Sky and Andy's old bedrooms. It will be so wonderful to have you both here!"

"Something that I'm looking forward to, Maud."

"Is Ace still with you?"

"Absolutely, he is. He'll be going down there with us. He's a great guard dog. Listen, I'm going to crash. It's been a rough day for me and I'm totaled, but happy. I'll call you when we hit the road, okay?"

"Sounds great, Gabe. And gosh, can I call you on your cell phone now?"

"Sure, you can," he replied, and he gave her the number. "It will take us two days to reach you. We'll probably stay overnight in Colorado and arrive late afternoon on the second day."

"Don't be a stranger. Stay in touch with us, okay?"

Chuckling, he sat up, placing his sock feet on the carpeted floor of his hotel room not far from the DEA HQ. "I promise. Tell Steve I love him, that I'm looking forward to some wicked chess games with him, and give him a big hug of hello from me when he comes in tonight?"

"You bet I will, Son. We love you. Night, night . . ."

Night, night. Those were softly spoken words Maud always whispered to him when she tucked him in his bed when he was a young child. How many times in high tension and dangerous nights had he replayed those words and imagined Maud's strong, lean hands ruffling his hair, smiling down into his eyes, filling him with her boundless love? *Many.* Gabe wanted to tell her that, to let Maud know just how much her love was an antidote to his undercover life. He'd make sure and not tell her about those dangerous situations, however. She worried enough.

Chapter Three

April 4

Anna pulled up at the hotel in her black pickup with a U-Haul trailer behind it. Gabe stood waiting out on the curb with his beautiful dog, Ace, on a leash. It was the third morning after the mission briefing. The sun had just risen as she arrived.

He was wearing his straw cowboy hat, a Stetson, he'd told her, a hallmark of ranchers in the West. She wasn't impressed, but he seemed to be proud of it in a quiet, disarming, almost bashful way. He wore the same scuffed wrangler boots, and a green-and-white plaid cowboy shirt, the sleeves rolled up to just below his elbows. She didn't want to admit she liked his muscles, and the dark hair sprinkled across his forearms. He was handsome in an interesting way, but didn't seem to realize it as some dudes did, who played upon their looks and body to attract a woman. She was pretty sure he was wearing the same Levi's as a few days ago, since they looked wrinkled and work-worn. There were three luggage cases near him as she braked to a stop. He tipped the edge of his hat toward her. A cowboy greeting? Anna wasn't too clear on what cowboys did except ride horses and herd cows. They didn't have cowboys in Guatemala.

She climbed out, coming around the front of her truck. She, too, wore jeans, a three-quarter-sleeve purple tee, and tan sneakers. She loved her long hair, but always had to capture it up off her neck when on duty. This morning's travel toward Wyoming made her put it into an out-of-the-way ponytail.

"Good morning," she greeted, coming to a halt, seeing what she thought was happiness or pleasure glinting in his gray eyes as he studied her. "This is Ace?"

"Sure is. Let me do the introductions so he knows you're not only friendly, but you mean something to me personally. He knows the difference." With a command, Ace stood up, his golden-brown eyes, large and focused on her, studying her. He had Ace sniff her fingers and then walked the dog around Anna, coming back to the front, where Gabe ordered the dog to sit.

"He's absolutely gorgeous with that black mask over his face and that fawn-colored body," Anna said. "We have a lot of Belgian Malinois in service as drug-sniffing dogs down in Guatemala."

"Ace is smarter than I am," he said, smiling a little, giving one of the dog's sharply pointed ears a caress. "He knows now that you're like family to me. And he'll guard you just as quickly as he will me. You can come and pet him if you want."

Grinning, Anna said, "Oh, in a heartbeat," and she crouched down, placing her hands slowly on Ace's head. He began to pant, his pink tongue lolling out one side of his mouth, his long, busy tail thumping. "Good sign, he likes me."

Gabe chuckled. "He'd be out of his mind not to," he

said, and then met her smile. "I'll teach you his commands on the way to Wyoming."

"Great." She ruffled his neck and she smiled as he licked her cheek. "Oh! That was a nice kiss! Sweet dog." She gave Ace a final pat and said, "Let's get going. I'll open up the second seat so Ace can get in."

"Roger that," he said, giving Ace a command to walk at his side. Once Ace was in the back seat, Gabe went over and picked up two of the bags. "Mind if I put them in the truck bed? It will give Ace the room he needs to stretch out. He's an eighty-pound dog."

She picked up the third one. "Not at all. We can place them in the trailer, if you want? That would be safer."

"Nah, nothing in here except clothes. The bags are waterproof."

"There's some rope in my metal tool chest," she said, and she pointed to it as they walked to the back of the truck. "Let's tie them in by their handles."

"Good idea. That way, they won't fly out. Have you had breakfast yet?"

"Yes, grabbed a bacon, egg, and cheese biscuit at McDonald's on the way over here." She hefted the dark ballistic blue nylon bag over the top of the pickup and set it gently on the bed. "You?"

"Let's stop at one on the way out of San Diego. Maybe at El Cajon? There's only one way in and out of San Diego if we want to go east and that's up through Interstate 8. Ace especially loves their Egg McMuffins."

Grinning, Anna said, "Roger that, Interstate 8," trying to ignore his maleness. They were close and she caught the scent of fresh soap, noting with her sniper's all-terrain alertness that his reddish-brown hair was damp and recently washed. He was clean-shaven, as well. In no time, after she gave him the rope from her toolbox, he'd expertly tied the bags in so they couldn't be lost in transit.

"You don't have much to move," she noted, straightening and standing next to him.

"Been two years undercover. I was rarely north of the Mexico border except for clandestine meetings in dark alleys somewhere in San Diego with my handler."

"Hmm, that explains it. Well, ready to go?"

"Yeah," he said, smiling over at her, "let's saddle up, pardner."

"Pardner? Is that Western slang for let's blow this joint?"

"Every cowboy has a buddy and we call them a pardner. Come to think of it, you'll need to be schooled on some of the Western sayings and things like that so you fit in as a wrangler at my new ranch and don't bring attention to yourself as an outsider. If they do sense that, people will become wary of you."

"Sounds good. Now that we're undercover," she said, and walked around and climbed into her truck. As she belted up, he climbed into the cab. "I'm all ears to slang." Pointing to the cup holders in the center between them, she said, "I bought you a large coffee. It's black, but there's cream and sugar in the glove box if you need it. Figured you might like some this morning."

He gave her a keen look, the corners of his mouth drawing upward. "You're good, Agent Navaro. Really good. Thank you for being so thoughtful." He fastened his seat belt and then took the coffee, taking a slow, pleasurable sip of it, making a sound in the back of his throat.

"You sound like a satisfied cougar after a kill," she noted wryly, pulling away from the curb and maneuvering back into traffic. Inwardly, she felt good about the look on his face. For a moment, that mask he wore dissolved, and the man she saw beneath it shook her deeply. In a good way. But not in a way she needed right now. She was on assignment and that meant no fraternization. It had to be all business. This time, she lamented that reality.

Chuckling, he said, "Call me Gabe. Where we're going? We need to lose the agent side of ourselves into the nearest dustbin. When we get home to Wyoming, first names are pretty much it, unless you meet a stranger and then it's Mr., Ms., or Mrs."

"Okay," she murmured, speeding up, taking the middle lane of outgoing traffic toward the mountains ahead that they'd have to climb. "I've never been undercover. Well, that's not true. As a sniper, I was ALWAYS undercover, but it was in a hide. What do people call each other in Wyoming? Do they have nicknames, too?"

"Well, since we're working together, we will be on a first-name basis. I noticed in the mission details that they're changing your last name to Dominguez and removing your real name, Navaro. I read in the report that the DEA gave you a passport from Buenos Aires, Argentina, to help cover your tracks."

"With good reason," she said, frowning. "I've got a one-million-dollar bounty on my head by Pablo Gonzalez."

Scowling, Gabe said, "I didn't know that. That info is not in the details I read."

"Well, it's a way of life. I came to the States for Marine Corps sniper school, graduated, and then went back to my home country, Guatemala, and began stalking drug lord top-tier people. I figure if I took them out, instead of the mules and drug soldiers at the bottom rung of the ladder, I could disrupt their movements." Her voice turned satisfied. "And I have. Continually."

"Which earned you the high price on your head."

"Bingo."

He watched the traffic, checking the rearview mirror.

It was just habit, memorizing cars behind them, in case there was a tail of some kind from a local cartel discreetly following them. "Being a sniper on the move all the time must have been pretty stressful?"

"No more than you playing a bad hombre when you really aren't and infiltrating drug cartels."

He sipped the coffee gratefully. "Where we're going? It's normal for you to call me Gabe."

"Then you can call me Anna."

Nodding, he continued his perusal as another, faster car, passed them. He trusted no one and there was a lot of drugs hauled up Interstate 8, up and out of Southern California, over the Cuyamaca Mountains and then down into Arizona and the golden sand desert. This highway was a well-known drug gateway. "You have weapons for us?"

"Yes. Pop the center lid," she said, and she pointed to it between the front seats.

He did and found two Glocks.

"Both loaded, bullet in the chamber of each and safety off," she warned.

"I'm assuming you have a concealed carry license for both of us?"

"Yes, California and every state in between here and Wyoming that we have to drive across. The DEA obtained them for us. I don't think we'll get pulled over by law enforcement, but in case we do, the papers are in the top of the glove box. I didn't think it would be smart to be carrying our DEA ID on us. I have my agent info on my iPhone, just in case."

"Same here. But I don't think anyone will pull you over because you're driving slower than the speed limit with that trailer behind us."

"Right on." They were approaching El Cajon now, the

Interstate 8 curving around, the stony Cuyamaca Mountains silhouetted in the distance.

He set his straw hat on the seat between them. "How are you feeling about coming to Wyoming?"

"I was bored with my surveillance job out of Descanso and the area surrounding it. Been doing it for a year now, and I wanted to do something else. I didn't know what," she said, giving him a wry glance, noticing the mask had not yet settled back into place. *Good.* She was far more curious about Gabe, the man, than she cared to admit to herself right now. "I'm really anxious to do something new and get out of my rut."

"Do you have any skills with horses, ranching, or cattle?"

"Not with cattle." She heard him chuckle. "But I'm a quick study. I grew up on my parents' estancia and was riding horses from the time I was eight years old, onward. My father preferred an agricultural farm instead of raising cattle. He believed in helping the poor and worked with food banks and kitchens in Antigua, with our leftover produce that was bruised or disfigured and couldn't be sold to grocery stores in the United States." Her voice lowered. "My father was well loved by everyone."

Hearing the loss in her low tone, he asked, "You grew up in a rural area, then?"

"Yes. Antigua is the old capital of Guatemala. Our estancia was on the outskirts of the city, in the agricultural district near Santa Ana. I went to an all-girls Catholic school there and later, received a scholarship to attend Yale and go after a degree in law. My mother, Maria, is a prosecutor with a degree from Yale and I wanted to follow in her footsteps."

"According to the bio they had on you, things changed after your father was murdered."

"Very much so. I don't regret it, though. The way I look at it? I'm in law enforcement instead of being an attorney, but it's still about righting wrongs and defending those who are innocent and unable to protect themselves from these bloodthirsty cartels."

"Interesting perspective," he said.

"Why did you get into dangerous undercover work?"

His mouth quirked. "I went into the Marine Corps at eighteen, a real headstrong risk taker. I later moved into black ops recon work behind enemy lines and really liked it. I also worked as a dog handler and located IEDs with my dog's help. After I got out, the DEA came knocking at my door. They were recruiting a lot of US-born Hispanic males to infiltrate the cartels across the border from San Diego. I went into it thinking I knew everything, but I learned very quickly, undercover work was different from my recon work. Ace went with me as part of my under-cover identification."

"That kind of work would make me feel like I was schizoid. I couldn't live two lives. I really respect what you did."

He nodded. "Yeah, you assume a whole new demeanor, a backstory, and pray to God that the DEA has gone deep enough into your personal record that your story holds. Luckily, it did."

"But you didn't like what you were doing?"

Shrugging, he said, "I was younger then and still had some risk taking to do. It was all right. I got satisfaction that we're sending some of the biggest Central American cartel lords to prison here in the US after extraditing them. That made me feel good about it."

"Didn't you miss your family, Gabe? I know I would."

"Especially around the holidays," he murmured fondly. "My parents really threw great holidays for the four of us kids. I think sometimes they were trying to make up for what we couldn't celebrate with our biological parents. The four of us were adopted."

"Your adoptive parents sound like incredible people," she ventured, giving him a sympathetic look. "I'm looking forward to meeting them."

"Oh," he teased, leaning back and spreading his long legs out before him, "you'll fit right in. My sisters, Skylar and Andy, are both no-holds-barred twenty-first-century strong women. They don't put up with this world we live in right now. They're just as independent and confident as you are. I'm sure you will take to them and vice-versa. BFFs."

"They sound like a perfect match for me. I like to be around can-do people, women or men. There's been times when I've been scared to death while I stalked a drug lord, but I just shoved it aside and relied on my muscle memory and training."

"And look where it got you. You're alive and well."

"I could say the same for you."

"For our age? We've done a lot, been through a lot in our twenties."

"That's funny, it sounds like you're pining for quieter waters now? The risk taker in you is satisfied and you don't want any more danger?"

He gave her a praising look. "You're really good at picking up on people's emotions, aren't you?"

It was her turn to shrug. "I've always lived on my feelings and gut. My father said he'd never seen anyone with the honed instincts that I was born with. I take that skill of mine for granted, but I realize many people don't trust their own inner judgment enough to work off it."

"No," he agreed, "they don't. In my business it was all instinct and gut calls."

"We're alike in that way," she murmured. She lifted one hand from the steering wheel toward a pair of golden arches to her left. "There's a McDonald's a few blocks off the freeway," she said. "Egg McMuffins! We'll go there to grab you a breakfast."

Ace whined, sat up, and thumped his tail, sticking his head between their seats, giving each of them an interested look. They laughed.

"Does he understand English?" Anna hooted.

"Egg McMuffin, McDonald's . . . yeah, he's got them memorized and the connection to it. He's a junk food dog."

Laughing heartily, Anna said, "Not a junkyard dog, but a junk food dog. That's good, Gabe."

"Oh, Ace IS a junkyard dog. You haven't seen him in guard mode yet. Right now, he's acting like a family dog out for a fun drive with the two people he loves most in the world." He held up the coffee cup. "When we get the food? I'll go in and order two McMuffins for Ace and then I want you to feed them to him. He'll connect that if you feed him, you're his family and to be trusted just as much as he trusts me."

"Interesting. Okay, I can do that." She started slowing down to take the off-ramp.

"You're a lifesaver, Anna, for both of us." He held up his empty coffee cup. "Thanks for being so thoughtful."

"You had some shadows under your eyes the afternoon we met. I knew you were probably tired and stressed out."

"I was," he admitted. "To my soul. I was glad my undercover with that cartel was finished. I was running on fumes, missing my family, missing a life I had growing up instead of lying all the time."

"Then," she said softly, making a turn to the off-ramp, "this is going to be a good assignment for you. You'll have your family nearby and you won't have to lie that much unless we come face-to-face with one of the Elsons, which probably won't be that often."

He sat up, constantly looking around. It wasn't anything obvious, but too many years of being hunted had taught him that hyper-alertness could save his life. "Yeah," he sighed, giving her a quick glance, "there's no place like home."

"I couldn't do what you did," she admitted. "I operate better alone and being my own boss. I don't have to argue with anyone or try to change their mind. I get along well with myself," she said, and grinned, turning into a large mall parking lot and parking near the fast-food establishment.

"Opposite of what I had to deal with," Gabe agreed, climbing out. "Can I get you anything? Another cup of coffee? Any other food?"

"Coffee sounds good. *El grande, por favor.* Large, please."

"*Bueno, señorita*, good," he acknowledged, nodding and shutting the door.

"I'm going to make a call to my mother while you're inside." The cab grew quiet. She liked speaking Spanish with Gabe, his accent real. She was sure no one would ever mistake him for being born in the USA. She wondered about his parents because in the briefing bio, it said he was adopted by the Whitcombs. Were they Latinos? The name Whitcomb wasn't a Spanish surname, that was for sure. Anna noticed immediately the cab didn't feel as warm and as inviting as before. Gabe had that kind of magical, unexpected effect upon her. She liked his easygoing ways, his sensitivity. *Dios*, God, how did he survive the brutality of undercover work with a cartel and still be sensitive like that? Cartels were a bloody business and she knew it. Maybe he was hiding that side of himself from her. People who went undercover were called chameleons for a good reason.

The traffic of El Cajon was mostly left behind after leaving McDonald's. Ace slurped up his two Egg Mc-Muffins from her, licking her palms in thanks. She fell in love with the warmth she saw in the dog's large, intelligent eyes. And then, he licked her cheek, as if it were a doggy kiss from him to her. She got very quickly that Ace was super intelligent—just like his master.

There was even less traffic on Interstate 8 as they passed Alpine, a small town in the foothills of the Cuya-maca Mountains. They would continue a slow, curving, and winding climb through the hills and begin heading over the mountain range that was roughly five thousand feet in elevation at its highest point. Anna was touched when Gabe brought back cinnamon rolls as a dessert they shared between them. As she drove, he would fork a small, gooey one and hand it to her while she kept her eyes on the road. At one point, there was a massive Border Patrol stop halfway into the mountains, something she had passed every day when working in the Descanso area. She knew all the men and women and they waved her through without searching her trailer.

"What is the weather like in Wyoming right now?" she asked.

Sipping his large coffee, he said, "Three months of summer and nine months of snow." He gestured to the Rocky Mountains, which showed off multicolored boulders beneath the rising sun. "From I-8, we'll get to the Arizona border. After crossing into Yuma, we go about fifty miles farther and then take I-10 out of Gila River, Arizona," he said. "We'll continue to stay on what is known as the 'the non-snow route,' because right now, there's snow blanketing Wyoming. And it will stay there until early June. We'll continue to take the southern route and then turn north to get to the eastern side of Wyoming via Colorado. We're lucky because we're between storm fronts right now and that means no snow falling, but the roads will probably be wet the farther north we go, and more potential for ice even when the sun is shining."

Wrinkling her nose, she muttered, "Snow? Ice?"

Laughing, he liked her sense of humor. "Yeah, lots of it."

"My blood is thin. I get cold easily."

"You were born in a jungle environment, near the equator. It's going to be quite a change for you."

"Will you drive when we hit snow or ice conditions?"

"Sure. I was raised in it."

"And I wasn't. I have no wish to slide off the road with a trailer behind us."

"I'll drive whenever you want to be spelled," he assured her.

"It's so sunny and beautiful up here at the summit," she said, gesturing around rocks and yellow boulder–strewn mountains for as far as the eye could see.

"Just wait," he promised.

"I'm really looking forward to meeting your family. We'll be staying there for a week or so before we drive down to the Rocking G?"

Nodding, Gabe said, "Yes, we need to get acclimated in a lot of different ways. Sometimes that area is hit with heavy snowstorms in April. We need to make sure that when we go down to our ranch, it's passable on that eighty-mile stretch of highway. According to my father when I talked to him yesterday, the Rocking G is in sorry shape. He has keys for the house and said the roof is leaking in several places, but that two of the four bedrooms are dry, so it looks like we'll have a place to sleep without getting wet."

Mouth turning down, Anna said, "What about heat and electricity?"

"My dad has got the electricity turned on, but heating is another problem. There's a potbellied stove in the kitchen, a huge fireplace in the living room, and plenty of chopped wood in a nearby shed. We're going to have to buy a lot of supplies from the Wind River hardware store like electric heaters to warm those bedrooms at night because the temperature will fall well below freezing."

"I think we should stock up on some electric blankets, too."

"Agreed. We can stop at any mall in Phoenix, Arizona, if you want, and get those kinds of supplies."

"I'm not freezing my tail off, Whitcomb."

Chuckling, he said, "I got it. By the time we arrive home, we'll make sure you have everything you need to stay toasty warm like a bug in a rug."

She gave him a jaded glance. "Is that some more Western slang? Or a biologist's saying?"

He grinned. "It's a Western saying."

"When we reach your ranch, I'll be all ears for how others use slang, too." She was curious about Western people, having grown up on cowboy stories of the Wild West. Was it really still wild? She was about to find out.

April 6

"Welcome to our home, Anna!"

"Thank you, Mrs. Whitcomb," she said, entering the foyer with Gabe and Ace. She liked the tall, thin woman's warm, sincere smile, watching as she leaned down and ruffled Ace's head while the dog wagged his tail in hello.

She heartily hugged her son and they traded kisses on each other's cheeks. Standing off to one side, Maud shut the door so the cold midafternoon air didn't steal the warmth from within the amazing two-story log cabin. There was a storm blowing in tonight and they had made it to the Wind River Ranch just in the nick of time.

"Anna, we are all on a first-name basis around here," Maud said, releasing Gabe and stepping forward, giving her a quick hug of hello. "Please, make yourself at home. *Mi casa es su casa,* our home is your home. We treat everyone as if they are family. Please relax and know you're welcomed."

After shrugging out of her jacket, Anna placed it on one of the many hooks. She deeply appreciated Maud's using Spanish. "Thank you."

"You both look tired," Maud observed. "Except for Ace, who looks like he could use a good run out back."

Gabe nodded. "That's what I need to do. I have his ball in my luggage. I'll get it out as soon as I can and get some of that energy released in the backyard."

Maud gestured to them. "Come on, I've got coffee and pastries waiting for you in the kitchen. I made some of my world-famous chocolate chip oatmeal cookies. Gabe's favorite, by the way."

Ace whined, looking expectantly up at Maud, trotting next to her down the hall.

Everyone laughed.

"He knows what 'cookie' means?" Anna asked him.

"Yeah, he's a foodie. Got 'em all memorized."

Ace whined again, looking up at Maud.

She leaned down, petting the dog. "Now, now, since we knew you were coming, Ace, we made you some doggy biscuits."

Ace barked, dancing around in front of them, more

puppy than the serious war dog that he was. His claws clacked loudly as they made their way toward the kitchen.

Anna couldn't stop laughing. "I swear, this dog understands EVERYTHING we're saying!"

Gabe made a happy sound of agreement and continued to walk with Anna. He leaned over and whispered, "Old habit of Ace because he came home here shortly after I got him and Maud fed him her cookies and he NEVER forgot it," he whispered. "And the human cookies are gonna be good, too. We'll take a lot of them with us for later munching."

Anna chuckled and they trooped down the long hall, the cedar floor an artist's mix of gold and coppery reddish colors swirling beneath their feet. With her sniper's attention to detail, she glanced around the fabulous-looking home. The cabin, if it could be called that, was at least four thousand square feet and two stories high. It was a lavish home, the kind that would be premiered in high-end socialite magazines. There was cedar paneling on some of the walls, but not all of them. Drywall had been strategically placed in between to break up the all-wood visual. The walls had been painted a cream color and gave the space a sense of subtle change without it being jarring. There was a lot of thought put into the building of this house. Just the placement of drywall with the paneling told her that. She spied the living room off to her right and the soaring, impressive two-story river stone fireplace roared with a welcoming fire. The river rock was rounded from hen-size eggs to grapefruit size, the colors dazzling white, black, tan, cream, brown, red, and gray. There was a huge butterscotch leather U-shaped couch system facing the fireplace. A long, L-shaped piece of etched glass topped the gorgeous cedar coffee table. She was too far away to see what the etching was, however.

There were Navajo rugs of varying colors and sizes placed around the huge living room, lending soft shades in earth tones to complement the cedar flooring. What a beautiful place! Gabe was lucky that he grew up in this Wyoming palace, she thought, smiling to herself. Anna reminded herself that her own family was very, very rich and she, too, lived on an estancia, unlike most people in Guatemala.

Maud Whitcomb wore Levi's and a pink fishhook cable knit sweater with a deerskin rust-colored vest, a silver concha pulling it partly closed. Her short black hair was peppered with silver strands and fell just below her ears. She wore no makeup nor fingernail polish, either. Anna was just like her. This was a woman who clearly was comfortable in her own skin and as an individual. Anna had never liked makeup because, as her mother said, it hid the real person beneath. And wasn't it more important for the real person to be seen and not hidden? Besides, in her business, she had to use scentless soap, no makeup or perfume. Someone with a keen nose would smell it and find her hide. *Not good.*

Slowing, they came into an L-shaped kitchen with a bank of windows framed by white, frilly curtains that paralleled the counter, making it look feminine and inviting. The entire counter consisted of swirls of cream-, caramel-, and sienna-colored granite. There was a huge aluminum double sink, and she saw a high-end and very expensive Wolf gas stove with several pots cooking on it opposite the counter. The scents of vegetables intermingled with a rich use of spices and meat made her mouth water. Maud pointed to the long rectangular kitchen table made of cedar inlaid with turquoise here and there. It was at least seven feet long, able to seat a lot of people at once. Above her were wagon wheels hanging from the ceiling with glass hurricane lamps around each of them, the LED lights lending plenty of brightness to the area, yet, their design and craftsmanship harkened back to a long-ago era.

"Sit down, both of you," Maud invited, pulling out one of the comfy chairs. "Coffee?"

"Absolutely," Anna said. "Are you sure I can't help you, Maud?"

"Nah, you two have to be tired from traveling for two days. Rest. I'll take care of us," Maud said, and she scooped up a plate of just-baked cookies, three saucers, and as many spoons. She also already had a doggy bowl filled with Ace's idea of biscuit cookies and placed them in the corner. He promptly trotted over and started downing them with gusto.

Gabe warned in a low tone, "Maud is a one-person band," and sat down, watching his mother fondly.

Anna sat opposite him. "Is the whole family like her?"

Gabe rubbed his jaw. He hadn't shaved this morning when they left Colorado after an overnight stay at a motel. "I think all the kids are driven in one way or another. All type A's, like my mother. My father is a very laid-back type B, by the way."

"I think it's a family thing," she agreed, taking the platter of cookies Maud handed to her.

"You got in before the weather closed us down," Maud told them.

"I told Anna about our snow and cold," Gabe told his mother. "She's from Guatemala and has thin jungle blood."

Pouring the coffee, Maud gave Anna a sympathetic look. "Well, the good news is, Anna, that we'll have two more months of winter, but the worst of it is over. Come early June, it starts with spring for about three weeks and then dives right into summer until mid-September." She placed two mugs of steaming coffee in front of them, then left to go back for her coffee.

"I see Gabe only wears a thin jacket," Anna said as Maud returned with a mug of coffee for herself and a small silver platter of sugar and cream, setting it down near them.

"We consider thirty-two Fahrenheit, which is freezing, very warm in Wyoming," Maud chuckled, sitting at the end of the table. "I'm sure it won't be warm to you."

"No, for sure."

Maud fixed her coffee and gave Anna a long look. "When we talked with Mr. Hardiman about this secret mission, he didn't mention who Gabe's partner would be."

"I'm it," Anna said, taking an oatmeal and chocolate chip cookie from the plate. "I think you and your family are very brave to even become a part of this mission."

"Steve, my husband, who, by the way, is in Australia on business, said we didn't have a choice. We either all work together to eradicate this cartel's encroachment into our valley like a deadly infection, or we'll pay for it in horrid ways later." Maud sighed. "I'm happy to have Gabe here, but it's a little unsettling to know you are both in danger down at the other end of the valley for God knows how long."

"I'll be there," Anna assured her gently. "I'll make sure he's kept safe."

"Gabe said on the phone before you left La Mesa that you're a Marine sniper."

"I am," she said, appreciating the brown sugar taste to the warm, soft, and gooey cookie.

"Many years in her skill slot, Maud," Gabe added. "Anna is the best. And this isn't going to be that danger-ous, so stop worrying. This is a surveillance mission. Anna will be setting up twenty-four-hour video, taking camera shots when she wants, and we report it back to the DEA in La Mesa. For the most part, I'll be outdoors being a wrangler, and so will she. It's going to look like people bought and moved into the Rocking G and nothing more to the Elsons next door."

She gave her son a look of relief. "Hardiman didn't give us the smaller details."

Anna reached out, briefly touching Maud's hand. "All we're doing is trying to identify and name the men who are taking part in this ring here in the valley. I'll be making a list and sending it to the DEA cloud, and their experts on facial recognition in Washington, DC, will do the rest. It's a very low-key mission." Anna saw Maud's face lose tightness that she interpreted as stress and worry for her son. She didn't blame the woman at all, but in this case, more information would help Maud relax and not let her wild imagination take over as she lay sleepless at night. "And"—she picked up some strands of her hair—"I'll be dyeing my hair red to cover my normal black color. My last name has been changed as well, and so has my birth country."

"That's pretty much it," Gabe said, not wishing to make his mother worry any more than she did normally, which was a lot when it came to her four children. He saw Anna give him a quick nod, as if in tune with why he wasn't going to say much else about the danger of their mission. The less his mother knew about it, the less she would worry.

"I feel much better now," Maud confessed, giving them a look of gratefulness.

"A very boring mission," Anna assured her, eagerly taking a second cookie. "These are really good, Maud."

"Thanks. Do you get to see your family very often, Anna?"

Anna was careful with her reply. "Between assignments, I get a month off and fly down to my country and visit my family's estancia."

"I'd want to see my family between assignments," Maud said.

"I'm always in touch via my cell phone and I talk with them at least once a week."

"Oh, that's good, then. Have your parents ever been to the US?"

"Yes. My father was a Marine general. He was often at Camp Pendleton, in Southern California. He sent his best Marines to your country to be trained."

"Your family serves your country and you must feel proud about that," Maud said.

"Just like your family does," Anna said. "You are all patriots in the service of the USA, too."

Maud gave them a kind look. "That's very true. I'm just glad you're here, safe and sound. Andy, my oldest daughter, just married Dev. They'll be here tonight for dinner."

"Is Sky around?" Gabe wanted to know. "And how about Luke?"

"She's on duty over at the airport for helicopter medical emergencies. You'll meet her tomorrow morning. Andy has the twenty-four-hour duty with her husband, Dev. Luke said he'd be coming in, but didn't give a time or date. That's typical of him," she said, and smiled fondly.

"Too bad Luke does wear a watch," he said, teasing. Luke was one of those people who marched to his own drummer.

Maud looked over at Anna. "Luke is a hotshot and right now he's over with a US team fighting fires over in

Australia. He does it year-round. He has a job here, in the valley, with the wildfire team, but this time of year, he's where the fires are at."

"That's not a job I'd want," Anna said. "Fire has a mind of its own."

"Ugh," Maud said, "tell me about it. Dev was saying that they want to hire him as a manager for the regional firefighter team here and he'd be working out of the airport, which means he'd be home. I want that so badly. Steve and I would love to have all our children come home and settle down nearby."

"Family is good," Anna agreed gently.

"Has Luke made a commitment to Pete Turner?" Gabe asked Maud. He saw Anna's confusion. "He's the boss of the air medevac and the wildfire unit at our airport," he explained.

Maud nodded. "Yes, he's given a verbal reply to Pete, but papers have to be signed and then it's a done deal," she said, pressing her hand to her heart. "He'll sign the papers and will be arriving any day now from Australia."

"For good?" Gabe challenged. "After all, he's the tumble-weed of the family."

Laughing, Maud said wryly, "All our children are tumbleweeds! Who are you kidding?"

Gabe grinned and drowned in Anna's warm, brief gaze. "Well, guilty, I guess."

Snorting, Maud said, "The four of you are all type A's. Steve has been in Sydney and he gets together with Luke out in the field over there, when it works. At least they have some quality time with each other."

"Then," Anna asked, "all four of your children are coming home for good?"

"It looks that way," Maud said, crossing her fingers. "We want them nearby. We miss them terribly."

Gabe reached out, squeezing his mother's work-worn hand. "And we've all missed you and Dad."

Anna saw the tears well up in Maud's eyes. What a tight family. One that loved one another and wasn't dysfunctional like the Elson family they'd be observing for the DEA. It made her miss her own mother acutely, but she said nothing. It was hard for her to talk about her father even though he'd passed many years ago. They, too, had been a tight family like the Whitcombs. That ache in her heart would never go away. How she wished her father were still alive!

Chapter Four

April 13

"The Rocking G looks like a disaster to me," Anna said, sliding out of the truck and joining Gabe at the front of it. Ace leaped out, staying at Gabe's right leg. He was so well trained that he could be trusted to remain with them and not run off and snoop around. Above them, low-hanging gray and white clouds pushed by the off-and-on wind, made her hug herself, the wind icy even at ten A.M. She wore a black felt Stetson, but her ears were freezing. And she'd bought a good down coat, a muffler, and thick, warm gloves, as well.

"Yeah," Gabe murmured. "Dad wasn't joking when he said it was in bad shape." He pulled out his cell phone, called his mother to let her know they'd arrived safe and sound. Then, he texted a message to the DEA in La Mesa and Salt Lake City that they had arrived on station.

Sweeping her gaze around the property, she saw everything was in a state of dishevelment. Wooden rails sagged because five feet of snow could easily be dumped in the valley during the winter, the weight of it bending hand-hewn rails that were probably fifty years old. Patches of the white stuff were all around them. The storm that had come through seven days ago had dropped two feet of snow, which was more than enough for her. She saw the Elson property less than half a mile away from where they stood in the muddy driveway.

The nicker of the horses in the horse trailer they'd brought along made them both turn their attention to a small, nearby horse barn. To Anna, it looked in good shape compared to the house. Her words turned into vapor. "Shall we see how the stalls are? Get the horses comfortable and settled in? Let Ace look around since he will be guarding our equipment for the second floor?"

"Yes." He glanced toward the Elson property, no sign of life except two pickup trucks parked on the side of the ramshackle single-story house. It looked almost as bad as the Rocking G house. "Let's go snoop," he said. He gave Ace a hand signal and instantly, he leaped up and stayed right with Gabe.

"Aren't your ears freezing?" she wanted to know as he opened the sliding barn door that creaked with need of oil and some care.

Chuckling, Gabe said, "Oh, yeah. You get used to it after a while." He gestured to her. "Go on in."

Anna saw a light switch and turned it on. The horse barn held four wooden stalls. There were a lot of cobwebs and dust on the rafters above, barely discernible, but alerting her that cleanup was going to be long and continuous. She spotted a ladder. "I'm going up there," she said, pointing a gloved finger up at the landing that rose above. "Want to see if I can find a good spot to locate the video camera and other equipment."

Nodding, Gabe said, "Watch that ladder, okay? It may have cracks in it. I don't want you to fall."

"I'll watch it," she assured him. Anna liked that he was protective, but not smothering. Most men who didn't know she was a sniper tended to want to do the latter. Checking out the ladder on the wall, she saw there were ten steps up to the landing. Using her hands, she gingerly tested each of the first five. They were old, but durable. On the fifth step, she checked out three above her. The good news was the ladder was safe. There were some nails that needed to be replaced or worked out from the wood, but a hammer would fix these issues in a hurry.

The landing was in gray light, and she found another switch and turned it on. There were several bales of hay, but they were covered with decades of dust and would have to be thrown out. The light from the bare bulb above in the rafters was enough for her to spot a small wooden door in the side of the building that faced the Elson property. Going to it, she pulled off her gloves, stuffed them in the pocket of her coat, and found a rusted latch. With patience, she was able to slide the lock back and the door creaked open.

Being careful, Anna knelt down and cracked it just enough so that she could see outside. The Elson property was in perfect alignment with her window. The video equipment could be placed here and easily used. Pleased, she shut the door and then took a good look at her new hide for her spy equipment. It was dusty, filled with cobwebs, and needed a good cleaning.

"How's it look up there?" Gabe called from below.

"Excellent," she said. "I'm coming down."

They spent the rest of the morning cleaning the debris out of the stalls, bringing the horses in after they laid cedar shavings, and putting the hay bales into the tack room area. With the horses watered and fed, the barn door left open so they could each look out the upper part of the stall door, they went to check out the house.

"Hungry?" Gabe asked, cutting his stride a bit.

"Starving."

Ace whined, cocking his head, giving Anna a begging look.

Gabe chuckled. "See? You fed him that first morning and now he's looking to you to continue it. That's a good sign he trusts you."

"I'll be happy to do that. Should we get his dog bowl out and feed him inside the house?"

"Yes, we'll all go over there and eat a bite."

They stopped at the truck and he pulled out a cooler filled with food that Maud and her cook, Sally, had made up for them. There was no nearby restaurant in this area, no takeout, no nothing. They did have groceries, and they would use the chill of the outdoor and freezing temps at night to keep certain foods cooled until they could purchase a refrigerator.

"Even my hide in a tree was cleaner than this place," she grumped, watching dust poof into clouds as they walked into the large kitchen after Gabe had switched on the electricity.

Gabe frowned and looked around. "A lot of mouse droppings, too," he observed. Ace was already casing the house, his dog prints in the dust everywhere he walked, smelled, and then moved on to another place to check it out.

"Mousetrap time," she agreed, hands on her hips as she slowly looked around, memorizing the layout. It was an ancient log cabin with white mortar between each of the logs. A lot of the mortar had cracked or been lost in the twenty-five years that the house had no upkeep. It needed a lot of repair. Without the mortar, cold wind would leak in, lowering the heat they would try to build with the fireplace in the living room. She followed Gabe from room to room. It was easy to identify where the roof was leaking in two of the four rooms.

"Take your choice," Gabe said, pointing to the two bedrooms that sat beside each other in the hall.

"I'll take the blue door."

He grinned. "I'll take the pink door."

Anna chuckled. "Is your masculinity cringing?"

Gabe opened the pink door once more and left it open. "No. Is yours?"

She laughed softly. "Not at all." She stepped into her bedroom, a small window in front of her, the once-blue drapes sagging, holes chewed in them by mice and no longer serviceable.

"Let's scout the outside of the house after lunch? Maud made us some prime rib beef sandwiches with horseradish on them."

"Sounds good. We need to look like two people just moving in, not the spies that we are."

Gabe was happy that his father had the plumbing in the house repaired and that they had running water, plus a new water heater that had been installed earlier. Maud had supplied them with a lot of rags that could be used in cleaning up the dust and debris, and he pulled one from one of the boxes he'd carried in earlier. Anna came over, grabbed one, and without a word, wet it at the double porcelain sink and began to wipe the dust off the square, wooden table at the other end of the kitchen. There was no question she was completely self-sufficient, but she was still a team person. He got busy wiping off the four wooden chairs around it. In no time, they had the surfaces clean enough to eat their food from, and they sat down opposite each other and eagerly ate beef sandwiches.

Gabe rummaged around and found some Cheetos in a sack and opened them up, laying them between them as they ate. Anna still wore her hat, and he suspected it was to keep the heat from her head from escaping and making her less warm as a result. "Your ears are red," he observed, giving her a grin.

"So are yours."

"Comes with the territory."

Groaning, she said, "Right now I'd like to trade this hat in for my knit cap."

"We'll bring in the rest of the boxes after we eat. You can wear the red baseball cap Maud gave you and pull the knit cap over it. It will cover your ears and the bill will protect your eyes from weather and sunlight."

"Sounds like you've done that once or twice yourself."

"It's the uniform of the day," he said, munching on the salty, cheesy Cheetos.

"The military is never going to leave you, Gabe."

"It had to when I was undercover, but here"—he looked around the kitchen—"it won't matter."

"I don't think the Elsons will come over here. Do you?"

Shaking his head, he said, "No, but I think your idea to reach out to Roberta Elson, their mother, is a good one."

"As soon as we get this place cleaned up, I want to bake some cookies, drive over to their homestead, and see her."

"Do it after the boys leave," he warned. "Catch her alone. Sarah Carter said Roberta was clearly abused by her husband, Brian, before he died. She knows right from wrong, is lonely, and would like to move into Wind River, but the boys want her to stay out here in the middle of nowhere."

"To feed them, do their laundry and stuff," Anna sniffed, a hint of anger in her tone.

"When we spoke with Sarah, she said Roberta was the epitome of an abused wife and housewife."

"I think Roberta can be manipulated from what Sarah

told us earlier in the week," Anna said, wiping her hands off with a paper towel from a roll that sat on one end of the table. "It might take us a couple of days to clean this house up and get everything online, but she's my target of opportunity."

"She's the only one we have a chance with turning or at least maybe getting some intel out of her."

"I just wonder how the Elson boys are going to react to me bringing over some cookies to them as their friendly new neighbor?" She filled Ace's dog bowl with kibble, walked over to a corner of the kitchen, and filled a large bowl of water for him. Soon, Ace was chomping down with gusto on his kibble between drinks of water.

"That's something you'll have to evaluate on the fly. If they buy our story that we've bought the place and you work for me, then they might stand down and be a little mistrustful."

"They're too ingrained into the cartel not to be wary, Gabe. I would just take it on SOP, standard operating procedure, that they may think we're agents."

He grimaced and finished off a handful of Cheetos, closing the bag. "Yeah, that's my take on it, too. But over time, as we start to ride fence lines, repairing all those posts that are down and stringing new barbed wire, they might change their minds."

"I want to go out to the barn, clean it up, and get my spy equipment set up this afternoon."

"Go ahead. I'll start on the house."

"I'm trading this hat in for Maud's baseball cap and my knit cap, though," she warned, picking up the wrapper and standing.

Laughing, Gabe said, "Roger that. Dad said he had a chimney sweep come out a month ago and clean out the soot in the chimney so it doesn't start a fire once we get wood in it to start heating up this place."

She took a lapel radio that was hidden beneath the collar of her coat, turning it on. "Let's do a radio check so we have comms between us?"

He stood, unsnapping his radio and turning it on. "We're on the same frequency. Let's do a test. You go out to the barn with your equipment. Once you're up on that landing, give me a test call."

"Roger that." She hesitated, her voice sounding humored. "You're easier to work with than I thought."

"Funny, I was thinking the same of you."

Anna met his grin. She liked this guy way too much! He seemed completely in sync with her at every turn. Far more than any other man she'd met. "I like working alone, Gabe, but you're changing my mind."

"Uh-oh," he deadpanned, walking over to the door and opening it for her, "we're in trouble, then."

Shaking her head, she saw the merriment glinting in his eyes, and that mouth of his—which was decidedly sexy to her—curved with good humor. "I'll send you a test in a bit," she promised, heading for the truck bed where the equipment was stowed beneath a heavy tarp.

By five P.M., Gabe had the house pretty much cleaned up. The stove worked, thank goodness, and he had a prime rib roast in the oven, warming it up for dinner. Maud had thought of everything, including some pre-baked potatoes in the many boxes she'd packed for them. He'd not seen Anna for a couple of hours. She'd come in and used the bathroom, which worked, thanks to the plumbers. She reminded him of Ace when he was on a scent, eyes somewhat narrowed and all business. By the time she came in at five, he'd had the table set with dishes Maud had sent along with them. The flatware was on the table along with paper towels that would serve as napkins for them. It was nearly dark, the house was actually warm as he'd fed the huge fireplace with well-dried wood. His heart expanded a bit when he thought that Anna would really appreciate that welcome warmth. Though he was trying not to like her too much, it wasn't working. Gabe knew he was in trouble of a different kind.

The door opened and closed.

He turned, smiling a hello at Anna, who pulled off her gloves after shutting the door.

"Wow," she murmured, pulling off her headgear, "it's actually WARM in here!" Ace greeted her, wagging his tail, licking her fingers. Anna leaned over, petting him fondly.

"Take a look," Gabe urged, pointing toward the living room, liking the surprise in her expression. Her hair was in a loose ponytail, and he wondered just how silky it would feel if he threaded his fingers through that dark red mass that had been recently dyed. She looked great with red hair, he decided, watching her walk into the living room, staring appreciatively at the crackling, popping fire. Finding himself wanting to please Anna, he forced himself to finish off getting dinner on the table for them. When he looked a moment later, Anna was standing in front of it, palms of her hands open toward the heat. There was a pleasurable look on her face, her eyes half closed, as she stood there like a sponge, absorbing the heat into herself.

"Hungry?" he called.

"Am I ever!" She reluctantly left the fireplace and headed to the kitchen, shucking out of her winter gear, hanging them on wooden pegs near the door. "And it all smells so good! Is there anything I can do to help, Gabe?"

"No, just come and sit down. Ace already got his kibble. I'm sure there will be leftovers and we can drop them in his bowl after we eat."

She went to the sink, which was spotless and a gleaming white. "Gotta wash my hands first."

He stood patiently beside the pulled-out chair. He'd found cushions, washed and dried them in the new washer and dryer that had been installed. "Take your time."

There was even a clean towel nearby to dry her hands. Turning, she hurried over. "You're treating me like a queen, Whitcomb. I'm going to feel spoiled." She sat down and thanked him in Spanish.

Going over to the oven, he drew out lightly browned homemade biscuits and slid them into an awaiting wooden basket. Handing them to her, he asked, "I would imagine in your job you didn't have much time for a relationship?"

"You're right. I never got serious about a guy because I would see him maybe once every three months when I'd come in for a rest before going back out into the jungle." She sniffed the biscuits. "Mmmmm, Maud makes the best!"

"Put two on my plate?" He set the heated-up prime rib between them. He'd seated Anna at the head of the table and he took the chair on the right side of where she sat. Ace politely lay down next to Anna's chair, chin on his paws, eyes half opened, his ears moving as they spoke to each other.

"Roger that. I'm taking two, also," she said, and she pulled a dish with bright yellow butter over, setting it between their plates.

Sitting down, Gabe got serious about eating and so did

Anna. For long minutes, only the clink of silverware against the flowery plates could be heard. Anna gazed over at the living room. "This house is surprisingly warm. It feels so good."

Cutting into his prime rib that steamed as he did so, Gabe said, "I've got the electric heaters set up in each of our rooms. Our goose down sleeping bags are spread out on the beds. I think it will be warm enough to sleep without us putting on headgear and sleeping with it."

"That's great," she said, voraciously hungry. Slathering lots of butter, salt, pepper, and then a huge dollop of sour cream on her baked potato, she enjoyed every scent, the delicious heat surrounding them from the fireplace.

After they were done with their meal, Gabe cleared the table, poured coffee, and brought out brownies that Sally had made them. "Let's go sit on that couch in front of the fire," he suggested. He first went over and gave Ace, who was waiting at his bowl watching him, the scraps from their meal.

"Sounds exactly what this jungle person needs," she admitted, rising. Anna took the two mugs of coffee, and he brought two small plates with brownies on them. The couch was a light tan leather, and even though it was quite old, it was still serviceable after being dusted off. There was a rectangular coffee table in front of it and she set their mugs on it. Sitting down, she slid Gabe's mug toward him and he handed her the plate with the brownies.

"I could get used to this," she admitted, biting into the dessert. Ace came in and made himself comfortable in front of the couch, watching his two favorite people.

"Me too." He sat on one end of the couch and she on the other end. There were about four feet between them. "I'm so used to sleeping on the floor, wrapped in my sleeping bag, in rat hole apartments with four or five other drug soldiers."

"And I'm used to a lot better circumstances thanks to your DEA. I had a nice apartment in La Mesa. No cockroaches or rats in it, either."

"Yeah, but according to your service record, you spent a lot of years in the jungle." He slid her a glance. "There weren't no brownies out there, I bet?"

She smiled a little, savoring the chocolate blooming in her mouth. "No . . . nothing like what we just ate, thanks to your mom and Sally."

He settled back into the corner and studied her silhouette. There was no other light on except the light of the fire, and it danced and shadowed her face in interesting ways. "I can't wrap my head around a young woman like yourself spending her twenties hunting down drug lords in a jungle."

Her brow rose and she lifted her chin, taking the cup of coffee in her hands. "My father was murdered by a hit put on him by a drug lord. Isn't that explanation enough?"

Shrugging, Gabe said, "A woman of your intelligence, your education, and in the upper crust of Guatemalan society, you could have done anything you chose, Anna. Your family was from a very old, rich lineage of ranch and farm people in your country. And stop me if I'm being too nosy or curious about you. Okay?"

She sipped her coffee. "There's something about you, Gabe, that doesn't rile me or make me feel like you're an intruder into my private life. I'd like to think you are sincere in asking me, not nosy just to be nosy."

"You're one of a kind, that's for sure, and yes, I am sincere about it. What I'm asking is really personal, though. You haven't known me that long."

"I have the same curiosity about you," she said, and she drilled him with a direct look, seeing his lips curve faintly.

"Okay, then, can we play twenty questions with each other?"

"Sure. And if I get too personal, just tell me."

"Same here. Do you want to go first?"

Anna took another sip and settled into the crook of the couch, watching the shadows move along his face. "Do you know your Hispanic origins? I know you are adopted. I was just wondering . . . I see Indian blood in you with your high cheekbones and a broad brow. My family was Castilian, coming from Castile, Spain."

"All the nobles and royalty came from the Castile area, if my history serves me. Right?"

"Yes. My family line was not royalty, although they had a lot of money in shipping concerns. And what about your family roots? Do you know what country you hail from?"

"No, I don't know."

"Did you ever want to know?"

He made a face. "Yes and no. It ebbs and flows in me. What good would it do to know? My mother abandoned me. Knowing that, why do I want to stir up the past and try to find her? I would rather look forward than back."

"Hmmm, that's a good argument. I was trying to put myself in your place, and in the place of your adopted brother and sisters. I guess my curiosity would push me to find out, but that's me."

"Maud and Steve left it up to us kids to do what we wanted with that information. They would pay to do the investigation. None of us have really pursued it."

"You are loved, and to me, that's more important than anything else."

"We are," he said, his voice growing softer as he stared

into the flames of the fireplace. "There was never a day that went by that we didn't know that, Anna. And for me, maybe that's why I never pursued my past. As a kid, I didn't realize how lucky we were to have been adopted by them, but as an adult, I sure know the difference in family dynamics. And I've always been grateful to them for their unselfishness toward us. It just doesn't get any better than that: being wanted and being loved."

"That's the bottom line," Anna agreed gently.

"My turn?"

"Sure."

"Why are you so different from other women?" And then he amended, "Not that you aren't a woman in the first place." He opened his hands. "It's just that most women don't become a sniper."

She gave him a wry look. "Even in history books, especially in World War Two, there were Russian women snipers who helped turn back the tide of the Nazi invasion into Russia. I'm sure there are more, but history is written by men, not women. And women, even if they can do the job and do it well, tend to not be written about by the patriarchy of male domination."

"That's changing today," he said, "and I'm glad. Is your mother a feminist?"

"I guess you could say that. My parents didn't see me as a girl. They saw me as an independent human being. My mother, especially, because she fought so much male divisiveness at Yale to get into law, swore that when they had me, I would be raised differently." She opened her hands. "For example? Instead of getting a doll when I was young? My parents laid out four different career toys for me. One was a doll with a wardrobe, one was a LEGO set, another was a doctor's bag and stethoscope, and the last was a microscope and other science-oriented toys. I went for the LEGO building-block set. I liked building things. The other part of this is my father would take me to the motor pool at the Marine base, and the guys there taught me everything a boy is usually taught, such as changing a tire, draining and putting fresh oil in the truck, and working on the engine. That, I loved. I excelled at it."

"So, you had a brain that was interested in how things worked. My sisters, Andy and Sky, are super mechanically minded and they ended up in the military as pilots."

"My father took me to the shooting range when I was ten years old, and I fell in love with weapons and shooting handguns and, eventually, hunting rifles, at targets. It just came naturally. It wasn't that I wanted to kills things, rather, the challenge of winning shooting competitions. By the time I was seventeen I'd won Central America weapons contests in rifles. I liked the military because it was organized and efficient. And I liked my life that way."

"After your father was killed, that all changed?"

"Yes," she admitted heavily. "Something wonderful died inside of me when he died. In its place was this white-hot rage and wanting to track down and kill the man who had put a price on my father's head. I wanted him dead." She chewed on her lip, gazing into the fire for a moment, and then slowly turned her head, meeting his shadowed gaze. "I had never wanted to kill anything, Gabe. Not until that moment."

"That had to be hard on you emotionally."

"It was. I realized there was evil in the world that wasn't going to be dealt with in any other way except an equal power from another source to deal with it. I sleep well at night, Gabe. I don't have any guilt over taking the lives I've taken. All I have to do is know how many more innocent lives would be taken if they were still alive, and I'm at peace with my decision."

"You said you were done with being a sniper. Right?"

"Yes. I'm changing. I can feel it. To tell you the truth, getting this assignment was like breathing fresh air. I had taken out the bad guys in Guatemala who were part of the Gonzalez cartel that murdered my father. I caused disruption and cost him millions of dollars. I feel I have vindicated my father's death and that's enough for me."

"And who knows what will happen with this mission? I was grateful you didn't let Maud know how dangerous this could become. She's a worrywart."

"I don't think any parent wants their child, no matter their age, in the line of fire."

"That's why I kept ninety-nine percent of my undercover away from my parents. They'll never know. I especially want Maud to think this is a low-level, very safe mission."

"I'm with you on that," she said, sitting up. "But the Elsons have a bad record. I've got the video and other equipment online and working up in the horse barn. I'll be reviewing it twice daily: once in the morning and once in the evening. It is all simultaneously going to the DEA cloud where they can view it."

"Good," he praised. "Tomorrow I'm going to be outside a lot. My first priority is to get our roof fixed."

She held up her hands. "I've repaired a number of roofs. Need a helper?"

He smiled a little. "You bet. Besides, it will look good for the mission. It's supposed to be warmer tomorrow and we'll have sunshine and blue sky. There's no sense going up on that roof until around noon. There's going to be frost on it through the morning hours."

"Sounds good. Looks like we have nineteen questions to go with each other," she said, and she looked at her watch.

"I don't know about you, but I'm whipped. You have to be also?"

"Yes, I am. I'm going to do dishes. Why don't you go get a hot shower and hit the hay?"

"Hit the hay?"

He chuckled. "Well, not in reality. That's a Western saying: Hit the hay means lay your head on a pillow and go to sleep."

She stood and stretched. "Did your Western people sleep on hay for a pillow at one time?"

He liked her sharp intelligence and her ability to piece things together, but that was what a sniper did, put the jigsaw puzzle together so it presented a full picture. "Our pioneers used straw to fill up a pillowcase or usually some kind of flour sack. A lot of straw was used."

"Glad those pillows we bought were nice, firm Styrofoam instead," she teased, picking up her saucer and emptied mug of coffee.

He rose. "Makes two of us. Set your watch for 0600 for tomorrow morning?"

"Done," she answered, walking out to the kitchen.

Gabe joined her, getting ready to do the washing and then letting the plates and utensils air-dry. "I think we're going to invest in a dishwasher very, very soon."

"I don't do dishes, Whitcomb."

"Next time we're in Wind River, I'm going to the Sears store."

"Better yet? Why not call your mother? She could buy one for us and a Sears van could bring it out here to us. Save you time and trouble."

Gabe had to admit, that was a far better idea. "Done."

She chuckled. "I'll see you in the morning. Thanks for a great dinner. I was starving."

He hadn't expected her to turn and place her hand

lightly upon his upper arm. She felt warm against the flannel of his long-sleeved shirt. There was strength in her long fingers, but she didn't use it on him. It was a butterfly-light touch. He looked down at her gold-brown eyes, seeing something in them he couldn't interpret. And then his gaze dropped to her lips that invited more inspection than he dared do. His voice was thicker. "I'll see you in the morning. Get a good night's sleep."

Her hand slipped from his arm. "Just to let you know, I've got an alarm set on my video equipment. If anyone comes over the fence that separates Rocking G land from the Elson place, or drives up to our house? The alarm will sound on my Apple Watch." She tapped it. "If that happens, I'm going to get to your room pronto, Gabe. I won't be knocking. Time will probably be of the essence because this place is lonely, forgotten, and we both know the only activity will be druggies."

"Good plan of action," he said, turning, leaning his hips against the counter. "I don't have an Apple Watch." He glanced down at Ace. "But I have something better. He'll start barking if he hears anything. I'll keep him in my bedroom with me at night until Ace gets used to the place, the normal, natural sounds, and he knows the house. I don't want him out guarding the barn when it's freezing cold. His hearing is excellent and if someone tries to get into the barn, he'll start barking and alert us."

"It's good to have him with us. On my end? I can sync it with my video equipment and camera that I've set up on the Elsons' grounds and house. Get DEA to buy you one. They did it for me."

He raised his brows. "Good idea. How far will that signal go?"

"As long as we have cell towers we can connect with, it will let us know. If we're away from this place and the

Elsons decide to come over and snoop around? It will sound the alarm and we'll hear it, provided we're in range."

Grimly, he muttered, "We have to expect them to come and check us out. Some way, somehow. That's why leaving Ace here to guard the premises when we have to be away is a good idea."

"Tomorrow, late afternoon, I'm going to bake some cookies and take them over if those two pickups are gone, and drop in and see Roberta Elson. We need to make contact and also ramp down their curiosity about us. Ace can stay here at the house with you."

"I don't know if I like the idea of you going over there alone."

Snorting, she gave him a playful punch in the upper arm. "Oh, come on! There're no damsels in distress here! I'll be fine and you know it."

Giving her a lopsided grin, he said, "I suppose you're right. It's my protectiveness toward women."

"I'll bet Maud didn't teach you to view women like that."

"She said women were a lot stronger than any man and I've found that to be true. My father is old-fashioned and still is very protective . . . and I can remember times when Maud would tell Steve to leave Sky or Andy alone and they'd handle any disputes their way. And"—he chuckled— "it always worked fine the way the girls wanted to do it."

"Your mother is like my mother. She doesn't suffer fools or overprotective males. It's not the way the world of today works. Women can take care of themselves just fine, and I'll do okay over there tomorrow. So, wipe that worry off your face, Cowboy. Good night . . ." She patted Ace on the head and told him good night, also.

Chapter Five

April 14

Anna could see the banked worry in Gabe's eyes, but he said nothing as she placed a cloth cover over the basket of cookies she'd just made. They were still warm to the touch, the chocolate chip scent in the air. Gabe would go out to the horse barn and watch through her binoculars as she drove over to the Elson home. The two sons had left hours earlier, so Anna knew this was a good time to reach out to Roberta. How would she react?

Anna had no weapons on her, something she'd waffled on while dressing in her jeans, a blue and white flannel long-sleeved shirt, and a rust-colored goose-down vest, and picking up her black Stetson hat. The weather was warmer at ten A.M., forty degrees, the sky cloudless and the sun's cheerful rays welcome. The snow that had fallen was still in large, glaringly white patches beneath the sunlight as she walked out to their pickup. Gabe followed her. She didn't need protection, and she knew he was a throwback to another age and time by now, after seeing the wranglers at his parents' ranch react similarly to all women. They would always tip the brim of their hat, call her ma'am, open doors for her, and were courtly, like knights from another age. It was chivalry, Anna had decided after spending seven days at the Wind River Ranch, not chauvinism. There was a huge gulf of difference between them and it was called respect.

Gabe opened the truck door for her. "Be careful. I know you will be, but I'll worry that those two sons could drive back to the house at any time. That leaves you vulnerable."

"I'll be okay," she promised, climbing in and placing the basket on the seat. "I have a recording device hidden on me they'll never find, and you'll be listening in on it so you know how it's going. Plus, any conversation is being directly recorded to the DEA cloud. They'll have it all. I'll be okay, Gabe."

His mouth twisted, and he stepped back, saying nothing. "I'm going to have to get used to twenty-first-century women who don't need any coddling or protection anymore."

She grinned. "I think it's sweet. I'll see you in a bit," she said, and she swung the door shut.

Gabe stepped back and headed for the barn. He was relieved that her hidden recording device would make all the difference to him about being worried out of his mind and just being stressed by the fact she had no weapon on her.

It took a few minutes to drive into the Elsons' gravel and muddy driveway. Anna felt confident after talking with Sheriff Sarah Carson about Roberta. She was to be pitied and was not violent, nor did she handle any weapons. She was a badly abused woman, a mouse living with violent male drug rats, as she saw it. If anything, she wanted to try to forge a true relationship with the woman. Grabbing the covered basket, she walked up the cracked concrete sidewalk that was wet from ice starting to melt. It led to the front door. She pressed the doorbell, which worked.

Looking around the area, she knew there was a small barn located behind the house. The boys parked their two big, honking trucks, gussied up with chrome wheels and bumpers, showing they were spending some of their drug money on tricking out their vehicles. It was so immature, Anna thought. Grown men, violent men, with the maturity and brains of a fourteen-year-old.

The door creaked and groaned open.

"Hi," Anna greeted. "Are you Mrs. Elson?" Anna tried to swallow her shock over the woman's narrow, sallow face, her thin lips compressed. She wore a gray cardigan sweater beneath a shawl of similar color, long black pants that were dirtied, and a pair of very well-worn black leather shoes. She knew from Sarah that Roberta was a drug addict. When she looked into the woman's eyes, she didn't see the pupils contracted, which was usually a sign that the person was partaking of recreational drugs. Maybe she had caught her between cocaine or heroin hits.

Roberta scowled, pulling her shawl around her thin shoulders. "I am. Who are you?"

Anna smiled, trying to disarm her wariness toward her. "I'm Anna Dominguez and my boss, Gabe Whitcomb, just moved into the Rocking G Ranch next to your spread." She held out the basket toward her. "I thought it would be neighborly of us to meet you, since you're so close to where we have our house and barn. These are chocolate chip cookies I just baked. Would you like to take them?"

Roberta's gray and brown brows rose as she eyed the basket of cookies. "Oh! Well," she said, reaching for the basket, "that's right nice of you, Mrs. Dominguez. Thank you. I sure never expected anything like this. We noticed you had moved in a couple of days ago. That place is in a really bad state of repair and has sat without humans in it for at least twenty-five years."

"Call me Anna. And I'm not married." She took off her hat. "I'm the wrangler Mr. Whitcomb hired. He and I are trying to get the horse barn in shape and the house roof patched right now. May I come in for just a moment?" It was a bold move on her part. She saw Roberta frown, look toward the highway, and then back at her. Did this woman have any social skills? Was she expecting company? Did they have drug drops here right now? Was she expecting one?

"Uh . . . why, sure, sure. Come on in. I warn you, though, the house is a mess! My two sons, Kaen and Elisha, are gone for a bit. They're drivin' over to Salt Lake City, Utah, and will be back later tonight." She stepped aside, looking fondly down at the basket she kept in the crook of her elbow and pressed against her body. "I know for a fact, they are gonna love your cookies. That was mighty thoughtful of you! Come in! I don't normally get company and it's mighty nice to talk to another woman."

Thanking her, Anna stepped inside. She guessed the Elson boys were taking drugs to dealers in Salt Lake City. The window drapes, a thick, dark green fabric, were all shut, making the foyer and the living room murky gray, depressed looking, and she was right: It was dusty; there was dirt across a carpet that looked to be at least twenty years old, ragged and torn here and there. This house reminded her of a hoarder's house. She stood, watching the woman shut the door and then slide three deadbolts in place once again. The wood on the door had been replaced, probably kicked in by who knew who? It was unpainted, recently installed and the deadbolts put back into place, Anna guessed. Her sniper's gaze did not miss anything in those fleeting seconds as she unobtrusively scanned the immediate area, however glum and underlit that it was. Addicts didn't like sunlight. She'd often seen drapes over windows to hide them from those who might be curious.

"Come into the kitchen. Do you like coffee?" Roberta asked, moving past her, gesturing toward where they were going to go.

"I love coffee. It goes well with cookies," Anna said, smiling at the woman whose shoulders were hunched forward. She felt sorry for Roberta, understanding that abused spouses often hunched forward to ward off a blow from an angry husband or partner. Her heart squeezed in sympathy for the woman who had been beaten. She was sure the four sons had also suffered the same fate from their father.

In the kitchen, dingy, unwashed yellow curtains hung and were open, showing the patchy snow across the flat property. All the wooden fences were broken down, the barbed wire lying in strands across the landscape. Obviously, this was not a working ranch at all. There were crumbs on the white plastic counter, puddles of grease here and there, the kitchen equally dirty. Roberta pointed to a square table with six wooden chairs.

"Have a seat. I'll make us coffee in a jiffy."

Anna sat with her back against the wall and in a position that gave her a view of the kitchen door as well as the hallway to her left. That door could be an escape route. Or maybe it's where the Elson boys came and went? Trying not to be obvious, she memorized the layout and the two exit points in case she needed to escape. It was good that the boys were heading for Salt Lake City. That was three hours from here. They would be gone all day, and she breathed a little easier. At least they wouldn't come barging in on them. She noted Roberta's hands shook as she made them coffee. Opening a cupboard door, she pulled down two cups. Anna wondered just how clean they were.

"Do you like milk and sugar?" she asked, turning toward her.

"I like mine black, Mrs. Elson."

"Oh," Roberta laughed, "call me by my first name, Roberta."

"If you'll call me Anna?"

"Of course," she said, bringing the basket of cookies over. Pulling the cloth off the top, Roberta leaned down, inhaling deeply over them. "My, it's been so long since I baked cookies and this smells so good!"

"There's two dozen," Anna said. "I saw two men at your home yesterday, and I thought I'd make enough for them, too."

"My sons Kaen and Elisha live with me and that's who you saw. This is a real surprise for them. They love sugar of any kind." She picked one up daintily, biting into it.

Anna saw immediate pleasure come to Roberta's thin, pale features. Her hair was not combed and desperately needed to be washed. It was straight and touching her shoulders. That ratty-looking gray shawl just made her skin look even grayer than it really was. Anna was no design maven, but a little makeup for Roberta would go a long way. The dark circles beneath her large, well-spaced eyes made her look positively ghoulish with that sallow skin. She wanted to say something, but bit down on her lower lip. She wasn't going to change this woman, an addict all her life. Anna had plenty of experience with them in Guatemala. If Roberta wanted to honestly quit her addiction, she would seek help, but according to Sarah Carter, she never had. That saddened Anna because clearly

Roberta liked her company and was probably thrilled to talk to another woman after living with four sons and a violent husband.

"Well, tell me about you being at the Rocking G," she urged, sitting down near Anna and watching the coffee maker chugging noisily along on the counter.

"Mr. Gabe Whitcomb bought the property," Anna said, sticking to the undercover script.

"He's one of the sons of Maud and Steve Whitcomb."

"Yes. He's come home to stay and wanted his own ranch because he wanted to remain in the valley."

Rising, Roberta went to the counter and poured the coffee. "My boys went to school with the Whitcomb kids. Back then, they were good friends. A lot of kids hated my sons, but the Whitcombs were always good to them and vice versa."

"Then the two families know one another," Anna said, thanking her for the steaming cup of coffee.

Roberta sat down. "Elisha and Gabe Whitcomb were best friends in school. Did you know that?"

Shaking her head, Anna said, "No, I didn't."

"Gabe went off into the military, as I recall."

"I didn't know that, either," Anna lied.

Sipping her coffee and taking a second cookie, Roberta became thoughtful. "My husband, who is now dead, would never let our four boys play with anyone. He'd tell my sons lies, that the others, any others, were no good. They didn't stack up to us. Elisha cried once when he was thirteen. He was on the basketball team with Gabe, and they were going to go on a school picnic before the end of school, but my husband wouldn't let him. It broke Elisha's heart. Brian never let any of our boys out to have a social life. He demanded they stay home, work around the house, and not venture out beyond that."

"I see," Anna said gently. "Did you want to venture out some?" She smiled a little. "You know how women love to get together and network. My own mother has a knitting club she loves to attend weekly. For her, it's a way to leave the everyday cares behind for a little, be with friends and have a good time together."

"Oh," Roberta whispered, "how I longed for that throughout the years!" She picked up the corner of the ratty gray shawl she wore. "My mama made this for me when I graduated high school. Every time I wear it, I feel like it's her arms goin' around me. The poor thing is so old, but it brings me such comfort."

Heart twinging, Anna tried not to be as touched as she really was by Roberta's whispered, sad story. "Do you knit?"

"Nah. I had my hands full raisin' four rambunctious boys who couldn't stay out of trouble." She grew pensive and added achingly, "There's days when I wished my life had taken different twist and turns than it did."

"I think we all have those regrets," Anna said. She munched on another cookie.

"Elisha is going to be shocked that the people next door to us was his best friend growin' up! Wait 'til he hears. I wouldn't be surprised if he wants to run over and see Gabe right away."

"Did they remain friends until Mr. Whitcomb left for the military?"

"No . . . things kinda went south when my youngest, Cree, kidnapped a local girl, carrying her off into the Salt Mountains." Roberta's mouth thinned. "It was wrong what Cree did. And he didn't do it once. He did it twice. He served hard time in prison for the first kidnapping. When the girl came home many years later, my son still had an obsession about her and he didn't learn his lesson. When he carried her off that second time, two county sheriffs and a whole passel of other law enforcement hunted my son down and killed him."

"That's a lot of history I'm not familiar with," Anna admitted.

"Only because you're an outsider and wasn't born or lived in our valley," Roberta said. She shook her head. "It was no fault of the girl who got taken. Cree knew better. I raised him better than that. But my boy was so lonely . . ."

"I'm so sorry," Anna murmured, reaching out and touching her skin, which was like cool parchment paper beneath her fingertips. "Listen, I have to get going, but I'd love to come over and have coffee with you from time to time, if that's all right?"

"Of course," Roberta said, her voice hopeful.

"If you make coffee, I'll bring the cookies," Anna said, rising, smiling down at the woman whose face was drawn with incalculable suffering, the grief clearly written in her watering eyes. "Can we agree to that?" she urged, wanting to reach out and hold Roberta gently. This woman had had nothing but awful and sad times in her life.

"Why . . . I'd dearly like that, Anna. But you're gonna be mighty busy over at that ranch."

"I'll find the time," Anna promised. She touched her shoulder. "I gotta go, but I'll be in touch. Okay?"

Roberta gave her a happy look. "That would be mighty fine . . . and thank you for these cookies. When Elisha hears that Gabe Whitcomb is over there at that ranch, I probably won't be able to have ten horses hold 'em back from goin' and seein' him. Can you tell Gabe that? They weren't friends after that girl got kidnapped. There's a lot of years of water lyin' between them."

"I'll let Mr. Whitcomb know," she promised. "I'll talk

to you next week, Roberta. Thanks for the coffee. It was really good."

"I didn't know you and Elisha were friends in school," Anna said, sitting at the kitchen table later with Gabe. She watched his expression carefully. "There was nothing in my report on you that said anything about this. Does anyone in DEA know about this relationship?"

He nodded, rubbing his jaw. "Only top-tier people know. We wanted this part kept secret for a lot of reasons."

She sipped her coffee he'd just made for them. Ace was happy to have her back. He was standing, resting his head on her thigh as she petted him. Outside, she could see the noontime blue sky and bright sunshine pouring through the windows at the end of the counter. "Want to tell me about it?"

"Yes," he said, giving her an apologetic look. "All the children in the valley, at one time, went to one school pretty much in the center of the valley. We had a twenty-five mile ride on a bus twice a day. The Elsons didn't always live where they do now. When I was growing up, they lived very close to that school. They didn't always have the bad name and reputation they have now. But now, no one likes them. They shun all of them mostly because when Brian was alive, he'd get even with anyone who tried to put one of the sons in his place. They were like a wolf pack, bullying others and then beating them up. They were constantly being called to the principal's office and being warned. Notes would get sent to the parents and that was when Brian would storm off to the school, confront the principal or whoever had written the report. He was dangerous and he was always on cocaine, so everyone at school started to learn that one bully, a father, put everyone on a threat-level alert."

"And Elisha?"

"He and I just vibed with each other. He was shy and quiet, like the youngest brother, Cree. We played sports together and got along. I really liked him. He was sensitive to others, not a bully like his two older brothers, Hiram and Kaen. Cree hid in the world of fantasy, later kidnapping Tara Dalton."

"What a messy, dysfunctional family," she muttered, shaking her head. "Do you have any plans to go over and see Elisha?"

Shaking his head, he said, "No. When we were juniors in high school, we kind of split up for good because he was getting into drugs and I wanted nothing to do with them or him."

"Do you think he'll drive over here and see you?"

"I honestly don't know, Anna. We were seventeen at the time. There's a lot of time and water under the bridge. I'm twenty-six now. He doesn't know I went into the DEA, either. And now? He's a drug runner and supplier working with a cartel."

Anna saw the pain in Gabe's eyes and heard the heaviness in his voice. "Wow, this is really complicated. If we have to confront them or bring in a DEA team to take them down, that's going to bother you."

He sat up, moving his shoulders. "It will in one way, for sure. Elisha was a ten-year-old freckle-faced kid who used to rescue butterflies and bugs from Hiram, who was going to yank their wings off them for fun. Elisha was always the one who had a true north about right and wrong."

"Do you think living in that rat's nest with Brian eventually wore him down, and he gave up and went into the drug business with everyone else?"

"I do," Gabe said, giving her a sad look. "And when I realized this was going to stress me a lot more than I thought because of our past friendship, I almost didn't take the mission."

"What made you decide to do it?"

"If we don't stop the present incursion into our valley by this cartel, it will only get worse, and a lot of people will be murdered as a result. It will be a slow-rolling bloodbath in the valley, and I just didn't want to see that happen. The buck stops with us."

Anna said nothing, but thought a lot. What-ifs were terrible. What if Elisha had turned bad and had no qualms about shooting at Gabe? Much less her? He couldn't be trusted, that was for sure.

She saw the torture for a split second when Gabe lowered his mask. It was then she realized just how much this was tearing Gabe up. He didn't know what Elisha would do if it came down to a fight at the OK Corral. And could Gabe shoot Elisha? Would the past stop him any more than it would his childhood friend?

"I didn't realize the depth of your predicament," she said softly, reaching out, touching his closed fist resting on the table. "I'm sorry. This is a real conundrum. You can't just suss this out and know what Elisha will do if we get into a firefight with him and cartel soldiers at some point."

"Yeah," Gabe gritted out, "that's my continuing nightmare, Anna." He looked up, pinning her with a thoughtful stare. "I don't know why I'm confiding all this to you. We're professionals. We've both worked in the drug world's underbelly for a long time. We know what can happen."

She removed her hand, feeling his knotted fingers relax beneath hers. "You keep surprising me, Gabe." He tilted his head, a quizzical expression on his face. "You aren't the typical undercover agent nor are you like the ATF, DEA, or FBI guys I routinely bump around in the night with. There's a sensitive side to you and you're not afraid to share it with me. Most of the men I work with are locked up tighter than Fort Knox. But you aren't."

"Does that bother you?"

She gave a short laugh. "No. But that's what is surprising about you: You aren't afraid to really talk with me. You've got your ego in check and I find that incredibly refreshing coming from a man. You remind me so much of my father growing up. He was always an officer of high rank in the Marines. I saw that stoic, gruff side to him, but never when he came home." Her voice lowered with fondness. "He would pick me up, smother me with kisses, cradle me in his arms, and talk with me, not at me. We had real conversations at the table and he always educated me, but not in a way that made me feel stupid. He would trade nights with my mother, reading a book to me before I went to sleep. I looked forward to hearing a story every week and I loved it. He always supported me, was kind, and never stern or harsh with me. I know now how lucky I was growing up because, as an adult, I've discovered most fathers are not like that with their children. They are more or less absent from their lives due to their work. My father never allowed work to interfere with big moments in my life. He was always there for me." She looked away, a lump forming in her throat. "To this day, Gabe, I miss the hell out of him. My mother has never gotten over losing him. They were so in love with each other."

"Your father sounds like mine. He's the same as your father was."

"I saw that the week we were staying at their ranch. We were both lucky and I think"—she gave him a faint smile—

"that Steve rubbed off on you and you're very much like him."

"So," he teased, withdrawing his hand from the table, "does that mean you can stand having me around for months to come? That I'm not a pain in the ass to you?"

She pushed back on the two rear legs of her chair, balancing herself. "You're spoiling me, Whitcomb. If I'm honest, I look forward to our time together, times like this," she said, and she gestured to him. "I just find it so refreshing to have a genuine, down-to-earth honest discussion with a man. That's rare or maybe it's just the men I draw. I don't know."

"No, most males are stoved up," he agreed, sipping his coffee. "It's the way they were raised, the expectations of the father to emulate him. I did emulate my father, but it was a healthy, positive thing in my mind."

"Mine too."

Silence settled in the kitchen.

"I kind of like having this wavelength with you," Gabe quietly admitted, studying her beneath his short, thick lashes. "For whatever that's worth."

"I do, too. It brings back good memories of my father." She touched her heart with her fingertips. "A warm fuzzy."

"I don't mind being a warm fuzzy in your life if you don't," he teased, smiling a little at her.

A flush of heat rushed up into her face and Anna realized she was blushing. If Gabe saw it, he didn't mention it, thank goodness. "I've worked alone for a long, long time," she admitted, her voice low. "I was thinking the other day that maybe I've grown lonely for some social interaction, that I need people . . . well . . . maybe I should qualify that. I've been unconsciously looking for someone who I could let down my guard with and just be myself. Share."

"And you can't share out on a sniper op," he agreed, holding her glistening gaze.

"You're an enigma to me," Anna admitted, "and I'm not sure how to deal with you."

"On a personal or professional basis?"

"Oh, I'm solid on your professional stature."

More silence.

"Maybe," Anna ventured, her voice barely above a whisper as she looked toward the kitchen, "we're both lonely and we're both wanting something different, something good to walk into our lives."

His brow arched as he thought about her admission. "That's another facet of you I like, Anna. You aren't afraid of calling the shots and laying it all out on the table. To me that's refreshing. I've always had problems understanding women because they have their own language they speak to one another. But when they speak it to me, I'm trying to translate it and"—he grimaced—"I've failed spectacularly at it at times. With you? There's no translation needed. You're straight to the point and I appreciate that. It helps me know where I stand with you, and if things get dicey outside this door someday with the Elsons, I won't have to second-guess what you need or tell me. Does that make sense?"

"Sure it does," she murmured, setting the chair down on four feet. She folded her hands on the table, holding his darkening gaze. There was something pure and good swirling between them and like a beggar who was starving, she secretly lapped up his openness with her. "Maybe we're both hungry for some good ole-fashioned socialization between a man and woman?"

"I've thought about that, too," he said hesitantly, opening his palm on the table. "In our business you know there can't be anything personal between a working team."

"I know that." She gave him a humorous look. "But we're not robots or heartless, either, Gabe. We might be in our cold-blooded business, but that doesn't make us less human."

"That was why I was glad to get out of undercover. I was having a helluva time stuffing my emotions so they wouldn't interfere in my daily survival."

"I couldn't ever go undercover like you did. I really couldn't. You have my everlasting respect." She sighed. "And in a way with the Elsons, and especially Elisha if he wants to make amends and become your friend again, you'll be undercover on this mission, too."

"I know," he growled, unhappy. "Elisha was always loyal to me and I to him. He respected what we shared until his father forced him into drug dealing. I always knew he didn't have a choice in it. It was either fold and give up or run away from that toxic family."

"In the end, he did the best he could, but my instinct tells me there's still something good and unspoiled in him. My money is on him coming over to try to bandage up the past and then move forward as friends with you once more."

"I hope not," he said sourly. "I don't want to lie to him, but I know I'll have to."

The sadness in his voice was harsh with recrimination. "Let's take it a day at a time. Maybe you can flip Elisha if he does show up and you two start to bond again. He could work for the DEA."

"That will never happen. The Elson family is tighter than fleas, Anna. They would never be a traitor to one another."

"Just a thought. You know them a lot better than I do." She scooted the chair back, stood, took their emptied cups to the sink, and rinsed them out. All the Elson boys had, at one time or another, gone to federal prison on drug running charges. Hiram was still there. As torn as Gabe was about Elisha and his past with him, she never questioned if he would do something to mess up the mission. And if she read between the lines of their burgeoning relationship, he was protective of her even though she didn't need that kind of shield. She worried more about that part of him because in a firefight, decisions were made in nanoseconds, and there was no way she wanted him to take a bullet for her. That concerned her more at this point.

She heard him push the chair back, and she turned as he headed to the living room to put a couple of logs into the fireplace. It was nicely warm in here without being hot. With so many leaks in the house, it was never going to get overly hot inside. However, there was heat in her heart toward Gabe. He was different in a good kind of way. What did she want out of this discovery? To grow closer to him because he seemed open to it without saying so? What then? What did SHE want? Her love life was more off than on. She craved a long-term, serious, deepening relationship with a man. Not a one-night stand and not one based just on sex. As a sniper, she was ultra-conservative, taking her time, having the patience to let a situation develop and see where it was going before she made decisions. Still, Gabe called to her sexually as well as emotionally. She didn't see any faults in him—yet. And she knew everyone had them. Maybe his fault was the broken relationship with Elisha and how it might affect him when the chips were down.

That left her feeling uneasy. Maybe Elisha wouldn't come over or try to make amends. That would keep things nice and tidy. Anna had too many hunts go south on her, too many missions take an unexpected turn where she had to throw her plans out the window and start all over again as she tracked her enemy.

It would be no different this time, she told herself, wiping off the counter with a wet washcloth. There were enough unknowns on the table right now without this new one. And Elisha was now a huge question mark: enemy or friend? And how would they know? And when would they know? The mother, Roberta, was harmless. She hated weapons of any sort. Sarah Carter had told her Roberta wanted peace, not war. Roberta wished throughout her marriage that her abusive husband would get out of the drug trade, but it never happened, and so she lived with more weapons than any one army needed in a home. She was the peaceful person in the group.

Maybe Elisha was the peaceful one, too? Anna wished she knew more. She washed out the cloth, wrung it, and hung it over the faucet. Hearing several logs being thrown on the fire, she turned, watching Gabe. He was ruggedly handsome no matter what he was wearing. Strictly female curiosity, she wondered just how beautiful he looked when he was naked. She buried that thought because it had no place in their mission.

What would tomorrow bring? Feeling unsettled, she knew her gut was never wrong. Did it involve Elisha? Roberta? Or worse, Kaen, presently the overlord and Darth Vader of the family? Grimacing, she dried her hands on a towel and headed for the door. Today they were going to patch the roof and stop the major leaks before another storm rolled in. At least she'd be working with Gabe, and that lifted her spirits. Anna didn't ask herself why.

Chapter Six

April 15

Rain fell heavily against the roof as Gabe woke up the next morning at six. Luckily, they beat the bad weather and got both holes in the roof patched yesterday. No more rain inside! It also meant that they'd be working inside, not outside today.

Sleet pinged against the frosted-over window. The empty room, with the exception of his bed and the electric heater that couldn't keep the place warm, didn't feel homey at all. Glaring at the cracks between the logs here and there that needed to have new mortar made and applied to close the leaks, Gabe pushed himself out of bed. He took a quick, hot shower, warming himself up, and dressed. Anna had gotten up earlier as evidenced by the damp bath towel hanging nearby, and the welcoming smell of fresh coffee met his nose as he opened the door. Ace was standing expectantly, asking him to please let him outside to do his business. Time to get going.

In no time, they had made breakfast after he had gone out to feed and water their horses. Ace loved having the horses around, going to each stall to smell each horse's muzzle as a "hello." Anna wasn't exactly good at American food and, instead, she'd made huevos rancheros, complete with some tasty, hot salsa on the side. For Ace, she made a four-egg scramble with bacon bits, which he happily slurped down.

Gabe and Anna sat at the table, eating the hearty breakfast along with fresh, hot coffee.

"We got work out in the barn and in the house," Anna said, wiping her mouth on a paper towel that doubled as a napkin.

"Let's work inside today," Gabe suggested. "I want to stuff paper into all those mortar cracks until we can hire a handyman to come out and fill them. In order to do that, the temperature has to be at least over sixty degrees and it's not going to reach that until maybe early afternoon."

"I'll help you," she said. Anna gazed at the cracked mortar. "Do you have someone in the valley who knows how to fix log mortar like this?"

"Yes," Gabe said, "his name is Charley Haverman, and I'm calling him today to get him out here to fix it. Mortar needs a certain temperature to set and it doesn't do well below freezing, so we'll probably have to deal with this in late May," he muttered unhappily.

"But it's warmer in here than outside. Can we have him fill mortar in when it's above freezing in here, then? At least, it would be a start."

"I intend to talk to Charley about just that. He's sixty-five and was raising log cabins in this valley since he was in his late teens. He knows raising and mortar like no one else." He grinned a little. "He'll be able to help us out."

"Mmmm," she agreed, thinking that they could be nice and warm if they slept together. The thought jarred her. Something was happening between them, almost magical and out of her control, for sure. She'd never been drawn to a man like she was drawn to Gabe. He was all at once intense, focused, and yet, laid back. Maybe being undercover taught him how to be like that, and it earned even more of her respect.

Disgruntled by the errant thought, she went about cleaning up the table after breakfast. They got to work plugging the worst offenders around the house with paper. By nine A.M., Gabe was on the only phone with Charley Haverman, and they settled on a time and day for him to come out and help them with the mortar.

Ace growled and went to the front door, tense and staring at it.

There was a heavy knock at the kitchen door. Ace barked.

Gabe called him to his side while Anna took a quick peek out the curtained kitchen window near it. Shock rooted her to the spot. It was Elisha Elson! He stood in a blue plaid flannel hoodie, his hands stuffed in the pockets, hunched over, dressed in his Levi's and work boots, making him look like a typical working hand at a ranch. His brown hair was partly hidden by the hoodie. What did he want? Instantly, she moved away from the window.

"Elisha Elson is at the back door," she whispered. She saw Gabe's brows rise and then draw into a scowl.

"Let me take this," he said. "Hang back in the kitchen, but stay alert." He gave Ace orders to guard Anna as she stepped deeper into the kitchen, her focus on the door.

Anna wasn't wearing her revolver, and she turned and walked into the nearby pantry, taking out her weapon, which was covered with a terrycloth towel on the third shelf. Gabe watched her as she came and placed the gun beneath a small kitchen towel sitting on the counter, well within reach if they needed that kind of weapon, but out of sight of Elson. Her throat closed momentarily as she watched Gabe draw himself up, as if to shield himself.

Gabe opened the door, meeting his old friend's gaze. "Elisha."

"Hey, Gabe, I had heard rumors of you buying this broken-down ole place. I came over to thank you and your lady friend, Anna, for bringing over cookies to my ma yesterday. We got back late last night and she told us about your kindness." He pulled one work-worn hand out of his pocket. "I wanted to come over and say hello and thank her for what she did."

Internally, Gabe relaxed a little. "Nice to see you again. Want to come in and have a cup of coffee with us? You can thank Anna yourself. Maybe catch up a little?"

"Oh . . ." Elisha said, and turned, looking toward his pickup truck parked out in the driveway. He returned his gaze to Gabe. "I s'pose I could. I was just makin' a neighborly call to thank her, was all. I don't mean to intrude or anything. . . ."

"She's my foreman, Anna Dominguez. Come on in. You can meet her. We were just sitting down for a break. We've been stuffing newspaper into cracks between these logs all morning. Colder than hell inside this place."

Laughing a little, Elisha pushed the hoodie off his head. "Yeah, I know that one. Ma's been on our backs about callin' Charley Haverman to do just that."

Gabe stepped aside.

Anna moved the hidden pistol farther back on the counter, behind the coffeemaker. Ace remained standing at her side, but his focus was on the man coming into the house.

Stepping inside, Gabe closed the door. There was a large hog bristle rug inside, and Elisha wiped his boots meticulously on it.

"Elisha, meet my foreman, Anna," he said, gesturing toward her in the kitchen.

His dark blue eyes gleamed as he turned, catching sight of her. "Hello, ma'am. I'm your next-door neighbor, Elisha Elson. I just dropped over to thank you for those mighty good-tastin' cookies you made for my ma yesterday. She was nice enough and left some for me and Kaen. We liked 'em, too." He stepped forward, his large hand extended in her direction.

Anna smiled slightly and nodded. "You're welcome, Mr. Elson," she said, and she shook his hand.

"Shucks, call me Elisha, will you? Ma said you were like a guardian angel dropped into her life. She was very touched by your kindness, ma'am."

Anna released his hand, missing nothing, automatically looking for weapons or a bulge in his hoodie jacket. Finding none, she took a step back from him.

"Ace is my dog," Gabe said, coming over and standing next to Elisha. He gave the dog a hand signal that meant the stranger was not a threat. Ace instantly sat down, but continued to watch him.

"Hey, nice pooch," Elisha said. "Really smart looking. You always had a dog growing up here, Gabe."

"Yes, we're all dog people, for sure. Listen, Anna just made a fresh pot of coffee," Gabe said, gesturing toward the kitchen table. "Come and sit down and let's have a cup?"

Anna watched the man who was a drug runner, waiting for any sign that he was dangerous to them. She knew the drill: Pretend nothing was wrong, act normal, and follow Gabe's lead. After all, he'd survived many years undercover and lived to tell about it.

"How do you like your coffee, Elisha?" she asked, pulling down three mugs from the cupboard.

"Oh," he said, "just black. Is it strong?"

Gabe chuckled and walked to the table, pulling out

some chairs. "Very strong." He made sure to sit facing the door and windows, and across from Elson, whom he did not trust. Anna poured the coffee, served it, and sat in the chair at the end, closest to the kitchen and to that weapon if they needed it. "Not much has changed, has it? We were drinking black coffee together at twelve years old."

Pushing his long, large-knuckled fingers through his uncombed and unruly light brown hair that hung to his shoulders, Elisha chuckled. "No, not much has changed and that's comforting to know."

"I'm sorry to hear your father is gone," he said.

There was pain and regret in Elisha's eyes. His mouth twisted.

"In a way, it was a blessing. He was beatin' up on my ma more and more. We couldn't be there to stop him. He had a pretty bad cocaine habit. Me and Kaen could leave when he was in one of those bad moods, but Ma didn't. She always wanted to be near him to help him, always afraid he'd die of an overdose. No one could stop him from takin' that stuff," he said, and he shook his head, remorseful.

"Your family has seen a lot of heartache," Gabe agreed gently, watching as Elisha knit and unknit his long fingers. Was he still doing drugs or was he clean? There was no way to tell since his arms were covered by a jacket. Did he have twenty or thirty heroin tracks on each arm? Was he on opioids like so many in America were right now?

"Yeah," he grumbled, pushing his hand across his unshaven face, his beard scraggly. "Some families are born underneath a dark star. I told you that when we were friends in school."

Nodding, Gabe took a sip of his coffee. He flicked a glance at Anna, who came and sat down at his elbow with Ace lying on the floor between them. She was listening to every word and cataloging every facial and body expression that Elisha had.

"Well, I hope things are better now than they were then." Of course, he knew they weren't. He didn't want to discuss the death of Cree, either, the other brother. Or that his grandfather and brother Hiram were rotting in a federal prison for life. "Bad seed" is what kids at school had called each of the Elson boys. Some families just seemed to be passing on something genetically dysfunctional from one generation to the next. A part of him felt sorry for Elisha. He had been a struggling but decent kid in school, trying to do right, but going home to that snake den every night, he couldn't escape it, so he finally succumbed to poison and toxicity doled out daily by his old man, who used to beat all four boys. Further he and Cree had been bullied by local groups of boys who taunted them, pushed them around, and demeaned them. They were abused children growing up, and sometimes Gabe wondered if all four boys didn't suffer brain damage from those beatings, because they were never quite "right" when it came to living within society in a healthy or positive way. They were seen as problem children to be avoided by other children.

"Tell me how you came to pick this place to live in?"

Gabe nodded, hands around his cup, giving Elisha a highly edited version. When he finished, he saw Anna rise. She refilled their cups and sat back down. He could almost see her cataloging Elisha. There was nothing weak about this woman warrior. It was nice to have a full-fledged partner on this mission; something he wasn't used to having. She had his back and he knew it.

"What about you?" Gabe asked. "There's been a lot of years that have washed past us."

Leaning back in the chair, pushing his palms down the

thighs of his Levi's, Elisha said, "I'm a part-time truck driver, long and short hauls. Whatever assignments I get out of Salt Lake City, is where I drive. Living out there"— he circled his hand in the air—"I can't ask for more work, so all Kaen and I get is part-time routes to California and the region whenever possible." Shrugging, he added, "It's better than nothin'."

"Where all are you driving to and from?"

"Well, like a few days ago, we got a long-haul assignment to San Francisco, California, out of a Salt Lake truck terminal. Me and Kaen took a load to the West Coast and then picked up another one in Southern California on the way back."

Gabe knew that drugs were funneled into large cities and then dispersed out to more rural areas and much smaller cities. Chances are they dropped one load of drugs in San Francisco and drove south to pick up another one. More than likely, with the way the drug lords had changed tactics, the drugs came in from a trawler that had originated out of Mexico, plied a hundred miles off the coast, handed the cargo off to a semi-submarine boat, and they would sneak into some small inlet where their truck loaded up the illegal drugs. All that was dangerous for Elisha and Kaen. If they got stopped by Border Patrol or the Coast Guard, they could have been discovered. These two brothers were rolling the dice in dangerous ways.

"What about around here?" he prodded Elisha. "Are you doing deliveries here in the valley?"

"Not so much," Elisha said. "We roll through Jackson Hole, cross into Idaho, and deliver goods to large and small towns in the southern half of that state."

"So, your trucking company is somewhat regional then?"

"Yeah, but the owner in Salt Lake City wants to expand.

Right now, most of our work is to the West Coast or points in the Northwest."

"Does your boss want to expand to other places?"

"Yeah," Elisha said. "We heard on this last trip he's wanting to move into Casper and Cheyenne, Wyoming. I guess his big prize is Minneapolis, Minnesota, and then he is always after having a truck terminal in Chicago, which he wants most of all."

Gabe kept his face carefully arranged. This was useful intel and Elisha was talking as if he could trust them. They understood only too well he was talking about a major regional drug contact under Gonzalez's grip. Well, wasn't that what they wanted? Although he was sure Anna and he never dreamed of the Elson boys coming over and having coffee with them. That blew Gabe away. "Sounds like a pretty goal-oriented dude," Gabe said genially with a smile. "Is he a good boss to work for?"

"Oh, yeah," Elisha said. "He's always giving us bonuses. Kaen and I like that a lot. Extra money is always welcome." And then he lost some of his boastfulness. "Ma needs a surgery. She's sixty and has five more years before Medicare kicks in."

"Oh? What's wrong with her?" Anna asked, concerned.

"It's her eyes. She's got really bad cataracts. She's partly blind right now. It cost ten grand to get new lenses so she can see."

"That's a lot of money," Gabe agreed.

"Kaen drives me nuts sometimes."

"Oh?"

"We're supposed to be saving for her operation, but he keeps blowin' the money on broads and beer." Elisha looked over at Anna. "Sorry, ma'am. I didn't mean to sound so rude."

"That's okay," Anna responded gently. "I was wondering

when I saw her why your mother always had her hand out in front of her. Now I know why. That must be awfully frustrating for her?"

"Yes, ma'am, it is. I save my bonuses in a mason jar I hide from Kaen, but he spends his. I'm tryin' to find a second job so I can save faster. So far"—he hitched one shoulder—"there's no jobs here in the southern end of the valley."

There were, Gabe knew, but they required people who didn't have a convict record a mile long like the Elsons did. That would stop Elisha from getting any job that paid well. "Keep trying," he said.

"Yeah, I'm gonna." Elisha gave Gabe a fond look. "Hey, this was great getting to sit down and connect with you again, bro. Maybe, if you want? We can kind of be buddies again like we used to be?" He rose and pulled up the hood on his head. "I gotta go. Things to do for Ma."

Gabe rose and so did Anna. "Nice seeing you again, Elisha," Gabe said, and shook his hand. "We'll stay in touch with each other, for sure."

"Same here." He turned and nodded to Anna. "Nice meetin' you, too, ma'am. Again, thanks for those great-tastin' cookies. That meant the world to Ma and us," Elisha said, and he pressed his hand against his chest where his heart lay. His expression lightened and he reached out, patting Ace on the head. "Beautiful dog. Really a looker. Nice meeting you, Ace."

Anna sucked in a quick breath, not sure what Ace would do when Elisha unexpectedly reached out and gently patted the dog. Would he bite him? Ace wagged his tail in a friendly fashion afterward, so the dog must know something about him that was trustworthy? Anna would ask Gabe later after he was gone.

"Glad I could make Roberta's day with the cookies.

Now that I know she has sight issues, if you and your brother are gone for days at a time, call me," and she jotted down a phone number and handed it to him. "That's my cell number. If Roberta needs ANY kind of help? I'm always here at the ranch only a quarter of a mile away. I can even take her shopping or anything like that, or if she needs to see her doctor, because I'm going to be driving back and forth for my boss, here, to get supplies from Wind River. Okay?" She pressed it into his extended hand.

Elisha stared at it, gulped, and then studied Anna. "That's right nice of you, ma'am. I think you're a mind reader or somethin'."

Anna smiled a little. "Why do you say that?"

"There's times when we're on a long haul and she's left all alone. I worry about her. Kaen says she'll be fine, but I'm never sure. She's older now, and since my father got killed, it's like she's moping around. I want to help her, but maybe she needs a good woman friend just to talk with. You know how women like to talk to one another," he said, and he gave her a loose grin along with an apologetic look in case she took his comment the wrong way. "My ma doesn't have any friends down here. She used to when we lived in Wind River, but that was a long time ago and it's eighty miles for her friends to drive out here. So, she lost them and I know she's terribly lonely."

"Well," Anna said, "she has me and you tell her that. I don't want her over there by herself, alone for days, if she needs help."

"We're close," Gabe said, walking him to the door. "We can help her if you want?"

"Oh, sure, sure, that would take a HUGE load off me, bro. Thanks so much!"

Ace came over and licked Elisha's work-worn hand. Delighted by the dog's affection, he rubbed Ace's head gently, smiling down at him. "You are truly a handsome dog," he told Ace.

Gabe opened the door as Elisha straightened and turned, letting him out. He clapped Elisha on the back. "See you later. I'm glad you dropped over."

Anna watched Elisha drive away. Gabe stood close to her left shoulder, behind her after the door closed. "What a surprise," she said throatily, twisting a look up at him. She saw pain in his eyes. Why?

"Damn, this is going to be harder than I thought," he muttered.

Anna swore she could almost feel the heat radiating off his tall, strong, capable body a bare foot between them. Tucking away her desire for him that was growing daily, she turned and rested her hips against the counter, palms resting on either side of the sink. "You look torn about something. What's wrong, Gabe?"

He moved beside her, leaning against the sink, his arms crossed, frowning. "Elisha caught me off guard. When I went undercover, I never knew the people I'd be in contact with. This is different," he said, and he rested his chin against his chest, frowning, his gaze on the floor between his feet.

"Because you knew him," she offered softly.

"Yes," he said, and he raised his chin, meeting her sympathetic gaze. "He was a vulnerable kid in school, Anna. Like a turtle without a shell. I was always protecting him. His other brothers, Hiram and Kaen, wouldn't or couldn't. Elisha was the kind of boy who cried if a butterfly's wing was tattered or torn off. Or if he found a baby bird that was knocked out of its nest, he'd put it in his pocket, climb the tree, and put him back in the nest if he could. Otherwise, he'd take it home and feed and raise it and then release it when it could fly. He was always trying to save others, even if they weren't human. Kids made fun of him. They bullied the hell out of him and Cree." He held Anna's softened gaze. "I always liked him. As I got older and more mature, I realized he was just one of these guys with a soft heart for underdogs."

"Even though he was an underdog."

Heavily, he exhaled and growled, "Yeah, him and Cree. Both beaten weekly by their father. They were both softhearted underdogs. When Cree kidnapped Tara Dalton at sixteen, carrying her off into the Salt Mountains, the whole valley was shocked by the event. But I heard my parents talking late one night in low tones. I stood outside my bedroom and listened. I heard them saying that it was a wonder any of the four Elson boys were even alive at that age because they didn't know what a parent's love was. They'd never been held, protected, or cared for like a child should be. Roberta tried to protect her sons as young children, but Brian wanted them toughened up so they could make it in this world of ours."

"So, Brian saw weekly beatings as the way to toughen them up," she concluded sadly, shaking her head. "How horrible for all of them."

"My mother said Cree was so starved for love that he'd fallen in love with Tara, who was his age. It was an obsessive love and I was too young to realize any of his focus on her. But looking back on her kidnapping, all he wanted was for someone to love him. It was a really traumatic time for everyone concerned."

"Did Tara get freed by law enforcement?"

"Yes, eventually. Cree went to federal prison for it. They tried him as an adult."

"Dios," Anna murmured. "I saw pain in your eyes, Gabe. What was that about?"

He dropped his hands to his side, giving her a long look. "That I'm going to use my friendship with Elisha, our past history with each other, to try and get info out of him that will benefit our side."

"That has to be hard," she agreed. "He seemed . . . well, he's rough looking, but he's actually quite sensitive and aware of others as well as what they may think of him. Even Ace liked him and that surprised me a lot. I was worried he would attack or bite Elisha."

"Yeah, I was surprised that Ace warmed up to him. The dog obviously senses that he's a decent person, deep down inside. Elisha's a nice guy caught in the vise of a drug family, and now he's thrown in with Gonzalez. Damn." Pushing away from the counter, he walked slowly up and down the length of the kitchen, in thought.

Anna remained where she was, feeling the depth and storm of his emotions regarding Elisha. "I hope I wasn't out of line offering to take care of Roberta if she needs something."

"No," he murmured, halting, giving her a pleased look. "I thought it was a masterful stroke of genius. What better way to get over there and see what you can find, and she's partially blind? I mean, I know that sounds harsh. I also sensed you did it out of human compassion, not the other."

"You're right, I did. She's not the center of this investigation. I have no doubt that under the circumstances she fights just to survive daily, and is not a part of the drug trade."

"I'm inclined to go there, too, but you'll still have to keep your eyes open and we'll need to verify her status."

"I will. Still, she's someone to be pitied, Gabe. She never told me she was going blind."

"Even abused people have their pride," he muttered, scowling. "I think in time, she'd have told you as you continued to forge a friendship with her."

"I agree." Anna wrinkled her nose. "Their house smells awful. There's rotting food everywhere. There's laundry stacked up that desperately needs to be washed. She spends most of her time in her bedroom watching soap operas, from what she told me. I can see why because that house is an unmitigated disaster of dirt, filth, lack of care and tending."

"Roberta might know her two sons' schedules, though, give you tidbits of info. Things that might help us piece together if they're making drug drops here in the valley or not. It doesn't look like it, but we need to verify it."

"I call them puzzle pieces." She inhaled deeply and released it. "I'm going to sit down and record everything. You should do the same, and then we'll compare notes. I'm interested in that terminal they named in Southern California."

"We're thinking along the same lines," he said. "We need to cross-check with DEA Salt Lake City about known routes that are on the cloud and see if these are new or not. If they are, it's one more inch forward in this case."

Gabe read Anna's thorough, detailed notes, not surprised by her precision. Snipers lived and died by subtle details. They sat at the kitchen table, several cups of coffee consumed between them as they studied and made notes on one another's eyewitness reports.

"We were caught flat-footed," Anna said, lifting her chin, meeting his gaze that always sent a frisson of quiet joy through her heart. "We need to have prearranged recorders that can easily be turned on without anyone knowing it. I want to work on that today. I've got plenty of electronics and gear with me in my bedroom. I'm going to bring them all out to the dining room table, lay down an oilcloth, and get to work."

"Good. This report of yours is incredibly detailed. Nice work."

She felt her cheeks heat up. "Thanks. We pretty much parroted each other on them."

"I'm going to fax DEA these notes and then convert them to a Word document and put it into their cloud."

"Did your ears perk up when Elisha said he was scouting around for a part-time job? You know him. What do you think of that? Everything I've read on the Elson family is that they moved and sold drugs together. That didn't make sense to me. Does it to you?"

His mouth twisted. "It jumped out at me, Anna. I don't know what to make of it. Maybe he's angling for a job here?"

"I had two paranoid thoughts. One, he's onto us and knows we aren't what we seem to be, or two, he's conflicted within his family gestalt and wants a second job to pay for Roberta's cataract operations."

"I thought the same. But Kaen would kill him if he tried to leave the family drug business. He's a cold bastard, a sociopath."

"So? Why would he tell you that, Gabe? I just got this sense there was such a deep, old, trusting bond he had with you. I felt as if he were reaching out for help. What did you get from it?"

"I'm not as intuitive as you," he said wryly. "I saw the pleading in his eyes when he said he was looking for a second job. I picked up that beneath it, he wants out."

"And it seems he's VERY devoted to his mother. Every

time he talked about her, his voice went soft. You could almost hear the yearning in his tone that he wished for a different life than the one he was leading."

"I agree. What else are you thinking, Anna?"

"That maybe you could give him a part-time job if you think it might work. That way, we would know when he was leaving and could alert the DEA."

"Elisha isn't the sharpest knife in the Elson drawer," Gabe admitted. "What you see is what you get. He's plain-spoken, and more emotional or at least wears his feelings more outwardly than his brothers. He looked tired with those dark circles under his eyes, and he was completely exhausted and stressed out."

"Hauling an eighteen-wheeler full of drugs would stress anyone out," she answered dryly, pushing her notes toward Gabe.

"We need to think through all the possibilities. I'm going to talk to our handler at the DEA in Salt Lake about it, float the idea of hiring Elisha part-time. I'm not sure I want him around here, especially with all that video and electronic gear up in the second floor of the barn."

"If Elisha ever sees it, I'm sure he'll put two and two together."

"Let's see what our handler thinks, give him a couple of days to digest our first face-to-face with an Elson."

She tilted her head. "What about you? I see the stress in your face and hear it in your voice. Are you okay? Is there anything I can do?"

He reached out and barely grazed her hands that were clasped on the table. "I'm finding it unsettling that you read me so well."

"But I'm safe, Gabe. My interest isn't professional, it's personal. I watched the strained dynamic between you and Elisha. I tried to put myself in your shoes. What if I had a longtime buddy from my younger days? And we had to painfully separate from each other because of Elisha's horrible, monstrous addict father? And yet, you had to go to the same school? It had to be very tough on both of you."

"Yeah," he admitted hoarsely, looking away for a moment, "it was. Elisha was the outsider. Cree tried to fit in with Hiram and Kaen, who were as cruel as their father. I never told my parents this, in fact no one, but as a kid, my heart hurt all the time for Elisha. With my kid brain I couldn't understand it all, because I truly liked him. We worked like a team, we played sports together and we did hiking and a lot of fun things after school together. He was the only Elson who ever came up to our ranch and had picnics and hikes or boating outings with us. Those were happy days for me and Elisha."

"I'll bet he's never forgotten them, nor have you." She opened her hands. "Listen, with all this other information you've given me I have a strong feeling that Elisha's trying to pull away from his drug world. He may not be telling Kaen or uttered a word of it to Gonzalez's drug cartel because they'd kill him."

Snorting, Gabe said, "Hell, they'd put a bullet through his head in a heartbeat. And they might through Kaen's as well as Roberta's. You know how they are. One defector and they snuff out the rest of the family back to uncles, aunts, and grandparents."

"Yes, I know that all too well. What if he is trying to defect, Gabe? What if he's reaching out to you in code, hoping you can read between the lines? He trusted you with his life growing up, I'll bet. Why wouldn't he reach out to you now?"

"Desperate people do desperate things," he agreed, pushing the chair back and standing, his hands going to his hips as he pondered her observations. "Damn, this is getting sticky in ways we never anticipated, Anna. I worry for you, too."

"I'll be okay, Cowboy," she teased him quietly. "I'm more concerned for you, the emotional tug on you."

"I'll remain clearheaded," he promised her gruffly. "Don't worry about that."

"I'm only concerned for the personal stress on you, Gabe. Professionally? I know you'll do what is by the book and what is right. I guess," Anna admitted ruefully, holding his wounded stare, "my concern is purely selfish, and I know we're not supposed to mix personal stuff with professional."

His hands dropped and he gave her a lopsided bit of a smile. "A little late for that, *mi corazón*, my heart."

Anna felt the world halt, her gaze narrowing upon his. Yes, she'd heard his roughened endearment, never expecting it. Okay, he had guts. She was going to be just as courageous. "You just said something out loud that I secretly feel for you, Gabe."

Chapter Seven

Gabe's heart thudded over her quietly spoken words. A new level of seriousness in her eyes made him lose his voice momentarily. Feeling the tension ratchet up between them, he felt paralyzed over his spontaneous admission. Rarely did his mouth get ahead of his brain. He sat down, holding her thoughtful gaze, not feeling any blowback from Anna. Gabe swore he could see her eyes glinting with amusement. It forced him to rasp, "Did I shock you with what I think of you, but never say?" He saw a wry twist of her lips, lashes dipping as she stared at her clasped hands on the table for a moment.

She stared up at him. "That was a dangerous thing to say, Gabe. Did you mean it? Or are you just flirting with me?"

"I don't flirt, Anna."

"Okay . . ."

"Look, I know I'm crossing a line here with you and I'm not at all sure you're in this with me . . . us . . . or not." Frustration tinged his lowered voice. "I've been fighting my attraction for you since the afternoon I met you." Automatically, his gut tightened, afraid that Anna didn't share his need of her.

"Are you ever in trouble, Whitcomb." She sat back in the chair appraising him. "I'll give you this: You aren't shy."

"I'm surprising myself."

They both gave a strained laugh, more out of relief. Pressure of something that had been building up within both of them had finally been released and was being aired.

"I thought this was coming," Anna admitted, shaking her head. "Whatever magic or cursed energy that's between us, it's mutual, Gabe. I've been fighting my attraction to you, too, telling myself I had no business sticking my personal wants or desires for you into this. That's the cursed portion of this. I could blame it on the fact I'm used to working alone, that I don't know how to share, but that would be a cop-out and I'm not about to do that. The magic that exists between us is something I want to explore, regardless, but I'm cautious."

He rubbed the side of his bristly cheek. "I've been going through all the same reasons, but you keep luring me toward you with your incredible intelligence. I don't mean it to sound like this is your fault, because it isn't. It's my issue. My curiosity, I suppose, about you."

"Oh. Then it's not my body but my brain that you're a moth to a flame with?"

He chuckled.

"I appreciate your dry, cutting humor," she pointed out, matching his bashful grin.

"Yeah, well I think people in this trade automatically develop it, don't you?"

Anna smiled a little more. "It's a symptom."

He became serious. "You fascinate me, Anna. You have from the outset. Every day it has become tougher for me to ignore you. There's times when I want to really let down and just explore you instead of keeping that professional distance."

"Said the scientist to the bug he'd just captured."

"No . . . not like that. You're not like most other women who are still finding their own personal power and absorbing it and then becoming it. You already have. You're ahead of them, and I guess, from the best I can figure out, and that's my fascination with you."

"Women around the world are awakening to their own power, finding their voice and becoming it," she agreed. "I just got a little bit of a head start, that's all. So? Me being a Marine sniper doesn't bother you?"

"No, just the opposite."

"You do know women are far better snipers than men, don't you? Even your military owns that one and admits it."

"It's a known fact," he agreed. "What about us? What's comfortable for you under this circumstance? I need to hear how you feel and what you want to do about it."

"You can't kill desire," she said dryly. "My biggest issue is learning to live in both worlds simultaneously. When to suppress my personal stuff in trade for taking a professional stance and vice versa. We have never talked on this level with each other before and I think we need to get a clear understanding about it first. Don't you?"

"Yes." Gabe compressed his lips for a moment. He returned his attention to Anna. "I had to develop a relationship, with a woman, in order to survive in the Tijuana cartel."

"Of course you would have. You had to fit in, not stand out."

"I needed a woman because everyone else had one. The relationship was one-sided. Maria never knew who I really was."

"But outwardly," Anna said, "you fit in and the cartel accepted you."

"That was the plan. I didn't like lying to her. She became collateral damage in a sense and it made me feel guilt over it. I had always wanted a loving marriage like my parents have. I dreamed about it as a kid and through my older years. Call me old-fashioned, but I grew up in a happy home where love was shown every day. Even though we were adopted, Steve and Maud loved us until we realized we were truly wanted and would never be abandoned again by an adult."

She stood up and went to the counter, pouring herself another cup of coffee. He came to her side.

"You want some?" she asked.

"Please. There's more I need to say, more I need to hear from you, Anna. How are we going to handle this?"

She filled his cup and then turned, resting her hip against the counter, studying him. "We know the obvious, that we can't get personal when things are going south or when we're in undercover mode."

He stood there and sipped the coffee. "Right."

"For me, Gabe, I need whatever it is pushing us together to unfold naturally, over time. I don't want to be chased, pawed, or think I can be used for sex when you want it. That's not going to happen with any woman in today's world."

"I'll always honor your boundaries and I'll respect them."

"My mother grew up with my father in Antigua. They knew each other as children, always having that closeness, that friendship that accumulates with one another over time. Later, my mother graduated and went to Yale Law School in the US. My father left to pursue military college. After they received their diplomas, they married and I came along a year later. I grew up like you did: with a lot of lavish love and being adored and appreciated. I was always close with both my parents." She stopped, frowning. "Maybe that's why my father's murder by a cartel struck me to my soul."

"And instead of having your family hunted, you became the hunter."

She sighed. "I did. My mother worried constantly and had to have guards at our estancia. She knew I was being tracked by the cartels in Guatemala. A price on my head didn't help her sleep at night, either. I was glad when this assignment came along, Gabe. I was wanting to get out of the business." She gave a fond look around the kitchen. "At least here? No one knows me. I'm not being hunted." Her mouth quirked. "At least, not yet."

"Your chances of becoming known here are slim," he reassured her. "And that has to alleviate some stress on you, right?"

"Better believe it." Shaking her head, she said, "Gabe, to be honest about where I'm at, is that I'm in a state of transition. I'm yearning, I guess, to settle down. I used to be fine working alone for months out in the jungle. I've found myself instead wanting to be in a backwater place where it's quiet, where there is no violence. My mother told me a long time ago that I would want family again. She was right. I want to find out what it's like just to have a regular life, not the one I've been leading." She saw his gaze warm on her and it felt damned good. "What about you? Are you going to continue to be in the DEA? You already said you were glad to be out of undercover assignments."

"Friendship is a good place to be at," he agreed. "I like that it doesn't make demands or expectations on either of us."

"Good," she said, relief in her tone.

"This is my last gig with the DEA," he said. "I only took this one because it involves my family and where I want to live and settle down."

"This is a mess for you, then."

He made an unhappy sound. "I worry for my parents, my brother and sisters, not myself."

"Well, I worry for you. . . ." She gave him a frustrated look. "So let's be friends? It's a good place to start. Being friends has no pressure or expectation to it. And I don't want any more than what we're in right now, with Elisha suddenly showing up at our door and hinting he wants a part-time job here. If he's allowed into where we're living, that's double jeopardy in my book. You may know him well, but I don't. For all we know, the cartel is putting him up to this because they want to use this area as a drug drop. We might be stepping into sensitive territory."

"You're right." He gave her an unhappy look. "I've thought about that, too. And there's no way to prove that Elisha is telling the truth or not."

"We're going to have to take this a day at a time with him if he shows up again."

He studied her. "We need to wall off our video gear up on the second floor of the barn. We can't have him snooping around if we're ever both gone from the property."

"Agreed."

"That's something we can do now. It's a good day to work inside while it rains."

"I'm not a carpenter, but I'm a good second pair of hands," she told him.

"My dad is a master carpenter, never mind he's a world-famous architect. He taught me because I showed an interest in it. Now"—he smiled slightly—"I get to use it."

April 30

    "Something's going on," Anna told Gabe as he met her up on the second floor of the barn. She held up the laptop. "Look at this. . . ."

    He leaned over her shoulder, feeling the warmth of her body, but he was careful not to get too close and make her uncomfortable. Watching the video, he saw Kaen and Elisha climbing out of their camouflage-painted truck. There was a huge tarp over the rear of it, with something stored beneath it. They had parked in back of the house and up against two open sliding-barn doors. The time on the video read four A.M.

    "What time did they leave?"

    "One A.M.," Anna said. "Kaen was driving, made a left turn out of their driveway, then he was out of range of the video. The truck bed was empty at the time he left. I suspect they went to a drug drop place and picked up bales of some kind, bringing them back here to their barn."

    Lifting his chin, he saw the tarp being pulled off by the brothers. Beneath it were what appeared to be one foot by one foot squares, each roughly three inches thick. They were all wrapped in dark green plastic and tied up with brown cord rope. "Looks like cocaine."

    "Maybe heroin, too," Anna said. "Both drugs come in that size of package and wrapping. It's probably all laced with fentanyl, anyway, which makes it deadly to the user."

    "That stuff is a killer," Gabe agreed, watching the two men take as many as half a dozen parcels into their arms and disappear inside the barn with them. There were no lights on except for a dull red one above the barn door. They hadn't turned on any lights within it, either. "We need to get over there and check it out," he said, glancing up at Anna.

He unconsciously inhaled her scent that always reminded him of a summer meadow filled with wildflowers. Her hair was tamed into a ponytail, warm clothing on because it was just above freezing in the barn. The last two weeks had been a special hell for him. He wanted to touch her hand, her shoulder, and let her know he craved a more personal and intimate relationship with her. Time wasn't on his side. He had to cool his own selfish needs.

"That's what I was thinking, Gabe."

He straightened. Anna shut off the video and sat down on a bale of timothy hay. "Do you want to contact Salt Lake City and get approval for it?" she asked. They couldn't just step into this without higher-ups signing off on it first.

"I'll call now," he said, and he looked at his watch. It was six A.M. "The night watch will be on duty and I'll ask for approval for tonight, say, around two A.M."

"With the brothers being there?" Anna demanded, shutting the lid on her laptop, frowning.

"Yes. You talked to Roberta last week. Were they going somewhere this week?"

"She didn't say anything to me even though I'd asked her about where her sons were."

Grunting, he pondered the danger level. "We need to get in there and be sure it's drugs."

"And even if we do?"

"The Salt Lake City task force for this area will probably want us to keep an eye on them and see if another truck comes in and takes the drugs for distribution. Or if the brothers leave with the drugs. They'll be followed, but it won't be by us. We're to maintain our cover here."

"Who's going to tail the Elson brothers if they go someplace with the drugs?"

"Salt Lake will alert the task force, give them the GPS, and they're going to have to follow them and see where and to whom the drugs are distributed. They'll be compiling lists at this point."

"Right," she said. "Good thing Roberta doesn't have a dog. That would make this even more dicey to get over there to check out the contents in the barn."

"Yeah," he agreed grimly. "Let me make that call. Are you coming in?"

"I need to upload the still photos to the cloud. I'll be in shortly."

"Okay," he said, taking the wooden ladder steps down to the first floor.

Anna liked the newly built video area. She and Gabe had worked two days to create a small shed that looked more like a toolshed to the casual observer on the second floor. It could be padlocked if they ever left the property and no one was here to keep watch over it. Gabe had installed a silent alarm within the shed that would send a signal to the Salt Lake task force, who would record it and then contact them. Luckily, Anna had synced her Apple Watch with the potential break-in and it would send her a signal, as well. Positioning smaller cameras hidden up on the beams of the barn on the first and second floor, they would get a good look at the perp who broke into the barn. If that happened, their cover was blown and that wasn't good. The danger was ratcheting up. Whether she wanted to or not, she worried about Gabe getting hurt, even though he was a toughened undercover DEA agent. He knew the drill. Still, in her heart, she worried.

May 1

"Ready?" Gabe asked Anna. Ace was in the house and told to guard it. They didn't need him on this foray. They stood just outside. It was two A.M., a moonless night with some high cloud cover. The wind was inconstant, a front heading their way tomorrow. He always considered wind an added plus because it could muffle their approach.

"Ready," Anna said quietly into the mic near her lips. They wore an earpiece and mic so they could converse if necessary. Dressed in black bodysuits, Kevlar vests in place, Glock pistols in holsters with a bullet in the chamber and the safety off, they began a slow approach to the field that yawned between them. There was no cover. And that is when, if the brothers were up and watching, they could be killed. That thought made her reach out, grip Gabe's hand. He turned, surprise in his eyes, but heat in them, too.

"I'll lead," she told him. Squeezing his hand one more time, she released it.

Gabe nodded, but said nothing. Anna was the perfect person to lead them. She was used to walking silently through jungles and hunting down her targets. He wasn't. The eyes of a sniper were unlike others. There could be trip wires, practically invisible to those who weren't used to knowing what to look for, around the barn.

He pulled the ski mask down over his face just as she had done. Her hair was tight in a bun at the nape of her neck. They melted into the night, keeping six feet between them. They would walk down their fence line opposite the end of the barn where the drugs were. Then, make their way through the weeds of the pasture and ease behind it.

The next ten minutes were tense as Anna kept her

NVGs, night vision goggles, aimed at the ground at her feet and just ahead of where she was going to step next. The wind came and went, gusts passing them. At times, she halted and knelt down on one knee, intently watching the house for any sign of movement, listening for a voice carried on the wind, or a light going on.

The house remained dark and quiet.

Easing slowly upward, she moved again. It was impossible to look down into the weeds until she was on top of them. Anna seriously doubted any wires were out here, but it would be foolish to think that there were none, either. Her heart was thudding slowly in her chest as the rear of the barn loomed before her. She had done this work for so many years that it did not raise her pulse nor did adrenaline start leaking into her veins. This was old-school. Boring, but it could kill her and Gabe just as easily, so her focus was fierce.

Behind the barn, they flattened their backs against it, taking a breather. The hardest part was crossing that open field, a quarter of a mile wide.

Gabe eased away from the barn, moving about six feet outward, looking for another entrance, a window or anything. Anna had pushed her ski mask up and took off her NVGs for a moment. Her eyes glittered, lips compressed, nostrils flared. He was breathing hard, too. It was actually more physically demanding to walk slowly than to run that distance. He pointed to his right.

"Window."

Anna nodded, slipped on the NVGs and pushed away, following him down the weedy area outside the old, unpainted wall of the barn, watching for trip wires or disturbed soil that could have an IED planted beneath it. As much as he wished Ace were present, the dog could present complications to what they wanted to accomplish.

Gabe halted, eyeing the window. It was dirty and he couldn't see through it. Running his gloved fingers upward, searching for a latch, he found one. Using one of his tools in his belt, he couldn't budge the window.

"Locked from the inside," he muttered unhappily.

Anna peered through the gloom. "Can't see a thing. We have to see if there's a window at the other end. Last thing I want to do is to try to get in through the sliding barn doors. Anyone in the house, if they were up, could see us out there."

"No lights on in the house to indicate that so far," Gabe said, turning. "Let's go . . ." he added, and moved ahead.

There was a second large window. Once more, he ran his fingers over the seam where it opened. The caulking that had been around the window was yellowed with age and cracked, and most of it was gone.

"Locked from the inside."

Anna cursed softly beneath her breath. "Okay, let me lead. They could have a wire or some other device in the front of this shed that could send them a silent alarm inside their home."

"Go for it."

Anna took the lead and halted at the corner. She knelt down, absorbing the darkened house that was about a hundred feet away from the barn. The tree branches around the house clacked as gusts hit the naked limbs. Everything was quiet. Easing to her feet, she intently watched where she stood. She would stop, look up, look down, searching for any device that might send a warning to the brothers.

Nothing. At least, not yet. Anna dragged in a deep breath and moved up to the slight slope of a graveled area.

"Padlock on the door," she reported, pulling out her locksmith tools.

Gabe came and stood behind her, placing himself as a

target, shielding her from anyone's view from the house. He had pulled out his pistol and silently watched the home and surrounding area.

"Open."

Music to his ears. He heard the one panel door being eased open, the rust on it making creaking, squeaky noises.

"I'm in. You're next . . ."

Looking over his shoulder, he backed into the barn opening. Once in, Anna shut it as quietly as she could. Turning, she swiftly surveyed the gloom. It was a large area and she could see the piled-up drugs in one corner between the two windows they'd tried to ingress earlier. "Let me search first for any alarm devices," she told him, holding up her hand in warning.

"I'm going to open whichever window I can get open after you okay the area," he told her.

"Good idea. I'll count packets, take photos, and then we'll vamoose."

"We'll have to have one of us come around and padlock that door once we're done," he said, looking around and up in the cobwebbed, dusty rafters above them.

"Roger that. I'll do it." She pulled a pair of thick, protective latex gloves on her hands and took a protective oxygen mask, unclipped it from her belt, and settled it over her nose and mouth. If fentanyl was present, and if she breathed in a tiny bit of the powder, it could kill her instantly. And if she didn't wear the gloves, just getting the drug on her fingertips would immediately absorb it into her bloodstream. It, too, could kill her. She made a motion for Gabe to remain far away so he couldn't be harmed in case one of these packets was that deadly drug. He nodded and stepped far away, next to the door.

Gabe watched her move in total silence. Fortunately,

the floor of the barn was swept, but everything else in it was filthy. It felt like an eternity, but it was only five minutes before Anna had reached the drugs and then checked out both window areas. Sometimes, druggies put silent alarms or baby cams up so that anyone entering would trigger it. This was not the case with the Elson brothers. They obviously felt safe enough here that no one in their right mind would try to come into their barn. They more than likely were counting on their dangerous reputation in the valley. A tight grin came to his mouth. Over the years, he'd found gaping holes in druggies' understanding of stealth. And, like Anna, he had acquired a lot of training and on-the-job experience looking for these holes. Drug soldier laxness was their gain as far as he was concerned.

Anna knew from experience not to open any of the packets. She had an instrument that, once it was placed on the packet, would identify what drug was within it. As she thought, watching her monitor, there was not only heroin and cocaine, but also packets of pure fentanyl. That scared her even more. It was so lethal. And druggies weren't pharmacists or doctors who knew what amount to give a person so that it didn't kill them. She was very careful not to move anything on the pile, preferring to take photos from the sides and top.

She counted the packets, fifty in total. They'd all been heavily taped and cord had been tied around each one. Taking photos with a special, small camera, she had everything she needed in five minutes. Looking up, she saw that Gabe had quietly eased open one of the rear windows. It was large enough for them to escape out of and not be seen on their exit. Dust fell in a cloud down below it as he gently eased it open, trying to minimize any sounds. She saw him pick up and carry over a plastic egg crate they could use to step up on and escape more easily. Moving toward him, she made a hand signal that she was ready to go. They had the evidence. That was all that mattered.

"I'll go around front and lock that barn door," he told her.

"No . . . let me," Anna said, tucking away her instrument and camera into pockets on her belt. "I don't trust that they couldn't have laid trip wires. I want to take my time getting to those doors." She couldn't tell much from his expression with NVGs and an oxygen mask on. She made the decision for him, stepping up on the egg crate. "Help me out."

In moments, she had pushed across the sill of the window and ended up on the ground on the other side. Scrambling to her feet, she turned, watching Gabe quietly maneuver through it. He was larger, wider, and longer than she was, and she held out her hands to help him. He gripped them, then made a quick push with his boots and launched forward. In moments, Anna had guided him out and to the grass.

As Gabe got to his feet and removed his mask, she said, "I'll go back into the barn and lock that window so they don't suspect we were in there. Then, I'll come out and padlock the doors shut. I'll meet you at the corner and then we'll leave."

"Copy that," he grunted, getting to his feet and pulling the window closed. "Be careful, Anna."

"Oh," she said, "always." She slipped away, trotting toward the other end of the barn, and made a turn around the corner, heading for the other side. Breathing through her mouth, she crouched at the corner that would take her to the front of the barn. The lights were still out in the house. Nothing moved. The wind gusted and then quieted.

Like a shadow, she crouched and made her way around to the front door that they'd slid open. In no time, she'd entered it and locked the rear window and turned. Her boot caught on something. In seconds, she fell. The sound scared her. She felt immediate pain in her ankle.

Dammit!

Remaining on the floor, she told Gabe, "Boot tangled in something. I fell. I'm all right." That would keep Gabe where he was. Getting to her feet, she tested her left ankle. It was tender and complained. But she could walk on it. Looking around, she saw she'd tangled with a gunnysack that had been thrown across the floor that they hadn't seen earlier.

Hurrying to the door, she quickly slid it shut without a sound, leaving just enough room for her to slide between it. In her gloved hand, she held the padlock. Peeking out, she made sure all was quiet and dark.

It was. *Good!* Slipping out, she quickly slid the padlock into place and locked it.

Done!

She swiftly moved with a slight limp toward the end of the barn. Turning, she met Gabe.

"Are you okay?" he demanded, gripping her upper arm.

"Fine. Probably sprained my left ankle." She pulled off her oxygen mask, stuffing it in a pocket and so did Gabe. "Let's go!" she said, and she pulled out of his grip, heading toward the field behind the barn, which would hide their exit. Luckily, the weeds were fairly beaten down, and unless the brothers were expert trackers, they would never find their trail. This time, they headed in another direction, just in case the Elsons could track, not taking the same one they'd used to reach the barn. It took more time, but Anna knew how to discourage trackers and by the time they reached the fence to their property, a good thirty minutes had elapsed.

It was 3:30 A.M. when they got to their barn. Quickly shucking out of their gear, they hid it in a nearby trunk against the wall and padlocked it shut. Using their NVGs, it was easy to get to the house. Inside, they kept the lights off. They moved to the one bedroom, shut the door, and turned on the light.

Gabe's face was sweaty and tight. Anna could see the worry in his eyes as she sat down on a nearby chair.

"You're limping more," he growled, coming over, kneeling down, and looking at her left boot. "What happened?"

"Tripped on a gunnysack under my feet," she said, shaking her head. "Rookie mistake. I should have looked more closely where I was standing. I need to get these photos uploaded, Gabe. Will you write up a report so I can send it with them?"

"I want to check your ankle first."

"Later," she said, standing. "I'm okay." She watched him unwind to his full height, no more than a foot away from her. Reaching out, she squeezed the upper arm of his black one-piece suit. "I'm fine. I'll check it out as soon as we get this intel into the DEA."

"Yes," he muttered, giving her a dark look, "we will."

Anna nodded, liking the "we" he'd said, hiding a smile as she brushed past him and out the door. She had to get out to the barn to unload the camera card, hook it up, and send the photos. "You can fax that report to them."

"I'm on it."

She could tell he didn't want to leave her side, that protectiveness on full display. Halting momentarily at the open door, she turned and said, "Really, I'm fine, Gabe. Don't mother hen me. It's just a sprain. I'll take care of it when I come back in."

"Okay," he said, halting, staring down at her.

"I'll be back in about ten minutes. See you then . . ." she said, and she turned carefully, not wanting to stress that ankle any more than she had to. As she hurried down the hall to the back door that would lead to the barn, she absorbed his care and concern. In a tense situation, Gabe had acted appropriately, and that served to tell her one more good thing about him as a partner. She'd been alone all her professional life and having someone at her side was entirely new to her. Never mind she was teased daily by his masculine presence. What was she going to do about it?

Chapter Eight

"You need to take your boot off so we can look at your ankle," Gabe said as she reentered the house fifteen minutes later. Ace had greeted them, wagging his tail, glad to see them once more. He ordered the dog to lie down near the table so he could examine Anna's injury.

"Yes," Anna said, shutting the door. She shrugged out of her coat, hanging it on a nearby hook. "I got the video and photos loaded up on the cloud."

"And I took your numbers and info on the packets and faxed it to Salt Lake City task force and DEA La Mesa. Now, we sit back and wait to see what they want to do with this intel." He pulled out a chair at the kitchen table. "Take a seat. I want to examine your ankle."

"Okay, Doc," she teased, sitting and leaning down, unlacing her boot. "Stop being a helicopter mother, okay?" She lifted her chin as he knelt down in front of her. "If I had a nickel for every scratch or injury I had out in the jungle, I'd be rich, Gabe."

"Well, it's different now," he said, resting his hands on his thighs as she unlaced the boot. "We're partners."

It was more than that, but Anna wasn't going there. *Not now.* "You're right. I'm not used to working in tandem." She grinned a little and lifted her head, meeting his narrowed gaze that clearly showed his worry over her injury. "Are you like this out in the field, too?"

"No. When I was undercover, I had no partner. I was on my own, like you were."

Grunting, Anna eased the boot off. She hid her grimace and took off her heavy sock, pulling up her trouser leg. "Crap."

Gabe saw the bluish-purple swelling around her ankle. In part, the high-top boot had given her ankle the support it needed. He watched the flesh swell now that the walls of the boot were removed. "I wonder if you've torn something," he muttered, and he cupped her heel in the palm of his hand and ran his fingers knowingly over the injury. "It's pretty swollen."

Unhappy, Anna still couldn't stop the pleasure rippling up her calf from the way he supported her foot in his large, calloused hand. His fingers were gentle, but probing, and she sat there privately absorbing his light touch. "It does look bad," she agreed. "But I don't think I tore anything, Gabe, or I couldn't have walked on it at all. It's probably just a bad strain. Lord knows how many times I've gotten them out in the jungle."

It was his turn to grunt as he looked up. "We have to get you to the ER at our local hospital. I want this thoroughly checked out."

"Oh, come on!" she protested, pulling her foot out of his hands. "I just need to get some Epsom salts in warm water and I'll soak it several times a day, buy an ACE bandage at the drugstore to wrap it up, and I'll be fine."

"No." He held her rebellious expression. "Not this time." He looked at his watch. "It's four A.M. I'll put Ace out in the barn to guard the contents, give him a warm blanket to snuggle down into. Then, we can take off and get to the Wind River Hospital in about an hour and forty minutes. The ER will be empty at this time of morning, and we can get you in and out pretty quickly. Ace will have water and kibble out there, so he'll be fine until we return."

She sat there, craving his touch again. If she hadn't have pulled her foot from his hands, she might have done something a lot more jolting to Gabe. She wanted to kiss this man and find out how his lips tasted beneath hers. It was unbidden. And stupid. And not the right action to take at the moment. Heaving a sigh, she said, "Well, we'd have to go into Wind River to get the Epsom salts and an ACE bandage from the drugstore, anyway."

He gently patted her exposed calf. "Good call. You won't get that boot back on because your ankle has swollen up to the size of a large orange. Let me get you a pair of your loafers. You can wear them, instead."

She appreciated his no-nonsense approach. "We agree," she said, tugging the sock back on. "I'll sit here and wait for you to retrieve them from my bedroom."

Rising, he teased, "I like that you don't keep fighting logic," giving her a warm look of praise.

Scowling, she growled, "Just get my shoes, will you, Cowboy?" She saw humor light up in his eyes, one corner of his mouth twitch into a slight grin as he turned and walked away. He wasn't a man who withered at her confrontational style. Anna liked that. Gabe was smart enough to know when to back off and give her room to deal with this situation. One more reason to like him, dammit.

Gabe felt sorry for Anna. She was a person of high confidence, didn't need help from anyone, and here she was hobbled like a three-legged horse, frustration clearly visible in her eyes. He drove out of the hospital ER parking lot, the sky lightening a pinkish color announcing the coming dawn. She sat in the passenger seat, pouting. She had a pretty lower lip and he entertained thoughts of kissing her. What did she taste like? What was the texture of those lips of hers against his own? Reluctantly suppressing his desire for her, he focused on his driving.

"I'm going to go over to my parents' ranch for about an hour. And then, we need to get back home. There's no one there to feed or water our horses if we both leave the ranch."

Looking down on the medical boot that was placed on her lower leg, she muttered, "At least I can walk instead of limping."

"Yes, but you're going to be hobbled for at least six to eight weeks." He gave her a wry look. "No more night runs for you. At least, for a while."

"Talk about rubbing salt in my wounds," she flung back, a grin edging her lips.

"We'll get through it together, Anna. I've been expecting someone to call us about what the higher-ups want us to do about our find last night."

"Won't be long in coming," Anna promised. "I think they'll follow the truck that either picks up that stash at the Elson home, or wherever the Elson brothers take it. DEA doesn't want us blowing our cover this early in the game."

Gabe slowed the vehicle, turning right onto a wide, graveled dirt road. A mile farther inland stood the heart of his parents' busy ranch. "I'm in agreement with you."

"At least you get to visit your parents. That's the only good thing to come out of this."

He gave her a sympathetic look. "We're alive. That's the real point."

"You have me there."

"I'm looking forward to seeing my parents. We'll probably be catching everyone at the breakfast table. We're coming in unannounced."

"Wise idea," Anna agreed. "Even though I don't feel we're being followed or the Elsons have some kind of tracking device to watch our movements, it's a good idea to stay way under the radar in order to protect your family."

"Better believe it." He grew less serious. "I'm sure my parents will be happy to see you, too," he murmured, slanting a glance in her direction. Her eyes warmed and the tight line of her mouth softened. She missed her family, too. Who wouldn't? He drove into the main area of the ranch, the road paved to the main ranch house. In no time, they were out of the truck.

"Want some help?" he asked, coming around to Anna's side.

"What if I told you I would because I like being close to you?" she asked, and she looked up, watching his surprised reaction followed by a gleam of pleasure in his eyes. There, more of the truth was out. What was Gabe going to do about her bold honesty? She was limping slowly along under her own power, but he remained nearby just in case she needed help.

"What if I told you I had a double reason for asking that?" he said, giving her a humored look. He opened the gate and stepped aside, watching her.

"What are the two reasons?" she asked, halting as Gabe latched the gate behind them.

Anna was an independent, intelligent, and confident woman. Most men would be scared off by that combination, but Gabe wasn't. "First, I'm going to find out if you'll take help from someone else when you need it," he said, approaching her. "Second, I'm doing this for myself, too. I like being able to touch you. I feel we have a nice, building connection with each other. You can tell me if I'm wrong."

"You're not wrong, Gabe. I like a man who isn't afraid of women like me."

"What's there to be afraid of?" he asked, and he held out his hand toward her. Anna came and moved beside him.

"We don't have enough men yet who aren't cowed by a fully empowered woman. That scares the hell out of most of them, pronto."

"Unfortunately, it's going to take time for most men to accept the fact women are equals to any man. Now? Would you like me to help you?"

"Yes, I'd like your help."

He noted the vulnerability she was sharing with him about herself. That meant a lot to Gabe. He slipped his hand lightly around her upper left arm.

"We do have a nice, building connection," she murmured, giving him a momentary glance as they approached the wooden steps.

"We need to talk about this on the way home. Okay?"

She saw the seriousness in his expression, but also, if she read him accurately, relief followed by happiness that they'd leveled the playing field with each other. That was what she felt: relief. His fingers were long, steadying, but not tight or controlling as he helped her up those steps to the front door. Halting, she said, "Okay, sounds like a plan to me, Cowboy."

Chuckling, he knocked on the door. "I like my new nickname."

"Oh, I have many for you." Anna's heart warmed as he gave her the look of a man wanting his woman. It sent her lower body into a storm of yearning on its own.

The front door opened. It was Maud. Her face lit up with shock and she pushed the screen door open.

"Gabe! Anna! What a surprise! Come in!" Maud said, and she stepped aside.

Anna followed him in and closed the door as Maud hugged her tall son. She smiled as Maud released him and she stepped over to her.

"Anna! What happened to your ankle?" she asked, and she gave Anna a gentle hug and released her carefully, eyeing the supportive device around her ankle.

"Tripped," she lied. "A bad sprain, nothing more. I'll be fine in about six weeks."

"Hey, breakfast is on?" Gabe asked, sniffing the air, pointing toward the kitchen down at the other end of the long hall.

"Sure is. Your dad is coming home tonight from Australia. Come on, join me. I'm eating all alone." She picked up Anna's hand and walked at her side.

"I was hoping to see him," Gabe said, falling in behind the women. "We're only stopping for an hour and then we have to get home."

"Figured as much," Maud said.

"Hi Gabe and Anna!" Sally Fremont called gaily, coming out of the kitchen area. "Good to see you two."

Anna lifted her hand toward the fifty-year-old woman who was dressed in a pink sweater, tan slacks, and a bright red apron around her waist. "Thanks for the welcome. We're hungry, Sally. Can we beg a breakfast from you?"

Sally smiled and smoothed the red apron over the tan slacks she wore. "Of course."

Maud motioned them to the table. "Sally has made me pancakes this morning, with a side of bacon. Interested?" she asked them.

"Count me in," Anna said, thanking Gabe as he pulled out the chair for her to sit down.

"Makes two of us," Gabe said, giving the woman a look of thanks.

"I'll be back in about ten minutes," Sally promised.

"I'll get them coffee," Maud called to her housekeeper.

"I can help you," Gabe said.

"Nah," Maud said, waving at him to sit down. "Pouring two cups of coffee isn't hard to do. And we have caramel-coated coffee cake as well."

Gabe looked around, a sense of relaxation overwhelming him simply because he was home. The only one he'd ever known. Being here was filled with nothing but good memories, incredible love, and happiness.

"How are you doing?" he asked his mother, taking the coffee and giving one mug to Anna and the second one for himself. He divided up slices of coffee cake to the three of them. Maud handed him two forks; one for him and one for Anna.

"Oh, fine. Everything is running like a top around here," Maud assured him, putting the tray aside and sitting down. "We're cranking up for spring. There's a lot of cattle leases that Jake, our foreman, is getting set up. It will be crazy time from late May through mid-June, thousands of cattle are being trucked up here to eat the nutritious grass we grow here in the valley."

"We never had cattle on our estancia. Only a milk cow that I learned how to milk," Anna said, sipping her coffee, a look of pleasure wreathing her face. "I really like your coffee, Maud. It's strong, hearty, but not acid-tasting."

"Blame that on me going to northern Costa Rica with Steve. We discovered an organic coffee grower and we've bought his beans ever since. Just nothing else like them.

They are grown in volcanic soil and I think that's what makes them so special."

"We pride ourselves in Guatemala because we raise coffee in the volcanic mountain areas, too," Anna said. "This reminds me of home, very much like our coffee. It's delicious."

Smiling, Maud said, "That's good to hear. Doesn't hurt to have a little taste of home. I'll have Sally bag up some beans for you so you two can enjoy it together."

"Wow," Anna murmured, surprised but pleased, "that's wonderful, Maud. Thank you!"

Gabe chuckled. "Now? We'll both bail out of bed with our hair on fire knowing that good coffee is waiting for us."

Anna laughed and so did Maud.

"So," Maud said, "how are things down there?"

"Going fine," Gabe reassured her, seeing the worry banked in her eyes. He wanted to ease her concern in any way that he could.

"It's quiet," Anna reassured her. "This mission is just about watching, is all."

Gabe felt his tightened gut relax. Anna wasn't lying to his mother, but she was shading the truth of it. There was the potential for danger every day living next to the Elsons.

"How did you get an ankle sprain?" Maud wondered.

"Oh," she said, "that. Really embarrassing. I tripped on a plank that was slightly above the floor of the barn and that did it."

"I've done that myself," Maud said sympathetically. "All our barns here on the ranch are a hundred years old. We work hard to replace old, weather-beaten planks, but there's always one that will catch you sooner or later."

"Well," Anna said dryly, "it was my turn."

"Will that interfere with your job?" she wondered.

"Not at all."

"That's why they sent two of us," Gabe said. "It won't hamper what we're doing down there."

Maud sighed and gave them a wispy look. "I've missed both of you so much. I know you don't want to be seen around here very much while this mission is going on, but it's awfully nice to see you."

"Breakfast is on," Sally sang, coming with two plates in her hands filled with pancakes and a side of thick, crisp bacon.

"Your mom, I think, is pining away for your company, Gabe."

Gabe drove out on the gravel road and onto the highway that would take them south to their ranch. "I know. I feel guilty, if you want the truth. That was the part of the mission I didn't like: being so close to my parents and then not being able to have much contact with them."

She smiled a little. "Maud understands the circumstances, though. I hope you don't mind that I fibbed about how I sprained my ankle."

"It had to be done." He set the cruise control, barely any vehicles on the road. The sun had risen, sending long, warming beams across the valley. "You won't be climbing that ladder to get up to the second floor for a while," he cautioned. "I'll take over your duties up there until you can do it yourself."

"I'm going to feel useless," she grumped unhappily.

"With the weather keeping the ground muddy and wet, there's not much we can do outside right now, anyway. I was thinking we could do some inside work on the ranch house, like put insulation in and then hang up drywall instead. You can be a second pair of hands and my chief helper. That will keep you busy. That place leaks like a sieve, and I really want to get it warmed up and stop the drafts once and for all."

She brightened. "I like that idea. Painting the drywall after we get it up and dried?"

"Sure. This is something we can do during daylight hours. We can keep an eye on the Elsons while we're at it."

She sighed and laid her head against the back of the seat. "I meant what I said earlier about us, Gabe," she said, and she rolled her head to the left watching him give her a brief glance. She saw his hands tighten briefly on the wheel and then relax.

"So did I." Mouth quirking, his voice became roughened. "Look, I've tried ever since I met you to ignore you. And I can't."

"It's not like I'm some kind of infection."

Chuckling, he saw her give that wry grin of hers. "I guess I had that coming. This isn't anyone's fault. I've lived so long undercover, pretending, that I was pretty much numb, emotionally speaking."

"I can't imagine the energy and stress it took to play at liking a woman who was a convenient cover to keep you safe in your mission."

"Yeah, I hated that. I didn't mind lying to the drug soldiers, but it was rough to lie to the woman involved as cover for me."

"So," she said, gazing out the front window, the sunshine bright and the sky puddled with what looked like white cotton puffs here and there, "maybe you're not numbed out emotionally after all if you're attracted to me. Right?"

"Right."

"Don't sound so glum about it. Worse things could

have happened. We could have been a complete misfit for each other. That would be hell on earth."

"I've never had a situation like ours before. Has it ever happened to you?"

"Me? *Nada*. I was always running and hiding in the jungles from drug soldiers who want that million dollars that was placed on my head. I didn't dare go home or be seen near our estancia, either."

"That's hard on everyone," he said, sympathetic. "We're attracted to each other, Anna. I know we've danced around this conversation before, but last night when you got injured, something deep inside me snapped. I said to hell with it, that I was going to tell you how I felt."

"I'm all ears. I want to see if it matches how I feel toward you."

"I think about you all the time. I feel like I'm going to die if I don't get some personal conversation time with you. I liken you to the air that I breathe. I want to know everything about you, your growing-up years, your parents, and how life shaped and molded you into who you are today." He slanted a look her way. "Is that asking too much?"

"As we drive home? Let me fill in the blank spots in my life for you," she said, meeting his gaze, feeling the heat radiate even more from her lower body.

It was nearly eleven A.M. when Gabe came in from feeding and watering their horses. Ace was more than happy to see Gabe and Anna return, and remained with him while he did the feeding. He smelled of alfalfa, a fragrance that Anna loved. There was an invisible connection throbbing between them. This time, it didn't bother her. She had an hour to tell Gabe much about her childhood and he listened intently. Only when she stopped would he ask focused questions. It brought her to tears almost because her father was so much like him. He, too, would listen with respect, even when she was a young child of eight, excitedly sharing her experience outdoors somewhere on the estancia, and he took it all in without interrupting her. And then, later, her father would ask questions that made her think hard and caused her heart to bloom with such fierce love for him. He might have been a Marine and a high-ranking officer, but with her, he was vulnerable in ways she'd never seen a man. Until now. Gabe was entrusting himself to her, little by little. And she reciprocated. Her parents' marriage had been based upon mutual respect, mutual trust, and a deep love for each other. Now, far more mature than her years, she recognized how fortunate she'd been to have the parents she had. Losing her father was the single hardest blow to hit her in her life. There were so few men like her papa.

"The horses are fine," Gabe assured her, shucking out of his denim jacket and hanging it over a peg on the kitchen wall.

"Did you let them out for a while?"

"No. There's a storm coming from the west," he said, pointing in that general direction. Sitting down on a wooden bench, he took off his barn boots and set them in what they called their mudroom. "I don't know if we'll get snow or rain."

"Or both," she muttered, shaking her head. "It was sunny until an hour ago. Blue sky," she added, and she looked out the kitchen window, frowning. "I really miss the sun."

He smiled a little, pulling on a pair of cowboy boots and standing. "It's coming. I promise."

"Did you go to the second floor to make sure our booth wasn't disturbed?"

He came over, standing near her. "Yes. Ace did a good job of taking care of the barn in our absence. The lock is on the booth on the second floor, untouched. In a little bit, I'll go out there and retrieve the video and get it sent to the cloud."

She washed her hands with soap and warm water, wanting to get back to the daily rhythm they'd established with each other. "Sounds good. I'll go to my office and see if we have any encrypted emails from DEA."

"How about we eat around noon?"

"Are you hungry again?" she teased, hanging up the towel, looking up at him. He hadn't shaved yet today and she liked the way the darkness of his beard accentuated his high cheekbones.

"I guess so. I'm a growing boy."

"Hardly, you're a man." She watched him give her a slight grin, his cheeks pinking up. Was he blushing? It was an endearing reaction. Timing was everything. Gabe wasn't even going to realize she was stalking him. She was very good at it, being a sniper who hunted their enemy. Gabe wasn't her enemy. He was someone she wanted to know on every possible level, and she was going to do just that: wage a stalk of attrition. Little by little, she was going to bring him into her arms. And not just for sex. Sure, that was a part of it, but there was so much more. She'd observed that in her parents as a child: the warmth of a look, an affectionate touch on the shoulder, sitting and listening to each other talk, laughing together, sharing tidbits of food, and so many other small but oh-so-important moments that said it was love, not just lust. However, Anna fully admitted that she lusted after Gabe, too. He was ruggedly handsome, in top shape, and there was nothing to dislike about him at all. She heard him give her a grunt, going to the sink to scrub his hands.

Soon, they were both busy with DEA information being sent to HQ. Outside the window of her office, she saw the pickup truck ease from behind the Elson house. It had an empty bed. Anna got up and went to the window. She stood to one side, watching as the two brothers drove out of the muddy driveway and make a left turn. Frowning, she called to Gabe to come into her office.

"What's up?" he asked, halting behind her near the window.

"I don't know. I just saw the Elson brothers make a left turn onto the road. It's the only highway that goes up into the slopes of the Salt Mountains. Why are they going there today? It's raining and cold."

Rubbing his chin, he muttered, "A good question. We're taking Ace. Let's follow them at a safe distance."

"That's what I think. The hair stood up on my neck when I saw them driving out and turning left. This is a feeder road and it connects with Route 89, the main one that goes up through the valley." She rubbed the back of it, limping toward the open door. "It's always a sign of danger."

"You know what? You should stay here, Anna. You're crippled with that sprain. I can get in the truck, follow and see where they're going."

"Like hell," she snapped. "If something happens, you may need me. There's two of them and we know they're armed and ready to shoot first and ask questions later."

Halting outside in the hall, he shrugged. "Okay, no argument. I'll get our weapons and gear. You get in the truck. I'll get Ace's leash and I'll drive," he said, and he gave her a look that didn't ask her for permission. Anna nodded. "Done deal. I'll go get our radios."

In a matter of five minutes, they were in the truck, strapped in with Gabe driving out onto the rain-slick highway that was empty of all traffic. Ace rode in the back seat. This road ended at a trailhead parking lot at five thousand feet. Glancing up at the low hanging gunmetal gray clouds churning in slow motion above him, he said, "Looks like snow at six thousand feet."

"Even more suspicious," Anna growled, placing a bullet in the chamber of each Glock pistol, releasing the safety and placing them between them on the seat. She had already called in the activity to the DEA in Salt Lake City, Utah.

"Our satellite phone isn't working and I sent it to be fixed down at Salt Lake HQ. We'll be without it."

Frowning, Gabe said, "They'll get it fixed sooner, not later. Until then, we're out of touch."

With the low-hanging clouds, no satellites could pierce it except for one that had infrared. It was due to fly over in forty minutes, luckily, in their area. That might be helpful, but Anna didn't count on the clouds miraculously parting so they could get photos of the area.

"We know the brothers aren't out in this miserable weather to go hiking," she said. The highway was straight and sloping into the mountains. Far ahead, a good four miles, she could barely see the truck. The rain was coming down more heavily, no longer a pitter-patter. It would soon make the truck disappear. Gabe had wisely left the headlights turned off, using the weather to hide while following the Elsons' vehicle.

"For sure. I wonder if there's been a drug drop?"

"I know druggies use bad weather to cover their drops and this is a perfect time for it."

"I was thinking the same thing. How's your ankle feeling?"

"Fine," she answered. "Stop worrying about me."

"Can't help it. Let me be a mother hen, okay?"

Snorting, she said, "Not today. We don't know what's ahead for us, Cowboy."

Chapter Nine

Gabe timed them arriving at the parking lot. He pulled off the road before entering the area. Instead, he found several smaller evergreens as cover, driving behind them and hiding their truck. Up ahead, he saw the Elson truck parked and neither brother in sight. Turning, he said to Anna, "I'm going to recon with Ace and try to locate those two." He took the radio, clipping it on the inside of his coat collar, placing the earpiece into his ear.

"Okay, but give me updates or I'll bail out of this truck to find you. I'm not sitting here long, Gabe."

"Roger that," he said, and he leaned over, kissing her temple quickly. "Later . . ."

Stunned, she sat there, staring at him. There was amusement in his eyes, that sensual mouth of his moving slightly upward at the corners. In moments, he was out of the truck and quietly closing the door. He had kissed her! She hadn't expected it. But she didn't dislike it, either.

Using the woods as cover, Gabe and Ace quickly moved through the squishy, slippery brown pine needles that covered the floor of the forest. He'd committed this area to memory and moved up a steeper slope, hunched over, staying low and using the massive tree trunks that rose fifty to eighty feet above him to hide his presence.

His breath came out in wisps and jets. Ace was ahead of him on a six-foot leash, ears up, and Gabe knew the dog could hear the two men even if he couldn't. The way his dog tugged against the leash, going up the slope like a rocket without hesitation, Ace was now in battle mode. The rain was pelting bits of ice and slowly turning to sleet. He pulled his black baseball cap a little lower to protect his eyes as he dug into the soft, wet floor with the toes of his boots, moving to the right, knowing that soon, the entire parking lot would be viewable.

Two minutes later, Gabe halted, hunkered down on one knee behind a large tree trunk, Ace coming to his side, panting, but all his attention farther up the heavily wooded slope.

There, below, was the Elson truck. Where were they at? Swiftly scanning the area around the parking lot, he caught a flash of an Elson's bright red coat far above him. Ace saw it too, a low growl in his throat. The slope was straight up and unforgiving, with black rocks poking out of the pine needle floor here and there. The mountainside went up to seven thousand feet and then dropped just as steeply back down into a large, oval valley below that was Rocking G property.

He quickly spoke to Anna, telling her that he and Ace were going to follow them. He gave his GPS coordinates, which she would convey to the DEA HQ. There was no way with her ankle in its present condition that she could do what he was now doing, and both of them knew it. He heard the frustration in her husky voice. He knew she wanted to be where the action was at.

"Stay safe, Cowboy."

"Roger that. Anyway, I have to know what you thought of my kiss," he said, and he grinned, signing off, springing upward, swiftly moving up the slope parallel to the Elson brothers, Ace lunging all the way ahead of him, on target. He would shadow them, keeping out of sight, but catching glimpses of them here and there as they struggled, slipped, and sometimes fell by stumbling over a hidden root beneath the pine needles. Ace was absolutely silent, unlike him.

It took twenty minutes to reach the seven-thousand-foot level where the snow was falling in big, fat, wet flakes. Gabe saw the Elsons halt at the top, a pair of binoculars in Kaen's hands as he looked at something below where they were standing. Hiding behind a large boulder, Gabe went to his belly and Ace mimicked, lying alongside him. The snow was not falling thickly, and he could see a bare white layer on the yellowed grass. His heart beat once, heavily. Watching where the Elsons stood, and where he was hidden, he craned his neck and saw bales wrapped in green plastic scattered throughout the meadow. Counting them quickly, he pulled out his cell phone, taking photos. And then, he rolled on his side, sticking his cell phone out from behind the rock, getting several more photos of the Elsons, who stood talking loudly, gesticulating several times at the bales below.

Hiding behind the boulder, Gabe told Anna what he'd seen and gave her the count on the bales.

"Are they different-size bales?" Anna demanded.

"Yes. If I had to guess, it's a mixed drug drop from a plane. There's three sizes and I would hazard that they are marijuana, heroin or cocaine, and the smallest bales are most likely fentanyl."

"Roger that. What are the Elsons doing?"

"Talking between themselves. My guess is they knew this drop was coming. Kaen has a notebook out and he's writing down how many bales are down there."

"It's starting to snow here, Gabe."

"Yeah, it's picking up here, too. I'm coming back with Ace. I'd like to get us out of here before we leave snow tracks on the highway to our ranch. I don't want them having a clue that we were following them."

"Get down here, Cowboy. We need to cover our tracks."

He grinned, slipping the cell phone into his coat pocket and zipping it shut. "Roger that. It will take me about twenty minutes to reach you. I'll check in halfway down."

"You'd better."

Swallowing a chuckle, he made sure the Elsons, whose backs were turned toward him, were still looking down at the meadow and not in his direction. They were. Gabe pushed slowly to his knees and then crouched, giving Ace the order to get to his feet. They eased silently farther away so that even as they paralleled their trail, they would not see him in his dark brown jacket or a brown dog with a black face mask. It was always smart to wear colors that faded into the surroundings, not stand out like that red coat that Kaen was wearing. Ace blended in perfectly, looking like a shadow between the trees.

The ground was slippery, a mix of water with sleet, and now a few snowflakes. Weaving in and out, Gabe cautiously took the downward slope, causing him to slip more than ever. Halting every minute or so, he wanted to make sure that the Elsons were not nearby. Ace was his first warning system, and he wasn't giving any, so they must be putting distance between them. At the halfway mark, he called Anna and checked in. He heard a bit of relief in her voice. The snow had suddenly stopped and he was glad, turning back to sleet and rain. There was a crack in the clouds, a sliver of sunlight stabbing through the gray day for a bit, before the beam was blocked once more.

He was concerned about the highway. If there was a layer of snow on it, even a quarter of an inch on the black road surface, the Elsons would see their tire tracks. As he approached the pickup, he saw Anna wave in greeting. He lifted his glove, made his way around to the driver's side, and opened the rear door. Ace leaped in and he unsnapped the leash from the dog's collar. Then, he climbed in.

"Wicked weather," he grumbled, taking off his cap and slapping it against his knee, and then resettling it on his head.

"Ugly. Makes me pine for the jungle. You okay?" Ace stuck his head between the seats, panting, but licking her hand as she brought it up to pet him on his wet shoulder.

"Fine. When I left, the Elsons were still up at the top, counting the bales down in the valley. They also had a radio. It looked like a satellite radio. They were talking to someone but I don't know who. I wasn't that close to them. I'm sure Ace heard it, but he doesn't understand English." And then he grinned off-handedly. "Except Egg McMuffins."

Ace whined, thumping his tail with excitement.

"No," Gabe told him. "Not today, big boy."

Anna laughed and she said, "Let's get out of here. The snow stopped. I'm worried that if we leave tracks on the highway, we're busted."

"Already with you," he said, putting the truck into reverse. In no time, they were gone. The light snow on the highway had already melted, much to their relief. That meant that unless the Elsons already came down from the top of the slope, they wouldn't be aware of them at all. Relief tunneled through Gabe as he pressed down on the accelerator, wanting to put as much distance between them and the Elsons as they could.

"I've been in touch with DEA in Salt Lake. They're on this. Do you have photos I could send them?"

"Yeah, got 'em on my phone. There's no cell towers out

here, so we'll have to wait until we get home to send them over your laptop."

"Let me call them and tell them they're coming," she said, and she was on her radio.

By the time they arrived home, it started snowing again, this time in earnest. He dropped Anna and Ace off at the house, then drove to the barn. He opened the doors, drove the pickup into the lower part of the barn.

When he entered the house, he knew she'd be in her office, sending the photos he'd taken on his cell phone to the Salt Lake task force office. Ace was licking his fur dry in her office.

Shedding his coat and hat, he changed out of his winter boots for a pair of sneakers. Walking to her office, he automatically glanced out the window near where she sat at her desk.

"They're back," he warned Anna in a low tone, standing to one side of the window so he couldn't be spotted. "Nothing in the back of their truck."

"Phew," Anna said, finishing off the sending of the photos, "that was close."

"They must have turned and left maybe five or ten minutes after we left," he said, watching the brothers drive around to the back of the house, their truck now hidden from prying eyes.

"Not much else they could do. DEA says there's going to be weather clearing around 0300 tomorrow morning. They are sending a predator drone to that valley to take a good, close look and get photographs."

Gabe nodded. The brothers must have gone in the rear door of the house as there was no more activity around it or the barn. He roused himself and moved over to her desk, sitting down on a chair off to one side of it. "What else has Salt Lake said? Anything?"

"Yes." She leaned back in her chair, studying him. "They want a count on these bales, which they'll get from the Pred. And then they want to keep it on station at about ten thousand feet and see if the Elsons go back to pick up the bales tomorrow. If they do, they're going to have the Pred follow them. Right now, I'll bet the Elsons are contacting regional buyers of these drugs in other states. HQ wants us to continue to watch and keep them apprised. We're not to do more than that."

"Do they know about your sprain?" he asked.

"What do you think?"

Chuckling, he said, "No, I don't think they know."

"Only you, Ace, and your mother know, Cowboy."

"I guess I wouldn't admit it, either," he drawled, giving her a look of praise.

"I've been in the field too long. I've pulled muscles and had strains out in the jungle, with no help at all. You just do what you have to do and keep going."

Gabe frowned, his voice lowering. "You deserve a helluva lot more care than that, Anna. You've put yourself on the line for too long, without a partner or any help."

She reached over, briefly touching his hand. "Well, now I have you and Ace. Don't I?"

"Are you happy about that?"

"More than you know."

Gabe studied the Elson home. "That's good to hear." He watched the house for a bit. "I have a lot of questions. How are they going to get those drugs out of that meadow?"

"You do realize that meadow is on OUR ranchland? We own it."

"I had taken a look earlier at our property lines. That

particular meadow is deeded to this ranch. It's not on forest service land."

"Another criminal act by the Elsons," Anna gritted. "They're using this ranch's property to drop illegal drugs on. I wonder how many times in the past they did it?"

He pulled the curtains shut and turned. "I worry what the Elsons are going to do about US being here now. That's going to change their normal plans to transport the drugs."

She snorted. "They've probably been running this gig for at least a year. That's how long they've been a part of the Guatemala drug ring. This ranch was abandoned. It was a perfect setup for everyone concerned who wanted to drop drugs into the US without anyone seeing it happen at all."

"If anything happens, Salt Lake will alert us," she said. "Until then? We wait and watch."

"This puts us in more danger."

She quirked her lips. "Yes. What we have to rely on is that the Elsons think we're stupid and completely unaware of their activities. They may leave us alone. At least, for now."

"I hope you're right."

"Hey, I need to soak my ankle in that horse bucket you brought in from the barn earlier. It's in the kitchen. Can you help me?"

Gabe knew she wasn't the kind of woman to ask for help. She was, in her own way, letting him know he was important to her, that she valued him. "Sure. Meet you in the bathroom?"

"I'll go sit on the toilet seat, take off my boot, the ACE bandage, and my sock. You do the rest?"

"Sure." It wasn't like this was new, because he'd been doing it since she sprained her ankle. Still, he looked forward to that brief contact with her. And he wanted to really be there for Anna, not just be a fixture in her life because of the mission.

In no time, he had the rubber horse bucket filled with very warm water and Epsom salts. As he knelt and guided her foot into the water, he heard Anna groan with pleasure. "I have a confession to make," he told her, looking up at Anna. Her hair was mussed and he wanted to thread his fingers through that thick, shining mass.

"Oh?"

"I like helping you. It makes me feel good, and I was wondering if it did you, too?" He saw merriment dance in her eyes.

"It's mutual. You're a great mother hen, Cowboy."

He moved the water around with his fingers. Sluicing the water on her lower leg gently over her swollen black, blue, and purple flesh, he said, "Our parents drilled into us that we never get through life alone. That we need one another." He pulled his hand out of the water and took a small towel, drying it off. "I really appreciated you telling me about your young life. I want to tell you about mine if you want to hear it."

"I'd like nothing better, Gabe. You've been pretty off-limits in a personal way to me since we've met." She gave him a smart tap on his broad shoulder. "You can't steal a kiss from me and not open up."

"I did steal it, didn't I?" he said, and he saw her lips curve ruefully, a glitter of challenge in her gaze.

"Yeah, you did."

"Truth be told, I wondered if it would be the last time I saw you. I knew following the Elsons I could get killed. It was selfish of me, I admit, but I wanted to see how you tasted, how you smelled, to touch you at least once."

"I like your excruciating honesty," she murmured, lifting her ankle out of the bucket.

Gabe provided her with a towel to wrap it in and stood, removing the bucket so she could set her foot on the rug. By now, they worked like the good team they were. He had a plastic bag of ice chips and he gently wrapped it around the ankle for about five minutes. The heat and cold were ordered by the doctor and helped by reducing the swelling and supporting better circulation in the injured area. "Are you pissed at me for doing it?" he asked, and he glanced up at her after gently wrapping the ACE bandage around the bag of ice.

"No. It took me by surprise, is all. But it was nice. I guess I intuitively knew what you were doing. You were going into an unknown situation and yes, if you were discovered, the Elsons would try to kill you. It was a dangerous moment. I felt Ace would give you first warning, though."

He rested his hip on the back of his boot, his other knee flexed, inches separating them. "Normally? I ask a woman if she wants to be kissed. I don't take for granted she wants me to do it."

"I like a man who asks and doesn't assume. But"—she touched her temple where he'd kissed her earlier—"I understood what you did and why you did it."

His lips twitched. "Were you thinking along similar lines at that moment, then?"

"Busted. Yes . . . yes, I was."

He chuckled. "We're a pair," he said, and he looked at his watch. "Another two minutes of icing."

"I can handle rewrapping it, Gabe." She twisted a look up at the curtained window. "I'm worried about what the Elsons are going to do next. I don't feel like hanging drywall or anything else right now. I want to check into the

Pred camera feed via my laptop. I really think we need to stay informed."

He briefly touched her shoulder. "I agree. Once you get your ankle wrapped and you're mobile, you can do that. I'll go out and fix us breakfast. Hungry?"

It was her turn to chuckle. "Yes. In many ways. But for breakfast? I'd like steak and at least three eggs over medium, please."

"You got it," he promised, and he left the bathroom.

May 2

Ace's loud, throaty bark ripped Gabe out of a deep sleep. What the hell?

A moment later, his radio went off, screaming a beeping warning that he had on his bed stand. Instantly, he leaped out of bed, feet onto the cold wooden surface. Dressed in a pair of dark blue pajamas, he rushed to the window that faced the Elson place. He jerked it open, and his eyes widened. There was an eighteen-wheeler backing slowly up beside the house, both Elson brothers and six other men at the rear of it, guiding it toward the barn. There was a bright light illuminating it, the sliding door open from what he could see.

"Gabe!"

Anna's voice was low, urgent as she pushed into his room.

"Over here," he rasped, holding out his hand toward her. She was in a long, flannel nightgown.

"My radio warning went off."

"Ace heard it and woke me, then my radio took off," he said, positioning her in front of him along one side of the window. It would be foolish to stand in the center of the window and possibly be spotted by one of those drug soldiers.

"The Pred has this all on video," she said, watching intently through the window. "Look at all those pickups! Where did they come from?"

"We don't know. Look at those men. They're armed."

"Drug soldiers," she spat.

Gabe was glad there were no lights on anywhere on their property. He didn't want to have these weaponized strangers looking at them as a possible threat. "Stay here while I get dressed. I want to get our weapons ready."

"Roger that," she whispered, her full attention on the Elson property. Ace remained with her, the ruff on his neck standing up. Taking her cell phone from her pocket, she turned it on while Gabe grabbed a pair of jeans, a long-sleeved shirt, and socks, disappearing out the door and moving toward the bathroom. Within a few minutes, he came back, dressed, their M4s locked and loaded. He placed them on the bed behind her.

"Go get dressed," he said, "I'll take over."

She handed him the cell phone. "Look, Pred video. It was running a loop between the valley and the Elson ranch. It will tell you everything. I'll be right back."

Urgency thrummed through Gabe as he watched both the video and what was going on next door. The truck turned off, all lights doused except the one above the sliding door to the barn. He watched all six men disappear behind the truck. He didn't have long to wait. The stash of drugs in the barn were carried out by the men. They were fast and efficient.

Then, he saw three of the men trotting out beside the truck, disappearing into the darkness. In a few moments, three pickup trucks were being backed alongside the eighteen-wheeler. In the beds, beneath tarps that were rapidly released, Gabe saw those huge bales that had been dropped in the valley. His mind spun with questions. Luckily, the video in their barn was taking all of this in.

"They've got the bales out of that meadow!" Anna said, coming back into the room, dressed. Her hair was up in a ponytail. Around her waist was a holster carrying her Glock. She stood opposite Gabe at the window, remaining hidden for the most part, watching the drug activity.

"They're efficient," he muttered. "They've done this dance more than a few times."

"Seriously," Anna agreed, scowling as she watched them. "No one seems to be paying any attention to us."

"Let's keep it that way. Are the Elsons crazy? Don't they realize that kind of noise from that truck would wake the dead?"

She shrugged. "Half their brains have been eaten away by the drugs they use. They don't think like normal people, Gabe. At least, that's my experience out in the jungles with these killers."

"I know you're right. Maybe we'll get off lucky tonight."

"We'll see," she said tensely. "They're backing those other three pickups to the truck now."

"Six drug soldiers, six pickups," he said. "Everything in the barn and their trucks are being put into that one eighteen-wheeler."

"I want to know where it's going," she said.

He handed her the cell phone. "There's a text from Salt Lake HQ," he told her.

Squinting, she read the text. "They're on top of this. The Pred video is being sent to them in real time, too. We're to remain where we are. Try not to arouse suspicion."

"It will blow my mind if the Elsons think it hasn't awakened us."

"They're too busy counting the money they've probably just been handed by the leader of that truck brigade," Anna growled.

"I'm sure Salt Lake is rubbing their hands in glee over this. It's going to give them a helluva lotta leads on regional contacts and city contacts and where they're taking this truck."

"I'm wondering if they won't stop the truck at some point," Anna said.

"If they let the truck go, DEA will find out where their stops are to offload the drugs and who the dealers are. They'll get a LOT more information that way."

"Yeah, but they don't want all those drugs on the street, either."

"It's their call, not ours. When this is all over? I want to go back to what the video showed up in that valley where the drugs were dropped. How did these pickups get up into that meadow? What's the route?"

"I was thinking the same thing. Also? How often do they do this drop into that meadow? I'm sure there's a plan in place. These drug lords aren't stupid. In the jungle, I would watch them place drug stashes in certain villages for dealers to pick up. They never dropped it twice in the same spot. They are really careful about that."

"Yes, they did that in Tijuana, across from San Diego. The drug lord I worked for had a lot of different ways to get the drugs across and into the US. About once every three months, he might have us drop the drugs in the same spot. Maybe four times a year. That way, Border Patrol wouldn't start putting a pattern together on these drops."

"Well, we're in the thick of it now," she said, giving him a dark look. "How much do the Elsons trust us? Do they think we woke up? What did we see? For all we know, the drug lord has already given the order to have us killed. That's what they do."

"They're done," he said. Looking at his watch, he said, "Fifteen minutes, tops." He watched the pickup trucks leave and then the eighteen-wheeler pulled out behind them. The Elsons slid the barn door shut, turned off the light, and disappeared into the rear door of their house.

It was dark once more.

Anna let out a sigh and straightened, pulling the curtains closed. "Let's go watch the Pred video from the valley and try to piece this whole operation together."

"I'm making us some coffee, first. It's three A.M. There's no way I'm going back to sleep. My adrenaline's up."

"Mine too. I'll go to my office. Bring me coffee? I need it, too."

Gabe nodded and headed out of the bedroom for the kitchen. Anna turned toward the office and Ace went with her.

"They've got a tidy plan in place," Gabe said, sitting next to Anna at her laptop later. The Pred video ended.

"We need to get a forest service map of that area. It shows they came in on a little-used dirt road from the west side of that meadow."

"No road showed up on the property blueprint," Gabe said, setting the emptied coffee cup aside. "The US Forest Service has roads like this all over the Salt Mountains. They are usually firebreak roads, so hotshot crews can get back in there to fight a wildfire, if it happens. They are nearly impassible except for a high-chassis pickup truck or maybe an ATV type of vehicle. From the look on that video, the road is muddy and pretty much ungraded or not cared for at all."

"But why would it be there in the first place?" Anna asked, sitting back in her chair, holding his scowl. "What's in that valley that makes it important to them to put in time and money and a grader and bulldozer in order to create it?"

"I don't know. We need to make a call to the Teton County office in Jackson Hole, and snoop around."

"What if the druggies made that road by simply running their pickups back and forth on it? I saw them do a lot of that in the jungles where they had important drop-off points."

Rubbing his unshaven chin, he said, "Good observation."

"Do we want to alert the Forest Service about this? Right now, it's classified and only the DEA and the ATF know about it. We should probably ask them first?"

"I will." He looked at his watch. It was six A.M. Already, the sky in the east was lightening. "Can you type a message to the night crew on duty in Salt Lake and get our marching orders?"

"Roger that." She sat up and began to type.

Gabe looked around the quiet room. It was chilly. This house, if it could be called that, was a leaky sieve. They both wore layers of clothes, a sweater and a flannel shirt, in order to stay warm. He looked at the soft tendrils caressing Anna's cheek. Her profile was one he could absorb twenty-four hours a day. He wondered if she didn't have some Mayan Indian somewhere in her history. Maybe not, because her family, from what she'd shared, were from Spain, Castilian, the upper class, whose skin was frequently white, which set them apart from the poorer people of that country. A hundred years earlier her ancestors left Spain forever and settled in Guatemala, where many of their descendants still lived to this day.

Anna's grandfathers were governors in the Guatemala province where her family had their estancia. Anna's father relied on his intelligence, abilities, and drive to climb the ranks of the military. Gabe knew how much corruption could be found in Central and South American countries. It had always been a part of them. Somehow, her father had resisted it all, a self-made man who worked hard and rose through the ranks honestly, earning his general's stars.

And Anna was very much like him. Now, Gabe understood why she still, to this day, grieved the loss of her father. He had been a beacon of hope to the people of Guatemala. Many wanted him to run for governor, but he refused. Instead, he had been intent on cleaning up the infestation of drug lords who were using his country. And he'd gone a long way toward doing just that. Anna not only carried Spanish blood in her veins, but also qualities far more important in Gabe's opinion: honesty, commitment, a penchant for hard work, and integrity. Her profile reflected not only of her strength of character, but also the softness he yearned to explore. He longed to share his growing love for her.

Gabe didn't sidestep the word *love*. He knew what love was and what it wasn't. And what he felt toward Anna was growing more within his heart every day. The last month, his sleeplessness and nightmares had turned into dreams of desire and, yes, lust for Anna. He was old enough to separate lust from love, although both of them started with an *l*.

Would there be downtime in this cat-and-mouse game with the Elsons to focus on Anna? Now that he knew she wanted him, it was merely a question of how serious she was toward him. Gabe wanted a deep commitment from her, but wasn't sure if it was at all possible. She was on loan to the US. Her home was in Guatemala, her mother was still alive and wanted her daughter to come home . . . but Anna couldn't go home. Not with that million-dollar bounty on her head. Until all drug lords were eradicated from her country, if she went home, her parents' estancia would become a target for all of them. And he knew too well that drug lords would kill innocent family members in order to wreak their revenge.

Sometimes, in quiet moments, he could see a faraway look in her eyes, and he sensed that perhaps she was home-sick, wanting to share time and space with her mother, or walk the land of the estancia that she loved so much. Maybe she wanted badly to go home and live there. But Anna wasn't stupid, and Gabe knew she wouldn't go back to her country and leave her mother and their home open to attack by the drug lords.

He felt bad for her. In a way, she too was orphaned, but for different reasons than his unknown mother abandoning him. Maybe that was part of what drew them to each other? The loneliness? The desire to create a family out of nothing? He'd come to appreciate the human need for bonding and family. His two adopted sisters and Luke, his brother, were in the same boat with him. Maybe when such things were taken away from a person, they pined for family even more? And at his age? He wanted a family more urgently than ever before. As he quietly absorbed Anna's profile while she worked on the email, the ache grew in his heart. He wanted this woman to be a part of him for the rest of his life. Gabe wondered if Anna wanted to create a new family. Was that a deep, aching part of her, too?

He had so many searching, intimate questions for her and none of them could be asked. Yet . . .

Chapter Ten

June 2

"I think I'm whole again," Anna told Gabe as she walked with him out to the barn. "My ankle is strong and reliable now." Ace trotted at her side, prancing around, giving her quick looks, as if to celebrate her healing.

Pulling his black Stetson a little lower on his brow, keeping the bright sunlight out of his eyes, Gabe nodded, liking the lilt in her husky voice.

For the last month, Anna had fretted and he understood why. During that time, Ace had shown his protective side, always being near her. At night, he went to sleep beside her bed and Gabe let him have that choice. Dog and woman were one now, no question, and he was happy about that. Anna was a woman who got things done and did not like being imprisoned by an ankle brace.

"You're walking just fine," he agreed. The morning was cool, in the forties, but the sky was a light blue, the sun strong and warming, the scent of lush green grass beginning to grow in earnest now that winter had finally left them alone.

They entered the barn. Earlier, Gabe had hooked up the

horse trailer. Now, with the horses saddled and bridled, it was time to lead them into it.

Today, their mission had changed markedly. Another twenty bales of drugs had been dropped last night in the same valley by a satellite flyover. Salt Lake HQ had alerted them. Earlier, Anna had called Roberta Elson to see how she was. She found out the brothers were somewhere in California, delivering goods with their pickup truck, but Roberta wasn't sure when they would return home. Translated, that probably meant drugs being driven over to the state, to specific street dealers.

So they weren't here to go up to that meadow to retrieve the goods. Somewhere along the line, Gabe surmised there had been a miscommunication. With the brothers out of town? It was a good time to go to the parking lot, ride the horses up and down into the meadow, and do some reconnoitering. The Predator was coming over tonight, to loiter at ten thousand feet in a wide oval between the Elson spread and that meadow. Right now, they had no eyes in the sky, and Salt Lake HQ wanted eyes on those bales. Today, Gabe and Anna would do it via horseback.

He'd placed their rifles and other weapons wrapped in a tarp in the front of the trailer. They'd gear up once they arrived, not sure what they would find. Roberta had said the boys would return tomorrow. They had a one-day window to find out what HQ wanted and return home, before nightfall, just to be safe. He glanced at his watch. It was seven A.M.

They'd gotten up early, fed and watered the horses, and then eaten a large breakfast themselves. Anna was fit and ready to go. Wisely, she wore an ACE bandage around the ankle to give it extra support. There was no telling what could happen today. Nothing, Gabe hoped. But his years undercover told him to never relax and never assume anything because things could go haywire in the blink of an eye.

As they loaded the horses and got them prepared for the drive, Gabe felt his heart twinging with fear. It was fear of losing Anna. This past month had been hectic and chaotic. Since that eighteen-wheeler had hauled out a load of drugs, they lived in constant fear that the Elsons might attack and try to kill them.

Anna had wisely kept in touch with Roberta. On three different occasions she had taken her to the grocery store in Wind River, and once to the doctor. Roberta was slowly going blind with cataracts growing in her eyes. She was afraid of the surgery. And because of that connection with Anna, they'd been able to more or less keep tabs on when the brothers were on the road selling drugs to buyers in other states, and when they would return from those jaunts. On those days when they were gone, Anna and Gabe slept better. But never completely.

He brought Ace over to the barn, ordering him to guard. Then, he locked the barn, dog inside. Ace would be their first line of defense should the Elsons or anyone else wander over to the barn, thinking to open it and peek inside. With Ace's deep, growling bark, anyone would be detoured. He'd put in plenty of water and kibble for Ace in case they weren't back by a certain time. Calling his parents, he told them where Ace was, that he and Anna were out on a mission, and that if they didn't hear from them within twenty-four hours, to come down and get Ace and take him home with them. Gabe didn't want to worry them, but he wasn't going to leave Ace locked up without adequate food or water, either. He told Maud where the key for the padlock was kept so that she could find it and unlock the barn door.

As he settled into the seat, shutting the door to the

truck, he waited until Anna had strapped on her seat belt.
Beneath their long-sleeved cotton shirts, they wore a level
two Kevlar vest. Unsure of what they would find or get
into, that vest had to be in place to stop a bullet if a firefight happened. Gabe slowly pulled out, not wanting to
jerk the horses in the trailer around. Soon, they were on
the highway, heading up the gentle slope that led them into
the Salt Mountains.

"I'm really getting frustrated with Salt Lake HQ," Anna
muttered, taking off her black baseball cap and setting it
on the seat. "When are they going to spring the trap
shut on this drug drop and the Elsons? They've allowed
the drugs to flow to sellers and yes, I know that DEA is
picking up a lot of network drug info on those dealers
and such."

"It's a trade-off," Gabe said, sympathetic. "The more
connections they make with local and regional drug dealers,
the wider the net can be cast when it's time to pull an
operation to get all of them in one big drug bust."

"Oh, I know . . . I know . . ."

"We're alive, that counts."

She wrinkled her nose. "I don't trust the Elsons. I sleep
light just like I did in the jungle."

"Sleep deprivation, for sure."

They were heading into the forest now, the morning
light touching the tips of thousands of evergreens above
them. Soon, they were bracketed by nothing but trees.
"I'm thinking we should go find that road the druggies
made into the valley."

"Yeah, it was a jolt to talk with the Forest Service, and
find out they hadn't made an official road into it."

In no time, they had pulled into the empty parking lot.
Unloading the horses, they placed the M4s into a rifle
sheath that hung off the saddle. They placed the holster

with the Glock around their waists and then covered it up with a lightweight, warm nylon vest that would hide it. Gabe wanted them to look like a couple of wranglers to anyone spotting them. And they, in the meantime, had to have sharper eyes and be more alert than any possible druggies that might be down in that meadow. How he wished for the Pred's eyes on it right now.

Mounting, Gabe took the lead, more familiar with the area than Anna. She would look around and keep their rear safe. He had the front end of their team and was constantly swiveling his head from time to time, looking for anything out of place or an unusual movement. One thing for sure, their horses would hear or sight a human around them long before either of them did, and so both paid attention to their animal's reactions and the way their ears moved. It was damp and cold in the forest. It had rained three days before, the brown pine-needled floor carpeted throughout squishing each time a horse's hoof came down upon it.

According to the map that Gabe had memorized, it would be about thirty minutes before they crested the top of the ridge and from there, they could access the road and the meadow. A blue jay nearby squawked a warning, flying low and in front of them, hiding in another pine tree, continuing its outcry. Other than that? It was that soft silence that Gabe had grown up with here in the valley and it was soothing despite the possible danger that lay in front of them.

His mind wandered for a moment, settling as it always did, on Anna. He wasn't sure who was more frustrated. He or she. It was probably equal, judging from the way he would sometimes catch her looking at him. The yearning between them was stretching to a breaking point. Both of them were smart enough to know trying to start a relationship in the middle of a mission was sheer stupidity. It was also a distraction and it could get them killed if they didn't rein in their runaway desire for each other. He, too, wished this mission was over. He wanted a chance with Anna. A real one. A forever one if he allowed his quelling heart to run free with what-ifs. Never in his life had he wanted to quit this job more than right now. Every morning he woke up, he dreamed of what it would be like to have Anna snuggled alongside him, their shared intimacy, a real life, a rich one full of promise ahead of them.

Gabe knew it wasn't smart to dream. Dreams never came true, except when he'd been young, and Maud and Steve adopted him. He was one of the lucky ones. And he knew luck didn't strike twice in a lifetime. People were lucky to get good fortune once. How could he hope for a second dream come true?

As they reached the ridge, Gabe and Anna dismounted, tying their horses nearby and crouching and lying on their bellies once they could look over and down into that huge meadow. Anna took photos with a long-range lens. Gabe lay six inches from her prone position, slowly moving the binoculars to see if he could spot human activity.

"Hey," she said in low tone, her lens on the bundles, "each one has a taped piece of cardboard on one end of it. I can make out an H, an F, and a C."

"Probably for the drug contained in them. My drug lord did the same thing to identify the contents. That would be heroin, fentanyl, and cocaine."

Pulling out her cell phone, which wouldn't work up in this area because there were no cell towers, she punched the info into an email and sent it to the draft box. Once they got down out of here and back into cell range, it would automatically be sent to Salt Lake HQ.

"I don't see anything," Gabe muttered. "I'd like to go down and snoop around. Maybe there's another road that can't be seen by the air? Drug dealers almost always have two exit/entrance points in case one was unusable, they had another chance to escape."

"Good idea." She sat up and tucked the cell into her vest pocket. "Ready?"

"Yeah," he answered, unwinding and standing. "Just because we don't see activity doesn't mean someone isn't down there."

She tucked the camera into a padded saddlebag and buckled it closed. "I know. Best thing is to use the cover of the tree line and stay inside it. I never exposed myself in a meadow or a valley."

"Be like the animals," he said, mounting. "How's your ankle feeling?"

She grinned, mounting. "My ankle is fine. My legs feel like wishbones and my butt is sore."

"Tenderfoot," he teased.

"Guilty as charged, Cowboy." Anna reached out, gripping his gloved hand, squeezing it and releasing it, falling back behind his horse.

His fingers tingled. Just her touch was enough to set him off. He gently pushed his personal need for Anna aside, and they began a winding, steep descent into the meadow two thousand feet below them. When they were within a hundred feet of the end of the tree line, Gabe pulled his horse to a stop, allowing him to rest for a bit. Anna pulled up beside him, their boots brushing against each other.

"I don't see anything," she said, her voice low. "I sure wish we had Ace with us."

"I know," Gabe said, "but he's of more value to us guarding that barn and the electronics inside it." He looked around. "I don't hear birds singing."

"Hmmm, good catch. That means a predator is around, then."

"Yeah," he said. "If it's a cougar, I don't mind."

"But if it's a two-legged predator, we will," she said, standing in the stirrups, looking around from where they had come. Settling back into the saddle, she said, "Let's recon?"

"Yeah. I'll go ahead."

"Hero," she taunted, giving him a playful smile.

Gabe absorbed her lips, that smile of hers. "No. Not a hero. I'm just as on guard as you are and scared."

"Another thing to like about you," Anna said. "You're honest."

"I don't like the other possibility. Do you?"

His boot brushed hers as he walked his horse past hers. "No. Let's stay alert . . ."

Guiding his sorrel gelding, Red, Gabe made sure a hoof didn't strike a downed tree limb, thereby breaking it, the cracking sound alerting anyone nearby. The bay gelding Anna rode, Top, wove slowly around half of the large, oval meadow. Anna would stop every now and then, photograph close-ups of each bale. Gabe waited patiently, knowing that the scrawled letters or numbers would mean something to the Elsons or whoever picked them up. It was a code. And just getting those codes would tell DEA which drug lord was involved, and where the bale and its contents were headed—if the code could be broken. He had many codes he brought with him to DEA after leaving his undercover assignment. That helped break not only the ring in Tijuana, but also capture the drug lord himself. He was proud to have been part of the team that took the Mexican drug lord down and put him out of business.

Red anchored to a stop, ears forward, nostrils flared. Gabe lurched forward in the saddle and gripped the gelding's barrel with his long legs to stop from being thrown over his head. He searched the shadowy grayness in front of them. Even though the sun was climbing, the evergreens were thick and one couldn't see too far among them. His horse was rigid and stood without moving. He heard Top, who was right behind him, suddenly stop and do the same thing. Cursing mentally, Gabe could see nothing. Had the horses picked up on a scent? It could be a cougar. Or a human. He didn't know which. Lifting his hand, he pushed the vest aside and pulled out his Glock, a bullet in the chamber. He knew Anna would do the same.

Suddenly, a bullet sang next to the tree where Gabe was. Bark splintered, cracked, and flew in all directions.

Red snorted and jumped sideways.

Nearly unseated, Gabe grabbed the horn to stop from being tossed off.

More gunshots shattered the silence around them.

The returning blast of Anna's Glock filled the air. The scent of gunfire stung his nostrils as he spotted two men on foot, dressed in military garb, running hard from behind them. They were drug soldiers!

Red grunted as Gabe reined him sharply to the left, toward a thicker stand of pine ahead of them. Anna fired slowly and methodically at the soldier running toward them. Snipers never fast fired, ever. Gabe heard a scream. One of the drug soldiers was knocked backward, Anna's aim deadly. She twisted around, digging her heels into Top, the dirt and pine needles exploding behind the horse as he leaped forward.

They raced up a small rise toward a huge black basalt group of boulders around seven feet high and twenty feet wide. More wood splintered and exploded from the trees surrounding them. The wind whipped by Gabe's drawn face as he leaned low on his gelding, urging Red to scramble at top speed toward that fortlike grouping of rocks. It was their only chance of safety.

There were more shouts behind them. Gabe jerked a look over his shoulder. More men! Red charged into the U-shaped arrangement of rocks that looked like a dark fort in the woods. He pulled the gelding to a stop. Dismounting, he wrapped the reins around his fist. Jerking a look to his left, he saw Anna clamber down out of the saddle, awkward, but landing on her feet. He held up his hand to silently tell her to wrap Top's reins around her hand. The horses were terrified, leaping around, jerking them as they held on to the animals.

Hunkering down, Gabe heard the gunshots stop.

Breathing hard, Anna moved to his side, watching through holes and cracks in the rocks. "Drug soldiers!"

"How many?"

"Maybe four. I wounded one. The other was still standing and firing at us."

He wiped his sweaty upper lip, peering intently through a crack in the wall of basalt rocks. "I swore I heard a shout to their right. Two more voices, maybe."

"I wouldn't doubt it." Anna wiped her eyes. "Damned bullets hit those trunks. Wood was exploding all around me."

"Do you have a splinter in your eye?" he demanded tightly, jerking a look toward her.

"No . . . I'm okay." She was on one knee and twisted toward him. "Where do we go, Gabe? There's no way out of here for us. Druggies usually travel in pairs and normally no fewer than six to eight men in a group."

He looked around behind them. "That way is the road. We didn't see anything on it. I think we can use this group of boulders as a shield, mount up, and ride hard down the slope toward it. We can then get on it, and hightail it out of here and get back to the parking lot."

"Wasn't there a lake nearby? I saw it on the map."

She had a sniper's memory. "Yeah, a small lake on the other side of this meadow. It flows into the Snake River at the other end of it."

She blew out a hard breath. "Damn, I didn't see them coming. At all."

"They're dressed in camouflage for this kind of area," Gabe said, "don't be hard on yourself. Our horses spotted them first, though."

"Yes," she said, and she scowled. "Our radios won't work down here, either. Too many mountains between us and Salt Lake City. Worse? Our satellite phone is in for repair and it's not on us. We're on our own."

"Yes," he admitted heavily. "That sat phone could be a huge help to us right now."

"What if this group is in the parking lot, Gabe? They would see our truck and trailer."

Grimly, he considered that. "I don't think so, Anna. My gut tells me there's a second road into this place. They might have driven up last night, taken that second, unknown route, and they were coming in here this morning to claim the bundles when they saw us."

"Uh-oh, six men twelve o'clock. Heavily armed," she said, and she pointed in that direction.

Instantly, Gabe peered through the cracks. Hardened drug soldiers, armed with AK-47s, wearing Kevlar vests holding six or seven clips in each one. They meant business. "Mount up, we're heading down to that road as fast as we can go. We're no match for them."

"Roger that," she rasped, throwing the reins over the horse's head. She didn't mount well, but she was able to scramble into the saddle.

Gabe swung up into the saddle in one smooth, unbroken motion. Whirling Red around, he aimed him down the steep slope that went for nearly a mile and dug his heels into Red's flanks.

With a grunt, the gelding leaped forward, past Anna, churning up the pine needles and moist dirt with its rear hooves and creating small clouds of debris behind him.

Anna stayed low, clucked to Top, who instantly took off, right on the rear of Gabe's mount. She pushed with her legs and hips, urging the horse faster even though they were already galloping at breakneck speed down a steep incline. Weaving, bobbing, and whipping around thicker stands of pine, she gripped the horn with one hand to stay aboard. Her mind raced with plans and possibilities. Anytime now, those soldiers would be at the rock fort.

Then, they'd sight them in a split second and lay down a wall of bullets. Their only hope was to drop below this shelf they were on and then they would be hidden and protected from bullets by the slope itself. She saw the black rocks poking up here and there. If a horse hit one of those the wrong way, he could stumble. Or bruise the inside of his hoof and turn up lame in a heartbeat. She watched where Gabe guided his horse, far more the horseman than she was. Her left hand continued a death grip around the saddle horn. She didn't have the strength built up in her legs like Gabe did to use them to hold on to Top. Instead, she was being violently jostled around, sometimes her butt in the air, praying she didn't fall off. Sometimes her butt slammed into the rear of the saddle.

The ground was a blur beneath them. She tried to emulate Gabe's method of riding. He was seamless, like liquid butter with the movements of his mount as he guided Red right, then left, avoiding dangerous rock outcroppings.

The shelf was coming up in a hurry! She sucked in a

breath, wondering how much of a jump it would be down off it to the slope below.

Suddenly, Gabe hauled back on the reins. The horse dropped instantly on his hindquarters to the ground, mud and pine needles flying upward. Leaning hard left, Gabe helped Red at the last moment and stopped him from jumping over that ledge.

Anna had no time to even croak in surprise at Gabe and Red's sudden, sliding stop. Top followed suit, almost sliding into Red's rump. She watched in horror, leaning back and leaning left like Gabe had done. Her horse's hoof barely missed Gabe's back! Both horses were sliding, inching closer and closer to that ledge!

A scream jammed in Anna's throat as she got her first glance over that ledge. It was a least a ten-foot drop-off! There was no way they could leap that! It would kill the horses! It would kill them!

Oh, shit!

She kept her cool—snipers did not get caught up in danger because they lived in peril constantly. Instead, she focused on every little thing Gabe did to help his struggling mount, who was now clawing desperately at the slope, to stop from sliding and then tumbling over the ledge.

At the last moment, Gabe let the reins go and launched himself out of the saddle, using his feet to propel him toward the upper slope and away from the ledge.

Stunned, Anna couldn't move fast enough to do anything. Top was leaning hard to the left, the left toe of her boot was snagging into the pine-needled earth, her leg against his barrel. She clung to the horn, her mouth open, nothing coming out of it.

Gabe tumbled upward on the slope, tucking himself into a ball, rolling away from his horse. Anna sat frozen in the saddle, Top in charge, unable to know what to do next.

To her left and ahead of her was Gabe rolling like a ball. Red found purchase, his hind legs like powerful pistons driving into the earth, inches away from the ledge. With no human weight on his back, Red made one last effort to avoid going over the ledge.

It was enough! Without Gabe's weight, the gelding was able to miss the ledge and struggle to the slope above where the rider was still tumbling.

Everything happened in split seconds. Anna saw them avoid that deadly plunge. Her own horse was in a better position, digging in with his heavy hindquarters, taking her away from that ledge. Somehow, Top threaded between Gabe, who stopped rolling and was leaping to his feet, and his horse, ten feet away from him, who was slowing down.

The sound of rifles being fired exploded around them once more. The firing was muffled by the thick woods.

No! Anna saw Gabe get up after she passed him. She pulled on the reins, drawing Top to a skidding halt. Red had just halted, turned, and trotted back toward her. She leaned down, grabbing the loop of reins just as he came up to her. Bark was flying around them as the bullets came through the air like angry bees singing around them.

"You all right?" Gabe panted as he trotted up to them, his gaze on her as he took Red's reins.

"I'm fine. You?"

"Okay!"

She watched him mount, guiding Red to a gallop downward another twenty feet, and then lurching to the right, seeking the protection of the shelf.

Anna prayed Top would not be hit by a bullet as she clapped her heels into his flanks. The gelding grunted, leaped forward, and followed Red around the end of the shelf. She clung to the horn once more, legs flapping.

Every bone in her lower body felt bruised and tender, but she kept up with Gabe. She could see that the slope was less harsh in its incline as they wove in and around the trees at high speed. Her eyes watered, the wind battering her nonstop. *Sweet Guadalupe!* She thanked her patron mother mentally as she urged Top on.

The firing stopped.

For now. Anna knew those soldiers had half a mile or so before they reached the ledge. While AK-47s were good at close range, they were terrible at anything more than a quarter of a mile, and they were at least half a mile away from the shooters. This rifle was designed to be a close quarters weapon, not like her sniper rifle with which she could easily take out a target down at one mile, even more, when necessary. She breathed a little sigh of relief. The road was much closer now, churned up, muddy, and with a lot of tire tracks creating high-peaked ruts.

The tension began to sift through her. They would be safe on that road. They could quickly gallop around the long curve of the hill and then no longer be targets of the six soldiers running like hell to catch them right now.

As they hit the flat of the edge of the meadow, she felt Top begin to slow. Gabe's horse was also slowing because they'd run so hard and long. Animals ran out of energy just like a humans did. Gabe brought Red down to a ground eating trot. So did she, getting bounced around even worse than before than at a gallop. Top's fur was soaked, gleaming with sweat, and he was snorting rhythmically through his nostrils, telling her how tired he was.

Anna saw that the road ended at the opening to the meadow. On the other side of it was a small rise covered with numerous pine trees. She watched as Gabe guided his horse to the edge of the road, where the ground was far more even. Red was staying clear of all those ruts that could trip him up. They swung to almost the tree line, just five feet or so between them and the road. She kept looking back. No soldiers. Not yet. But she knew they were coming.

"Anna, look out!"

She jerked her chin up looking at where Gabe was pointing. There, on the edge of the curve that was almost a mile away, she saw four ATVs speeding toward them with soldiers carrying rifles directed at them.

This time, she croaked, "WHERE?" Where could they go? They were being bracketed, an age-old military tactic. And the men riding those racing ATVs were wearing the same clothing as the six who were somewhere up on that mountain slope.

Gabe cursed and launched his trotting horse directly into the woods in a straight line and as fast as it could get into the protective tree line.

Anna followed, feeling like a bag of jelly at this point, her body numb with bruising. She couldn't fall off! She just couldn't!

Gabe slowed enough to allow her to come alongside of him. "There's a lake a mile from here. Those ATVs will never make it through these woods. The only way they could find us is to walk through it. We can get to the lake and go around it. They can follow horse tracks because the ground is soft and I'm sure these dudes can track. There's a heavily graveled area on the other half of the lake. We need to reach that and it will make our tracks disappear. I want to get to where the lake empties out at the Snake River. Okay?"

"Okay," she said, her voice sounding hoarse.

"Can you make it, Anna?" he asked, and his gaze dug into hers.

"Hell yes! You lead, I'll follow!" She saw him give her a tight grin, pride in his eyes for her.

"The horses are tired," he told her. "I'm going to push them until we reach the lake. By then, we should have plenty of miles between them and us."

"That sounds good, Cowboy. Let's rock it out."

Nodding, Gabe swung in front of her, guiding Red in and out of the trees at a trot. By now, it was noon from what Anna could tell. This was a nightmare. And she wasn't sure how it would end.

They continued weaving through the forest, which was now silent. A little more relief trickled through her. The horses maintained a good, steady trot and she swore she could feel her mount beginning to be more rested from that crazy run they'd made earlier.

The lake never looked so good! It was about a mile long and half a mile wide. She couldn't see the Snake River at the other end; the land curved downward a bit on a grassy slope. There was an endless carpet of forest surrounding it. The green grass grew richly around the banks. There were ducks flying out and she saw a great blue heron lift off as they approached the edge of the water. Gabe was right about the horse's hooves sinking into the wet soil. He guided his horse farther away, the soil more dried out and more stable. She kept watch by looking back every five minutes or so. The last thing she wanted to see was an ATV or a drug soldier coming at them on foot from these thick stands of evergreens.

Finally, on the other side of the lake, Anna saw the soil turn to a lot of gray, black, and white gravel. And sure enough, the horses' hoofprints no longer showed, thereby covering their escape. She saw a long beach of gravel embracing the edges, and there were young cattails growing up after the long winter. More ducks came out of the reed patches as well, startled by the two riders and their trotting horses. Looking back, Anna could see that they were now below the lake greenery, no longer viewable by anyone coming from the opposite direction. A bit more relief dripped through her.

Gabe pulled up his horse and waited for her. He turned, so he faced her. Running his long, spare fingers down the sweaty neck of his valiant horse, he said, "We've run them hard. They aren't going to be able to blow out a mile or more for quite a while. We need to find a place to hide and rest up."

"Okay, you know this land. Where's a good spot?"

Gabe pointed to the forest. "Let's dismount, give our horses a well-deserved drink of water, and then we'll walk them deep into the tree line. I don't know what's in there, but we have to find someplace to hide ourselves. Red and Top are our ticket out of this mess. We have to let them rest."

"My ass needs to rest," she muttered darkly, gently rubbing it tenderly.

He gave a low chuckle. "Yeah, that wasn't a quaint little ride. I'm proud of you, Anna. You hung in there like a champ. I thought for sure you'd fall off."

"Give me a break! I rode horses as a child and a teen. I might not have riding legs like you do right now, but I know what it takes to hang on."

"Thank goodness for saddle horns, right?" he teased, leading Red out to the water.

"For sure," she whispered, doing the same, clucking to Top to follow her.

The horses drank deeply and long. Finally, they had their fill. Gabe had saddlebags like she did. Both had packed food and water. He took out a plastic bottle of water, opened it, and handed it to her.

"Drink up."

"Thanks," she whispered, touched that he gave it to her first. She took only half of it, understanding they only had so much to share between them.

"Finish it," Gabe urged, leading his horse out into the gravel.

"No, you drink the other half, Cowboy. We're in this jam together." Anna saw a warm light in his eyes, and for a moment it erased the danger they were in. On its heels was a question that ate at her: Could they get out of this alive?

Chapter Eleven

It was four P.M. and Anna sat, her back resting against a pine tree, watching and listening. The birds were still singing here and there, flitting around. There was no outcry from them—yet. Had they lost the drug soldiers? Or not? She felt as if she were back in the Guatemalan jungle, being tracked, chased, and hunted. There was never a day that went by when she wasn't. A million-dollar reward was on her head. So of course, drug soldiers would want to find her. Her thighs ached. Her knees felt bruised, tender, and slightly swollen from the gallop to flee the hunters. After they'd watered the horses at the lake, they'd taken refuge within the tree line of the forest.

Rolling her head slightly to the right, she saw Gabe checking the horses' legs thoroughly, making sure there were no cuts, bruises, or stones found in the inside of their hooves that could make them go lame. Her heart opened to him, despite the danger that hung around them. She saw the strain in his features, the sweat gleaming on his face and neck as he gently patted Top. Turning, he gave her a silent thumbs-up, meaning her mount was sound. Next, he moved to his gelding, Red. Within minutes, he was finished with his examination.

"All good," he told her in a low voice, sitting down opposite her, facing her and crossing his legs beneath him.

Nodding, she continued to slowly look around. "Thoughts? What are we going to do?"

"I'm sure those soldiers are here to pick up this latest drug drop. If they give up on finding us, I'd like to use the hill that is on this side of the meadow to watch and record them if possible."

"I'd like to find if they use the road we were on or another one as they move the bales out. Wouldn't you?"

"Yes," he said, taking off his Stetson, wiping his face with his hand. He settled the hat on his head, giving her a long, intent look. "Most of all? I want us to live through this. We have no comms until we can get at least three or four miles down the highway in order to reach cell tower range."

"Don't you think Salt Lake HQ might be worried by now? We had a check-in with them by noon. It's four P.M. We were supposed to be home by that time."

"Yes, I think they are aware something's happened. We don't know if they have a Pred in the area or not. And the only other way to find out is by satellite and we know it's not going over this particular latitude right now." He gave her a grim look. "And add to this, Salt Lake is about four to five hours away from us."

"We could be dead or captured by the time they got anything moving our direction to try to find us," Anna agreed glumly. She reached out, sliding her hand into his. Instantly, his fingers closed around hers. "I want to get out of this alive, too," she said, her voice trembling. "I want quality time with you, Gabe. With this happening? If we make it out alive? I'm turning in my badge afterward and telling DEA I'm done."

He lifted her hand, kissing the back of it. "Makes two of us. Something's happening between us, Anna. Something damned good and I'm old enough to know it's serious. I want the time with you. Safe time. Not always being on guard or being in the crosshairs of a drug lord."

She sat up, went to her knees, pulled her hand from his. Placing them on the sides of his face, she whispered, "I'm going to kiss you, Gabe. You don't know how long I've wanted to do this . . ." and she leaned down, her lips fitting warmly against his. She heard him give a low groan of pleasure, his hands cupping her shoulders, drawing her against his searching mouth, the wetness shared between them sending her soaring with joy. Her world of danger, for one moment, melted away and dissolved. In its place was the unique scent of the man she was kissing, the pine surrounding them, a heady mix that made her lower body begin to ache for want of him in every possible way. His mouth was strong, not dominating, but cherishing her, as if she were priceless to him. As his fingers caressed her hair that was up in a mussed ponytail, she shivered with anticipation of what it would be like to lie with him, love him fiercely and passionately as she had dreamed of doing so many times before.

Their breathing changed, was swifter. Their lips clung to one another, the urgency mounting between them, and it took everything Anna had to ease away from Gabe's hungry mouth. She barely lifted her lashes, staring into his slitted eyes, feeling his strength, his utter need of her in every way. Allowing her fingers to move through his short hair, she whispered unsteadily, "I've been falling in love with you since the day I met you. . . ."

Gabe's eyes widened and he allowed her to ease back and sit on her heels, her hands entwined with his. "Me too," he admitted thickly.

"When did you realize it was more than just sex and lust?"

"About a month ago." His mouth quirked. "I fought it, Anna. I knew it wasn't the right time or place to tell you how I felt about you."

"Did you want to?"

"Yes, with every cell in my body. When I realized you wanted the same thing as I did in our growing relationship, it was a hundred times tougher to keep my mouth shut."

The corners of her mouth curved faintly. "Same here." Anna looked around, listening for sounds that would tip her off that soldiers were lurking nearby. The birds continued to chirp. Moving her gaze to his, she admitted, "I love you, Gabe. I can't put a finger on exactly when I knew that. And today has done nothing but make it very clear to me what's really important in my life. It's not this game with drug soldiers that may get us killed."

Caressing her fingers, he rasped, "We'll get out of this. One way or another. Right now? The only important thing is us escaping alive."

"I agree. DEA has plenty of Pred and satellite info on this meadow now to launch an all-out assault on this drug lord and his soldiers. They can stop this meadow from being used ever again. Later, they will find another one, somewhere else."

"But hopefully outside of Wind River Valley. That's what I want for us, Anna: time to let our hearts decide what we mean to each other and doing it in safety."

She nodded and pulled her hands from his. "If I don't stop touching you, I'm going to jump your bones, rip off your clothes, and have my way with you." She saw a slow, heated grin come to his perfectly shaped mouth. Her lips still tingled with the memory of him against her lips.

"Believe me, it's my fantasy, too."

"Can't happen here, Cowboy."

"No, ma'am, it can't." He slowly unwound and stood up. Looking at his watch, he said, "It's four thirty P.M. My gut tells me that gang is in the meadow stacking the bales in the rear of those ATVs."

"If they've got four ATVs, they aren't going to put twenty-plus bales into all of them just one time. They are going to have to make at least two trips."

"Yes, and probably to that other road we don't know about." He scowled, hands resting on his hips, in thought. "I don't think they'll be hunting us. They'll probably think we rode off, and they don't have that kind of time to hunt us down. They have to get those bales out of the meadow and to the Elson barn. That takes a while."

She stood up, pushing pine needles off her Levi's. "I agree."

"We can't wait to see if Salt Lake is reacting to us being out of contact or not."

She stood beside him, inches separating them. Anna wanted to be close to Gabe, and she knew better than to touch him again. She felt the explosiveness palpating between them, that hunger to become one, to seal their hearts with each other. Would they live to do it? To come together? She wasn't sure.

"Can we walk the horses through the woods toward the other end of the lake where we can get eyes on them?" she wondered.

"Yes. We'll ride. We'll have to make sure the horses don't step on any larger pieces of limbs that are down. The noise could give away our position."

She grimaced. "And let them know that we're still lurking around. I think they'd tried to go after us again, but it would have to be on foot. Those ATVs will never make it through the thickness of this forest."

"My bet is that they're going to focus on the bales. Ready to saddle up, partner?" he asked, giving her a warm look.

"Let's go," she said.

"I'll bet your legs are killing you," he said, lightly placing his hand on the small of her back as she walked at his side.

"I'm ignoring them . . ."

He helped her mount, handing the loop of reins into her waiting hand. "Follow me, *mi corazón*, my heart."

She gave him a loving look, picking up the reins, their fingers touching. Her heart burst with anguish, but she said nothing because it was the wrong time and place. Reaching out, she caressed his roughened, sandpapery cheek.

Within moments, Gabe mounted and they faded deeper into the darkened woods. As they approached the end of the small lake, Anna could see the meadow. Right now, it was empty of ATVs and soldiers, with six large bales left to be picked up.

Gabe nudged his horse into a trot, remaining hidden in the forest, heading for the other end of the meadow.

Anna knew he was looking for that other road. Where they had been, it was impossible to know if the ATVs had gone out the regular road or a secret way. She grimaced, her butt taking a beating on the saddle as Top remained close to Gabe's horse, who was at a fast trot.

The light grew as they got closer to the tree line. Anna saw Gabe unstrap the Glock. She did the same. She focused on her doglike hearing, wanting to pick up the sounds of ATVs returning to the meadow. Right now, no birds were singing.

The forest was still. As if waiting . . . waiting . . .

She wished for a sniper rifle. In most instances it put a lot of distance between her and her target. Here, the only weapon would be close quarters use of pistols at seventy-five yards or less. *Not good.*

To her surprise, they came upon a nearly indistinct roadway that was used very little. Gabe dismounted and so did she. They were still within the tree line, within fifty feet of that road. Anna could see ATV tracks on it. A lot of the pine needles that had once covered it were removed by the thick, heavy tire treads, showing them that the soldiers had left out of the meadow on this unknown route.

Gabe made a signal with his hand indicating that they take the horses deeper into the forest. They walked for ten minutes before finding a suitable place to tie them up on a low-hanging pine tree limb. Together, they jogged silently toward the road.

"They'll be back," Gabe said in a low voice as they moved swiftly toward the tree line ahead of them.

"Yeah. Wish I knew when."

"We don't know how long this other road is. No idea . . ."

"What do you have in mind?"

Gabe halted, looking warily up and down the road, and then toward the meadow. There was nothing that said the soldiers couldn't come in from the other end. He was taking no chances. He squatted and Anna joined him. They remained close to keep their voices from being heard.

"Let's use our cell phone video. We can at least identify the soldiers that way."

"Plus, show them in the process of hauling the bales on the ATVs, which the prosecutors will like," she said, and she gave him a sour smile. Gabe nodded, his face hard and unreadable. Now, she was seeing the soldier in the field and it made her only love him more. This was a man who was a fierce opponent, but also a fierce protector of those he loved. Anna could literally feel the energy pouring off him and in her direction. She wondered if he was trying to find a way to keep her out of the line of fire. Fat chance that would happen! They were heavily outnumbered and no way able to take on close to a dozen heavily armed drug soldiers who would kill them on sight.

"Wait . . ." Anna rasped, sitting up, craning her head to the left, to the road. "I hear them! They're coming our way."

Gabe rose, nodding. "Let's head this way. I want a good video angle on them in the meadow."

Anna followed his long-legged strides parallel to the road but angling into the forest more to remain unseen. Her heart never amped up with adrenaline. Snipers had been medically recorded with normal heart rhythm and pulse even though they were being hunted or being the hunter. She knew that SEALs of the US Navy had been recorded doing the same thing. Maybe, she thought as they jogged rapidly into a darker area, their bodies knew that because they were hunted all the time, there was no use getting amped up and anxious about it.

Gabe halted. He saw a huge black basalt promontory spanning twenty feet. He signaled her to remain at one end, and he took the other. Both pulled out their cell phones, setting them up for the video recording.

Anna had a perfect view of the entire meadow. She had eighty percent on her battery. That was good. She threw Gabe a thumbs-up, letting him know she was ready. She missed the radio contact between them. Hand signals and simply reading her partner's intentions would have to do.

The ATVs drew closer, their sounds drowning out the

quiet of the forest. Anna remained on one knee. She set her phone down on the dried pine needles and pulled out her Glock, putting a bullet in the chamber and then settling it back into the holster.

Soon, the first ATV drove by with four soldiers on board. From Gabe's end, he got the first look at them, and by the time they reached Anna's end, she had excellent profile photos of each man on board. They were hard-looking, lethal, and she knew the type only too well. The second and third ATV roared by. She spotted the two Elson brothers on board the fourth.

Within minutes, the foursomes in the vehicles were out in the meadow, the men leaping off and hurriedly carrying the last of the bales, one to each ATV. Anna filmed the entire sequence. Between her and Gabe's video, they would have a complete picture to show the DEA and the prosecutors. *Good!*

She saw Gabe stand. He signaled her with his hand to take off toward the hidden horses. Crouching, Anna ran. She could hear the ATVs starting up. Digging the toes of her boots into the soft floor, she ran hard, wanting to get much deeper into the forest so the soldiers wouldn't know of their presence.

The ATVs passed them just as they reached the horses, the sounds of the growly engines muted and softened within the forest. Gabe untied the horses, giving her the reins to her mount.

"Put your cell phone in the saddlebag and make sure it's buckled up so it can't be tossed out."

"Roger that," she said, quickly unstrapping the leather bag and placing her phone in it after she'd shut it down.

"We're going to follow them," Gabe said. "They'll leave us far behind because of their speed, but we have to find out where they are gathering for these drops."

"Yes," she said, getting into the saddle. The sounds of the ATVs were barely discernible now.

Gabe turned his horse, trotting swiftly through the forest, paralleling the road. When he could no longer see it, he moved them closer to the tree line where they'd have a good view again.

Anna tried to key her hearing to any ATV noise, but heard nothing. They were now following the road that took a long, arcing curve over a thousand-foot slope. Gabe tried to keep them within the tree line, but sometimes the road made a sudden sharp turn here or there. They skirted around another large basalt rock area.

Suddenly, they were out of the tree line as the curve opened up.

Anna gasped. They had trotted into a large, oval area of flattened brush and grass. Right in front of them were three pickup trucks, the ATVs off to one side, the bales being tied into the trucks, flaps going over them so no one could tell what they were.

Anna croaked. She jerked Top to a hard stop. Red was already sliding to a halt.

Too late!

They were spotted!

Damn!

Anna saw three of the soldiers pick up AK-47s. A fourth screamed, pointing at them, running for his weapon next to a pickup truck.

Gabe sank his heels into Red's flanks, heading straight back into the woods. Top was hot on his heels.

Wood exploded as a hail of AK-47 bullets screamed around them. A branch was hit, falling right in front of Gabe and his horse. It nailed him in the shoulder, nearly knocking him off.

Anna wasn't so lucky. Another overhead branch was hit. It fell straight down, striking Top's head.

The horse jerked to the left, trying to avoid the blow, but it was no use! Anna lost her seat. She went flying and tumbling end over end ahead of Top. The other end of the limb struck her in the right shoulder, pain racing into her upper chest. Anna bit down hard on her lower lip to stop from crying out, and tucked. She knew hitting the ground in a ball would lessen impact and potential injury to herself.

She hit with an "ooof!" and rolled. Top had stumbled and fallen, crashing to the ground so near to her that she could smell the sweat of the terrified animal's fur.

Stopping her roll, she leaped to her feet, feeling the pain in her shoulder. Top was dazed but got up, a little wobbly on four legs for a moment.

Gabe rode back to her and dismounted, his expression contorted with worry.

"I'm okay," she said, heading for Top, who was shaking his head. On one side of it was blood running from where the overhead limb had struck the gelding.

Gabe, holding the reins on his own spooked animal, walked up to Top.

More bullets were whining and flying into the woods.

When would they quit firing, Anna wondered, patting her shaken horse.

Gabe handed her the reins, quickly examining all four legs of her mount. He wasn't lame. The cut above Top's left eye was an inch long, bleeding, but it wasn't deep. Gabe took his handkerchief out of his back pocket and applied pressure to it. In less than two minutes, the bleeding stopped. Top snorted and nudged Gabe's chest in thanks for his help.

"It's a mild cut," Gabe told her. "Nothing to worry

about. Top will be fine in a moment. He's just rattled but he'll regroup."

"Thank the Lady Guadalupe," Anna whispered, taking the loop of reins and mounting.

Gabe fluidly mounted Red and waited those minutes to allow Top to get himself back together. He noticed the horse's brown eyes were alert and shining, not dull or disoriented, which would indicate Top had a concussion. "We have to gallop now," he said hoarsely. "Ride careful."

Galloping in this thick of woods seemed like a crazy thing to do to Anna. The horses had to run in and around huge pine tree trunks as if they were in a pole-bending contest. The jerks, moves, and leaning one way or another on Top in order to remain upright was so dangerous for both of them. She barely was able to hang on.

The gunfire stopped!

Gabe slowed to a trot. He fell back to where Anna was bumping along in the saddle. "You okay?" she asked.

"Top seems okay. What do you think?"

"He's his old self," Anna said.

Gabe's face relaxed a little. He looked around. Nothing. "*Vamoose*," he told her.

"Yes . . . yes . . . let's just get out of Dodge!" She had no idea where they were. They had no maps on them, as they'd thought they were taking a simple ride to look at a meadow. She swore she'd never make that mistake again.

IF they got out of this jam alive.

Gabe waved his arm, asking her to follow him.

He always seemed to know where he was going. They didn't even have a compass to share between them.

Now what? Were the drug soldiers running after them? Trying to locate them? It would be impossible for them to use the vehicles because they didn't have the room necessary to drive through this forest without crashing into one of these massive pine tree trunks. Her mouth was dry as if cotton balls were inside it. She was sure after this hellish run, both horses, shaken up and jittery, were as thirsty as she was. They'd need to find a water source.

What the hell were the drug soldiers doing right now? How Anna wished for a Pred to be flying silently overhead. But even if there was one, they were out of contact with Salt Lake HQ and wouldn't know it, see it, or hear it.

They were in a very, very dangerous situation. And no help was coming to get them out of this hot mess alive. *Oh, Dios!*

Chapter Twelve

"That was those people from next door," Kaen growled to Elisha as they helped get that last bale hoisted into their ATV.

"I know," Elisha said, hearing the disgust in his brother's voice.

"You don't sound very upset by it," Kaen said, taking the driver's side of the ATV. "Get in! We're moving!" he said, and he threw a thumbs-up to their leader, Jose, who was in the lead ATV and pulling out of the meadow.

Elisha settled into the passenger seat, wrapping his hand around the strut as Kaen gunned the ATV, the noise buffeting his sensitive ears. His heart twisted. What were Gabe and Anna doing up here on this mountain earlier? He'd been in the group who had spotted them. Kaen was the first to fire at them knowing full well they were their neighbors from next door. He knew drug soldiers shot first, asked questions later. Elisha had deliberately shot at them, but purposely missed them. He couldn't kill them. They had been so kind and caring to Roberta, who needed their almost daily help. She lived alone and relied on Anna and Gabe since they'd moved next door. It had been a godsend to Elisha, who took the full-time responsibility of caring for his mother.

The ATV bumped and jumped, the tires spinning and shrieking in protest, throwing up a spray of mud and grass as Kaen guided it swiftly to catch up with the other three machines. By the time they left the meadow, they were heading down the little-used muddy road where their pickup trucks were parked. His mind lurched between their duties to the lieutenant, Jose, and the drug lord, and the fact that Gabe and Anna were on the run for their lives.

Once they arrived at their destination, the team of men, one of whom was badly wounded in the first fracas with the ranchers on the mountain, were sitting in one of the trucks.

Elisha went to check on Manuel first, and found him dead. He tried to quell his rolling stomach, the acidic nausea climbing in his throat, wanting to vomit. He hated this work! But there was no way out. He wanted to care for his mother, who had been beaten by his father all their married life. She had suffered numerous fractures and was not only broken in spirit, but bodily, as well. It had been Anna who had first come over when they arrived at the ranch next door, to see her, to be there for Roberta. Elisha had been relieved when Anna, and then Gabe, would come over and help her. They took her to Wind River to shop for groceries. They took her to several doctor's and dentist's appointments. They didn't have to do that, but they had. Elisha felt guilt eating at his conscience as he walked over and told Jose that Manuel was dead.

Jose merely nodded.

"Get a shovel," he snapped, helping to load another bale into a truck. "Dig a grave. Bury him."

Nodding, that's what Elisha did. *Dig a grave.* There was no mercy from Jose. Ever. He hated being around the Guatemalan lieutenant who was favored and trusted by Gonzalez, their drug lord. There was no way he wasn't going to obey him, either. He'd seen Jose mercilessly shoot others in the head, killing them without any feeling whatsoever.

Elisha went to the pickup, where there were shovels and rakes in the bed. He grabbed a shovel and looked for a place to dig a shallow grave. He knew that no matter how deep he dug into the wet soil beneath the brown pine needle mat on the floor of the nearby woods, a hungry grizzly or black bear coming out of hibernation would happily dig into it and eat what was left of the soldier. That was the way of nature.

Elisha got to work, unhappy, but glad that he hadn't been wounded in that fray. He wondered, as he dug, if Gabe or Anna had been wounded. It didn't seem like it. They rode like fire itself and quickly disappeared around the end of that ledge drop-off. Later, they had been spotted again as they'd driven their ATVs around that long, curved corner, utilizing the other road to get into the meadow. Again, they'd ridden off, disappearing quickly into the thick, nearly impenetrable forest. Why were they hanging around? They had found the dropped bales in the meadow, that was a fact. Why were they so curious? Curiosity killed the cat. Elisha tried to put himself in their place. It wasn't every day a person would see big, black plastic-wrapped things in a meadow. They were probably up in this area scouting around, acclimating to the size and extent of the property. And this meadow was owned by the Rocking G. That was a more than suitable explanation.

Sweat dripped off his brow as he continued to dig. What were they thinking when Jose and Kaen started shooting at them? He was sure they were scared out of their minds, confused and fearing for their lives. He'd have taken off just like they had. The only thing that didn't fit was that Anna was firing back at them with a pistol. And she hit Manuel. His brows drew downward. She was one helluva shot. She was the only one of the two returning fire against them. But she was a rancher. And all ranchers knew how to use a rifle. Manuel had been killed with a pistol. Jamming his boot sole down on the shovel, he dug the first foot of the black, damp soil.

"Hurry up!" Jose yelled over at him. "We don't have all day!"

Glancing in Jose's direction, Elisha scowled, said nothing, and dug faster and deeper. In another ten minutes, Elisha had a makeshift grave created. Kaen came over to help him take Manuel's sagging body to the grave. Together, they threw the heaps of dirt upon the body. Mentally, Elisha prayed for Manuel. These were hard men, but they had souls. Well, all except for Jose; he didn't think Jose had one at all. He was a sociopath. Elisha had looked the word up online and Jose's behavior fit that definition completely. It also made him far more distrusting of their boss. He'd seen Jose shoot two other soldiers in the head on different missions because they weren't fast enough or had given Jose some lip, which he didn't like. Out came his Glock pistol. And he cold-bloodedly killed each of them without an afterthought.

Elisha wanted out of this job. He had been uneasy when Kaen had contacted the drug lord, asking to be a part of his sprawling gang that moved drugs from Central America and were pushing aggressively into North America. The pay was better, but Elisha had argued with his brother and lost. His argument was that he didn't want a drug lord coming into Wind River Valley. They had always run drugs locally, peripheral players in Wyoming. They didn't make a lot of money, but they'd made enough to survive. Pablo Gonzalez, the Guatemalan drug lord, had paid them five times the amount they made on their own. And Kaen couldn't resist the money.

Giving the black soil a mournful look, they finished burying Manuel. Kaen grabbed bunches of brown pine needles, covering up the freshly turned soil, trying to hide it. Elisha doubted that anyone would ever come back to this meadow, it was so far away from civilization. No one but a hungry bear would find the grave. No one.

"HEY!" Jose screamed, jabbing his finger at the road. "RIDERS! SHOOT THEM!"

Elisha gasped, his eyes rounding. Gabe and Anna! Again!

"Damn them," Kaen snarled, running for their truck to get their weapons.

Gunfire erupted.

Elisha ran after his brother, confused and upset. By the time they got to the truck, Gabe and Anna had disappeared back into the tree line. Gone! Like ghosts. Gasping for breath, Elisha had his AK-47 in hand, but there was nothing to shoot at.

The gunfire abruptly ceased.

Jose was screaming at all of them to get into the trucks. They had to get out of here!

Relieved that they weren't going to chase them, Elisha put the safety on the rifle and set it on the floorboards. Kaen was making sure that the bales they had were hidden beneath the tarp before getting into the driver's seat.

"Damn those nosy ranchers!" he spat, putting the truck in gear, jamming his foot down on the accelerator. "What the hell is the matter with them? Jose will want them dead."

Elisha hurriedly put on his seat belt, the truck swerving and revving through the mud. "He doesn't know they're our next-door neighbors."

"Doesn't matter," Kaen bit out, his glare straight ahead, following the other trucks out of the area and down that barely used road.

"But if we don't tell him they're our neighbors," Elisha said, holding on and bracing himself as the truck fish-tailed down the slope, "Jose won't know. We can play dumb, Kaen."

"Shut up! You're talkin' crazy. Jose will find out!"

"Don't tell him!" Elisha said more strongly. He gripped the seat and placed his large hand against the door, the swerving knocking him around.

Kaen cursed. "You're too damned softhearted! You always have been!"

"You can't tell Jose, Kaen. You cannot!"

Kaen's eyes slitted and he jerked a swift look in his brother's direction. "I don't know what I'm gonna do. They live next to us! They've seen the bales in our truck just now. They've seen us. They probably can identify us. Has that gotten through your thick, stupid head? Has it?"

"They've been good to Mama. You know they've cared decently for her! They're good people, Kaen. They try to do right by others. They probably rode up here in the first place just checking out their property, is all. I'm sure they never expected to run into bales dropped in that meadow. And by the way? That meadow is ON their ranch property! They had every right to be up here!"

"I know, I know. Dammit! But they'll turn us in! We shot at them! Who knows? Maybe they've been winged. Maybe they'll die out here somewhere. We can always check on them when we get home once we stash the goods in our barn. And tomorrow, we gotta take the truck and goods and drive out to California to drop the drugs off to the dealers."

Elisha sagged against the seat as the trucks moved from

the hidden back road and onto the highway that would take them home. Already, the other three trucks were speeding at least eighty to ninety miles per hour, wanting to escape what had just happened. "They're innocent," he argued heatedly. "I'm not gonna be part of killing them, Kaen. I just won't."

"Don't let Jose hear you say that, you stupid idiot! He'll pull out his pistol and put a bullet into your head for that!" Kaen yelled. He stomped on the accelerator, the truck roaring, leaping forward to catch up with the other three fleeing vehicles.

Wiping his sweaty brow, Elisha said nothing. He knew what his brother had said was true. "What can we do?"

"I don't know! But what if those two get back to their ranch and then call the sheriff? What then? Chances are they've identified us. We'll get arrested. We have drugs in the barn. They'll find them because they'll come to our house with a drug-sniffing dog. Hell! I don't know what to do!"

"We can't hurt them! They take care of Mama when we're gone!"

"Yeah, well, we'll be in prison again thanks to them snooping around! I don't think they are gonna let this go." Kaen shook his head. He picked up his cell phone, punching it to get in touch with Jose, who was in the lead truck.

Elisha stared in horror at Kaen. "No!" he cried, making a grab for the phone.

"Damn you!" Kaen yelled, pushing his hand away.

The truck swerved.

Elisha hung on as Kaen regained control of the truck. "You can't tell Jose! He'll have us kill them! I won't kill two innocent people!"

"Shut up!" Kaen said, and he got Jose on the phone.

Breathing hard, Elisha sat there, feeling nauseous,

scared, his mind moving between Jose ordering a hit on Gabe and Anna and them going to prison once more. He hated prison! He didn't *ever* want to go back to that cage! Oh, if only they hadn't seen them! Would Gabe and Anna call the sheriff's department in Wind River once they got cell-phone coverage? And had they identified Elisha and Kaen? Did they see them? If so, Elisha was sure these two innocent ranchers would tell the sheriff. And then . . . they would be arrested or a warrant put out for their arrest. The sheriff would hassle their mother, too, if they were not found to be home. Miserably, Elisha shut his eyes, torn up and not wanting to kill anyone. He hated killing. Kaen enjoyed it, but he never had. Kaen had always called him a "mama's boy." Told Elisha he was weak and unreliable. That he didn't have the balls to be a real man.

Trying to shut off the conversation Kaen was having with Jose, Elisha sat there, numbed out, tense and wanting to scream in utter frustration. If only his neighbors hadn't seen them on that mountaintop. If only . . .

If they were found and put into prison? Then their mother would be on her own. Would Gabe or Anna take care of her despite what happened? He found them to be honest, stand-up people, ranchers who, when they gave their word, it was an honor they would carry out until their last breath. Roberta dearly loved Anna. She had called her the daughter she'd never had, but wished she had. Anna was so kind, loving, and gentle with Mama. Elisha had felt so beholden to the two ranchers for their kindness. Out here in Wyoming, people relied on one another all the time. They gave one another help and support when needed, without asking, and they were always there. Ranchers were the heart and soul of Wyoming. Stand-up men and women who were good for their word. Rubbing his sweaty face, Elisha heard Kaen end the conversation. He dreaded what would come next.

Gabe was torn between the injury of Anna and her horse and trying to escape once more. He didn't think that the soldiers would follow them, however. They needed to get those bales out of sight as soon as possible. Red jogged along and they kept moving in and out of the trees, heading deeper inland. This forest had saved their lives twice with its wealth of heavily wooded hills and slopes. No ATV or truck could ever drive through it to catch them. But were there other roadways that they didn't know about? Could they drop the bales in the trucks and send someone back after them?

The June sunlight was lower on the horizon, sending golden slats and streamers through the woods, lighting it up like a lantern pushing away the gloom. It made it easier to see. His heart was in anguish over Anna's horse falling. She could have been killed. Gabe knew the personal emotions he was wrestling with had no place in this mission right now, so he jammed them down deep inside him and pushed his horse to a faster trot. He wished to hell he could know what was in the minds of those soldiers. Who was the leader? What were his plans? Would they just blow Gabe and Anna off and forget about them, focused instead on the drug drop? Or not? Worse? The Elsons knew the color of the horses they had on that ranch. They would recognize them. Even trying to go back to the ranch would be risky. The Elsons could be waiting to take them out if they ever made it back home. Helplessness overwhelmed him for a moment.

"Hey," Anna called, riding up behind him, "can we rest a moment?"

Gabe pulled his horse to a stop. "Yeah. You okay? Is Top limping?"

"No, he's fine. I just need to put feet on the ground for a moment." She twisted around, looking behind them. "Do you think we can? Or do you think they're on our tail?"

Gabe looked back and then down at her. He saw how stressed Anna was. "Sure, let's take a ten-minute breather. We've put at least two miles between us and them. If they are following us, they're on foot. And these pine needles cover our tracks. The minute a horse's hoof presses down on them, they spring right back up. We are very, very hard to track." He dismounted and dropped the reins on his horse. Both were ground-tied trained. It meant to the horse that if the reins were on the ground, they didn't wander off.

Coming around, he said, "Drop your reins. I'll help you off." He saw several bloody scratches on her cheek where she'd fallen when Top had stumbled and fell. Placing his hands around her waist, he easily lifted her out of the saddle. He saw the surprise in her features, but she didn't protest. Instead, Anna placed her hands on his broad shoulders as he eased her to the ground.

"Ohhh," she moaned, gripping his upper arms as he allowed her to take the weight, "I'm so damned sore, Gabe."

He kept his hands around her waist, assessing her. This had been grueling for Anna. "You probably have more bruises on your body than you know right now," he said gently. "Can you stand or do you want me to hold you for a moment?"

She looked up, her lips twisted. "Give me a second . . ." she said, and she moved her weight from one foot to the other, making sure she could stand on her own. "My legs feel like two wishbones," she griped.

Gabe nodded, seeing her grit and courage. "This has been one helluva day. It's bad enough we're being shot at and chased. But to not have rider's legs or even remember how to ride a horse on top of it all, I think you're pretty special. I'm proud of you, Anna."

"Thanks . . . the insides of my thighs feel raw."

"They aren't, but our flesh is pretty tender on the insides of our legs and it doesn't take much to make it feel like you've been skinned." He wanted to hold her more but she took a step back, releasing his arms, so he let go of her waist. Studying her, he saw the exhaustion in her eyes, too.

"I was thinking," she told him, looking around again. "The Elsons know who we are. What's to stop them from waiting for us when and if we get out of this situation? They could put the drop on us when we drive back to our ranch."

He took the reins from her horse and let them go. Sure that the horses could use a breather, too, he slid his hand around hers. "Come on, let's walk around a little bit and get our sea legs back. We'll both keep watch."

As they walked a slow circle around the standing horses whose fur was dripping wet with sweat, Anna said, "We aren't even sure the soldiers didn't find our truck and trailer. They could have hot-wired it and it's gone, too, Gabe. We could be really stranded."

"It's a possibility. Or, they could be hiding nearby our truck and trailer, waiting to bushwhack us, too. Be hiding up on that slope that's covered with trees. We wouldn't be able to see them until it was too late."

"This is a mess." Scowling, Anna said, "You have any ideas on what to do?"

"We have to try to get back to see if our truck and

trailer are still in the parking lot. That's our best option on a list that sucks."

"There's so little traffic on this dead-end highway to this parking lot that we'd never be able to stop another vehicle and get some help from the driver," Anna muttered, shaking her head.

"It would be pure luck if that happened, and I don't count on luck in a circumstance like this."

"Neither do I," Anna growled unhappily. She looked at her arms, which were protected, part of her jacket torn when she hit the ground earlier.

"Have you ever been in a similar situation like this tracking down your target in the jungle?"

"Yes," she admitted. "I had just taken out my target and thirty drug soldiers flowed into the jungle surrounding the villa afterward. I had to hotfoot it out of there pronto. They'd have killed me if they'd found me. Luckily, I found an old, rusted-out and unused water pipe and I crawled into it, covering the front of it with plant branches and debris, to hide myself. They walked all around the area. I sweated it out. They never found me, but it was too close for comfort."

He gave her a concerned look. "I'm glad I didn't know you then," he rasped. Framing her face with his hands, he felt her startle, not expecting this at all. "If I had, Anna, I don't know what I'd have done." He leaned down, his lips hovering scant inches from her own. "Now? It's different, my heart, *mi corazón*. I want time with you. I want to share my life with you," he said, and he leaned down, tenderly moving his lips against hers, feeling her instantly react, a low moan in her throat, her arms coming up to surround his shoulders, pressing herself against him. For that molten moment, danger didn't exist. He tasted the pine upon her lips, the strength of her, strong yet soft, giving and taking. As he inhaled the scent of her skin it made him dizzy with need. Reluctantly, he broke contact, staring into her drowsy-looking eyes. "You are precious to me," he rasped, his voice breaking as he caressed her flushed cheek with his thumb. "We're going to survive this, Anna. Somehow . . . we will . . ."

She released him, closed her eyes, and rested her cheek against his chest, the pounding of his heart against her ear. Encircling his torso, she whispered brokenly, "Ever since this happened, Gabe, I've realized that all I wanted was you. Time with you. Away from all this danger . . . possibly losing our lives . . ."

He heard the catch in her low, raspy voice, understanding this was a woman who didn't cry over little things. Her tears wet his jacket and he slid his fingers over her tousled hair, part of it still captured up in a ponytail and the rest jerked free when Top fell. "We want the same thing, the same thing . . ." he rasped, and he closed his eyes, resting his jaw lightly against her temple, savoring the contours of her body against his own, memorizing this moment because he knew it might be the last time they would ever embrace each other.

Easing away from him, Anna stared up into his troubled gaze. She could clearly see the love he held for her. And it had to happen now. In the midst of the worst day of their lives, with no guarantee that they would get out of this fiasco alive. Her voice was choked with tears. "I want a life without violence . . . I want quiet, peace, and loving you . . . just you . . ."

It felt as if an icy hand had gripped his heart as those whispered and torn words washed across his soul. Gripping her, he held her tightly against him, kissing her hair and her temple. "I love you, Anna. With everything I have, I love you . . ."

They stood there another minute, both realizing that they could be followed by soldiers who wanted to take their lives. As they unwillingly broke apart, Anna looked at the horses. They were exhausted, their heads hanging. They needed water. And rest. Their ears were not perked up and they weren't looking in any particular direction, which would have alerted her to humans on their trail. Like all animals, they had exquisite hearing. For now, they were safe.

"We need to turn our focus on them. Let's find a water source?" she asked, pointing to the horses.

Gabe nodded. "On the main road into that meadow, there's a nearby creek. I think we should try to make a semicircle around to it." He looked up at the darkening blue sky. His watch read six P.M. By eight P.M., it would be fairly dark. "We need to get to the edge of that meadow, get the horses a drink, and then try to make it parallel to that road and head out toward the parking lot. That map showed this road leading to it."

Nodding, she picked up the reins and pulled them over the head of her mount. "I can't think of a better plan. The soldiers could come at us from the mountain above the meadow, or by that road or the less-traveled road. We don't know which one they might have used."

"Or they might have forgotten us," he said. Walking over, he lifted Anna up into the saddle so she didn't have to struggle to mount. He saw how tired she was. They were all running on fumes.

"I doubt they've forgotten about us. And even if they did," she said, urging her horse close to his after he had mounted, "we have to hope the truck and trailer are still there."

He turned his horse. "Doubtful. Drugs are their focus. If it is stolen, then we have a long ride ahead of us. We can't risk going back to our ranch or being near the Elson place. They could be waiting for us at the house to show up."

"Do you know this area at all?"

"I saw the maps. There's a forest road that splits off this one and heads north. From there, it stays pretty much paralleling the foothills of the Salt Mountains."

"Where does it end up?"

"Near a small town called Harley. We passed it on the way down to the ranch. Remember it?"

"Yes, it's really small."

"What we can do, once we're north of the parking lot, maybe a few miles? We can reach Highway 89, which will probably be six or so miles. We get cell coverage around that highway. We can call into Salt Lake HQ."

"But we're out in open sight by that highway, right?"

"Yes. Can't help it. If we stay on the slope of the mountains, we're out of range. We'll have to show ourselves and hope like hell they aren't looking for two riders in the dark. It's a chance we're going to have to take."

"And it will be hell trying to flag down a motorist, anyway. It will be pitch-black by the time we get there."

"*If* our truck and trailer are gone. If it's still in the parking lot, then we have to see if they've set a trap for us or not. They could be waiting for us up on that slope, hidden by the trees, and we'd never see them in time."

She grimaced as Gabe started off at a slow trot. They had to save their horses. "If they haven't, then what's the plan?"

"Once we get north on Highway 89, we can call Sarah, the sheriff. We can let her know what's happening. Plus, you can be calling in to Salt Lake City, notifying them of what happened to us. I intend to drive right into Wind River and park outside the sheriff's office so we can coordinate everything. I'll call my parents and ask them to bring a couple wranglers up here to transfer the horses to their ranch."

"Sounds good," she said softly. *If only it will work.*

They broke out of the tree line, and located the small creek in the dying light. Gabe ignored the beauty of the orange and red sunset to the west. Once he got the horses back into the forest, they dismounted and allowed the thirsty animals to drink their fill. He shared their last bottle of water with Anna. The exhaustion was written in her face. From where they stood, they could see where the road was located. There were no lights, no hint of movement in the dusk. But that didn't mean there wasn't someone out there waiting for them near the parking lot.

They ate the last protein bar between them, hoping for some energy. Anna knelt down at the stream, sluicing handfuls of water on her face and neck, wanting to wash off the smelly sweat and dust. She took off her neckerchief, wet it, and gave herself a spit bath, washing her hands and lower arms, as well. Gabe did the same.

"We'd better get those cell phones on us," Anna cautioned as they prepared to mount up.

"Good idea." Gabe removed his from the saddle bags and tucked it beneath his vest and into his shirt pocket. Anna did the same. He gauged the nightfall coming rapidly upon them. "If we ride out onto the plain right now, we can be spotted. We're going to have to wait until it's dark and then move."

"How I wish for a pair of NVGs," Anna groused, coming and standing next to Gabe.

"We're going to have to trust our horses." He pointed toward the flat plain on the other side of the roadway. "This used to be a marsh, as did this meadow, but with climate change they've dried up. I think the horses will be okay going cross-country on it and not sink up to their hocks in some hidden mudholes somewhere."

"Ugh," she said, looking toward the mountain, studying the darkening road. "What's that?" She pointed toward the Wilson mountain range to the west of them. "I saw a flash of light."

Gabe scowled. "Weather. It's a night thunderstorm. We get them in the summer."

"It sure looks like it's coming our way."

"Maybe that's not a bad thing," he said, reaching out, squeezing her hand gently. "Rain can cover our movements. Not only that, if anyone's around looking for us? They don't want to be out in a thunderstorm getting soaking wet, either. That gives us an edge."

She returned the squeeze. "In the jungle, it stormed nearly every night for half of the year. I got used to being wet and miserable."

"Yeah, well, I don't like being cold and wet," he grumbled good-naturedly. "We're going to lose light real soon. Are you ready?"

"Anything to get out of this saddle sooner, not later," she joked wearily.

"Once we cross that flat, we've got to head toward the parking lot. That's a mile away. If everything is gone, then we head north and intercept Highway 89. That's about five miles farther. Then? We can call home for help."

"I'll bet your parents are going insane with worry for you."

He leaned over, kissing her lips lightly. "I'm sure everyone is. My parents care for you, too, Anna. Just hang in there. Step one is the parking lot. Let's do it," he said, and he released her hand, helping her mount.

The running was over. They were going to find out whether the drug soldiers had found their vehicle and trailer. Gabe mentally crossed his fingers as he mounted, pushing his horse to a fast walk, heading for the tree line.

Heading to whatever lay there waiting for them.

Chapter Thirteen

The thunderstorm hit just as they came to a halt at the edge of the parking lot, and they were still hidden by the tree line. Flashes of light danced above them, cloud to cloud, followed by long rumbles of thunder echoing across the valley. The rain was coming in big, heavy splotches, striking Anna in the face. She was glad for the baseball cap she wore, the bill shielding her eyes.

Tension thrummed through her as they both watched and studied the truck and trailer still in the parking lot. It had not been stolen, and that sent a ribbon of relief through her. It looked as if no one knew it was there. Could they be so lucky as to have been overlooked by the drug ring? Had they used the two roads in and out of that meadow and avoided this one and only place to park? Were they completely unaware of their presence in the lot? No, Anna didn't think so. Drug soldiers were not stupid. They had to question where the two riders on horseback had come from. A good leader would know about this parking lot and send a soldier to check it out. She became uneasy.

The wind roll, a long, horizontal cloud that wrapped around the front of any thunderstorm, came through, roaring and whistling with gusting fury at fifty miles an hour.

Anna watched the trees above them sway and bend in the sudden onslaught of wind-driven blasts. They buffeted her and Top, and the horse moved a little sideways but then anchored. Horses feared wind more than any other element. That was when a predator could sneak closer to them without the horse hearing their deadly approach. Top defied his own instinctual fear faithfully listening for her commands.

The rain intensified just as the howling gusts suddenly slowed, drops soaking through her clothing. In no time, she was dripping wet. Top shook his head from time to time, getting rid of the water running down his face and into his eyes. With every flash of light, Anna peered into the tree line and so did Gabe, who sat tensely on Red. That is where the drug soldiers would be hiding and waiting for them to show up. Her throat tightened. Rain slid down her cheeks, dripping off her chin, the water falling inside the neck of her clothing.

Winds became inconstant, swirling around as the lightning increased, the thunder sounding like bass kettle drums being played right on top of them. It was then that Gabe urged Red out of the tree line and walked him onto the edge of the asphalt that connected with the edge of the slope. He aimed the horse toward the truck and trailer that were three hundred feet in front of them.

After taking the safety off her Glock, Anna pulled it out of the wet holster, holding it down, next to her knee, on guard. Nudging Top forward, she kept her gaze pinned on the hill above them. That is where the attack would come from. Rain blurred her vision momentarily, and she muttered a curse beneath her breath, wiping her eyes free of the water.

Suddenly, Gabe's horse shied in front of her. It nearly unseated him.

Top snorted and planted its front feet, gaze riveted on the dark slope.

Gabe was tangling with his frightened horse. Red had been spooked by something that was coming down the hill at a full run. She heard the snap of a branch being broken above her. Anna brought her pistol up, unsure of the figure bolting down the hill. It was a shadow of a man. Without a weapon.

"He's unarmed," Anna yelled at Gabe, who had just gotten Red back under control.

Elisha Elson skidded to a stop at the edge of the asphalt, screaming, "Don't shoot! Don't shoot!" and he threw his long arms up into the air. "I'm unarmed!"

Digging her heels into her horse, she trotted to where Elson stood on the asphalt, breathing hard, his chest rising and falling sharply. As she came to a halt, her Glock aimed at him, she yelled, "Who else is up there, Elisha?"

Gabe rode up, hearing her yell at the man. He blinked the water away from his eyes. It was Elisha Elson! What the hell!

Breathing hard, his hair bedraggled, face wet, Elisha kept his hands up. "Just me, Anna, just me! Honest to God, I'm alone! I'm alone!"

Another bolt of lightning ripped across the sky, lighting up the whole area like a fifty-thousand-watt cosmic flashlight. Gabe could see everywhere and he saw no one else up on that slope where Elisha had been hiding.

"Frisk him," Anna told Gabe.

Dismounting, Gabe went over Elisha and expertly searched him for any weapon or knife. There was none on him. "Lower your arms," he growled at Elisha. "What the hell is going on?" He gestured sharply for Anna to join them.

Elisha leaned down, hands on his knees, gasping for air.

Dismounting, Anna arrived momentarily. She holstered her Glock, though still wary.

Elisha looked at them. "We don't have much time! We gotta get outta here! Now! Kaen is coming back from the house with three of Jose's soldiers. They're out to find and kill both of you!"

Anna snarled, "Then why did they leave you here?"

"B-because they wanted me to stay on as a watchman." He hauled out a radio wrapped in plastic to keep it from being destroyed by the rain. "I was supposed to call Kaen, let him know if I spotted you. I didn't call him. I swear I didn't!"

Anna jerked a look over at Gabe, his face hard, eyes narrowed slits, evaluating Elisha.

"Why are you warning us?" Gabe demanded.

"I-I don't want to see you murdered. And Jose will want your bodies to prove that Kaen and the soldiers did just that." He jerked a thumb at the truck and trailer. "Get your horses in there right now. Unhitch your truck. We're takin' it! We've got to get out of here pronto!"

"But they'll know we're gone," Anna said.

"Yeah, but they'll think you killed me. Maybe they'll look for me up on that slope before they do anything else. They won't hurt the horses. They could care less about them." Elisha wiped his bedraggled, wet hair off his face, and his voice turned raw with pleading. "Both of you have helped my mother so much. I'm against having you harmed. I know you'll turn us all in at the sheriff's office and I know you saw us in that meadow. I want to go with you. I'll turn myself in. I'm not gonna kill either of you, but they will sure as hell kill the three of us! And I worry

about my mom. They could kill her, too, once they find
out I turned against them. That's what they do: murder a
man's whole family!"

Gabe nodded. "Okay, okay," he snapped, "let's get the
horses in the trailer. Elisha, you and I will unhitch the
trailer afterward."

"No, I can unhitch it now," Anna called. She handed
Elisha the reins to Top. "Get them loaded!" she yelled,
running toward the truck at full speed.

Gabe gave Elisha a distrustful look. "You'd better be
telling us the truth or so help me, I'll kill you."

Raggedly, Elisha said, "I'm tellin' you the truth! We
gotta leave! They'll be here any time! You won't stand a
chance against them!"

Gabe tugged on Red's reins, and he broke into a trot
with Elisha following him with Anna's horse. He'd lost
sight of her and remembered he had the keys to the truck.
Pulling out the fob, he aimed it at the cab. Lights flickered.
That meant the doors were open. Now, she could unhitch
the trailer.

Anna worked at the speed of light. In three minutes,
she had the trailer unhitched. By the time the horses were
clopping loudly into the trailer, she had unhooked the
chains from the truck and let them drop to the ground. She
heard the main door close and latch on the rear of the
trailer. They were finished loading the horses. They would
be safe until they could be picked up later.

Gabe came up to her and gripped her arm. "I'm putting
Elisha in the passenger seat next to me. You sit in the rear
seat and keep your pistol on him. He could be lying. This
could be a setup."

Grimly, she wiped her face. "I had the same thought."

"We have to take the same highway out that Kaen and
his men are using. It's the only route in and out of here."

"I know," she huffed, jerking open the rear door and climbing in.

"Get your seat buckled up, Anna," Gabe ordered, opening the door so Elisha could get in.

Elisha jumped in, slamming the door shut.

In moments, Gabe was in the cabin, turning on the engine, the truck roaring to life.

"Headlights," Elisha cautioned in a rasp, holding up his hand toward Gabe. "Try to drive with only your parking lights on. This highway is nothing but up and down gentle hills, but Kaen will have his brights on. If we're lucky enough to see their lights before they see us we can get on the berm and try to hide in the tall grass alongside the road. There's a huge ditch on the other side of the berm with five-foot-tall weeds. You'll have to douse your parking lights and try to hide in that ditch until after he passes us."

Gabe nodded. "Good plan," he said, jerking the truck into gear, keeping the parking lights on as the tires spun and squealed. He wrenched the wheel one way, and then the other, hitting the accelerator as they skidded and slid out of the parking lot.

"Anna, try to use the radio! See if it will work!" he called to her.

"Roger that," she said, digging into her wet jacket to locate it.

"Mine works!" Elisha said, pulling it out of his jacket.

"Are you sure?" Anna demanded.

"Yeah, we use very strong radios. I'm sure it can reach the sheriff's office in Wind River!" He turned around and thrust it into her outstretched hand.

"Our radios aren't that strong," Gabe said. "Use his."

"Gabe, do you have a flashlight in the glove box?" she asked breathlessly. "I need it to set this radio to the right frequency in order to reach Sheriff Sarah Carter's dispatch."

"Yes, we do. Elisha, dig in the glove box for her," he ordered, his gaze and focus on the road ahead of them. The lightning was less now, the worst of the thunderstorm having moved by them. But he saw another cell behind it, moving swiftly. They'd hit that one in less than half an hour.

Instantly, Elisha twisted around, fumbling with the glove box. It fell open. Making a squawking sound of triumph, he grabbed the light and thrust it toward Anna. "Here!"

"Great!" Anna laid her gun on the seat, quickly fixing the frequency. In moments, she was calling the sheriff's department.

Gabe was focused on the hills that they were moving up and down on. He was going sixty miles an hour under some very bad conditions. Rain puddles had gathered on the highway, and huge rooster tails of rain fanned out on either side of the speeding truck.

"Tell me their plan," he demanded of Elisha. He kept one ear keyed to Anna, who had made successful contact with the sheriff's dispatcher.

Elisha nodded. "They were going to kill you as soon as they found you. Jose had orders to take your bodies back to our barn and cover you up with a tarp. We're to leave tomorrow morning with our drug bales on our regional circuit. Jose is taking a motel room along with three of his best soldiers in Harley, along Highway 89. They're gonna wait for us to pull in tomorrow morning and he checks to make sure your bodies are in there. Then, we get paid by him and he's leaving for a flight outta Salt Lake City in the afternoon."

"I heard that info," Anna called. "I'm transmitting it to the dispatcher."

Gabe's mouth tightened. "Do you see that?" he asked Elisha, making a jab at the windshield.

"Yeah," he choked. "Headlights comin' our way! Get off, get off the road now! Douse those parking lights! If they see us? If they realize it's your truck? They'll turn around and come after us. They got AR-15s on them with bullet-piercing rounds. They mean business!"

Gabe brought the truck to a screeching halt. A brief flash of lightning revealed that the weeds were nearly six feet tall off the berm. Below was a shallow ditch filled with them. Could they get in there and then get back out? The berm held firm as he guided the truck upon the surface.

"Hold on!" he yelled to them, and guided the truck down into the wide ditch.

Anna was jerked around. She gripped the radio, talking all the time, focused on getting their GPS position to the dispatcher.

The truck suddenly lurched to a stop.

Breathing rapidly, Gabe put down the window on his side. He wanted to hear what happened as the vehicle came past them or if it suddenly braked and turned around after spotting them.

Jesus, protect us, protect us. Don't let us be seen . . . he prayed.

"Everyone down. Here they come!" he yelled, ducking down.

Elisha hit the floorboards, his tall, lean body bent into a pretzel shape of sorts, his hands over his head.

Anna lay down on the seat, continuing to speak, giving life-and-death info on what could happen to them. She didn't have time to pray.

It had happened so fast!

Gabe heard a truck screaming by, water thrown up in huge veils.

"They didn't see us!" Anna cried, peeking out the rear window. "They're still heading out toward the parking lot area!"

Elisha sat up, twisting around, his eyes huge with relief.

"Hang on!" Gabe shouted. "Now, we gotta get out of this ditch!" Could they do it? Would they get stuck and become a target of opportunity?

Anna grabbed the door handle and held on. The seat belt bit deeply into her body as Gabe gunned the truck. It roared and raced down the center of the ditch, and then Gabe expertly turned the wheel just enough to climb up that weedy, slippery ditch wall.

The truck growled. It lurched upward. The water in the ditch was minimal. She heard mud slamming into the bottom of the truck as the tires spun and screamed. The pickup clawed and roared its way out of the ditch.

They were out! They were free!

Gabe switched on the headlights, the beams shooting outward, revealing the gleaming asphalt highway ahead of them. He stomped on the accelerator.

Anna gave a little cry of relief and told the dispatcher what had just happened. Looking at her watch, she saw they were five miles from Highway 89. From there, it was a straight shot north, sixty miles, to reach Wind River.

"Oh!" Elisha croaked, his voice tearful. "You did it! You did it! We're home free! Drive fast, Gabe! Real fast! Once Kaen reaches the parking lot and finds your truck gone, he's gonna put it together. He'll come racing down this highway at a hundred miles an hour, trying to find you two."

"Does he know my truck color?" Gabe demanded.

"Oh, yeah," Elisha said, wiping tears of relief out of his eyes. "He misses nothing."

"Well," Gabe growled, "he just missed us in the ditch, didn't he? So much for his stunning ability."

Anna signed off. She leaned forward. Gabe was a damned good driver. She saw the speed was seventy miles an hour. On a wet surface like this? That was dangerous and the truck could hydroplane, but they had no choice.

"Kaen will drive like the devil's on his tail," Elisha warned, looking back, his voice heavy with terror.

"He's gotta find us first," Gabe countered grimly, gritting his teeth.

They raced by their ranch and the Elson homestead. Ace would be much safer in the barn, than in this truck. In a matter of minutes, they were at the stop sign. Gabe slowed down, but he didn't stop. Highway 89 rarely had night traffic on it. Tourists drove during the day and stayed in nice hotels at night. They weren't out on a night like this. He doubted they'd meet anyone on this road for those fifty miles. The valley shut down at sunset.

Anna signed off. She pulled herself forward, leaning between the seats and leaving the radio beside her on in case there was a call back from the dispatcher. Raising her voice over the racket of the rain hitting the truck and the sound of water beneath the tires, she said, "Sarah is alerting DEA, ATF, plus the FBI. They all have to come out of Salt Lake City."

"That's hours away," Gabe gritted out, fighting the wheel and the rain-slick road.

"I know. Sarah is calling in the SWAT team from the Teton County Sheriff's Department north of us. There's thunderstorms all over the area and it's going to be like this most of the night, she said. They can't use their helicopter because the weather has too many dangerous conditions."

"SWAT will come in their van?" Gabe demanded.

"Yes. All twelve of them will. The Teton Department is emptying out all their deputies on duty and they're calling in others to replace them. Sarah is doing the same thing in our county. Between them, they have eighteen deputies and they'll all be armed for combat."

"How soon?" Gabe demanded, his heart beating hard in his chest.

"Sarah is leaving with her five cruisers in"—she looked at her watch—"ten minutes."

"We've got a long way to go before they reach us," Gabe said in warning. So much could happen in that space of time.

"Best that can be done," Anna said apologetically.

"What about Jose and his men at Harley?" Gabe asked.

"Sarah is sending the SWAT team to apprehend them."

"That's a good plan, but that bastard will fight back tooth, hammer, and tong."

She grimaced. "That's what I told Sarah over the radio."

"Sarah has AR-15s, right?"

"Yes. But no armor-piercing rounds."

"Well," Elisha broke in, panicked, "Jose and his men sure do!"

"I'll call Sarah right now and let them know. They only have Level 2 Kevlar vests."

"Hell, they need Level 4 with those thick ceramic plates to stop a round like that!" Gabe said. "SWAT will get cut to pieces as it is!"

"All I can do is call the dispatcher to warn them about the situation. Hold on," she said, picking up the radio.

"Jose won't go down without a fight," Elisha warned them. "He's a cold-blooded killer . . ."

"I know the type," she said, returning her attention to the radio. In moments, the info was sent. Anna turned off the radio, her heart aching. *Oh, Dios, Jesus, and Lady Guadalupe, protect everyone, everyone!* How soon would Kaen realize that Elisha had gone with them? How soon? This was FUBAR. A hot mess. She loved Gabe! Would they get out of this alive? The only one who was safe was Ace, in the barn. And she knew Maud would come and get him tomorrow morning. Anna didn't know how this was going to end. Now, her heart was beginning to pound because she had absolutely no control over their outcome.

She noticed a second thunderstorm coming their way, west of them. They were going to hit it, too. Damn! Gabe would have to slow down. She kept turning, looking for headlights behind them. So far, nothing.

"Is it like Kaen to go look for you if you were missing?" Anna asked Elisha.

He turned. "I don't know. I honestly don't. He's heartless, Anna. He doesn't feel anything anymore. He's got orders from Jose to find and kill you two. If I don't show up? He may think I'm dead somewhere on that hill and take off without me."

"Might he yell for you once they get there?" Anna asked urgently.

"Probably . . . maybe . . . I dunno. I'm sorry, I don't know . . . I wish I did."

Gabe shouted, "Headlights behind us!"

Anna instantly turned around and looked. She saw the headlights at least two miles away on the long stretch of highway.

Elisha made a strangled sound, watching through the rear window of the truck. "It's gotta be Kaen," he choked. "No one is out driving in this stuff."

"Roger that," Anna said. She picked up the radio, giving the dispatcher the new information.

"ARs become dangerous at five hundred yards," Gabe

warned them. That was fifteen hundred feet and one of those bullets could hit them. "That's roughly three-tenths of a mile."

"And that's when they can start putting armor-piercing rounds into our truck," Anna told Elisha.

"What kind of firepower do you have?" Elisha demanded, his voice strained.

"Two Glocks," Anna told him. "We lose accuracy at seventy-five feet. It's like bringing a water pistol to a military combat fight. A Glock will never outshoot an AR-15."

Elisha made an incoherent sound, his eyes growing huge with terror.

"All we have is our speed and a damned good bit of luck," Gabe growled. He pointed to the thunderstorm off to the left of them, still over the Wilson range of mountains. "The water is diminishing on the highway now. If we can outrun this storm, we'll have dry pavement and that means I can push this truck to its limit."

Ifs, so many ifs. Anna nodded, watching the headlights behind them. "That has to be Kaen."

"Is he gaining?" Elisha squeaked.

"I don't think so. The water on the highway is worse in his area."

"What kind of truck is he driving, Elisha?" Gabe asked, pressing down on the accelerator.

"It's a 2004 super cab Nissan Frontier."

"And this is a Dodge Ram three-quarter ton, a 2017," Gabe said. "I'm just wondering about speed. Anna? Can you see if your iPhone can connect with the cell tower? I don't know how close we are to it yet. If you can? Find out top speed on a Nissan truck versus our truck."

"On it," she muttered, pulling out her cell phone.

Please let us be within the cell tower reach. She pressed the phone on. Waiting was excruciating.

"We've got connection!" she crowed, excitement in her voice.

"Good!" Gabe muttered.

She quickly went and typed in the question. A lot of information popped up. "They're not giving miles per hour, just engine torque," she muttered.

"You have a 2004 pickup truck versus a three-year-old Dodge Ram," Gabe said. "There's no question torque is on the Ram's side of this argument. We can probably outrun them, but not by much. We just need to keep that distance far enough so that their AR-15s aren't accurate."

"Roger that," Anna muttered.

"Kaen musta hit that parking lot, figured it out, and turned around. Otherwise, he wouldn't have gotten near us so fast," Elisha squeaked.

"And he has to be driving like the devil," Anna muttered.

"There's other criteria," Gabe said. "How much gas does Kaen have in that pickup? Do you know, Elisha?"

Shaking his head, he said, "No . . . I don't. Kaen always drove. He never trusted me to drive."

"We've got a full tank and that will get us to Wind River, no problem."

"All I want to do is meet Sarah on the highway between here and there," Anna said.

"Stay in touch with her?" Gabe asked.

"I'm going to try calling her in her cruiser. I know her cell number."

"Call her," Gabe rasped.

"Roger that," she promised.

"Elisha? You keep watch on if Kaen looks like he's

gaining on us," Gabe said. "I'm hitting top speed in this Ram. The highway is almost dry."

Anna glanced out the window toward the Wilson range on her left. "We need to beat that storm coming at us, Gabe."

"Yeah," he muttered, shaking his head, "I know." Because he couldn't go over a hundred miles an hour on the wet road. That would be deadly for all of them. But would Kaen do it? Gabe thought he would.

Elisha turned, watching out the back window. "It doesn't look like he's gained."

"Good. Let's hope that 2004 Nissan is low on fuel, too," Gabe said. He heard Anna speaking directly with Sarah, but couldn't make out the conversation. Relief flooded him momentarily. Just having phone and radio contact was going to help. But it wasn't going to stop Kaen from trying to outrace them. He heard Anna give a yip. Forcing himself to keep his eyes on the road ahead, praying that no deer would cross in front of them, he wondered what that yip meant. Was it bad news? So far, they had nothing but bad luck except for dodging Kaen on that back road.

"Hey," Anna gasped, leaning between them after she got off the phone, "there were some Army Black Hawk DAP helicopters that landed at the Jackson Hole Airport last night. They were on a combat flight mission. Sarah called the FBI before she left to find out if any military planes or helos were in the area." Her voice grew excited. "There's four Black Hawks spooling up right now. DAPs can fly in ANY weather, and they're going to take off in the next five minutes. Sarah has asked two of them to escort the SWAT team to Harley where Jose and his men are holed up in that motel. The other two are coming our way. They already know the situation because the dispatcher has patched in the commander of the group with them. There are two of them coming down toward us and they're going to try to intercept Kaen and his men before they reach us. They have our GPS position."

"If the vehicle is Kaen's," Gabe warned. "It could be another innocent civilian. They need to confirm it before they do anything. I don't want any collateral damage."

"I know. I told them that. They won't do anything until the identification is solid. They don't want civilians killed in this fracas, either."

"What's a DAP, Gabe?" Elisha asked.

"It's a Black Hawk helo version MH-60L. DAP stands for Direct Action Penetrator. In other words, it's a combat helicopter armed to the teeth with guns, the Hellfire missile, and rockets. It's combat ready in every possible way."

"They're gonna fly with storms all around us?" Elisha demanded, disbelief in his voice.

"DAPs fly in damned near anything," Gabe told him. "Right now, we're between storms. That means these helos, which are fast and lethal, can probably reach us before that storm on our left hits this immediate area."

"What will they do?" Elisha asked.

"If they are able to ID that it's Kaen and those soldiers?" Anna said. "Sarah gave the commander orders to try to take them all alive."

"I know the plate number on the truck," Elisha said, and he gave it to Anna, who then reported it in to the DAP commander.

"Once they confirm that license plate on Kaen's truck, that will ensure no casualties by mistake," Gabe said, giving him a tight grin. He'd seen DAPs at work and their lethality.

"I'm now linked up with the flight commander, Captain Dunaway," Anna told them. "Anything I say to dispatch will automatically be fed to the Army DAPs as well as to

Sheriff Sarah Carter in her cruiser, as well as to the SWAT commander."

"It's important we're all on the same page," Gabe agreed.

"Hold on . . ." Anna said, and sat back, her phone to her ear, listening hard.

Gabe held his breath. This was good news! DAPs were bristling with armament of every type. They even carried the lethal Hellfire missile! He wasn't sure what these birds were carrying, but at a minimum, he knew they'd have .50 caliber machine guns and that would be enough right there to blow Kaen and his men away in that truck in short, efficient order. Elisha had no military background, so he was perplexed by what a DAP could do. Gabe didn't want him worrying about Kaen's life. If Kaen were smart and if it was him following them? The moment those two Black Hawks appeared out of the night and made themselves known to him, he'd stop his truck, get out, and hold up his hands and surrender.

Would he?

Gabe wasn't sure.

"Do the headlights look closer?" he prodded Elisha.

"Yes, it looks like they're gaining on us."

"Because the pavement is drier where they are now," Gabe said, his hands tightening on the wheel, his focus only on the road in front of them.

"Oh . . . well, yes, that'd make sense," Elisha said. "They do look closer, Gabe."

He heard the terror leaking into Elisha's voice. "How much closer?"

"Well . . . uh . . . I can't estimate . . ."

Anna turned. She gasped. "Oh hell, Gabe! He's a MILE away from us!"

Elisha sucked in an inarticulate gasp.

"One mile?" Gabe gritted out, disbelief in his tone.

"Yeah. I'm used to estimating because I'm a sniper. You can count on my accuracy. We have a mile sitting between us."

"How the hell can that little Nissan go that fast?" he muttered.

Anna sat up on her knees, facing the rear window. "Damned if I know, but he's coming at us like the hounds of hell!"

Chapter Fourteen

Anna didn't want to die. The specter hung over her as they raced at over a hundred miles an hour in a truck roaring down Highway 89. She saw the terror in Elisha's shadowy face as he was riveted to the rear window, watching those headlights inching closer and closer to them. How must he be feeling knowing it was probably his brother behind them and Kaen was intent on murdering not only them, but Elisha himself?

She had had so many moments like this, when time seemed to be suspended as she hid in the trees of the jungle to avoid the drug runners hunting for her. Watching them pass beneath her, barely breathing, Anna would remain still and unmoving. And the sense of delicious relief once they'd passed her hiding place, moving on, disappearing into the green of the moist, humid Guatemalan jungle, would nearly overwhelm her. Life was so precious.

It was a moment like this when she didn't know whether she was going to live or die. Her gaze moved to Gabe. The pressure on him. The responsibility for all their lives in his hands in this haunting moment. His focus was solely on his driving and what the headlights shattering the darkness of the highway ahead of them would reveal. At this time, Anna knew all nocturnal animals were active, eating, foraging, and hunting. If only they would not stray onto this highway, a deadly barrier to them as they raced down the asphalt road. It would mean instant death for all of them if they hit a deer or elk.

Life was such a fragile thing. And right now, she didn't know from one second to another if they would be destroyed in such an accident. No one could penetrate the blackness outside of the vehicle.

Anna tried to set aside her love for Gabe. Would it ever see fruition? Or end up shattered somewhere up ahead on this highway? Life was so cruel and unforgiving. Her father had been taken out of her life like someone blowing out a candle's flame. No warning. No . . . nothing.

And it could happen again . . .

Just then, her radio came alive. Instantly, she answered the call.

"Gabe," she called after she signed off, "the DAPs are going to be here in five minutes!" She swallowed convulsively, her voice hoarse. "Five minutes . . ." *A lifetime . . .*

Gabe gave a brief nod. "Are they going to confirm whether or not that vehicle behind us is Kaen?"

"Yes, they have the intel on the make, model, and color of the vehicle, too. They'll take a photo of the license plate to verify."

Elisha gave her a relieved look. "That's really good!"

"Roger that," she said. "They'll check first." She craned her neck, looking through the front windshield. "They're at two thousand feet, well out of range of the AR-15s. No running lights. They're coming in like the ghosts they are."

"Smart," Elisha said. "What will they do?"

She heard the worry in his tone. "They'll make sure it's your brother and the soldiers."

"But," he stumbled, "will they kill them?"

Grimly, Anna said, "Not unless necessary, Elisha."

"Oh . . ."

"Here they come!" Gabe warned. "They've just turned off their running lights. They don't want Kaen to know they're above him and checking him out . . ."

Squinting, Anna saw nothing. The DAPs were painted black to match the sky so no one on the ground or in the sky hunting for them could spot them. By FAA rules, they had to have their red and green running lights on the outside of the helicopter so that other civilian air traffic could see them. She knew they doused their lights to fly in like ghosts, unseen and unheard by Kaen. They'd never know they were there.

"How can they tell if it's my brother or not?" Elisha demanded, terror mounting in his voice.

Anna realized Elisha was losing it. In a calming voice, she repeated what she'd said before. "They have instruments on board," she told him, "that can check out the license plate. They'll find it, take the numbers, and call it into the sheriff's department and verify it one way or another."

"And if it isn't?"

"They'll not take action."

Her radio came to life. It was one of the crew members on one of the DAPs.

"Be apprised it is confirmed that this is a drug runner's vehicle. Over."

"Roger that," Anna said.

"We've already verified with the Lincoln County Sheriff's Department. Vehicle is one mile from your vehicle."

Anna said, "Copy that."

"Stand by. We are going to warn them . . ."

"What does that mean?" Elisha cried out, his voice breaking, twisting in the seat, staring out the rear window.

"I don't know," Anna said, turning, watching behind them.

"Are they gonna shoot to kill them?"

"I doubt it," she said, hearing the terror and emotion in his voice. "Not unless they are fired on by Kaen or his men. They want them alive, Elisha. To stand trial."

Gulping, sweat popping out on his brow, Elisha stared hard at the blackness behind them except for the two white headlights in the distance.

Suddenly, a red stream of tracer bullets was fired several hundred feet in front of that truck.

Anna was sure whoever was driving wasn't expecting that. The headlights suddenly veered and swerved off to the right. And then the left. And then, it appeared that the truck was spinning around on the highway.

"Vehicle disabled," the DAP operator told her on the radio. "It has slid off the road, it rolled four times and settled upright in a field. We're watching to see if anyone gets out of the vehicle. There's either steam or smoke coming from the engine. Stand by . . ."

"Roger," Anna said, her voice low with strain.

Gabe slowed the Ram down. It quickly decelerated and he pulled off, backing around so that they were now looking down that long, dark stretch of road toward the activity. No one could see anything, the DAPs without any running lights, hidden by the darkness and hovering somewhere above the incapacitated truck.

"I'm staying out of AR-15 range," Gabe told them. "We'll hold here for now."

"Do you think they know there's military helicopters buzzing around them?" Elisha asked hoarsely, gripping the seat with his large hands.

"I doubt it," Anna said. "It's too dark. They won't see

them, although if they disembark from the truck, they might hear them. That one helo descended enough to fire those warning tracer bullets across the highway in front of Kaen's truck. And they probably sucked in air, gaining altitude after that, in case anyone was going to start firing at them, even if they couldn't see them."

"Those dudes in the truck are probably pretty scrambled," Elisha said, his voice squeaky with terror. "Are they dead? How can we tell?"

The DAP radio operator came back. "Be apprised that there are four men exiting the vehicle. It shows they are carrying weapons. They're running away from the highway, into the field. Hold . . . sheriff on the line . . ."

Anna wished she could pierce the darkness, but she couldn't.

"Kaen's alive?" Elisha asked urgently.

"Yes, all four of them are," Anna told him. "They're trying to escape now, is my guess."

"They won't get far. How long before the deputies get here?" Gabe asked.

"Another seven minutes," Anna told him.

"But," Elisha said, alarmed, "no one has proper protection against those armor-piercing rounds my brother and the soldiers have in their AR-15s."

"I don't think the DAPs are going to let the deputies get near Kaen and his men. They're plugged into our network and listening as well. They won't take stupid chances, believe me."

Just as she finished talking, she saw a huge spotlight glare snap on, shining down from one of the DAPs flying directly over the escaping soldiers, several hundred feet above them. Before Kaen and the soldiers could stop and lift their weapons to fire at the helo, she saw more red tracer bullets stitching a circle around the four soldiers. While one DAP kept the glaring spotlight on them, the other did the work to surround the startled group. She could see what looked like stick figures in a field, but that was all. She pressed a button and the window lowered. Now, she could hear the thudding thumps of the two military helos coordinating their attack. Like hounds from hell, they were upon Kaen and his men. Anna smiled to herself. By now, they had to have figured out that if they didn't drop their weapons, the next group of tracers would be on them and they'd be dead in seconds.

"Throwing arms down," the radio operator told her, his voice triumphant. "Our sister helo is using an external megaphone, ordering all four men on the ground to lie on their bellies, arms outstretched in front of them."

Anna heard the smile and satisfaction in the operator's voice.

"Do you have men on board with you?"

"Roger that. We're descending to the ground. As soon as we do, we'll disembark the Army Delta soldiers on board with us, to cuff them and get them ready for the sheriff and her deputies who are coming our way."

Anna grinned. So did Gabe. Relief sped through her. Even Elisha look relieved. His brother would live.

"Here come the deputies," Gabe warned, hooking a thumb behind him.

Sure enough, four cruisers, lights flashing, sirens screaming, raced by them, heading to the side of the road where the DAPs had contained Kaen and his men. The garish light from the DAP hovering overhead made it look like a Salvador Dali surrealist painting. Was it over? *No.* Anna worried about the SWAT team heading for Harley and that motel where the regional drug leader and his men were holed up.

She clicked the radio and asked the DAP communications operator if they were heading toward Harley to help the deputies down there.

"That's a roger," he said. "Our Delta Force cuffed them. Now, the deputies are getting the four suspects on their feet and herding them toward the highway where their cruisers are located. Our Delta Force contingent is already loaded up in the other DAP that landed nearby once it was safe. We're getting ready to leave right now to assist your SWAT team. It will take ten minutes to reach where they're presently at on Highway 89. Over."

"Thanks for all you've done. We were in a real fix. Just take care down there. Out," Anna said.

She turned and saw the worry on Elisha's face, and could see the anguish in his eyes. He'd sold out his brother. Elisha had saved their lives. "Gabe? I think we need to head into Wind River and take Elisha to the sheriff's department to be booked."

Elisha nodded. "Yeah, let's do that. I'm not runnin' anymore." He gave Anna a pleading look. "I realized tonight you two aren't who I thought you were. Are you cops?"

"No, we're DEA undercover agents." Anna wasn't about to go into the guts of their mission with him.

"But you were kind and caring to my mother. Are you going to be in that ranch next door to our home after this is all over?"

Shaking his head, Gabe said, "No, that ranch was a prop. Something we used to watch you. We won't be down there after this mission is over."

Seeing the consternation in Elisha's eyes, Anna asked, "Why can't your mother come to Wind River? Sell your homestead. She's getting old and she's incapable of taking care of herself much longer, Elisha. Maybe you can talk her into doing that? There's a new care facility being built right now in Wind River. She's approaching sixty-five, so Medicare can help defray her costs. She would be well cared for and the hospital is only blocks away, if she needed it. What do you think?"

Pushing his fingers through his stringy hair, Elisha muttered, "Somehow, I'm gonna have to persuade her to do just that. Kaen doesn't care. He never did, but I do." He sighed heavily. "I know I'm going back to prison. So is Kaen. No one will be there for her."

"Look," Gabe said, turning the truck around and heading toward Wind River, "I'm going to have a talk with Sheriff Sarah Carter. I'll tell her how much help you were to us, how you saved our lives, Elisha. I'm sure in a court of law, a prosecutor may reduce your sentence. How much? I don't know. But it means you could get out earlier rather than later. You could be there to care for your mom, maybe."

Anna nodded, giving him a gentle look. "Gabe has influence in this case, Elisha. And I'll testify on your behalf, as well. You've always been the caring son to Roberta. And I think now she'll need you more than ever."

"I still worry about my mother, though. Jose is well known for murdering the family of someone like me to get even when they turn and tell prosecutors the truth."

"Have you thought of going into Witness Protection?" Anna asked. "Turn over evidence on the drug ring you worked for. I'm sure you and your mother would be taken in, your names and identities changed, as well as locating you somewhere other than Wyoming, so the drug lord can't ever find you. At least you'd have your freedom, a way to start a new life together."

"I've been thinkin' about that," he admitted slowly, lifting his hands and pushing the hair away from his face.

"I'm a pretty good carpenter. Maybe I could make a living for my mother and me that way."

"I'm sure you could," Anna said.

"Do you want me to discuss this with Sheriff Carter, then?" Gabe asked him.

"Yes. Would you?"

"You'll be given an attorney, Elisha," Anna said. "This discussion first needs to be shared with the attorney who will represent you in court. Then, Gabe can put in a good word for you."

"Okay. Yeah." He gave her a watery look. "You were always there for my mother. She always talked fondly about you when we got back from drug drops."

"Listen, as long as I'm here, I'll make sure to drive down and see her, see how's she's doing. Okay?"

"Can you let me know? The feds will probably throw the book at me and I'll sit in jail with no bail until my court date comes up. That could be a year from now."

"Don't worry," Gabe said quietly. "We'll take care of Roberta. Take that off your plate of worry, okay? You focus on what's best for you in this mess."

Anna saw tears well up in Elisha's eyes, and he quickly dropped his head, looking away, self-consciously wiping them from his eyes. When he spoke later, his voice was hoarse.

"I don't know how I'll ever thank the two of you . . . I really don't."

June 3

On the way home to Gabe's parents' ranch, Anna called them. They had dropped Elisha off at the sheriff's office and let Maud and Steve know they were driving in to see them. Anna sat up in the front seat, talking with them on a speaker phone they had in Steve's office, giving them a quick sketch of what had happened.

Their horses in the trailer at the parking lot would be brought home shortly. Steve had dispatched two of their wranglers in another truck, and they would be arriving to care for Red and Top.

Most of all, Anna liked that Gabe had reached over, squeezing her hand, giving her a look that made her heart melt, the fear for their lives draining away from her. They'd survived. Best of all, one of the deputies had already stopped at their barn, retrieved Ace, and was bringing him back in the cruiser to them. All was well.

"We'll spend some time with my parents," he told her after she got off her phone with them. "I told them we're dirty and need showers, but they begged us to come and see them first. Then? We're going back to our apartments in Wind River, shower, and get clean clothes. I need you, Anna. I want you close to me. I want to hold you, kiss you, and love you. Ace can remain outside our bedroom."

The sting of tears burned in her eyes as he gazed at her briefly while still keeping most of his attention on the road in front of them as he drove. Her fingers tightened around his. "I want the same thing, Gabe. And I'm sure Ace is going to be overjoyed just to be with us, even though he's not invited into our bedroom tonight."

"He'll be fine out in the living room." He rasped, "Life is too damned short," and reluctantly released her hand.

"That fact hasn't been lost on me."

At the ranch, Maud and Steve met them out on the porch near dawn. The sky was still dark, but a ribbon of pink outlined the mountains surrounding the huge valley. Maud hugged Anna and Steve embraced his son. And then the reverse happened. Anna was surprised and touched by the family accepting her as part of their own.

The sheriff's deputy carrying Ace rolled up. Ace leaped out of the car once the door was opened, heading like a bullet for Gabe and Anna. The dog was all wriggles, licks, tail wagging, and whining. They both knelt on the ground between him, lavishing him with murmurs of love, hugs of welcome, and lots of petting. Finally, Ace settled down and they rose to their full height, with him following between them and heading for the front door.

Sally Fremont was inside, setting up the coffee table in the living room where a fire roared in the river stone fireplace, sending waves of welcoming warmth to every corner of it. She had set out coffee along with another caramel coffee cake, plates, forks, and napkins. Anna hugged Sally and so did Gabe, both of them thanking her for all her help.

Gabe noticed that Maud had taken a few swipes at the corners of her eyes, too. Gabe went over and offered her a white linen handkerchief he always carried in his back pocket, placing his arm around his mother, giving her a tender embrace. He knew it had been hard on his parents. They probably thought they were going to die in that race to outrun Kaen and his drug gang. He sat down, patting the leather on the couch next to him, giving Anna a silent invite to come sit next to him. She did. Ace sat at their feet, happily absorbing their nearness, his pink tongue lolling out, his tail thumping. Sally brought in a huge bowl of water for him, and he slurped until filled.

Maud sat with Steve opposite them on one of the other two couches.

"Come on, you have to be thirsty and hungry," she urged, slicing up the coffee cake and placing the servings onto the wildflower-trimmed plates.

Anna sat up, took two plates, and handed one to Gabe.

"I'm still in some kind of daze at the lightning speed of what happened."

Steve grimaced. "We can only imagine. While you two were driving up here from Wind River, I got a call from Sarah Carter. She said to tell you that between the DAPs and the SWAT team from Teton County, Jose and his three men gave up without a shot being fired, and surrendered. They've cuffed them and are transporting them to the Lincoln County jail."

Gasping, Anna said, "Really? I thought they'd shoot it out with them."

Shaking his head, Steve said, "From all that Gabe had told us, I thought so, too, but I'm glad they didn't."

"The deputies are all okay, then? And the SWAT team members, too?" Anna asked urgently.

"Not a scratch on any of them. Sarah said the DAPs made a huge impression on Jose and his gang. They'd already heard from Kaen, who had him on the phone during the ruckus with them, and he knew these were military helos with Delta Force operators. I guess that scared the living daylights out of Jose and he came out unarmed, hands in the air, with his gang following him."

"Wow," Anna said, giving Gabe a look of relief, "that's incredible. I'm so glad these two DAPs were in the area!"

"Otherwise," Gabe said more grimly, pouring himself and Anna coffee, "it would have been a bloody confrontation. Not one wanted that."

Maud sat back, sipping her coffee. "Anna? How are you doing?"

"I'm fine, Maud. My days of being a sniper in the jungles of Guatemala served me well on this run to safety. I was used to being trailed and tracked. There were many times I had to climb a tree, remain unmoving, and let the drug soldiers pass beneath where I sat, never knowing I was there."

"I don't know how you did it," Maud murmured, giving her a look of awe. "I couldn't do that. You two have some special kind of nervous system and courage, truly you do."

"I've run out of whatever it was I ran on before," Gabe told them, getting serious. He glanced over at Anna, and then at his parents. "Anna and I swore if we got out of this alive that we'd hang up our DEA spurs and call it a day."

Steve's brows flew upward. "Are you serious, Gabe?"

"I am."

"So am I," Anna said. "But since I'm on loan to the DEA, there's some fancy footwork I'm going to have to do in order to stay in the US." She slid her hand into Gabe's. "I love your son."

"And I love Anna," Gabe said simply, giving her a tender look. "We had been fighting our growing love for each other since we met months ago."

Anna smiled a little, sidling closer to Gabe. "We were both mule-headed about not telling the other how we felt. We kept avoiding it, hiding it, and trying to ignore it."

"Didn't work, did it?" Maud asked wryly.

"No," Gabe sighed, "it didn't."

"But it wasn't for lack on our parts," Anna said. "What happened to us yesterday afternoon, getting shot at by drug soldiers up on that mountain, and then being relentlessly pursued by them, did it."

"We knew we were in a life-and-death situation," Gabe told them heavily, his brows moving downward as he held Anna's hand between his own. "We honestly didn't think that we'd survive it, Mom and Dad."

Maud gasped, her hand flying to her lips, her eyes widening. "You never told us any of this. Oh . . . God . . . I had a horrible feeling when we couldn't contact you.

We tried and tried to call you on your cell phones, but we knew wherever you were, you were out of cell phone range."

"And I remember our phone call," Steve said darkly, scowling, "that you told me you two were going up into the Salt Range today to reconnoiter and look around."

"Yes, we were," Gabe agreed. "But what we didn't count on was running into the drug ring swarming around up there. I'm glad I called you to let you know where we would be going."

"That's why Maud got this chill, always a sign that something bad has happened to someone she loved, which sent her into worry. I told her about my phone call to you earlier and that you two were going to be in the mountains. And we both know there's no cell towers out that direction and that you would be out of reach." He gave his wife a sympathetic look. "Maud had been right, all along."

"In a way," Maud whispered, distraught by the details of their escape, "I'm glad I didn't know. It's just too much . . . too much . . ." and she took the linen handkerchief and dabbed her eyes.

Gabe felt like a knife was twisting in his gut. "I'm sorry you had to worry so much, Mom," he murmured, meaning it. "That's why Anna and I are quitting."

"And we're glad to hear that," Steve whispered fervently.

Nodding, Gabe lifted Anna's hand, pressing a light kiss to the back of it. "We are going to go home now. We're whipped. What I'd like to do tomorrow morning is call our boss at DEA and we'll both hand in our resignations. Anna isn't a citizen of the US, being on loan to us from Guatemala, so that means we have a lot of paperwork to fill out to see if the DEA will support her staying here, with me . . . with us."

"We'll figure it out," Anna said. "I need to call my mother and talk with her. She's known for years what I do as a sniper and she'll probably cry with relief when she hears I'm quitting."

"But," Maud said, "won't your mother expect you to come home, Anna?"

She glanced over at Gabe and then over at them. "He's my home now, Maud. What you didn't know is that I have a million-dollar bounty on my head by several drug lords in my country. I couldn't go back there to live even if I wanted to. And I couldn't stay at my mother's estancia because then, she'd become a target of them also."

"Oh, dear," Maud said, stressed. "I'm so sorry, Anna."

She shrugged. "Gabe and I have a lot to talk about and this is part of that conversation we're going to have. We haven't had a chance to say much to each other about the present, much less our future."

"We'll figure it out together," Gabe said quietly. "We love each other, Anna. That's all that really counts."

"And everything else," Steve murmured, "will eventually fall into place after that."

Nodding, Gabe said, "May we come over for dinner tomorrow night? We should have more information on everything, plus we'll have turned in our resignations. We'll know more about that and we'll share it with you."

Maud sniffed and blotted her eyes. "I hope you want to stay near us, Gabe. You're the son who has been gone the most and we've missed you so much."

"And I feel the same," Gabe assured her. "Anna and I have to look for new jobs, and that's another thing we have to discuss."

"Lots of jobs opening up here in the valley," Maud declared, hopeful.

"Hold that thought," Anna told her. "I know how much

Gabe has missed you two and this valley. I need a place like this where it's rural, quiet, and I don't have to be looking over my shoulder."

Heartened, Maud whispered, "We'd love for you kids to stay here!" She pressed her hand to her heart. "Nothing would make us happier."

"But we want you two to be happy, also," Steve said. "You're right, you have a lot to sort out."

Gabe rose and released Anna's hand. He stepped around the coffee table. Maud stood up and he wrapped his long arms around her slender body. Kissing her cheeks, he rasped, "No more worry, okay? I'm home. I'm in love. And it doesn't get any better than that."

Maud hugged him long and hard, muffling, "You're right, Gabe. I love you so much! I'm so happy you're going to be out of danger." She kissed him on the cheek, smiling up at him.

Gabe went over and hugged his father, each slapping the other heartily on the back.

Anna came over and embraced Maud. She kissed the woman's cheek and whispered, "It's all going to work out. Don't worry."

Steve had come over and he too hugged Anna. "We're here for you two. Just let us know how we can help. Okay?"

Anna drew away, and gave him a nod. "We will. I promise."

Gabe called Ace and he leaped to his feet, joining them in a split second, ready to go where they were going.

Chapter Fifteen

"First, a shower," Anna told Gabe at the door of her condo. She felt a bone-deep tiredness overwhelming her and she saw it in Gabe's features as well.

He caressed her cheek, leaned down, and brushed her lips. "Shower first."

Anna was so glad to shed her muddy, sweaty clothes, allowing them to drop on the tiled bathroom floor. The rain-like shower of water, as hot as she could stand it, revived her. She washed her hair and scrubbed her skin. How luxurious it felt to wrap a pink, soft towel around her body after she got out. She combed and dried her hair until it fell into a gleaming sheen. Her heart, her mind, were focused on Gabe and finally being in his arms and loving him.

She had just wrapped a lavender chenille robe around herself when there was a soft knock at her door. Looking through the peephole, she saw it was Gabe. He was dressed in his dark blue robe, and she hoped that the only thing beneath it was him, naked. Opening the door, she gestured for him to come in. Ace came with him, licked her hand in hello, and then with a gesture from Gabe, went into the living room and lay down.

"Aren't you tired?" she teased, giving him a knowing grin as she closed the door behind him.

"No. You?" He turned, threading his fingers through her hair, leaning down, inhaling the scent of lemon on the gleaming strands.

"Mmmm, not at all. Not now." She eased away, gripping the lapel of his robe. "Come with me," she said, and she led him to her bedroom door, which was open.

She pushed the door closed with her bare foot and turned, opening his robe, pleased to see he was naked, her hands splaying eagerly out across his darkly haired chest. Making a soft sound of pleasure, feeling the contraction of his muscles wherever she grazed his flesh, she heard him groan. Gabe eased his hands beneath the opening in her robe, caressing her naked shoulders, closing his eyes.

"You don't know how many times I've dreamed of doing just this," he rasped.

"Ohhhh," she said huskily, "yes I do. . . ." She fully opened her robe, the sash falling to the sides, seeing his eyes gleam as he absorbed her from head to toe. Just touching him, leaning in, her nose against his chest, the hair tickling her, dragging in his masculine scent, made her whole lower body clench with need. "There is nothing I don't like about you," she whispered, placing small, wet kisses across his chest as she guided his robe off his shoulders, falling into a heap behind him. He followed her lead, easing the robe off her shoulders. Now, they were naked and she liked the warmth of his body, the tautness of it as she moved forward, sensually rubbing herself against him, his erection pressing against her belly.

His groan reverberated through her like sweet music. How long had it been? Far too long, Anna admitted. She slid her hands down his shoulders, feeling the ropy muscles of his long back, cupping his tight butt, pulling him against her.

"Keep that up and I'm coming before I want to," he growled into her ear. "Come here," he said, and he lifted her easily off her feet, carrying her to the queen-size bed, laying her down upon it.

She scooted to the center, tugging on his hand. Wanting him. Now. "I want you," she rasped, holding his narrowed, gleaming eyes as he came to her. Gabe reminded her of a jaguar on the hunt. She'd run into the cat many times in the Guatemalan jungle, especially from one of her many tree perches, watching one hunt, that same look in his eyes as in Gabe's right now. She guided him, silently asking him to lie down on his back. His lips twisted and he smiled up at her, hands sliding around her waist, lifting her up on him, her thighs bracketing his hips, her wet core sliding seductively against his erection. Closing his eyes, he relished her slow movements back and forth upon him, thrusting his hips upward, wanting to please her as she was pleasing him.

There was sex, and then, there was love. And when the two combined, it was bliss, as it was right now. Anna arched her back, feeling him penetrate her, sliding effortlessly within her, joining them as one. She moaned, her head thrown back, her fingers barely touching him as he gripped her hips, deepening their hot, pulsing connection with each other. Sex was great. But with love? Well, this was the first time she had both joined within her and she felt as if she were flying, her orgasm exploding within her. She cried out, shifting forward on him, bringing her weight to bear down upon him, feeling the orgasm blossoming within her like hot, flowing lava. Gabe knew how to help her sustain it, and that luscious, pulsating, pleasurable rippling effect just widened and deepened within her until she felt as if she were out of body, colorful lights going off like the Fourth of July behind her tightly shut lids. Oh! Never had an orgasm felt so good, so deep and gone on for as long as this one!

Moments after she started to return to her body, she heard Gabe groan deeply, his hands gripping her hips tightly, arching and freezing beneath her. Now, it was her turn to lengthen and help him enjoy the volcanic explosion. The pleasure was all hers as she opened her eyes, watching his face, teeth clenched, eyes tightly shut, caught in the glory and pleasure of his release. Moving her hips, sliding on those juices that comingled, danced, and joined with one another, the scent of good sex tickling her flared nostrils, she continued her hungry assault upon him, draining him just as he'd just drained her earlier.

Afterward, Anna gave a muffled groan and lay down across him, her brow against his damp temple. Both were breathing hard, their chests rising and falling against each other, sweat shared between them. It was pure lust they'd just shared with each other, laced with love. Anna understood the need to confirm life over death in one hungry act shared between them. It was swift. Life-confirming. Beautiful. Her whole body radiated and glowed from within and she savored Gabe within her, still hard, reminding her of the beauty of him and his dark, jaguar-like masculinity. As she lay there, sliding her hands beneath his damp neck, cuddling with him, holding him as he tightly held her with his long arms wrapped around her body, nothing had ever felt as right as this moment in her life. It was the first day of her life because she'd never fallen in love before. Until Gabe. Until now . . .

* * *

"We should be dead tired," Anna muttered, lying against Gabe. The sun was coming up, the bright bold rays shooting from the eastern window of her bedroom, across where they lay in a tangle of sheets, and illuminating the closed door to her bedroom.

Gabe managed a rumble in his chest, his fingers trailing down her damp back. "You're telling me?"

Laughing, she rolled away and sat up, legs crossed, her one knee resting against him. "I like us naked. I like that we loved each other off and on all night long. It was nice to wake up and discover you beside me."

"And then you couldn't keep your hands off me," he said, and his lips twitched.

Lips she loved to feel beneath her own, so strong and yet, achingly tender as he kissed her, caressed her, and loved her. She reached out, patting his taut, lean belly. "Nor could you."

"Nope," Gabe said, tucking his hands behind his head, watching her. "I counted six orgasms last night to my three."

"Seven. Most I've ever had." She sighed, closed her eyes, and whispered, "I think it's because I love you so much . . . you inspire me, you inspire my body. You are a jaguar in the disguise of a man, *mi corazón*, my heart. You are dark, dangerous, cunning, and powerful. All the things I've looked for in a man and never found, until now."

"We got off to a rocky start when we met," he said, capturing her hand, kissing her fingers, and then resting it against his belly.

"I didn't want a partner, Gabe."

"But you wanted out of your detail as a sniper," he reminded her gently.

"Yes, and that's what made me decide to throw in with

you and the mission. I just wasn't expecting . . . well, I was not looking for a man or a relationship." She gave him an evil smile, got up on her knees and faced him, her hand moving appreciatively across his chest. "When I saw you, I saw a jaguar. I swear. It was as if his spirit was around you as a man. I thought I was loco, sleep-deprived and depressed. I told myself what I saw was my imagination, that I would do almost anything to be out of the sniper business."

"I like being compared to a jaguar," he rasped, holding her hand against his chest. "And this is really funny, Anna."

"What?" She tilted her head, drowning in his warm gaze.

"When I saw you in person for the first time, you reminded me of a female jaguar, territorial, strong, dangerous, and so damned sensual. It took me back a few paces and I wondered the same as you: if I was going loco because I wanted out of undercover with the DEA."

"Hmmm," she purred, leaning over, kissing him for a long, long time, and then she said against his lips, "I wonder if we aren't both from the jaguar clan of humans, eh? Look at our undercover work, *mi corazón*. We are dark people. We work at night or in your case, undercover." She reluctantly broke contact with him and sat up.

Giving her a mirthless smile, he picked up the edge of a sheet. "Undercover, huh? Good pun."

They laughed together.

Anna moved and sat down, legs crossed against Gabe. "I think we need to get serious here." She glanced at the clock on the bed stand. It was seven A.M. "In two hours, we'll call the DEA in La Mesa and tell them we're walking away."

He outlined her splayed fingers against his chest. "Yes.

Then, we need to think about jobs. Neither of us will get a pension from the DEA. We have to look for a way to sustain ourselves."

"I want to stay near your parents, Gabe. I love this valley. I love the people in it. I feel as if it and you have breathed new life, new hope, into me. I don't want to leave it. Do you?"

He shook his head. "No. I don't want to leave it, either, Anna. My folks are right that I've been the son who has been missing more than any of the other kids."

"What do you want to do?"

"I want to talk to my folks about learning the ropes of ranching. Luke has firefighting. Sky and Andy are pilots. They love the ranching life, but they have no interest in learning it and then living it. I'd like to try my hand at it. Besides, at some point, our parents are going to be too old to do this kind of demanding work. I'd like us to be there to help and support them when they decide that the time has come to pass the ranch on to the next generation."

"I agree, ranching is hard work and you have to be young enough to do it. The body gets old and can't do it, even if one's spirit is willing."

He studied her for a moment, silence warming between them. "Then? You'd like to be a rancher's wife? Take your rightful place at my side? Be the good team we are?"

"The one thing I've found, Gabe, is that rural life suits my spirit. I've been another person while here in Wind River Valley. I like riding horses even if I got bruised by our wild rides escaping those drug soldiers. I like being around animals of all kinds. I grew up with chickens, goats, and cattle. I was a happy child on the estancia."

"Could you be happy at this estancia? Wind River Ranch?"

She smiled fondly. "Oh, yes. I have a head for numbers

and I like what Maud does. She's the bookkeeper, the person behind the scenes who keeps the place humming and organized. Your father is gone a lot. Maud basically runs the ranch by herself."

"I agree. But we'd both be focused on running it together. I wouldn't be gone for long stretches of time like my dad has been."

She squeezed his hand. "I'd like it that way. I'm interested in Maud's expanding business of having a dude ranch. Only, I'd want it tailored toward city children who have never been out on the land, around animals, or stood by a stream and felt the embracing energy from it. And I'd like to have my mother visit us during each summer, if she's open to it. We'll never allow the estancia to be sold while she's alive. I may not be able to go back to it, but she can live there and care for it. I've been thinking about talking to her about putting the ranch into a trust of some kind, to bring at-risk children in the city out there to learn about farming and ranching. To inspire them, to give them hope so they aren't looking at gangs to join, or go into the drug trade business. My mother is a very powerful and influential woman in politics at the highest levels of my country. This is something I'd like to speak to her about at some point."

"So," he murmured, moving his fingers down her arm, "you're focused on children and helping them? Is that where your heart is at?"

She gave him a sad look. "I've taken a lot of lives, Gabe. Now? Maybe because of my age or maturity I want to do something positive, something hopeful and healing for our children. Every man I killed had been a little boy at some point. I often wondered what his story was: Was he poor? Starving? Had no way to make a living other than enter crime? Children have always been a priority in my life. My mother has done much to help the poor and starving people of my country. She has created many avenues to help children be educated, especially little girls. I grew up with it and as I got to be older, around twelve, I saw how rich and well off I was compared to those who lived in the cities. My mother often took me on trips around the country with her so that I could see the poverty, the terrible living conditions these children grew up in. I thought everyone had a bed like mine, but I was never so wrong. These kids slept on hard-packed dirt floors with a rug wrapped around them. That was their bed."

"I saw it all the time when I was undercover," he said, frowning. "It hurts to see it. I wanted to do something, but couldn't."

"Well, maybe we can, now. At some point, my mother will be old and need more care and attention. Maybe I can talk her into allowing our estancia to become a beacon of hope for children in my country."

"Maybe she could come and live up here with us at some point?"

"I'd like that, but that's a few decades off. I'm not sure my mother would like eight months of snow and cold."

"Maybe Florida then, eh?" he teased.

Laughing, Anna nodded. "I think we could talk my mother into that. We could always have her stay with us during the summers. That's three months. And then she could fly back to Florida for the rest of the year."

"We could visit her every other Christmas or other major holidays and spend the other half here with my parents?"

"That works for me. My mother has missed me so much, so our ideas will sound like heaven to her. At the right time, I'll call her and start the conversation, find out what she would like."

He sat up, arranged the pillows, and leaned against the headboard. "Come here," he urged, pulling Anna into his arms, settling her across his lap.

"Mmmm, this is nice," she murmured, sliding her arm around his shoulder and neck, brow against his jaw. "I like being in love with you, Cowboy."

Chuckling, he kissed her hair and moved his hand against her hip, holding her close to him. "So do I. My dreams never matched this reality. I like this one even more."

"So?" she said, leaning back, holding his gaze. "Are we going to set a date to get married? My mother would never accept us living together. She's very old-fashioned. I feel your parents believe similarly?"

"Yes, they do." He kissed her brow. "Want to go down to the local jewelry store sometime later this afternoon? Choose something you like for a wedding ring set?"

"And you will put the engagement ring on my finger?" She watched him grin, his eyes alight and shining with love for her. Heart swelling, she savored this precious moment. Never had she dreamed of getting married, much less like this! Life was full of surprises, and sometimes, they were wonderful ones, just like this moment. "Well?" she prodded archly.

Laughing, he hugged her tightly, holding her, just holding her.

"That's a yes," she said, kissing his corded neck, her arms around his shoulders.

"Yes," he said roughly, laughter in his voice.

"Then," she said, scooting off his lap and bed, standing and facing him, "let's do this. Help me make a big breakfast. I'm starving! And I'll bet Ace is hungry, too! We'll make him some eggs and bacon. He'll love it."

* * *

It was seven P.M. and they had just sat down with Maud and Steve at the dinner table at the ranch. Gabe sat next to Anna, Maud and Steve at the ends of it. Ace was sitting in the living room. Sally brought out beef stroganoff, buttered green beans, and garlic and Parmesan French bread browned from the oven. For tonight's dinner, there was a glass of red wine for each of them. Maud thanked Sally and she got ready to leave for the evening.

"I don't know what we'd do without Sally," Maud admitted, digging into the tender beef smothered with a light brown sauce that was fragrant with rosemary.

Gabe nodded. "She's a gem. A part of our family. She helped raise us."

"That she did," Steve volunteered, using the bread to soak up some of the delicious sauce. "Mom number two, for sure."

"While we eat," Gabe suggested, "we'd like to tell you all that's happened today."

"I can hardly wait!" Maud confessed.

"Go for it," Steve invited, smiling.

Gabe launched into the DEA part and he saw his parents' faces sag with relief that he had resigned. Anna then told them their idea of working at the ranch, learning the ropes of ranching from them. Again, he saw delight in their expressions, almost shock. Why?

"How do you feel about this?" Gabe asked his parents. "Do you think we're up to it? Learning the business of ranching?"

"Oh," Maud gushed, "of course we are, honey! I guess I am in serious shock that you wanted to do it, was all. We thought the four of you would fly to the four winds as adults. Steve and I never expected any of you to take over the ranch."

"But we want to," Anna said, "with your blessing and help."

"You have our blessing, believe me," Steve said, serious. "I've been gone a lot and Maud has handled this primarily by herself. We're older now. I'm no longer traveling as much, but the ranch still falls squarely on her shoulders. I'd like to see that pressure and stress taken off her. She has other ideas, other dreams she'd like to tend to and if you two want to handle the ranch, that would be a godsend and a blessing."

Maud became emotional. "For so long, I had hoped one of our children would WANT to become the next owners of our ranch. You have no idea how many times I cried about this to Steve. We wanted to leave it in family hands, but it looked like all of our children were very happy in their careers. We couldn't ask any of you to come back here and work hard to keep this ranch flourishing, to keep it the hub of the Wind River Valley." She sniffed and pulled out a tissue from her pocket, daubing her eyes, giving them a look of apology. "This is a dream come true for me . . . for us. I've loved every minute of being out West. My spirit wanted to be here even though I was born back on the East Coast." She gave Steve a look of pure love. "And when this cowboy walked into Princeton proudly wearing his black Stetson and wrangler outfit, upending the tradition of wearing a blazer, tie, and pants at that university? I fell in love with him. And I'm still in love with him to this day."

Anna gave her a wobbly smile. "That's so beautiful," she said, and she looked up at Gabe. "That's what we want, too. I know marriages nowadays are throwaways within five years."

"Or, people just live together and never marry," Steve said, regret in his tone.

"Anna and I want to get married," Gabe said. "You want to tell them we've settled on a date?"

Smiling, Anna said, "Gabe proposed to me on the way this afternoon to the jewelry store. All I wanted was a plain gold wedding band, something that wouldn't get hooked on something and the diamond pulled out of its setting." She held out her hand toward Maud so she could see it.

"That's so wise of you," Maud said, holding her hand and noticing the band had tiny leaves with a stem connecting each one etched in it. "It's beautiful and functional."

"I really liked it," Anna said.

"I'll show you the wedding band after dinner," Gabe said. "It has flat, rectangular diamonds so they can't get caught on anything, either."

"That sounds beautiful," Steve said. "Being an architect, I always wanted to marry beauty with commonsense construction."

"We wanted to talk with you about a wedding next June, here, at the ranch," Anna ventured. "We want to live together, if that's okay with you two. Maybe live nearby on ranch property?"

Maud sighed. "Am I dreaming, Steve? Can I believe what we're hearing?" she asked, and she smiled at her husband.

"I can believe what you heard, sweetheart," Steve said. "Music to my ears, too."

"Oh, good!" Anna said.

"Double that," Gabe agreed, smiling. "We were thinking this coming weekend, on Sunday, when you have the family dinner here, we'd announce our engagement. We can let Andy, Sky, and Luke know what has happened. They know nothing about any of this."

"We'll make it happen," Maud promised, gushing with joy.

"After dinner tonight," Steve suggested, "let's go into the living room for coffee and dessert, and we can hammer out more details there."

"Yes," Anna said, pointing her fork at her plate, "or our food is going to get cold!"

"Gabe mentioned that your other children showed no interest in running this ranch," Anna said to Maud as they sat in the living room with their coffee and a slice of chocolate cake for dessert. Sally had brought Ace a huge Milk-Bone as a treat, and he promptly chowed down on it at the end of the couch where his people sat.

"That's right," Maud said.

"Do you think there will be any ill will about Gabe and me taking over the ranch eventually?"

Maud shook her head. "No, there won't be. In our will, each child will receive a very large sum of money when we are gone. They will not want for anything. There's no reason to fight over the ranch, which is now very successful. Each child will go their own way in life but never have to worry about having enough to carry them on to the end of their lives."

Anna felt relief. "That's good to know. Gabe and I were concerned that it might be a point of contention among them."

"There will be no jealousy or competition for the ranch," Steve assured them, slicing into his cake. "We didn't raise our children to be like that. We raised them to set them free to do and be who they wanted to be. We never made any of them feel like they had to hang around us or the ranch."

Maud's eyes glimmered with joy. "Somehow, and don't ask me how, I always knew, Gabe, that there was the earth in your blood, the land. I had admitted this to Steve off and on over the years. In my heart of hearts, I hoped that you would come home to us, Gabe."

Gabe shook his head. "You have always had a powerful intuition," he told her.

"When did you realize all of this?" Steve asked him.

"Shortly after I met Anna," he admitted. "I was tired and run-down from the continual stress of being undercover. I wanted my life back and I wanted to come home. It was really driving me."

"Maybe the land was calling you home," Anna whispered, touched.

"Of all our children," Maud told her, "Gabe was the one who was always out with the wranglers, on the land, riding and working. The other three kids, not so much. It was then that I wondered if, someday, he might want to run the ranch."

"Anna? How do you see yourself fitting into ranch life?" Steve wondered.

"I want to work with Maud. Her ideas, visions, and goals have lifted this valley out of poverty. I love children and I'd like to see more welcoming of them to your ranch. I grew up on an estancia and had a similar experience. But I see too many children in cities who are disconnected from nature, from the beauty and energy of life that we live with here in the Wind River Valley. I'd like to share that with them."

Maud made a happy sound, setting her empty plate on the coffee table. The wood in the fireplace, which was behind a glass enclosure, snapped and crackled. "Anna, you and I are far more alike than I could ever imagine! On my vision board in my office, I have plans that I'm going to begin this winter, to take a part of our ranch, about five hundred acres, and make it into a children's educational area. There will be all sorts of features to lure the children to try hands-on activities and see if they like it. My mother, Martha, is working right now with underprivileged children of color, whether black, Latino, Asian, or Native American, and coordinating with them. I'm asking each of these groups to give me their ideas. And with those ideas, I can move forward in creating a children's ranch of sorts. And for those who don't want to know about ranching, I'm going to have one on farming, gardening, and how to grow organic food for our community. Like you, I feel our children are our future. We want to support them and allow them to discover the rest of the world they know nothing of."

"I love the whole concept!" Anna whispered, her hand against her throat, tears brimming in her eyes. "I've dreamed the same dream, Maud. We have the same issues in Guatemala."

"Then," Maud whispered, her voice low with feeling, "let's you and I dream it together. Gabe will be very adept at running the ranch. We can bring the ideas to fruition. We can give children a whole new view of reality, a much better one than the squalor of living in inner-city areas."

"This is unbelievable!" Anna said happily. "And you're going to have the organizations who are sponsoring them pay for each child's visit?"

"Yes, my mother is working on some mega donators she knows to underwrite it all, so that our ranch doesn't lose money providing the services. She feels strongly they will come through with nearly a billion dollars. With that kind of money, you and I will dream really big for the children. I've even let my imagination roll forward, and I'm thinking that we keep each child for a full week. And in that week, they'll have indoor classes, demonstrations, experiments, and then take it into the outside world to watch their ideas at work. I want this as imaginative as possible for them."

"And with that kind of funding," Anna agreed, "you can bring in the best teachers in each area, to educate the kids."

"Yes, and they will be paid what they're really worth," Maud said darkly. "Teachers need to be paid a LOT more than they are receiving right now. Martha is working with a number of lawmakers in Washington, DC, to have a law passed on this issue. No more teachers' strikes. No more teachers buying items for their children in their class- rooms. The school should be paying for it and so should the taxpayers. Without our children truly being given a good, all-around education, they won't flourish, the econ- omy flattens, and it's a loss to the world at large, as well. We want our kids prepared fully for the twenty-first cen- tury."

"I'm in full agreement," Anna said.

"Pretty soon," Steve deadpanned to Gabe, "this ranch will become a new type of educational center that can be mimicked around the world. Maud has a way of cloning her ideas, and they always take off for the good of this country and our world, in general."

Gabe chuckled. "Mom has always been a wild horse with her tail on fire."

Steve joined him. "We'll reach out to our other kids and we'll have a wonderful Sunday dinner together."

Anna gave Gabe a smile. "You're home, Cowboy. My nickname for you has come true. I can hardly wait to see their faces when they all find out you're the new sheriff in town."

Chapter Sixteen

June 5

"OMG!" Andy exclaimed, holding Anna's left hand, looking at her simple engagement ring. "This is so beautiful! I love the vine with leaves etched into it," she said, smiling, and she released her fingers.

Anna smiled. "Thanks, Andy." She liked the genuine happiness dancing in her green eyes for her and Gabe.

Andy stood with Dev in the center of the living room where the family was gathering for their weekly Sunday dinner with Maud and Steve. Ace knew his place at the end of couch in the living room, alertly watching everything going on. Maud and Sally were busy putting on the final touches for the coming meal in the dining room. Steve was hobnobbing with Luke and Sky. Luke had arrived early this morning, here to take the wildfire assistant manager job over at the airport. That meant he'd be staying permanently in the valley. And, because he was in management, Luke would be remaining in the office, not fighting fires as a hotshot anymore. That made Maud and Steve very happy.

Sally had brought out small mugs of apple cider with ice cubes earlier, placing them on the huge coffee table in the center of the room. Even though it was early June, the weather in this part of western Wyoming could be below freezing in the morning, warm up to the sixties during the day, and drop back to the high thirties by late evening. Right now, it was in the fifties and everyone was dressed up and wearing clothing for semi-chilly temperatures.

Dev gave Anna a smile. "So, when's the big day, gang?"

Gabe, who stood next to Anna, said, "We're looking at June twentieth, next year, when it's a little warmer for an outdoor wedding here at the ranch. We're marrying each other, and it's symbolic for the two of us to marry on the ranch, promising to take it forward to the next generation."

Clasping her hands to her heart, Andy said, "That's so wonderful! You know? Luke, Sky, and I never wanted to be ranchers. I don't know why, but we just didn't. We all worried if it would be passed on down through our generation or not."

"It will be in the family now," Dev said, a nod toward Gabe and Anna.

Gabe smiled and placed his arm around Anna's shoulders, giving her a quick hug and then releasing her. "It's going to stay in the family, for sure. When you two decide to have kids of your own, they'll be able to come over here for visits and be on the ranch, know its history, and who knows, maybe one of them might be interested in being a wrangler someday."

"Well, no babies right now," Andy said. "I'm not ready for that yet. Mom and Dad have offered all of us kids a plot of land on the ranch. Dad wants to build homes for each of us on the property and I think that's a great idea."

"Yes," Gabe said. "We're hoping that all of you will agree to have a home built on the ranch."

"Will you take them up on it, Andy?"

"Yes, we will." She smiled up at Dev. "Steve is working on design plans right now. We're excited about it."

"You'll have to share your dream home blueprints with us," Gabe said.

Sky and Luke wandered over.

"Hey, I hear you're engaged to this brother of ours, Anna. Can I see your engagement ring?" Sky asked.

Anna held out her hand to the woman pilot. "Sure can."

Luke shook hands with Gabe. "Hey, Bro, congratulations. This was a big surprise to all of us. You've always operated in stealth mode and here, you sneaked in a marriage proposal, catching all of us off guard."

"Well, you had plenty of time to find the right woman, Luke," Gabe teased, releasing his hand. "I just beat you to it, under the radar."

Scratching his head, Luke gave him a merry look. "I didn't think I'd ever settle down. I liked traveling between North America and Australia. I like fighting fires. But things are changing in my life. I'm older and beat-up enough physically that I've stopped my hotshot days and decided to go into a fire management position like this one at the airport." He grinned. "Who knows? Maybe I'll find the right partner, huh?"

"Never can tell," Anna said, reclaiming her hand from Sky, who had gushed over the ring.

"No," Luke murmured, "you're right. But hey! I'm glad you two birds are going to take over the Wind River Ranch whenever Mom and Dad decide enough is enough and retire."

"Oh," Sky hooted, elbowing Luke in the ribs, "you know Mom is never going to retire! She might say she is, but she's an idea machine for this century. She's always got something new up her sleeve that she wants to do here at the ranch to improve it."

"That's true, Sis," Luke agreed, pushing his fingers through his short brown hair.

"And me?" Steve said, joining the group, "I might slow down on our architect jobs around the world, but I'll never truly retire from it."

"If you love something," Anna told them, "you'll do it all your life."

"I think we've all found our passion," Sky agreed. "And if you love what you're doing? Why should you ever retire from it?"

"Makes good sense to me," Steve said, grinning. "But not having the ranch to juggle daily at some point in the future will be helpful. Especially for your mother, who has more ideas than she has time here on this Earth."

They collectively laughed and nodded. Maud was a powerhouse, no question.

"I hear," Dev said, "that Anna and Maud have some great ideas for future directions for our ranch home?"

Anna nodded. "We do. And I'm sure Maud will tell you all about them when we sit down to eat."

"DINNER'S ON!" Sally called at the entrance to the living room.

Gabe picked up Anna's hand. "Come on, let's go." He gave Ace a hand signal and he leaped up happily at their side.

Everyone laughed because Sunday dinner was a constant in their lives growing up. And there was a seat designated for each person. Gabe liked that. The "herd" moved as one and walked down the long hall, chatting and laughing.

It felt so good to be home. As a child, after he'd finally come out of his shell, thanks to Maud and Steve's gentle and patient loving, Gabe felt free, happy with parents who truly loved him, and had healed many of his abandonment wounds. Joining the DEA and going undercover had been a move into a dark place within himself, once again. He knew he'd done a great deal of good on the war against drugs, but he'd grown exhausted by the emotional and stressful game of maintaining his cover. The last few days, sharing them with Anna, loving her, being loved, he felt like a butterfly that had been trapped inside a hard, un-yielding chrysalis, and was finally emerging from it into the pure light of day. Of hope. He glanced over at Anna. She was wearing a light wool pink pant suit that she'd bought in Jackson Hole with Maud yesterday. The color matched her cheeks, and he absorbed the sparkle in her eyes, the love in them for him, and it made his heart soar.

Sally took Ace into the kitchen where she had a special dinner waiting for him. She presented everyone seated at the long table with a platter of bison roast, a family favorite. There were steaming mashed potatoes, a dark, fragrant gravy, sliced and colorful zucchini, carrots and pearl onions in a garlic sauce, applesauce sprinkled with cinnamon, and toasted, buttered French bread, hot from the oven. Everyone clapped and thanked her for her hard work and efforts. She smiled and told them, "I have Gabe's favorite dessert: bread pudding with caramel sauce."

The whole crowd made oohing and ahhhing sounds of pleasure in unison. Luke, who loved it just about as much as Gabe did, rubbed his hands in glee.

"I'll skip dinner and just go straight to dessert, Sally," he said, grinning.

The whole table hooted at him.

"No way," Maud said, waving her fork in Gabe's direction. "You always tried this as a child, too."

"Well, you know? What works, works, Mom."

"Didn't work then, and it won't work today," Maud said firmly, giving him her best motherly scowl.

Everyone laughed, the meat platter, the veggies, and applesauce being passed from one to another as they filled their plates.

Gabe savored Anna at his right. This was the first family gathering where they were engaged to be married. For him, it was a special late afternoon, one he would not forget. He appreciated the slats of sunshine pouring in through the crocheted white curtains over the windows, making the dining room glow. Earlier, Steve had driven to the small florist store in Wind River and bought an arrangement of flowers, mostly highly fragrant spring freesia, in many bright colors, which now sat in the center of the table in a cut-glass vase.

Talk ranged around the group, with Maud filling them in on the idea of putting together a children's mini ranch and farm. Everyone thought it was a great idea. Sally brought a bottle of white wine and a bottle of red to the table. Everyone poured what they wanted and sipped it with their meal.

Sky and Andy told stories of their flights to help others who were injured, sick, or in an auto accident, taking them to the hospital via their helicopter. Luke told stories from his months spent in Australia, fighting fires.

They were all, to a person, glad to hear that Gabe and Anna had resigned from the DEA. Everyone confessed they were worried for Gabe being undercover. So was he, but he'd not admit that to the group.

"Do you think you'll be happy doing something so pedestrian as learning to run a ranch?" Sky asked Anna. "I mean, you've done heroic, bold, and courageous things for your country and ours, as well."

Anna held Sky's sincere gold-brown gaze. "You mean being a racehorse and suddenly deciding to gear down to plow horse speed?"

The whole table smiled and laughed at her analogy.

"That's good," Sky congratulated. "Yes, to go from high stress and danger to something, well, more quiet, peaceful, and safe."

"I've been wanting to get out of the sniper business for some time now," Anna admitted to them between bites. "I'm tired of being hunted."

"And," Gabe added darkly, "Anna has a million-dollar bounty on her head in her country. She can't go home even if she wanted to."

The table grew silent, scowls, worry, and surprise in everyone's expressions.

"That's awful," Sky whispered, shaking her head. "What is your mother saying about all of this?"

"I've been on Skype with her a number of times the past few days since we announced our engagement," Anna told the table. She pulled the French bread apart and laid it on the edge of her plate. "I've convinced my mother to donate the estancia where I grew up, that's been in the family for over a hundred years, to an international organization that will utilize it to help underprivileged children from around Guatemala. They will make a school out of it. I can't think of a better change for the estancia than that. She would do that when she's ready to retire. Maud and Steve have talked with her and he's drawing up plans for a mother-in-law house here on the ranch for her. She likes the idea of staying with us during the summer and then going to a new home in Florida where it won't be so cold the rest of the months of the year."

The table nodded in unison over her mother's decision.

"My mother will continue to work at the highest levels of Guatemalan politics. She's a force for good in our country. But from June through September, she will fly up here to be with us after she retires. Until then, she'll take vacations from her duties with the government, as she can."

"Wonderful!" Sky murmured.

"We are going to build her a home here on the ranch," Steve told everyone. "I'm working with Maria on architectural drawings right now. We trade PDFs of it and she gives me guidance, feedback, and I think we'll be done by midweek."

"Which means," Maud said happily, "we can begin building it now."

"Yes," Steve agreed, "and we'll get it enclosed by September and finish the inside, as well as furnish it with Maud and Maria's direction, in time for her to come next June for the wedding. And speaking of that, I'm also working on plans for Gabe and Anna's home, which will be about a mile from where the main ranch house is at. We'll have it enclosed before the snow flies this September, too."

"I'm sure looking forward to that," Anna told them. "For years, I've not been able to stay at the estancia and put my mother in danger. Here, she can stay with us for three weeks, and I'm sure going to enjoy it."

"We're really becoming a family once more," Sky sighed, giving Anna a warm look. "I loved growing up here with everyone. We were thick as thieves then as we are to this day."

"That's an understatement," Steve said, grinning down the table at Maud, who rolled her eyes.

Everyone laughed.

"Well, Anna," Luke teased, "you are now a member of the original Gang of Four. We've already voted Dev into it."

Sky giggled and poured gravy into a second helping of mashed potatoes on her plate. "Oh, Anna! Wait until the four of us tell you ALL the trouble we got into here on the ranch growing up!"

Anna raised her eyebrow at Gabe. "And I'll bet you were the ringleader . . ."

The table burst into laughter and quick nods of agreement.

"Guess I've been caught red-handed," Gabe admitted wryly, giving his siblings a sour look.

"Even as a kid," Sky said, "Gabe always flew under the radar. You never saw him coming."

"No," Luke opined, pretending agony, "it wasn't until after he gotcha that you knew you'd been had."

Anna snickered. "Hey, he's black ops, people. That's just the way we operate."

"And so," Luke teased her mercilessly, "we now have a second black ops family member."

"Wrong, dog breath," Andy said, giving Luke a sly glance. "Dev here was in black ops, too, as a Nightstalker pilot in the Army. He was undercover, also. We've even got an animal on the ranch that's black ops!" Everyone laughed and nodded their heads knowingly.

"I guess that means we all have to watch our step, eh?" Sky said, giving everyone a merry look.

"Well, one thing for sure," Maud told all of them, "there's going to be no secrets among us."

"But the black ops types," Andy said, "will be the first to find them out if there are."

Steve chuckled and shook his head. "Who knew we would become a stealth family?"

"Really," Maud said, finishing off the food on her plate.

"But," Anna reminded all of them, "people in black ops will ALWAYS have your collective back. To me? It's like a huge insurance policy on our family. We in the black ops community know the good guys from the bad ones. We'll spot them coming a mile away. We can warn the entire family more quickly. That's a good thing."

"Yep," Andy agreed, "we'll circle the wagons on the ranch and family and stay safe."

"Well," Maud intoned dryly, "I feel sorry for anyone who wants to defraud, lie to, or dupe any of us."

There was a serious nod of agreement by everyone at the table.

"Speaking of that," Gabe said, "you all know that Elisha Elson saved our lives. I'd like to give you an update on his working with the FBI. Earlier, he helped us, warned us, and the prosecutors are working with his defense attorney to turn evidence over on the Pablo Gonzalez drug ring from Guatemala. He and his mother, Roberta, are going into Witness Protection. Elisha is going to continue to work with prosecutors on indicting a far larger group within the drug ring, as a result. And when the time comes, he'll give evidence against them in court. He's not going to federal prison like his brother Kaen is."

"That's terrific," Sky said. "What will happen to the Elson homestead?"

"Roberta has sold it to us," Steve said.

Brows shot up around the table.

"We wanted to help Roberta out," Maud told them. "With the money from their homestead and ranch, they are going to be financially stable."

"They can start a new life without worry about money," Gabe said.

"That's right," Steve said. "And, we're in negotiations via our Realtor to legally buy the Rocking G, the ranch next door, from the DEA, who has agreed to sell it to us."

"It's a done deal on both properties," Maud assured them. "We're just working through the mountain of paperwork to make it so."

"WOW!" Luke said, "You're buying up a huge chunk in the southern part of the valley!"

"We have plans for it," Maud said slyly.

The children laughed and shook their heads.

"Maud and Steve are going to turn the Rocking G into a working cattle ranch during the summer months," Anna shared. "There's everything there we need to teach inner-city children about how a ranch works and runs. It will become the center to teach inner-city children about ranching and animal management."

"And," Gabe added, "the infamous Elson homestead will be torn down, rebuilt as a school and dormitory, and will be called Wind River Farm. Steve is working on plans for cottages and a school, plus huge gardens and greenhouses, for the property. Kids who want to learn how to farm, grow crops and food, as well as raise animals like sheep, goats, and milk cows will learn hands-on starting next July."

"Right now," Steve said, "I'm drawing up architect plans for both structures. We have already contacted local contractors to start building the cottages on each property for children and their adult supervisors."

Maud smiled dreamily. "And Steve has configured both places to be able to handle twenty-five children at a time. We are giving the children a two-week training that they can take back to their schools come fall. A lot of handouts, PDF booklets, an interactive website, as well as workbooks will be created for them. And every child will not only receive a tablet with WiFi and internet when they arrive, but they will also take it home with them, plus lots of lesson information that their teachers can share with the whole class. The kids will tell their personal experiences and stories of what they've discovered at the ranch or the farm. We're hopeful that when that happens, other kids will want to come. They will be flown out free by several airlines who are here at the regional airport and have donated the flights to the children. I've just wrapped up a five-year agreement with three airline companies. This will allow us to pay for things from our side of the ledger so we're not in the red, either."

"It's important to make a business solvent," Steve agreed. "And we knew that going into this new area of education, our payback will be children who will be educated, aware of our environment, of rural living and what it's like outside of city living. That will pay America dividends in the long run. Sometimes, there are things money cannot buy and this idea is one of them."

Maud smiled happily. "There's even more, kids. My mother, Martha, has gotten twenty-five colleges and universities around the country to agree to give any child who goes through our program a full scholarship in one of the rural minor or majors of their choice. That means each child who completes our two-week farm or ranch course has a guaranteed full scholarship, including dorm facilities, for two or four years, depending upon who they choose to receive their education from. It can be in agriculture, science, or medicine."

"That's incredible," Luke said, awed. "Double wow. What an opportunity for those kids."

"We're focusing mostly on children of color and new immigrants to our country, because we want to support them in becoming fully involved citizens of the US," Steve added.

"But that doesn't mean impoverished white children are left out, however," Maud said. "We've worked out an algorithm that gives ten percent to each group, so that no one gets more of a share than the other. There will be fifty percent girls and fifty percent boys. It will be fair and balanced for all."

"That's good," Andy said. "We don't need some group pointing a finger at your efforts and saying it's skewed or prejudicial in some way."

"All children deserve a break," Maud said. "They are our future."

Andy sighed. "This is all such good news. There's a win-win for everyone involved. Mom, you are just incredible in your vision and how you see helping others who have less than we do."

"Your grandmother Martha pounded that into me at a very early age," Maud replied fondly. "They traveled often and always took me around the world with them. I got to see third-world countries and they had so little water, medicine, or food available. It left an indelible impression on me and I never forgot it."

"I think," Steve said, "that if more Americans traveled abroad, they'd see how rich America really is, and begin to understand just how lucky we are."

"Yes, more inclusion, not exclusion," Anna said. "There's only one planet and whether people want to believe this or not, we're all in this together. Why not work together to make it the best for everyone, not just a few rich billionaires or trillionaires?"

"Well," Maud said, irony in her tone, "my parents are billionaires, but they're using their money and giving back to lift humanity upward and bring that idea into alignment with the belief everyone deserves an education. And when you educate a child? You've given them their freedom to be all they can be. That's what this country is all about:

the dream that we can be whatever we want if we work hard enough."

"Are you tired?" Gabe asked. They had come back to the condo an hour earlier, after the sun had set and they'd left the Whitcomb home. It was now nine P.M. Ace had been gifted with a huge doggy bed by Maud and Steve tonight, much to his delight. That bed was in the living room, which was his favorite place to hang out.

"Yes," Anna admitted, putting the last of the dishes into the dishwasher. She rinsed her hands at the sink and towel dried them off. "A good kind of tired," she added, turning and sliding her arms around Gabe's neck. Their hips met and she lingered on the shape of his mouth, always hungry to press her lips to his. "A lot has happened in a short amount of time."

He moved his hands down her shoulders, following the curve of her back, coming to a halt at her waist. "In the space of a week it's as if our old world of DEA has been blown away and replaced by a new, better one," he agreed, kissing the top of her head. "Maud and you get along so well together. I honestly don't know who has more ideas: you or her."

They laughed together.

"It's going to take until next June to move into our new home on the ranch. Just in time to be ready for our wedding."

"Maud's already trying to get you to start furniture shopping online," he chuckled, shaking his head.

"And don't forget the paint swatches, and her suggestions for the colors inside," Anna said, grinning.

"I think it's very nice that she is in Skype touch with your mother. Those two are going to be dangerous together."

Her lips curved. "My mother is just as much a type A as your mother is. They've started a lovely friendship with each other. I can hardly wait until they meet."

"Those two will huddle in Maud's office and we'll never see them again. They're world changers and visionaries, but of the best kind," he agreed.

"On a more serious topic, Gabe, I'm glad the Lincoln County prosecutor has agreed to help Elisha and his mother get into the Witness Protection program. That was a big load off both of us. He deserved something for warning us and saving our lives."

"Yes," he murmured, bringing her fully against him, her head resting on his shoulder, brow against his jaw. Times like this were what Gabe savored: the intimacy. It wasn't always about sex. It was about loving Anna and her responding in kind to him. "They're starting a new chapter in their lives just like we are."

"Do you think Luke and Sky will find their mates?" she wondered, closing her eyes, sponging in his warmth, strength, and tenderness.

"I'm sure they will. Sky has admitted she wants to be home and she's glad to be working as a medevac pilot with Andy and Dev."

"What about Luke? He seems like such a Western tumbleweed."

"No tumbleweeds in Guatemala, huh?" he teased. He felt her laugh and she kissed the side of his neck.

"No, none, but I've already seen them up here in Wyoming and Luke is just like them: always on the move." She frowned. "I almost feel like he's running from something . . . maybe the fact he's adopted and he doesn't know who his parents are. And now he's just taken a job that will really tie him down. No more gallivanting and flying around the globe chasing wildfires."

"Being adopted is something we all wrestle with, *mi corazón*. It can't be helped. It's part of who we are. I think Luke unconsciously doesn't believe he is lovable or that someone would love him and that's why he hasn't settled down. That's a wound adopted children always have. Some get over it. Others don't, and I think he's one of them. Maybe settling here in the valley will help him lose that wanderlust. When he sees how happy Andy and Dev are, and you and me? It may rub off on him."

"Well," she sighed, moving her hands slowly up and down his strong back, "let's hold him in good thoughts. I never dreamed of being married, either. Or of finding the right man to love. It just never crossed my mind. Luke's probably in the same lane as I was."

"Because you were a lot like Luke: always on the move. As a sniper, you had to be or the cartel would have found you."

"I suppose you're right," Anna admitted. "From the first time I met you, I felt this almost magical connection to you, Gabe. I sure fought it."

"But," he whispered, kissing her cheek, "love won out. Didn't it?"

"Yes, yes it did."

"We have a bright, hopeful future, Anna. Together."

She snuggled her cheek into his shoulder. "Forever, *mi corazón*. Forever . . ."

If you've missed the previous book in the
WIND RIVER VALLEY series,

WIND RIVER PROTECTOR,

turn the page and enjoy a quick peek!

The book is available at your favorite retailer
and e-retailer!

"Well, hell!"

Captain Andrea Whitcomb hissed out the epithet. She was in trouble. Her harness bit deeply into her shoulders as she hauled back on the stick of her A-10 Warthog, having swooped within fifty feet of a hill peppered with Taliban guns firing back at her. The Gatling gun beneath the nose of the aircraft made her entire body shake from the firepower she'd just delivered against the enemy.

It was dusk, the lurid red color of the sunset dying behind the Afghanistan mountains to the west. Her A-10 had a helluva lot of armor, especially around the seat of the cockpit where she sat, but bullets had done damage to both engines on her stalwart close air support jet. Her gloves were sweaty with adrenaline as she felt the gravity pinning her back against the seat. She silently pleaded with the ailing combat jet to climb and get the hell out of bullet range of her attackers.

Jerking a glance to her left, looking through NVGs, night vision goggles, she saw the Black Hawk helicopter was trying to make an escape out of that deadly valley. It had just dropped a SEAL team near the wall of the canyon when it came under fire. She had been called in from another mission to protect the Army helo. It was always dangerous dropping or picking up black ops, and it was done after dark, if possible.

This time? She was in trouble. And so was the Black Hawk. The Taliban weren't stupid. They had the helo caught in a bracket, heavy fire aimed at its rotor assembly area. Their enemy knew if they could destroy that one mechanical mechanism, the helo was grounded and everyone on it would eventually be killed—by them.

Sucking in a breath of oxygen through her mask, eyes narrowed, Andy saw the warning black smoke issuing from the helo's two turbo engines. *Not good. Not good at all.* There was a mountain range to the north end of this box-canyon-type valley and the helo was hobbling along, clawing for air and trying to get away from the bullets of the Taliban, too.

Her gaze snapped to the engine indicator, the dials telling her she was in equally bad shape as that limping-along Army helo. From muscle memory, she went into ejection-seat mode. First, mayday calls to Bagram. Her combat jet would have to be destroyed, provided she could safely eject out of the crippled craft. Nothing could be left of it to be picked through and then sold to China or Russia, who would want avionics, for starters, from the jet. There were so many top-secret black boxes on this jet, they had to be destroyed, instead of hoping a fire or explosion would do the job. She set the detonation assembly.

Her gloved hand flew over the cockpit array, prepping the jet for the series of internalized explosions that would be initiated upon crashing to the ground. Hopefully, with her ejected, the parachute opening and being far enough away from where the A-10 augered in, she'd survive this. A landing area was critical. She had a GPS radio on her flight suit and that would continually broadcast her whereabouts. That way, she could be picked up by either the Air Force or some other rescue operator helo that might be nearby. Sweat stood out on her upper lip, her mind moving at the speed of a computer.

The Warthog's engines, that specific whistling sound that was protected by the helmet she wore, couldn't be heard. But she could feel it lag and then a burst of surging power, and then her indicators would drop once more. She was losing power and altitude little by little. Barely at six thousand feet, heading north into those mountains, she could no longer see the Black Hawk because it was below her somewhere, barely creeping along at about fifteen hundred feet or so. Was it carrying a three- or four-man crew on board? Andy didn't know. She completed her eject list and searched the rugged mountains looming up ahead of her. The ravines were covered with hardscrabble trees that clung to their rocky surface. The tallest peaks were at ten thousand feet. For the next minute, she homed in on where she wanted to eject, what the terrain looked like and if she could survive it once she jettisoned out of the cockpit.

The first engine flamed out. The craft listed for a moment before she used the rudders beneath her flight boots, and the stick, to keep the Warthog flying level, flying toward her objective in the darkening sky. *One down.* An A-10 could handle losing an engine and make it back to base provided it wasn't shot up and coughing, like the second one was doing right now.

For a moment, the faces of her adopted mother and father, Steve and Maud, flashed before her eyes. She had been put on the step of a fire station and a firefighter had found her one cool May morning. She had been abandoned. Andy never found out who her mother was, but as luck would have it, she had been adopted months later and greatly loved by her new parents, who lived in Wind River, Wyoming.

She didn't want to die! Not like this. Andy had spent years in the Air Force, and every rotation back into Afghanistan provided close air support to men and women on the ground. She loved her life, her mission. But now things were coming to an end. And she wasn't sure if she'd survive.

For a moment, her attention was torn to eleven o'clock, to the left of where she flew. There was a small explosion, and she knew it had to be the Black Hawk hitting the rocky mountainside below and to the port side of her jet. It was the same area where she was going to eject into. Praying that the crew and two pilots made it out safely, her gaze flickered between the engine dial and where the small fire was below her. Then she focused on her own plight.

And then there was a huge explosion, a rolling red, yellow and orange fireball bursting out into the ebony darkness, lighting up a huge area around the helo. No one could survive that second explosion. Her heart ached for the crew.

The second engine sputtered and died. It flamed out, and she shut off the fuel line to it.

Automatically, her muscles puckered. Grabbing the lever, the cockpit Plexiglas separated with a loud bang around her.

Wind slammed and pummeled her masked and helmeted face. She was glad she had the NVGs in place over her eyes. Gritting her teeth, she initiated the ejection. In seconds, there was an explosion beneath her seat. Andy bit back a cry as her tightened nylon harness bit hard into her shoulders. Thrust into the cold darkness, the seat blew away from the now plummeting A-10.

Enclosed in darkness, Andy kept her elbows tightly pinned against her body. She kept her hands and arms stiff, holding them in place as the seat continued skyward. Just as the seat separated from her, she tumbled, hearing her chute begin to open somewhere above her.

Would it open completely? Her mind rattled between dying and wanting desperately to live. She was twenty-six years old, her whole life before her. If she made it out of this crash? She would leave the Air Force and find something in aviation. She loved to fly; she did not want to give it up, but she had to find something safer. The future wasn't an issue; surviving this situation was.

She swung like a pendulum through the night, wind gusts pummeling her. She could see she was going to land somewhere along the edge of a ravine. There were scrub trees everywhere. There was no way she was going to avoid tangling with one of them.

Just then, the A-10 plunged down onto the mountain-side to the right of her. It was a thousand feet higher in elevation from where she was presently drifting downward. Automatically, she opened her mouth to balance the pressure inside and outside her lungs. The pressure waves from the crash were like fists slamming into her. Yellow and orange fire erupted into several fireballs, telling her the string of explosions were the ones designed to destroy all the avionics. The whole area lit up in a surreal, shadowy reddish glow for a few seconds. It blinded her; she'd stupidly looked at the explosion and it blew her vision in the NVGs. She swung several more times in the sky, several smaller explosions occurring at the crash site.

The ground came up fast. Getting some of her night vision back, she saw the trees looming beneath her dangling boots. She kept her knees soft and slightly bent. In seconds, she slammed into a tree, branches and limbs snapping and breaking off beneath her. Leaves, twigs blew up around her. Andy's legs were pummeled as her ascent slowed dramatically, her body crashing through the tree, bruises blooming all over her legs and arms.

She hit the ground, rocks biting into her one-piece flight uniform, letting out an "oooffff . . ." The straps of the chute gave her a soft landing. And then they untangled from the branches and the chute collapsed nearby.

Heart pounding, fear tunneling through her, Andy had no idea if there were Taliban nearby. They did not have night vision equipment and were known to camp at dark. Was she safe? Not safe? Was there a group in this ravine? She didn't know.

Disoriented from the landing, she pulled off her helmet, setting it nearby. She unstrapped her pistol, keeping it easy to reach after sliding a round into the chamber, the safety off. Now, after all those yearly training sessions for just such a situation, Andy knew what to do. She made sure her GPS radio was on and broadcasting an invisible location beacon signal to anyone who might be hunting to pick her up.

The explosion she'd seen earlier showed she was about half a mile farther up on the ravine than the spot where the Black Hawk had crashed. Had anyone survived? She looked around, trying not to sob for air, adrenaline making her gasp. With trembling hands, she unsnapped the chute from her harness, dropping it to the ground.

Through her NVGs she couldn't see far because of the thickets in the ravine itself.

First things first. She started to get up as two more minor but powerful explosions went off above her. Andy stood on shaky knees as she scrambled up the hill, slipping, falling on the field of rocks. Luckily, her Nomex gloves were on, protecting her hands from being sliced and cut, but her knees didn't fare as well. Getting to the chute, she gathered it up between her arms. Taking it down to the tree she'd crashed through, she pushed it toward the trunk, getting down on her hands and knees, digging a hole to hide it from prying enemy eyes.

She wasn't going to need the helmet either, so she dug another hole with effort, her knuckles bruised from all the smaller rocks she hit. It was nearly impossible to dig deep enough because there was more rock than soil. Andy wondered how these trees survived on this windswept ridge. Lucky it was August and not the snow season. She wondered how anything survived in this godforsaken place known as the Sandbox.

Pulling up the cuff of her flight-suit sleeve, she saw it was 2100, nine p.m. Standing, she looked around. Above and below her, there were two fires: the Black Hawk burning below, and above, her beloved A-10.

She looked up into the cloudless sky, the stars so close she thought she could reach out and touch them. It was a moonless night. Keying her hearing, she took off the rubber band and repositioned her shoulder-length chestnut hair into a ponytail. Where was the enemy? She didn't know. Never had she felt so naked and vulnerable as now. And scared. It was as real as it would ever get for Andy. The adrenaline was still pounding through her veins, and her hands were shaky as she touched the butt of her pistol, which lay across her chest on top of the Kevlar vest she wore.

The wind was powerful and came blasting through the area in unexpected gusts, sometimes pushing her a step sideways or backward. She was glad her flight suit was a desert-tan color so it wouldn't stick out like a sore thumb night or day. Not that the Taliban traveled at night. They rarely did.

For the first time since joining the Air Force, Andy wished she wasn't in the military. She knew the dangers of A-10 jet jockeys being hit by enemy fire. It had happened to her many times before, usually bullets down the fuselage. Tonight? The enemy had gotten lucky and she was the unlucky one. Would an Air Force helo pick her up? How soon? She knew she had to try to call in and pulled the radio from her pocket.

Her night vision goggles had been affixed to her helmet, but she'd taken them off and hung them around her neck. She didn't want to bother with them at the moment. Time was of the essence. However, without moonlight she couldn't see her hand in front of her face. It was that black. Fingers trembling, she brought the radio up to her eyes, barely seeing the outline of it. Frowning, she couldn't find the green light on it that indicated it was working.

No . . .

Taking off her flight glove, she stuffed it in a leg pocket. Running her fingers across the top of the device, she cut her fingertip. Her heart sank in earnest. The top part of her radio was broken. That was why there was no green light. She must have struck it with the limbs of the tree as she parachuted to safety.

Looking around, fear snaking through her, Andy knew without her GPS radio working to signal where she was located, there would be no help coming except from the A-10 seconds before it augered in. Lifting her chin, she saw the flames of her crashed jet rapidly dwindling, more like a candle in the ebony night instead of the bonfire before. Her only hope was to remain near the wreckage. Someone, somewhere, would have to have fixed the last location of the GPS. They would send a helicopter crew out to the area and rescue her. She had to remain here. If it was cluttered with Taliban nearby? Her rescuers would not pick her up.

A shiver went through her. It was ass-freezing-cold on top of the ravine. She wrapped her arms around herself after pulling on the glove once again. It was bitterly cold. And until daylight came, Andy had no idea how far away her jet was, or how to get close to it to be seen by a rescue crew. And Taliban could be anywhere. If the jet was out on a bare spot on the slope, she would be seen by some sharp-eyed enemy for sure.

Heart sinking, she remained near the tree, unsure what to do. Her radio wasn't working, so no one would be able to find her. All she had on her flight vest were a few protein bars in her thigh pockets. And no water. This didn't look good.

"Hey!"

Whirling around, Andy stumbled and nearly fell. Her heart banged in her chest, her throat closed as the deep male voice came out of the night.

"I'm friendly, don't shoot!"

Her hand was already around the grip of the pistol as she righted herself, eyes huge as a dark shape—at least six feet tall—emerged from the inkiness of the ravine. "Who are you?" she demanded.

"Lieutenant Dev Mitchell. Are you the pilot from that A-10?"

Gulping, relieved, her eyes narrowed as the man came toward her. She could barely see the outline of his flight suit. "Y-yes. You're from the Black Hawk that crashed earlier?"

He halted. "I am. The only survivor. Who are you?"

"Captain Andrea Whitcomb, US Air Force. I was flying that A-10 until I got hit in both engines."

He gripped her arm. "Are you injured? Can you walk?"

She felt the strength of his fingers around her upper arm. Under ordinary circumstances, she'd have jerked away. But these weren't ordinary circumstances at all. "I'm okay . . . just bruises. Shook up for sure."

"Did you hide your chute?"

"Under this tree here. My GPS radio is damaged. No one can find where I'm at."

"I found you."

She saw his teeth white against the deep shadows of his craggy features. "How?"

He pointed to a set of NVG goggles around his neck. "These. Where's your helmet? Are the NVGs good on them?"

"Yes," she said. "I took them off my helmet before burying it. They are here, around my neck."

He released her. "We gotta get the hell outta here. The Taliban will come in at dawn, looking for us, searching for black boxes on both aircraft. We can't hang around here."

"B-but," she stammered, fear rising in her, "don't you have a GPS radio?"

"I do and it works, but we can't stay around these wrecks. Even a SAR, Search-and-Rescue, crew can't land in the middle of the Taliban closing in on where those birds are located. We have to leave. I'm in touch with them. SAR will track and follow my GPS coordinates until it's safe to come in and pick us up. This is very heavy enemy territory. We gotta leave. Now."

She turned, then moved to beneath the boughs of the tree, trying to stay out of the wind. So much of her fear had abated because the other pilot was there. And he sounded like he knew what he was talking about. "You seem to know what to do."

Again, that cocky grin. "Yeah. Not my first rodeo, Captain. You good enough to travel? The farther away we get from here at night, the better off we'll be. It's August; the sun's gonna come up early. We need to find a cave or someplace to hide when dawn comes. Right now we're in Taliban central. We need to head west," and he pointed across the ravine. "There's a firebase about forty miles as the crow flies in that direction. We have to climb up and over the mountain range to reach it."

"Forty miles?" she managed, her voice raspy. "We're walking to it?"

"Yeah. It's that or stay here and get hunted down by Taliban, who will sure as hell behead us, and we'll show up on videos across the internet. I don't think you want that."

"Hell no!" She heard him give a low chuckle.

"You saved our ass after we unloaded that SEAL group. They got away and blended into the wall of the canyon and made their escape. Thanks."

"What about your other crew?"

She heard his voice lower, a lot of hidden emotion behind it. "Dead. We crashed. I was the only one who got out."

"Oh, God . . . I'm sorry, so sorry."

"Ready?" he rasped. "We're going to go down into this ravine and climb up the other side. We have about five hours of night to hide us, and then we'll have targets on our backs."

"Roger that." Andy settled the NVGs into place over her eyes. The wind shifted, and she could smell his flight suit, the strong odor of smoke and grease contained in it. "Are you okay? Did you get hurt?"

"Some first-degree burns on the back of my neck and

top of my ears is all. I'm okay. I have some water bottles in my leg pockets. Are you thirsty?" He pulled on his NVGs and then gripped her gloved hand with his.

"No, but I'm sure I will be. I have no water on me."

He grunted. "You'll have it whenever you want. Come on."

Andy could barely see Mitchell's face. It was his soft voice, with almost, she swore, an Irish lilt to it, that helped her steady her own fear. She wished she could see his face. Was he married? Have a wife and kids at home? Most likely. What must they be feeling right now? She knew without a doubt that her own parents would be receiving a call from the Pentagon that she was MIA, missing in action. Andy's heart filled with anguish; she knew it would tear them up, and her three adopted siblings.

His hand was strong and guiding without hurting her fingers. He led her down the steep, rocky slope, and they were quickly devoured from anyone's sight beneath the scrub trees that stubbornly lived in the unstable ravine. There was no time to talk and no time to look around. She could see his broad set of shoulders against the nap of the trees sometimes. He was four inches taller than her, his stride ground-eating. Picking up on his urgency, very soon she was out of breath, rasping and forcing herself to keep up with him. They were at a high elevation and her body wasn't used to it. All she could see around them was darkness and the outlines of trees. The NVGs made everything a grainy green, and she kept her gaze down so she wouldn't stumble or trip over the rocks, some of them the size of cantaloupes and watermelons. It was a hard, rugged landscape, no question about that.

* * *

Dev Mitchell cursed silently as the Air Force pilot who had saved his life struggled to keep up. They had spent three hours on the run, getting as far away from the crash sites as they could. She was a trooper, had grit and never complained or asked him to slow down. The price of physical weakness would be capture, something he wanted to avoid at any cost. Once they breasted the first ridge, he stopped and told her to sit down and rest under a group of pine trees. Handing her a bottle of water, he stepped out to get the best radio signal he could find and called Bagram.

No stranger to the routine of being found by a SAR crew, Dev gave their GPS location. The answer he got in return chilled his blood. He had stepped away from Captain Whitcomb to make the call. She was green to what it meant to crash and then survive in this hellish country. Oh, he knew she had gone through all kinds of training, but this was the real thing, which was very different. Pulling out his notebook, he quickly wrote down some coordinates, shoving the pen back into his shirt pocket. Signing off, he quickly moved back to the pilot. Through his NVGs, he could see she had an oval face, a clean-looking nose and a nicely shaped mouth. Maybe in her mid-twenties at most. He was twenty-six himself. Liking her self-reliance, her pluck and determination, he knelt down in front of her, pushing up his NVGs.

"I contacted Bagram," he said in a low tone, his face inches from her, not wanting his voice to carry in case Taliban were nearby. "They've given me coordinates for a place for us to hole up. It's about a mile down the other side of this ridge."

"Hole up?"

He heard the fatigue in her voice. The alarm. His mouth thinned for a moment. "I was informed we're right in the middle of Taliban central. Where those birds crashed? We were a mile away from a large group of one hundred soldiers. Bagram has our location. They want us to go to a tunnel complex just down a mile on this ridge and hide out there. They can't bring in a Search-and-Rescue, SAR, to fly us out until the Taliban leave this area so it's safe enough to pick us up."

Groaning, she said, "How long?"

"As long as it takes. No one knows. We'll be safer resting in a cave or a tunnel complex during daylight hours."

"Yeah, but the Taliban use them, too. Did they tell you that?"

He grinned. "Yes. This isn't going to be easy, Captain Whitcomb."

"My name's Andy."

"Call me Dev. Nice to meet you. Are you hydrated? Are you ready to hoof it?"

She nodded. "Let's go." She handed him half a bottle of water. "You need to drink, too."

Taking it, he stood up and backed out of the grove, drinking the water she'd saved for him. There was a lot to like about this feisty female pilot. She was a team player; she thought of others and not just herself. As she joined him, he stuck the emptied plastic bottle into one of the thigh pockets of his flight suit. He didn't want to leave evidence behind. The Taliban would spot an American water bottle like a hawk spotting his next meal. It would tell them they were on the right path to finding them and he wanted to avoid that at all costs.

"How you holding up?"

"Sore and tired. You?"

"Same. If we get lucky, we'll find a place to hole up and then we can sleep."

She snorted. "Someone has to stay awake and play guard dog."

"I'll take first watch," he assured her, smiling. He pulled down his NVGs, seeing that pretty mouth of hers twist into a wry grin. She was a good partner to have. "Let's go."

The first time she actually saw Dev Mitchell was when he located a series of tunnels and found a cave that had a water source in it, plus light coming in from the top of it through a craggy, broken opening. It was the gray of dawn when he led her into it, after going in first, pistol drawn, to ensure no Taliban had taken up overnight residence in it. The place was empty.

The first thing he did after getting her in the cave was to walk outside, call Bagram and give them their GPS. When he returned, she saw the exhaustion in his face. He had red hair and the greenest eyes she'd ever seen. His beard darkened his oval face and strong jawline. There was nothing weak-looking about Dev Mitchell. The darkness beneath his eyes, however, told Andy he was suffering over the loss of his crew. As he took off his gloves, she saw they, too, had been burned, his hands reddened with first-degree burns, as well as his wrist area, where his Nomex fire-retardant flight suit had ridden up to expose his flesh. Her heart was heavy for him.

"Bagram has a Reaper drone at ten thousand feet flying over our area. It has a camera and it knows our GPS. The operator is watching for any Taliban wandering into our area and they'll call us if that happens."

"How long until they can rescue us?"

Shrugging, he put his NVGs on a rocky ledge near where the water seeped into a small nearby pool. "Unknown. This place is crawling with Taliban because it's close to the Pakistan border." His mouth flexed. "They think in a day or two."

"I found two protein bars in my pocket," she offered.

He gave her a one-cornered quirk of his mouth. "I have four. We'll share."

"Well, I wanted to lose a few pounds anyway."

"I like your spirit, Andy."

She warmed when his voice dropped to a deep, almost velvety sound. "Black humor comes with being in the military." She pointed to his reddened wrists. "Those look like more than first-degree burns."

He sat down, leaning against the wall, tipping back his head and closing his eyes as he stretched out his long legs. "The wind blew the Black Hawk into the slope. We crashed on the right side, the pilot's side." Grimacing, his voice soft, he rasped, "I couldn't save him. And our crew chief died on impact. Fire was everywhere. I cut his harness and tried to drag him out, but the fire drove me back." He opened his eyes and touched one of his blistered ears. "I couldn't do it. I was choking on the smoke, couldn't see, and I finally fell back and out the sprung door. I crawled away and made it to safety before the main explosion occurred." He rubbed his face wearily. "It was a bitch of a mission. If you hadn't been on station to suppress the Taliban fire, the SEALs wouldn't have gotten into the brush and escaped."

"I couldn't pull it off," she offered quietly, giving him a sympathetic look. "Whoever those guys were on the ground? They had armor-piercing rounds. Usually they don't. But this group did."

"Yeah, believe me, when those rounds came tearing into our Hawk, we knew we were in trouble." He gave her a grateful look. "You tried to save us. I saw how low you flew, taking their gunfire away from aiming at us. You put yourself in the line of fire so we could get away."

She sighed and nodded. "It wasn't good enough. I'm sorry. So? You had only one crew chief on board? Usually there are two."

"There were supposed to be," Dev admitted. And he lifted his chin, holding her gaze. "I guess the only good news is our other crew chief stayed behind because his wife was having a baby and they had her on a video feed."

"Thank God," Andy whispered unsteadily. "At least he didn't die. And you didn't either, so that's the second piece of good news out of all of this, Dev." She wanted to use his name, and it rolled easily off her tongue. Almost like a prayer. "You saved me, too. I didn't know where the hell I was, my radio was broken and I knew how much trouble I was in."

"Three pieces of good news out of this," he agreed tiredly. "Look, you need to eat a bit, drink water," and he handed her a bottle, "and then go to sleep. I've got purification tablets to put into our bottles to keep the water in is pool from giving us some parasite. Plus, we'll refill ottles tonight before we leave. Water is everything."

wake me in two hours? I'll take over the watch."

"No, I'll let you sleep four hours."

"Can you stay awake that long?" she asked, opening up her protein bar. She ate half and gave Dev the other half.

"Fear will keep me awake," he answered wryly.

She laughed softly, not wanting the sound to carry. "You're tough, Mitchell. Really tough." Her heart expanded when he gave her a little-boy smile, his face lighting up.

Most of all, she liked the freckles across his nose and cheeks. Surely of Irish descent? Maybe they'd get time later to talk.

"I think it's called a will to live instead of die," he responded dryly, quickly eating the other half of the protein bar. He pulled out the third bottle and drank half of it, then offered her the rest. Andy took it and thanked him.

"Even though we're Army and Air Force, we're getting along pretty good together," she teased, finishing off that water.

Dev dropped tablets into the three empty bottles and held them under the small stream coming out of the wall of the cave. "Yeah, we are." And his eyes sparkled as he gave her an intense look. "I'm just sorry I didn't meet you under better circumstances."